Praise for
CITADEL OF THE SKY

"Make room, GRRM: Chrysoula Tzavelas knows how to bring on the pain.... This is a rare book that I have every intention of re-reading before I read its sequel, which, frankly, I would like to get my grabby little hands on right now."

— C. E. Murphy,
author of *The Walker Papers*

INFINITY KEY

"Fast-paced.... In a genre that tends to emphasize young women's romances with male supernatural beings, this focus on female friendship and solidarity is deeply refreshing."

— *Publisher's Weekly*

WOLF INTERVAL

"Absorbing... this is a satisfying standalone novel that explores the lives of endearing characters to good effect."

— *Publisher's Weekly*

BY CHRYSOULA TZAVELAS

CHRYSOULA TZAVELAS

DIVINITY CIRCUIT

SENYAZA
BOOK 5

DREAMFARMER PRESS
DREAMFARMER.NET

Dreamfarmer Press
www.dreamfarmer.net

DIVINITY CIRCUIT
ISBN: 978-1-943197-12-5

Cover art by Ravven Kitsune
www.ravven.com

DIVINITY CIRCUIT

Maybe you've got a monster in your head?
This one's for me and you.

I aim to make most Senyaza stories 90% self-contained. But this is a story about consequences. So I thought I'd provide a very brief recap of some of the lingering points in the two stories this directly follows (along with notes on how the other two books fit in). If you've read the rest of the series recently, feel free to skip ahead to the story.

MATCHBOX GIRLS

Anxiety-ridden grad-school dropout Marley discovers she's a nephil, the child of an unknown angel, and saves the lives of twin girls prophesied to destroy the world. There's an angel, Ettoriel, who wants to use them in a ritual to erase the magical Hush, which prevents angels from dominating the world; Marley eventually defeats him with the power of information. Along the way, she meets fellow nephil Corbin; discovers a whole hidden world of nephilim, angels, Fallen and wizards; and becomes the full-time babysitter of the twins, Kari and Lissa. Meanwhile, her friends Branwyn and Penny find themselves pulled into supernatural trouble of their own. They all come to the attention of Senyaza, the communications corporation that originally created the Hush. Normally Senyaza would have stopped the angel, but they had a crisis of their own around the same time...

INFINITY KEY

Penny is in a coma, with her soul mostly burned out by Ettoriel in the previous book. While Marley deals with being tugged romantically between Corbin and the twins' guardian Zachariah, Branwyn focuses on finding a mortal magic that suits her and will allow her to do the impossible task of saving Penny. She makes contact with the faeries and is pulled into a plot to fully unleash them back into the world, which only partially succeeds. In the process of saving Penny, Branwyn learns how to enchant mundane objects and even give them rudimentary life, which is a magical skill long missing from the supernatural world. She repeatedly runs into a particularly annoying fallen angel called Severin, who has a knack for upsetting her, especially when he saves her life. One object she wakes up is the Senyaza skyscraper known as Titan One. She also manages to give Penny a prosthetic soul made from fragments of celestial Machines, the vast heavenly engines that power and structure the underside of Creation.

WOLF INTERVAL

This is a spin-off that follows AT, a supporting character from the other two books. Marley and Branwyn make an appearance near the end of Wolf Interval, but it has very little bearing on the events of Divinity Circuit.

ETIQUETTE OF EXILES

This is a collection of short stories, in which Branwyn forges a hammer from a Machine fragment and Penny's new soul causes her some problems, among other side adventures.

1
MARLEY

There was something about being over a thousand years old that made a man resistant to reasonable arguments, Marley mused. Especially when it was an argument that he should change all his plans based on her suggestion. She could predict the exact course of the discussion she and her employer were having, but she had to have it anyhow, to lay the groundwork for the future.

As she anticipated his response, she sat in a deck chair on the grass outside his beautiful house and watched her employer's children splash in a sprinkler. It was a sizzling July morning, and she was conscientious. It was, after all, just possible the sun might get to them, through the layers of sunscreen and her own magical guardianship.

Zachariah, said employer, leaned against the wall of his house. *He* was watching *her*. "In any case, nephilim have always been schooled at home."

"I wasn't," Marley pointed out. "And I wouldn't be who I am now without the friends I made in school. It's just kindergarten, Zachariah." She stroked the head of the extra-tall cat lounging beside her chair, as if she could draw patience off the calico fur. It would be so nice to convince him to see reason without having to chart out lots of debates in advance.

"It's dangerous," he said. "And not just for them."

"*Nothing* has happened to them since you hired me. Based on the evidence, it's not going to be that dangerous. And you don't actually care about anybody else," Marley pointed out. "Your turn," she added, as the splashing became hair pulling, because it was too much to expect she could protect the twins from *each other*. She saw a flicker in his aura and added, "If Kari bites you, it'll hurt."

Zachariah strode onto the lawn and into the fray, without the slightest concern for the water spraying everywhere. As he wrestled the fighting twin girls apart, the water soaked through his t-shirt, outlining the strong muscles of his torso and damping his black hair. Marley's cat, Neath, sat up and purred as she watched him intently.

Marley said, "Yes, yes, I know." She sighed. Zachariah was attractive enough that even a cat noticed.

The ancient nephil employed her to protect and care for his children, because she had inherited a rare guardian magic from her unknown mother. But it wasn't *just* a job and Zachariah made no attempt to hold her at a professional distance. Really, it was the opposite. He was always trying to draw her in closer. And sometimes she wasn't sure why she resisted.

There'd been nights after the children had been sent to bed when she'd been lonely or worried and he'd comforted her. On other nights she'd thought she sensed cracks in his steely self-control and reached out. And he'd welcomed her, held her, made her feel good. But the sense of a gulf between them never really faded.

Zachariah's mouth, so often hard and unyielding, softened as he inspected Lissa's bruised arm and Kari's tender scalp. "Girls. You have to be gentle with each other."

Marley watched him, her eyes narrowed against the brightness. It was when he was directly handling Kari and Lissa that she found him the most attractive, and when she most doubted his intentions toward her. She *knew* he loved them. There was nothing he wouldn't do for them.

That was part of the problem, though. She couldn't trust that he cared about her beyond her ability to supernaturally protect the kids. He never softened like that with her.

The other problem—the bigger problem—was that she never felt right about it the next day. She always found herself looking at her phone, hoping for a message from somebody else. A very particular somebody else, whom she hadn't heard from in months.

As the girls hugged each other and returned to playing, he strode back to Marley, slicking water off his shirt. "Let's compromise. How about a private school? I have interests in several private institutions. They begin at middle school but I'm sure I could convince one of them to start a kindergarten program for a year or two."

Yes, there was *nothing* he wouldn't do for the twins.

Marley blinked up at him, startled. She'd *thought* she'd known how this conversation would go. He'd say no, she'd drop it for the moment and bring it up again later. Maybe the twins would get a chance to try an ordinary school by third grade. "Let me get this straight. You're offering to buy a private school as a compromise solution."

He shrugged, expressionless, and went back to leaning on the wall. "Your protection fades with distance. You'd have to attend with them. It's the only way to be safe."

"No," said Marley. "Absolutely not. They have to learn how to interact with ordinary people, without having us hovering over them all the time." She glanced at the splashing girls, then tossed

Neath's favorite ball into the spray. Doglike, the cat sprang into the wet after it. The girls shrieked in delight as Neath batted it through the water to them.

Marley lowered her voice and said, "Look, I've been reading your own books. What happened last summer—the valence event—won't reoccur for another seven years. And the valence event was the only reason the angels... meddled."

'Meddled' was a very kind euphemism for 'tried to kill two little girls' but Kari had finally stopped having nightmares every evening, and Lissa's art had become a little less grim. Why wreck that?

"No, it wasn't. It wasn't even the only reason we're aware of, Marley," said Zachariah calmly. He was always calm. It made her feel like she was the unreasonable one, even when she'd done her research and laid out her evidence. "And they're not the only threat. Others know what's expected from the girls; others will try to influence what comes."

"Well, they haven't in the last year," said Marley testily. "Nobody has tried anything." Zachariah, over a millennia old, could be endlessly patient; Marley, not even thirty, hadn't learned that knack.

"And what if that's because you've been present? Don't underestimate what you do, Marley."

Marley couldn't argue. Her guardian magic, while it was limited by details like distance, number of targets, and the target's own willingness to be protected, *could* work as a bulletproof vest. But it had a more subtle effect, too. Thrown stones were more likely to go wide, or the thrower would get distracted before releasing his missile, or change plans at the last minute. Absorbing a physical attack was only necessary when somebody was really dedicated to doing premeditated harm.

She shifted uncomfortably, fidgeting with her sunglasses. This wasn't quite going the way she'd planned. But it was *important*. The twins had a frightening amount of power and how they were brought up was going to matter.

The angel who had tried to kill the twins had shown Marley a dark vision of a destroyed future. It was, he'd claimed, his motivation for what he wanted to do. He was saving the world. Marley had set herself directly against that. She didn't believe the girls, with their enormous magical potential, were *destined* to be destructive—but she did believe they could be *made* that way. They could grow that way. Zachariah's urge to wrap them in cotton had to be balanced by giving them connections to the rest of the world, and she was the only one who could do that. She was the only one with the leverage to get Zachariah, isolated from so many of his peers, to shift his position.

While she was marshaling her next argument, Zachariah counterattacked. "Move in with me. We can drop them off at school each morning—or put them on the bus, if you insist on that too—and you can use that danger sense of yours to assess the day ahead. If you're around the rest of the time, that's an acceptable tradeoff. For them *and* for me."

Marley's breath caught in her throat. She'd avoided having that particular conversation for so long, dismissing his hints lightly, laughing at the kids' suggestions like they were jokes. She didn't want to deal with saying no, and she wasn't ready to say yes.

Neath left the water, homing in on her distress like a magnet. The big cat jumped into her lap and hissed at Zachariah, who was unfazed. The sudden infusion of wet fur, followed shortly by wet, curious children, was a serious interference to Marley's already wildly careening thoughts.

"Won't you play with us, Marley?" asked Kari, tugging on the swimsuit strap beneath Marley's tank top.

Lissa looked between Marley and Zachariah, then at Neath. "Are you two fighting?"

"Are we?" Zachariah asked, raising one eyebrow at Marley. "I didn't think so, but look how upset Neath is."

Just what I need, a mood-ring cat. Marley shoved Neath off her lap, which left an opening for Lissa to move in. She hooked an arm around Marley's neck and whispered, "It's okay, Marley." Then she kissed Marley's cheek, exactly like Marley soothed her when she was upset.

"What's okay?" asked Kari.

"I don't know," answered Lissa. "I thought maybe she'd seen something scary. Like maybe a shadow blaster from Pixiebots."

"I didn't see anything scary. I was just surprised by something," Marley told them, painfully aware that Zachariah's eyebrow was still raised inquisitively.

Her phone beeped an alarm, and Marley scooped it up gratefully. "Hey! Time for you guys to go make lunch with your uncle, and time for me to go meet Penny and Branwyn."

Kari pouted. "Why can't they come have lunch here?"

"It's a special place Penny chose," Marley explained, dumping Lissa gently off her lap. "Just us girlfriends. Reconnecting. You'll make friends like that someday, when you go to school."

"Reconnecting," said Zachariah, deadpan. "With the friends you talk to every day."

"Well, you know, as an employee I'm entitled to a lunch break and days off and a paycheck, and it's up to me how I spend them." She couldn't raise one eyebrow so she raised both at him as she stood. Something flickered in his eyes and she couldn't tell if it was amusement or annoyance.

"Are you worried about losing your paycheck, Marley?" His voice was suddenly low and seductive. Shivers ran down her spine, as she remembered other times he'd sounded like that.

Firmly she shook her head and knelt to hug the girls. "Your

uncle is being silly. What's a silly thing to have for lunch? It's the right time to ask."

Kari's eyes brightened. "Whipped cream chocolate chip crepes." She turned toward Zachariah and moved in like a cub stalking a full-grown tiger. Marley smiled and then went inside to the downstairs bathroom to change into street clothes. Lissa and Neath both followed her into the bathroom.

"Neath says *something* upset you," accused Lissa as Marley reached over her head to close the door. Neath sat down and started licking the water from her fur.

"Does she?" Marley gave Neath a dark look. The calico never talked to *her*. "How exactly does she talk? Does she lick her paws once for yes and twice for no? Twitch her whiskers in code?"

"She just does," said Lissa uncomfortably. "Everything talks. You just have to listen. Why are you upset?"

Marley bit her lip and scanned the girl's aura. As always, a set of images representing possible futures flickered over the girl's head. Because Lissa was under Marley's protection and nothing unusual was happening, the strongest image—a sense more than a visual, really—was of safety and health. But she could say the wrong thing here, oh yes. Even without her magic, she knew that.

Carefully, fumbling for the right words, she said, "Zachariah and I were talking about grown-up things. You don't need to worry about it because it isn't going to change things between you and me at all."

Lissa stared at her for a long minute, her electric blue eyes intense until abruptly she relaxed. "Business stuff. Okay." She tilted her head, listening. "Oooh, crepes!" Then she flung open the door to vanish down the hall.

Marley relaxed too. Addressing a four-year-old's self-interest so often seemed to be the best option. Quickly, she finished dressing in street clothes and brushed her chestnut hair. Neath watched her intently.

"Whose side are you on, anyhow?" Marley asked the cat. The cat meowed, as if she understood every word Marley said. Since Marley was assured by various experts that the cat was actually an angelic construct, it was probably true. The cat certainly had plenty of other powers, like the ability to join Marley no matter what barriers stood in the way.

Marley thought about one of those experts, the one who she hadn't talked to in months. Corbin. Then she glanced in the mirror, inspecting the magical charms inlaid on her spiritual Geometry. Corbin had crafted two of the seven.

Zachariah, a much older and more experienced wizard than Corbin, had been trying for months to get her to let him replace Corbin's charms with more polished spells. She'd steadily resisted. As long as she had the charms, she felt connected to their creator. One of them was an inactive life-support charm. She was pretty sure if he was badly hurt or dead, the charm would fade from its node. Checking it on it reassured her that whatever he was doing, he was probably fine.

She emerged from the bathroom and found Lissa and Zachariah waiting for her in the hall. Lissa held a spatula. From the kitchen, Kari shouted, "Woohoo, I'm whisking!"

"That's going to be a mess," Marley pointed out.

Zachariah shrugged, unflappable. He glanced at Lissa, who was holding his hand tightly.

The little girl tugged on his hand and said, "You two hug and make up. No biting."

Zachariah snorted, but shook his hand free of Lissa's and crossed to Marley. "Her Majesty commands it," he said softly, and held out a hand to her.

Marley stepped into his arms, slid her hand around his neck, and gave him a kiss on the cheek. "We're the adults, you know."

He pressed his nose against her hair. "Oh, I know. Let's finish that conversation later tonight. We can persuade each other."

Marley wanted to nip him in direct contradiction to Lissa's instruction, but he would have taken it the wrong way. "Maybe. We'll see." Then she pulled away, and hurried out the front door.

2
MARLEY

Before Marley could meet Penny and Branwyn, she had to take Neath home. Too-big tagalong cats made the wait staff nervous, even if they stayed on patio seating. Neath was never, ever a fan of being left at home, though. Marley had read that cats didn't like leaving their territories, and it was clear Neath regarded Marley as her territory. And locking her in the bathroom didn't really help.

"I promise not to pet any other cats while I'm out," Marley told her, as she carried the cat into the house. Neath purred, and Marley rubbed her cheek against the cat's. Neath was strange and magical, but she was always willing to cuddle and never left Marley's side for long. There was something to be said for that.

But, of course, she was still a cat. And after a moment she meowed plaintively, letting Marley know cuddling and protecting her turf took a lot of energy and she was going to starve to death soon. So Marley put her on the couch and went to open a can of cat food. If all went well, Neath would eat and then nap, instead of getting bored or worried and showing up to check on Marley.

It had worked before. Sometimes.

As Neath settled into eating, Marley should have slipped out. Instead, she looked around the apartment she shared with Branwyn. It was messy and increasingly cluttered as their lives got busier, but it was also, to Marley, warm and homelike. She didn't want to leave it, even if everything else had been great with Zachariah. She liked having all her stuff where she wanted it to be. Zachariah was organized to a fault, in Marley's opinion. She thought he'd go nuts, too, if she was there all the time, messing up his stuff and not giving him any time to put things back the way he liked them. He couldn't be thinking it through properly, not on any level except protecting the twins.

Neath looked up, giving Marley a speculative look, which reminded Marley that she had someplace she was supposed to be. Hastily, she backed out the door and shut it before Neath could get out.

On her way down to her car, her phone chimed again. This time, it was a call from her mother: the human mother who had raised and loved her, not the celestial mother who had birthed her and abandoned her, save for possibly sending a magical cat. Madeline Claviger was her *real* mother, in every sense that mattered.

Except Madeline Claviger still didn't know that her daughter wasn't quite human, that her daughter took after her birth mother more than anybody could have imagined. Marley hadn't worked out how exactly to explain that, because she didn't really want to. The whole world was changing rapidly with the return of the faeries, but her relationship with her mother was precious and powerful and she didn't want to risk it.

Marley frowned and let the call go to voicemail. She'd call her back later, when she wasn't driving somewhere. She could never talk to her mother while driving. She needed room to pace and twist things in her fingers and run her hands through her hair.

Even when Marley wasn't keeping secrets, talking to her mother was distracting.

Instead she drove to Old Pasadena. Les Sirenes, the restaurant Penny had picked out, was chic and expensive looking. The scents of fish and fresh bread wafted through an airy interior. A low decorative fence divided a large patio from the shopping alley so diners could show off exactly what the shoppers were missing.

Penny was already seated on the patio, drinking something tall and iced and staring off into space instead of reading the magazine she'd brought. When Marley sat down across from her, she came back to herself with a start.

"Hi! I hope my text didn't interrupt anything good?" She smoothed her hair, already perfect, back from her face.

"No, it came at exactly the right time. Just like I expected. Thanks." Marley squinted at her friend.

Penny was both Latina and Persian by descent, but there'd often been a pallor under her dark skin in recent months, ever since she'd recovered from a magical attack with a huge dose of magical help. The magic that had saved her had made it hard for Marley to read her aura. Marley's magic seemed to think Penny was *safe* no matter what happened, without consideration for all the emotional trauma and mild physical harm that Marley could read in others' futures.

It was annoying, but Marley reluctantly accepted that it was possible her magic was right, at least about the physical safety. What had been done to Penny had changed her in ways that nobody yet understood. Marley had personally done a lot of research in the early days, after Penny woke up and couldn't stop crying all the time. And as far as her research told her, nobody had ever had a prosthetic *anything* made from a Machine stolen from Heaven before, let alone a prosthetic soul.

Then again, it was just as likely that the prosthetic soul was confusing her magic senses. Who knew? Nobody really wanted to experiment with grievous harm in order to find out.

"How are you doing?" Marley asked.

Penny gave her a dazzling smile. "Oh, I'm fine."

"Were you fine five minutes ago?" Marley knew better than to trust Penny's smiles. Penny could smile the stern frown off a stone general on command.

"Well, you know," said Penny airily. "Just thinking about my particular boy problems. And yours, too." She frowned. "I'd rather think about yours. Marley, it worries me that you had to put together this kind of planned escape just to have a serious talk with that man."

Marley sighed and picked up the menu. "Can we save the intervention until Branwyn gets here? You know she'll sulk if you start without her."

Penny gave a little smile and spread her hands, her mouth closed: an invitation to talk without being interrupted. She remained silent while Marley looked over the menu, and while Marley ordered something with rum in it. After that, the quiet became too much to bear, and the words started tumbling out of Marley.

"He asked me to move in with him. Directly. Right before you called."

Penny raised her eyebrows, bringing her hands to her mouth. Silently.

"Every time I think we're beyond this, I'm so happy, Penny. I want what's best for the girls, and I really like him, but I love the ability to get away. I'm still figuring out who I am after last year. I haven't even told my *Mom* what I am yet. And he—" Marley closed her mouth. She wasn't ready to admit to her friends her suspicion that he didn't care who she was, so much as who she'd inherited her magic from. That any daughter of her birth mother would have attracted him. That he only wanted more protection for his very special children.

"Let's just talk about something else for a while, until Branwyn gets here?"

Penny stretched her fingers. "All right. I got an official letter today banning me from the faerie convention."

"You mean the Extraworlder Conference," corrected Marley, smiling at the name. "Why in the world would they ban you? You weren't planning on going, were you? The Senyaza gala is this weekend too." She knew several faeries had visited Penny since her recovery, curious about the capacities of her new soul; she *suspected* one of them might be the 'boy problem' Penny had mentioned. At least, she hoped if it was anything supernatural, it was one of the faeries. A faerie was better than the angel who had almost killed her. Penny could defend herself against faeries now.

With a touch of irritation, Penny said, "No, I wasn't planning on it. I've seen enough faeries already to last me a lifetime."

Marley suggested, "Maybe they want you to come and it's reverse psychology?"

"Hah. No, they think that banishing faeries is… a calling for me or something, not just… who I am now. I didn't exactly choose my shiny new soul's faerie-banishing power. But they're afraid I'll show up and wreck the party."

"Tell them you're going to the Senyaza party instead. They'll love that. And then you could hold a party of your own and ban *them*."

"And have to spend all my time enforcing the ban? No thanks," Penny said sourly. "Maybe I'll get out of town after the Senyaza thing. I've got a few invitations I could take up. DC, New York…." She flipped idly through her magazine until she got to a photo spread showing a few reckless Congressional Representatives posing for photos with faeries. Even when the faeries had dressed appropriately for visiting Congress, they were easy to identify; each and every one of them looked like they'd been digitally enhanced far, far more than their photo buddy. Even the texture of the light on their skin looked different.

"Not much escape there," Marley pointed out.

"No. The invitation to DC isn't a compelling one. Signing up for civil service never interested me."

Her magazine gave a muffled beep, and Penny moved it aside to look at her phone. "Yes, Branwyn, we see that you're late. We saw that ten minutes ago," she said to the message displayed on the screen.

"What's she doing? Can we order without her?"

"Caught by her family somehow. Go ahead. I suppose you probably have to get back to nannying."

Marley shrugged, and caught a waiter's attention. After she ordered her lunch and Penny ordered an appetizer, they talked about television for a few moments. Then as Marley started eating her sandwich, Penny leaned back, finishing her drink and watching the pedestrians. Abruptly she said, "What happened to that one guy? Corbin? He's the one who tried teaching Branwyn magic, right? You used to talk about him all the time last year. Where is he these days?"

Marley stopped eating. She shook out her napkin and then folded it into a square, concentrating on making each edge sharp and clean. "I have no idea. He was doing some work for Senyaza in Japan or Europe somewhere and then he dropped off the radar."

"Japan or Europe," said Penny dryly. "What a narrowly pinned down location. So you two weren't close? I was kind of out of it when I first woke up, but I got the impression—"

"We used to talk a lot," said Marley hastily, one of her corners slipping awry. "Then we kind of drifted apart." But she still thought of him almost every day. She still reassured herself he was alive because she had his charms. He had a good reason for not talking to her. But she hoped that someday, once the rest of her life had been sorted out, they'd talk again.

As she habitually did each time she thought of him, she turned on the magical sight he'd given her and looked down at her torso, where the life-support charm was affixed to her magical core.

She blinked. The charms were self-contained spells woven from the Geometry, the massive lines and whirls of magical energy that underlay everything in Creation. All humans started with seven looped nodes along the thick line that ran through their bodies: knots of energy that spells could be affixed to. Wizards constructed and placed charms, but once placed, the charms drew on the bearer's strength and responded to the bearer's will.

Marley had been studying magic since she discovered it existed, first under Corbin's tutelage, and then on her own. She hardly qualified as a wizard, but she knew a lot more than Penny and Branwyn did. For example, she knew that it was almost impossible for anybody but the creator to casually remove a charm from a node. It took time, and a wizard's workshop. Marley had heard that a Queen of Faerie could do it with a wave of her hand, but she didn't know anybody else with that degree of control over the Geometry.

And yet: the life-support charm Corbin had given her was unraveling. She stared at it for a heartbeat. Then she tried to gather up the strands of the Geometry and hold the charm in place. It didn't work, and only a moment after she looked at herself, the charm was gone.

"What's going on?" asked Penny, alarmed. "Why are you muttering 'no, no, no, no?'"

Marley didn't answer, looking around wildly. A black bird flew down from the roof. Faeries could be almost everywhere these days, but not the Queens, which meant if somebody was removing Corbin's charms, it had to be—

A tall, lean man in blue jeans, a plain white t-shirt and sunglasses was walking down the alley away from the restaurant. He had dark hair. She stared hard at his back, and then she was sure. *Corbin.*

"Hey," she called, standing up. He didn't stop, didn't turn around. *He was walking away.* She lunged forward, as if she could catch him, and only succeeded in tangling herself in the decorative fence around the patio's edge.

Penny said, "Whoa, are you all right? Is that—? Let me just—" but Marley barely heard her. She seized Penny's hand, pulled herself to her feet and plunged over the fallen fence. Then she raced down the sidewalk. "Corbin, wait!"

"Oh my God, Marley, don't just run off and leave your—"

Marley collided with somebody. It wasn't Corbin, so she pushed past them, looking around wildly. At the end of the alley, she emerged into the crowds of shoppers on the sidewalk and paused. She tried to think past the buzzing of panic and confusion. Then she fumbled for her phone and realized it was in her purse, which she'd left in the restaurant.

A black bird swooped overhead and she saw Corbin crossing the street down at the crosswalk. She hesitated, staring at the distant profile.

"Is that really him?" inquired Penny, shoving Marley's purse into her ribs. "I saw him watching us and I thought of your friend, but I've never met him before... have I?"

"Once, briefly, when you were sick," said Marley, and fought her way through the crowds to the crosswalk. "You're taller, please don't take your eyes off him!" She kept her own eyes on the sky, watching for ravens.

"He went down the other alley," Penny reported. Marley pulled out her phone and tapped three buttons to call Corbin. It rang twice before being disconnected.

Hurt and anger battled for space. She pushed both reactions away and focused on activating several of the charms she had remaining: a charm to enhance her reflexes so she wouldn't trip again, and a charm to give luck a little nudge in her favor.

The light changed as soon as the luck charm activated. She charged across the street, cutting across the corner. Weaving around the people on the street, she turned into the alley. It was much less crowded and in the distance, halfway down the alley, she once again made out the white t-shirt.

Penny caught up with her again. "Are you sure chasing him is a good idea? Most guys who run like that aren't worth the effort of catching."

"He stole something from me," said Marley, and ran. People cleared out of her way, some because they saw her coming and some because they coincidentally—luckily—decided to head into one of the buildings.

He turned to look back at her, the long line of his nose achingly familiar. Then he stepped out of sight around the corner.

Penny grabbed her arm, hauling her to a stop. "Marley, don't do something stupid. Or if you *must*, stop leaving me behind. There are so many ways this could go wrong, especially if you keep running off!"

"Fine," Marley muttered. She grabbed Penny by the hand and power-walked her to the end of the alley.

"This empty alley is creepy enough. If he leaps out at us, somebody's getting hurt. And I know maybe you want to be alone with him after so long, but I'm not very comfortable with that. I'd be sad if something happened to you because I let you outrun me. Although, God, I've got to ramp up the jogging, when did you get so fast? You don't even exercise—"

There was nobody around the corner, no Corbin anywhere on the street. Marley hesitated, Penny's nervous babbling trickling in past her distraction. She looked at Penny with her danger-sight. The other woman's steady untouchable glow hadn't changed. Not *exactly* reassuring given Penny's special situation, but Marley's magic didn't work on herself at all: not her danger-sight and not her shields.

"Did we lose him?" asked Penny.

Marley turned her magic sight onto the street, looking at both the tangles of the Geometry and the auras her natural danger-sight provided. The Geometry sight wasn't one of her intrinsic powers. Corbin had built it for her: a custom charm that integrated her danger-sight and a few other visual perks. She didn't usually use her danger-sight on large groups of people because it was extremely upsetting to see all the possible ways strangers might hurt themselves in the next few hours. But she didn't want to waste time focusing if she caught a glimpse of Corbin. She wanted to know anything she could, right away.

The city street was a jumble of Geometry lines, nodes, matrices and loops, all crashing into each other. At the end of the street was a park. The Geometry there was less chaotic, the points of life fitting together into constellations that hovered on the edge of recognition.

Something strange was moving down there, she realized. Somebody who didn't have an aura. Dread uncurled in her gut as she recognized Corbin. She ran toward the park, towing Penny after her. When he moved deeper into the green area, past the playground, Marley had to shut down her danger-sight. Looking at all the children playing dangerous games was simply too much for her. But she couldn't give up the chase. Not yet. Not until she knew why. And how.

She paused to look again on the other side of the playground, in a stand of enormous old trees.

"Enough, Marley. Stop." It was Corbin, his voice rusty and barely recognizable.

Penny jumped and then laughed nervously, squeezing Marley's

hand tightly. Marley spotted Corbin's profile leaning against the side of the tree. He'd taken his sunglasses off.

"What's going on, Corbin?" She furrowed her brow, studying him, trying to understand. His face was drawn, almost gaunt, and there were lines around his eyes that she didn't recognize. He looked like he hadn't had a good night's sleep for weeks. His clothes didn't quite fit, as if he'd shopped in a hurry.

And to magic Sight, it was worse. His eyes glowed, one blue and one black. That was familiar. But the black webbing that clung to him, veiling his charms, was not. Red flared along his spine, as if his magic was cracking open, and something churned beyond it. It was like nothing she'd seen before.

And he was utterly invisible to her danger sense. That was new, too, and just as upsetting.

"What's going on?" she repeated when he didn't answer. "What happened to you? Why did you—"

"Stay there!" he said sharply, and Marley realized she'd moved closer to him, still towing Penny. "Stay away. Stop following me. I didn't come here to talk to you."

"What, you only tracked me down to steal back the charm you gave me?" demanded Marley.

"Yes," he said coldly. "And I should have started with your Sight instead. You can get Zachariah to replace it. Go away now, or I'll take that too."

"Corbin," Marley whispered, shocked nearly speechless. The man she remembered helping her, teaching her, and holding her had *never* spoken to her like this. When she'd been at her most neurotic and confused, he'd been gentle. When she'd been frightened, he'd helped her see her own strength. And when she'd been indecisive, he'd been patient.

But she never *had* decided. He'd left on a mission from Senyaza rather than demand things of her she wasn't ready to give.

Something changed in his posture, and his mouth curved in a smile both alien and familiar. "Shoo," he said. "Go play with the children."

Maybe she deserved the coldness, but there was more going on. Marley shook her hand out of Penny's and moved closer. "Something's wrong, Corbin. I can't see you with my magic, but I can tell that you're not well."

He tilted his head, watching her approach. He was taut as a bowstring, practically quivering as she got closer. His eyes dilated. "Can you?"

"Let me help you," Marley coaxed, reaching for him. Her protection magic could do so much to help somebody, but only if they allowed it to work. "What happened to you?"

He flinched as if she'd struck him, and his hand wrapped hard around hers, his fingers long and strong and warm. "You can't help me now, Marley. I made sure of that. I just wanted to see you one last time."

She held his hand to her cheek, barely hearing his words as she remembered being even closer to him. He'd left for good reasons but oh God, she'd missed him. She swayed closer, inhaling his sandalwood scent.

His eyes, so dark a blue as to be charcoal, widened and he gasped, pulling away from her and backing up as if she'd burned him.

"I said stay away!" He kept moving. "Don't come near me again. You, Penny? Explain to your friend that I'm not interested in this conversation. I'm not interested in *her*."

Then he backed into another tree, twisted the Geometry around him, and vanished into the Backworld.

Marley's hand dropped to her side and curled into a fist as Penny joined her and said apprehensively, "Are we done chasing him?" She slid her hand around Marley's arm.

Marley leaned on her, her legs suddenly unsteady. "For now."

3
BRANWYN

B ranwyn tapped her foot as she stared at the video chat with her youngest sister on her tablet screen, waiting for Meredith to get her act together. She'd decided to complete the paperwork for Meredith's new music school at her own studio instead of at her family's house, because her family's house was endlessly noisy and distracting.

It had been a good idea. But she'd failed to get all the bits together in advance. And filling out paperwork for a school was a lot more complicated than Branwyn had realized. Or at least *this* school. She hoped fervently it was the only school she'd be doing paperwork for in the next decade.

The chat session had already gone on longer than she'd hoped. Meredith fumbled through a file folder, babbling a mix of cheerful apologies and enthusiasm. Their mother, Holly, hovered in the background behind Meri. "You can just bring it by and I'll get it done, sweetheart."

"You've got enough to do, Mom. I said I'd send Meri to this place, so I'm going to do the paperwork," said Branwyn, digging deep into the patience reserves. She was so, so glad Tristan, one of her middle brothers, could do his own paperwork for the drama seminar she was sending him to.

"It's just so generous of you," said her mother anxiously. "Are you sure you don't want to save the money for a rainy day instead?"

Branwyn laughed, looking around her studio at the detritus of a dozen very profitable commissions. "I have a *waiting list*, Mom. I'll be busy for years."

"Yes, but it's for all these... magic people," said her mother fretfully. "How reliable can that be?"

"Found it!" said Meredith, pulling a sheet of paper from the folder.

"It'll be fine, Mom. I'm ready, Meri," Branwyn lifted her pen.

"I just don't want you to get in trouble like Jaime did," explained Holly.

"Mom, go away," said Meredith impatiently. "She's going to send me to *Gleason Academy of Music*. Dad already signed the form. Why are you trying to talk her out of it?"

Holly shook her head and moved out of the line of sight of the camera.

"Quick, while she's temporarily defeated," said Branwyn, and Meredith read off the information Branwyn needed. She noted it down neatly and then slid the final form into the envelope. "There we go, brat. I'll send it off today and you'll get a letter in a couple weeks. And now I have to go, because I'm already late for lunch." She ended the call mid-gush without a twinge of guilt. Meredith's enthusiasm could devour hours.

"That kid does go on," said a familiar voice fondly behind her. Branwyn grabbed her backpack and turned to see Rhianna, the oldest of her younger sisters, leaning on the open door of the studio.

"Hey, Rhianna," Branwyn said, rising and looking over the

younger woman curiously. She'd cut her red hair recently—exactly the same hair that Branwyn would have if she didn't keep hers dyed green—and had smoothed the curls so that it framed her face in a sleek bob. "Mom didn't mention you were in town."

"I haven't told her yet." Rhianna moved into the studio and looked around. "You've changed the place." It was true. What had once been Branwyn's art studio was almost a storage space now, with boxes of supplies stacked as high as Branwyn could reach. In one corner a partially open door had been painted on the wall, and the darkness beyond had a depth to it that hinted at its true nature: a passage to the Backworld where Branwyn did much of her real work. Rhianna only gave the door a glance before her gaze fell on the large inscribed metal hammer laying on the table beside Branwyn's tablet. There was a black gem embedded in the head. "Nice war hammer."

Despite the fact that Branwyn was standing, Rhianna seated herself in the nice chair, the one Branwyn normally offered to potential clients. She spun the chair, lifting her feet out of her shoes to make it go faster.

"Ah, you're not even pretending this is a casual trip. What's going on?" Branwyn let her backpack slide down to the ground again, but she didn't sit. Rhianna worked for the federal government, in the kind of job she couldn't admit to having. Since the previous October, when the faeries had emerged back into the human world, she'd only been home for the briefest of weekend trips.

"What makes you think something's going on?" asked Rhianna absently, watching her feet as she flexed them in and out.

Branwyn stopped the spinning chair. "Your hair looks nice. Different, but nice. How do you chew on it when you're studying, though?"

Rhianna gave her a small smile. "I haven't figured that out yet."

Branwyn waited for a moment but Rhianna didn't say anything

else. "You didn't come for a commission, did you? I mean, I've been a little surprised that I haven't heard anything from your crowd but it's all good. I've got a three page waiting list of private customers."

"In a way, that's why I'm here," said Rhianna and sighed.

It was the sigh that did it. It was too much. "You're softening me up," said Branwyn flatly. "Either spit it out or come back later, because I'm late for lunch."

Rhianna gave her a subdued smile and Branwyn felt a twinge of alarm. Either Rhianna had become even better as an actress, or something really was bothering her. Rhianna wouldn't hesitate to use her own trauma to manipulate somebody else, but she was usually delighted to admit it when Branwyn caught her.

"All right. Do you remember the key you gave me last October?"

"The key to this very studio that I impulsively gave you and then regretted later because I'd locked myself out? Yes, I remember." Branwyn had used her artificing magic on the key before giving it to Rhianna, waking up the inert metal into something with a Geometric node and the beginnings of an intrinsic nature of its own. "Did it become something useful?"

Rhianna took a deep breath. "Yes. It did. It was incorporated into a device that allows a supernatural entity to fully manifest in our world." Her eyes widened innocently. "They can't normally, you know. There's a field in place that inhibits them. But the device erases the field for the wielder."

"It's called the Hush," said Branwyn slowly, staring hard at Rhianna, trying to see through all her projected body language. "It was incorporated…. And who did the incorporation, Rhianna?"

Rhianna shrugged. "A lot of us contributed something, but it was overseen by our Senior Adviser."

"Your Senior Adviser," Branwyn said. "I want to know more

about your Senior Adviser. Is he the one who put those empty charms on you?"

"My protections? Oh yes." Rhianna gave her a sunny smile. "He's a supernatural entity too, but he's not like the faeries. He wants to *protect* people."

Branwyn remembered Penny saying something similar a year ago. It was back when Penny had been entangled with an angel who wanted to destroy two little girls as a way of 'protecting people'. She sank back into her desk chair, feeling sick.

"What's wrong?" asked Rhianna, moving closer, her smile fading.

"You're not in love with this guy or anything, are you?"

Rhianna drew back in surprise. "You're kidding, right? Oh my God, Branwyn. He's like my boss's boss's boss. And a lot more freaky than the faeries, to be totally honest. We're glad to have his help but he's an adviser, not some kind of celestial playboy."

Branwyn stared at her searchingly, and then relaxed in relief. Rhianna lied sometimes but she wouldn't lie about that, not to Branwyn. After a minute, she pulled herself together. "Senior Adviser sounds more *governmental* than you usually admit to. What's up with that?"

Rhianna looked self-conscious. "It seemed like the right corporate term for him would have been 'angel investor.' Nobody was really comfortable with that."

Branwyn laughed despite herself and stretched her legs out. "All right. Your Adviser is a supernatural entity who took what I gave you and made a device that would let him fully manifest on Earth."

"Yep! It's even better than what you and Jaime did for the faeries."

Shooting a dirty look at her sister, Branwyn said, "I used the faeries to save Penny; I didn't give them anything in the end."

Which was a little bit of a lie, but in the context it was true enough. "And they used Jaime to get around their door; he didn't do anything for them on purpose."

Sweetly, Rhianna said, "And now here they are, running all over the world causing trouble. Don't you watch the news?"

"I do, but I hardly need to. I have an up close, personal understanding of how dangerous they—and other supernaturals—can be, Rhianna! Penny almost died because of one who *wasn't* a faerie, and I—" Branwyn stopped herself. She tried not to think too much about her own brushes with a fate worse than death at the hands of monsters. "But never mind that. You're not worried about your supernatural guy *at all?*"

"Nope. I wasn't before, because we've got nothing else to help us against the faeries and I've seen the unpublicized reports on what they've been up to the last year. And I'm definitely not worried about him now. I've got something much better to be worried about now."

Branwyn wondered what the secret reports said. She'd heard bad things about some of the stuff happening in the rest of the world. In the USA, the most popular face of the faeries was the Nightwell movie production studio that had formed in Hollywood. They were friendly and sociable with the media, and very happy to put on demonstrations of magic. According to interviews they were positively thrilled with the idea of entertaining the masses with special effects-laden films. Their announced list of projects was… ambitious.

But pretty faeries in Hollywood aside, there'd been some awful clashes between some of the faeries and humans. A lot of the faeries who'd emerged from their Backworld prison weren't particularly trying to integrate themselves. Many, many humans refused to welcome those who wanted to try. And the faeries had enormous power when they chose to exercise it: over the weather and nature, over the minds of the unprotected, and over illusions.

On the other hand, humans had numbers and, while less well known, their own magic. It was a problem to be solved and Branwyn was secretly glad that her sister was part of an organization with the resources, information and willingness to try. But…

"What are you worried about now?"

Her sister reached for a strand of hair that was too short to chew on. "I'm worried about how the device has been stolen."

Slowly, Branwyn leaned her chin onto her palm, letting the silence drag out as she thought of who she didn't want to have stolen the device. Then she took a deep breath. "All right. The million dollar question: why are you here telling me? Do you expect me to make you another one? Because—"

Rhianna laced her fingers together. "Well… you've been doing a lot of work with Senyaza. We've got the records. You're tight with them right now. Do you know about their history with my organization?"

Branwyn narrowed her eyes. *The records.* She'd given up most of her privacy a year earlier, in a dangerous deal with the faerie Queen of Stone. It had been a serious wrench. But she didn't think Rhianna had been talking to the Queen of Stone about her work schedule. No, Rhianna had *records*, because she worked for an organization that had zero respect for anybody's privacy.

And it didn't bother Rhianna at all. How had Branwyn's sister's ideals ended up so far from her own? It was mind-boggling.

Her irritation spilled over. "Given that your organization doesn't even have a name, how could I possibly know about any mutual history?"

Rhianna flashed a smile. "You don't like Acme Integrated Solutions?" Branwyn just gave her a steely look and she added, "The President calls us the Office of the Unexpected. OX."

Her throat tight with conflicting emotions, Branwyn asked,

"Rhianna, have you met *the President?*"

Pursing her lips, Rhianna said, "Met? No. Been in the same room while he talked to my boss's boss? Yes. Anyhow, OX has been monitoring the exploitation of supernatural resources—magic—for a long time. A lot longer than the faeries have been running around. We used to be just a little office in a basement. But we've gotten quite a bit of a budget boost lately."

"Yes, I can imagine."

"So… Senyaza is the biggest collection of magic users around. OX has never been exactly happy with that. But as long as magic was on the down low and they didn't use it to influence the economy or anything, all we had to do was monitor them and the other magical weirdoes. And Senyaza was so good at managing uncontrolled magic that when trouble did start we could just sort of help out with paperwork after. It's not like we had the resources to do anything else."

"How long has your Senior Adviser been on the scene?" Branwyn interrupted.

"Oh, a while. Years. Though he didn't always have a formal position. For the longest time there was just my boss and my boss's boss as the human staff, stuck in a basement below Acme Integrated Solutions. *Anyhow*, a couple of weeks after our talented stepfather's song unleashed the faeries, OX contacted Senyaza to find out if they had a remedy planned. We spent a couple months talking about how to send the faeries back where they came from, but apparently there were problems on Senyaza's end?" Rhianna gave Branwyn an inquisitive look.

"I wasn't involved in any of this. All I know is that you were home for a weekend in February, and I made Mr. Black a belt that lets him talk to Titan One."

Rhianna shrugged. "February was a quiet month, comparatively. Anyhow… March was the Congressional hearings, and we had to manage those so the faeries didn't influence them—"

"Yes, it would be just *awful* if Congressional hearings for deciding what to do about a group of people were actually influenced by those people."

Rhianna gave her a scowl and went on. "Meanwhile Senyaza started—" then hesitated and backtracked. "Actually, wait, really, Branwyn? Really? You really think it was wrong of us to not allow entities with both the ability to influence minds *and* the ability to manipulate natural forces into the Capitol? They don't let in people with bombs either, even if they're discussing what to do about terrorists. At least the faeries were allowed to present video statements."

Branwyn ground her teeth. "I'm sorry. Go on."

With a severe look, Rhianna went on. "Senyaza started planning a big company meeting, and we started making our own plans. With a lot more fingers in the pie, because yay, Congress. In May Senyaza had their meeting. They invited most of their contractors and OX was invited to observe. All very nice and polite."

There'd been an invitation, Branwyn vaguely recalled. She'd been in the middle of something, and she hadn't been able to imagine why anybody thought she'd want to go to a Senyaza company meeting. She'd assumed it would involve boring financial figures and maybe a few product demos.

"So, um, yeah, it started nice and polite. But the new initiative the Secretary of Homeland Security gave OX didn't really go over well in the pre-meeting briefing and tensions kind of… flared during the meeting and there was a pretty vocal disagreement and that's why we think Senyaza has stolen the device." The words tumbled out of Rhianna in a flood.

Branwyn, experienced with Rhianna trying to obfuscate something, zeroed right in. "New initiative?"

"It's not really relevant to the topic at hand," Rhianna said airily.

"What I'm hoping for is that you can use your connections to Senyaza to discover if they took the device."

"Rhianna, clearly I'm going to be angry when I find out about this new initiative. I'm already angry now. Let's get it out of the way so I won't have to change gears later," Branwyn urged. "It will be more efficient for everybody." When Rhianna still hesitated, she added, "Otherwise I'll learn out from Senyaza. Wouldn't it be better to hear about it from my own sister?"

Rhianna stood and deliberately moved so the chair was directly between Branwyn and herself. "They—the government—*we* want to license magic users. I mean, we license drivers. So we need existing magic users to register. Including the faeries and the nephilim." She squeezed her eyes shut as if afraid of a conflagration.

"Including faeries and nephilim, who can't *not* be magic?"

Rhianna nodded.

Branwyn put her hands behind her back. "Right."

Rhianna opened one eye and then the other. "You aren't mad?"

"I'm furious," Branwyn assured her. "I'm going to tell Grandma that you're working for cryptofascists. You'd better go visit the kids while you can because once I talk to her you're going to be disowned and barred from the house."

"*Branwyn!*" Rhianna protested. "Don't be a jerk. These people are dangerous. We have to find some way of managing the situation and this lets us track who's willing to work with us. It lets us identify those who are willing to *try* to avoid being dangerous. It's barely more than an extra field on a census form. And the faeries, at least, *are* undocumented. And once the licensing system is in place, we can provide training, we can provide verification, they can sell their services to ordinary people who have some recourse against scams—"

"Were you *surprised* when Senyaza didn't like this idea?" Branwyn demanded.

Rhianna looked at her sidelong. "No."

Nodding, Branwyn said, "That's your guilty conscience at work. You know it's wrong to declare an entire group of people illegal just for existing."

"We're not doing that," said Rhianna sullenly. She went over to look at Branwyn's hammer, avoiding Branwyn's gaze.

"I have no idea how you expect to compel the faeries or Senyaza to register—oh my God, no wonder you think Senyaza stole the device, no wonder you *built* it. It's your enforcement stick. What did Senyaza actually say at the meeting?"

Rhianna gave her a wide-eyed look that reminded Branwyn of a child about to confide an impressive discovery. "Um… they told my boss that they were more powerful than the federal government. In not very nice language."

Branwyn laughed despite herself and guessed, "Your boss said, 'How do you expect to stop us?' and somebody there said, 'Fuck you, that's how.'"

"Pretty much," Rhianna agreed. "So will you help us?"

Branwyn groaned and pushed her hands against her head. "Rhianna. Why should I? You pretty much know that there's no way I'm going to support some kind of Nonhuman Registration Act, even if you dip it into training/licensing/profit chocolate."

"Well," said Rhianna earnestly, "We're *pretty sure* Senyaza stole it, but we'd like to be *absolutely* sure. Because if Senyaza stole it, we're not worried they're going to *use* it. They'll just stick it in that Repository of theirs. But if somebody else stole it…. We may have a bigger problem. So if you could confirm Senyaza has it, it would be *so* nice."

Once again, Branwyn thought of who she hoped *wasn't* involved. There was one—and another—and another. So many. She didn't want *any* celestial able to manifest completely. Once even one could, *everything* was going to hell fast. She dropped her face into her hands, contemplating the horrifying possibilities ahead.

"I'll see what I can learn."

4
MARLEY

Marley didn't argue when Penny demanded her keys. She was too busy trying to understand what had just happened. Corbin had said he wasn't interested in her anymore. She didn't believe that, but the thought still hurt so much she had trouble breathing.

Penny said cheerfully, "I'll take you home. It would have been a very nice lunch but we can try again later when some bastard doesn't show up and ruin your day, all right?"

The mention of lunch roused Marley from her self-absorption. "Did we pay for our food? I wasn't thinking—"

"*I* paid for our food. And grabbed your purse. Don't thank me, it's what I'm here for. Did you park in the garage? Let's go there."

Marley let Penny guide her to her car, and then drive the car home. Penny chattered for part of the drive before falling silent, but Marley only distantly noticed any of it.

At last Marley said, "I thought he was fine. I would look at his charms and think, even if he hadn't talked to me lately, he was fine. Someday we'd talk again. But he's not fine. There's something seriously wrong with him. And I had no idea."

"Yes, I saw that too," said Penny, subdued. "Like he's literally tangled up in something."

A spike of pain passed through Marley's head and then vanished. It had been a headache-inducing day. "I was such an idiot. I'm not going to let him just walk away again."

Absently Penny said, "Of course not." She shot Marley a glance. "Though he did make it pretty clear—"

Marley pulled at her hair. "Then why did he come back, Penny? We were out of each others' lives. He didn't have to track me down and take back what he gave me. If he hates me that much now—" She shook her head and looked out the window.

Penny said, "Don't ask me. I find men just as inexplicable as magic."

When they got to Marley and Branwyn's apartment, Neath was waiting outside the front door, her tail lashing. As soon as she saw Marley, she wound her way around her legs and then went to claw at the front door.

"You got out, cat, you can get in again," said Penny, but opened the door anyhow and pulled Marley in. "Sit down, sort things out. Call work."

Marley sat on her couch and was promptly knocked back by Neath. She blinked at Penny, startled, and then realized that Zachariah was expecting her back again that afternoon. She couldn't bear the thought of it, and as long as she was a paid employee, she was entitled to some time off. But she had to tell him something.

"Hi," she said into the phone after he answered. "Something personal has come up. I can't come over this afternoon. Can you manage without me?"

"Personal?" he inquired, surprised.

"I really can't talk about it now," she said hurriedly. *Or maybe ever.* Things with Corbin had been complicated partially because of Zachariah. They'd been friends once. They weren't anymore.

"All right," Zachariah said mildly. "But are you all right? The girls will want to know."

She should have just texted him. "I'm fine. Mostly. Look, I'll call you tomorrow if I'm not going to see you."

"Marley. Be careful, please."

The apartment door slammed open and Branwyn stood there, glowering, her green hair flying about her face like a cloud. Marley said, "I will," and hung up. "Branwyn, I—"

"I need to go visit Senyaza," announced Branwyn. "Can you come, Marley? They like you more than me. Hi, Penny, sorry I skipped lunch. My sister decided to bring me her problems again."

"Yes," said Marley, standing. "Yes, I'd like to visit Senyaza too. I have some questions for them I'd rather not wait for callbacks on."

Penny looked between them. "Can you drop me off so I can get my car?"

Neath meowed and then head-butted Marley's shin, as if shooing her out the door. Marley noticed because it was odd. Like Corbin saying he wasn't interested in her anymore. Another spike of pain passed through her head at the memory and she thought she might cry.

Instead, she said, "Let's go."

When Marley told Branwyn about Corbin, Branwyn said, "I'm just going to add him to my list of people to track down and shake the stupid out of."

"Oh no, there's a list now? What did your sister actually do this time?" Rhianna had gone on more than one 'adventure' in high school that Marley had to help cover for.

"I should blame myself. I should have known. Wait, what am I saying? How could I have known? Tarn said nobody had learned this magic of mine in centuries." Her gaze went distant. "Tarn… I wonder…"

"Branwyn, that's a stoplight! Pay attention or let me drive!"

Branwyn refocused on the road. "Sorry. I'll talk to Tarn later."

"Is he on the shake list too?" Marley guessed.

"Not yet. Though no bets on how long that lasts." Branwyn fell silent, either brooding or concentrating on driving. Marley decided it was best to not distract her more. Instead, when her mother called her again, she answered that.

They chatted for a while about her younger brother's adventures as a summer camp junior counselor, her mother's annoyances at work, and her father's project building a gaming table. Family gossip. It was casual, easy chat that left Marley plenty of room to do her own brooding.

Madeline Claviger and her husband had adopted Marley when she'd been abandoned as an infant in a basket in their carport. Once upon a time that had probably been an acceptable way of getting rid of an unwanted baby. But times had changed and Marley had never been able to forgive her biological mother for not dropping her off at a fire station or a hospital, let alone filling out the forms that would have made her adoption go quickly and smoothly. Discovering her mother had been an angel hadn't improved her opinion on the subject. Sure, legitimate paperwork might have been harder, but celestials had the power to smooth out all sorts of obstacles.

Marley had worried about who her biological parents were when she was a teen. But it had never been because she was unhappy with the mother who had raised her. Madeline had endured *so much* when Marley had been young, and loved her so well. Which was why Marley wasn't telling Madeline that her biological mother wasn't human.

Keeping secrets from her mother bothered Marley, but she was afraid talk about her involvement with the newly public supernatural world. Branwyn flaunted the magic she'd learned from the faeries, but there were still so many secrets. The fact that some people had angels or demons for parents was one of them, and it was one that would have a public backlash, at least in the United States of America.

Her mother would worry. Her mother would probably even get upset. And it was just imaginable that discovering her daughter's heritage would be the final straw that made her realize Marley was far too much trouble to love. It was a ridiculous, irrational thought, the thought of a panicked thirteen year old, but it still made the words dry up in Marley's mouth each time she considered confessing the truth.

"...And Aunt Leila was asking me when you were going to come out of the closet and I told her about that *nice* young man of yours we met when we came over for Easter but I don't think she was buying it, kiddo."

Marley's hand jerked and the phone almost flew out of her grasp. She fumbled and caught it and then jammed it back to her ear again. "Mom! Aunt Leila thinks I'm gay?"

"She's not being judgemental, sweetheart. She's just old and wants to be supportive. She doesn't want you to live a lie, and she sees you and Branwyn living together. Neither of you have boyfriends or even date and she thinks that's a *terrible* closet but that you should at least be honest with your family."

Marley stared at the dashboard. Family was *so* comforting. "Do you think I'm living a lie?"

Far too calmly, her mother said, "You're certainly hiding something major about your life. I suspect it has something to do with that *nice* young man that you're so definitely not dating."

Marley's mother was a screenwriter. She rarely used clichés like 'nice young man' by accident. Marley squirmed in her seat as she wondered what her mother actually thought about Zachariah. "He's not as young as he looks," she mumbled.

"That's a shocker, let me tell you," said Madeline placidly. "Well, I told Aunt Leila that you'd let us know what was going on in your own time. You know, as long as you stay true to yourself, whatever you are is fine."

Marley tried to find a way to brush the whole topic away, but she couldn't find the words. "Thanks," she muttered. She remembered the last Christmas card she'd received from her mother's aunt, addressed to both herself and Branwyn and added, "But you can at least tell Aunt Leila that Branwyn and I aren't a couple."

Marley's mother sighed. "And she was so looking forward to the wedding, poor old soul. She wanted to know if Branwyn would wear a tux or a gown."

"You know, maybe I'd wear the tux," said Marley, annoyed.

"Nobody *has* to wear a tux, dear. But Aunt Leila sketched a cute knee-length dress for you—"

"*Mom!*" wailed Marley. "She didn't. You're making all this up."

"Hand to God, I'm not," said Madeline cheerfully, but Marley just *knew* that she'd encouraged the conversation along.

Branwyn took the phone from Marley's hand. "Hi, Madeline. You know, I think I'd go for a sort of tuxedo-skirt hybrid. There's probably a name for it but we left Penny at home. Yeah, Marley and I will have to fight over whether Penny's the maid of honor or the best woman. And now I have to drag Marley off to do terrible things to her. No, you don't want to know. Sure, I'd love to. Give my love to Aunt Leila!"

She offered the phone back to Marley, smirking. "We're here, by the way."

Marley hunched in her seat and looked at the entrance to Titan One, the Senyaza skyscraper that served as shopping center, office building and apartment complex. "I wish I could just tell her. It's wonderful that your family knows all everything."

"Not everything," said Branwyn, prodding her with the phone until Marley took it from her. "There's quite a lot they don't know, and the way Mom and Jaime 'found out' wasn't exactly pleasant."

"Yeah, but you don't have to hide what you do all day, or why you do it."

Branwyn gave her a pointed look. "Neither do you."

Marley shrugged and sighed. "I know. I keep telling myself that and then I just get... afraid." She changed the subject. "You have to tell me what's going on before you attack Alejandro or I'm going to have to defend him from you and today has been too awful to add that on."

Branwyn made a face. "Let me sum up: The government has an angel. My sister works for him. They made one of my creations into a Hush-canceling device." Marley's mouth opened and Branwyn said, "No, wait, it gets worse. The device got stolen. Rhianna thinks Senyaza is responsible, because they totally reasonably don't want anyone getting around the Hush."

Marley processed that for a moment and then got out of the car. "Do you really think Alejandro will know if they did? Or that he'd tell you?"

"He'll know gossip," said Branwyn confidently, falling into step beside her. "Alejandro has the *best* gossip. That's why I like him more than George."

George was the Specialist Project Manager who was technically Branwyn's point of contact with Senyaza. He signed her checks and formally offered the contacts for the various projects she'd engaged in for Senyaza.

Marley said dryly, "And not because George is an old-fashioned charmer who doesn't approve of your magic?"

Branwyn ran her fingers through her hair. "He doesn't approve of *me* having my magic. He'd be fine if somebody like him had it. An old-school wizard, properly trained by another old-school wizard, who developed their skills reading books."

"There's nothing wrong with learning from books," protested Marley, the ex-college-librarian. They went over to the office level elevators next to the parking garage.

"Yes, dear," said Branwyn, patting her on the shoulder. "Anyhow, they assigned George to *manage* me. They assigned Alejandro to *coordinate* with you. I like coordination better."

Another spike of pain passed through Marley's head and she stumbled against Branwyn. Branwyn slid her hand down to catch Marley's elbow. "Hey, you okay?"

Marley shook her head, wincing. "Just a headache. Probably from looking at all of Old Pasadena with magic sight. I'm not going to be doing that again, let me tell you."

Branwyn made a face. "If they can't tell you anything about Corbin, I'll see what I can find out."

At the security desk, Marley negotiated the secure sign-in process that would let her bring Branwyn in as her guest. She knew that when Branwyn came to Senyaza alone, she had to wait for George or some other Senyaza full-timer to come pick her up at the checkpoint. Marley, on the other hand, had her own badge and was allowed in and out as she wished.

And what had Marley done to deserve that privilege? She'd been born a nephil, and agreed to be on-call for Senyaza for one project or operation a year. They would have given her a studio apartment in Titan One or one of their other buildings if she'd wanted one, too. Senyaza believed in taking care of its own.

The disparity made Marley uncomfortable, even though Branwyn basically approved. They were equally supportive of their human employees. It was just that humans had to go through Senyaza's strenuous hiring process for full-timers first. They didn't simply have to be born and say 'yes' to a standing offer made to all nephilim.

"Are you coming or not?" asked Marley, once she'd received Branwyn's temporary badge. Branwyn left off covertly marking up a posted flyer informing the employees of the upcoming gala event and joined her.

"What were you doing?"

"They're planning on introducing *my* project at the gala. I can't let a flyer advertising my work look like that ugly. It had to be fixed."

"Hah," said Marley. "Did you sign it, too?"

Branwyn gave her a little smile but didn't answer.

The sign on the outside of Alejandro Martinez's door read, "Associate Director." Marley wasn't sure where he fit into Senyaza's org chart, other than belonging to the vast and possibly misnamed Information Technology department.

Information technology was, after all, the entirety of Senyaza's public-facing business, what with all the cellphones, televisions, and computers. Radios had been incredibly important to some of the Senyaza victories. Even the Hush itself, that field that suppressed the celestial ability to influence humanity wholesale, had only been possible with the assistance of nephilim radio-like magic.

Marley knocked on the semi-closed door and Alejandro looked up from his desk. He was a short, slim man with immaculately groomed dark hair and a tiny beard. He dressed in the kind of business casual that was, according to Penny, worth every cent. As soon as he saw Marley and Branwyn, he smiled. "Marley! Of course you're here; we were just discussing you upstairs. You know these things, eh?"

Marley blinked. "Not really…?"

The smile became a roguish grin. "No? Well, I'll be recording the coincidence just in case. Sometimes talents do expand, you know. And I see you brought Ms. Lennox, who has been doing such stellar work on integrating the Nakotus system. I did not expect to see you before the gala! So what brings you here? Did I miss a message, or were you just in the neighborhood?"

"Branwyn wants gossip," said Marley. "I wanted to check in with you before I go see Special Investigations, since everybody gets grumpy if I don't. Why were you talking about me upstairs?"

Alejandro picked up a tablet and tapped its edge on the desk, like he was aligning a stack of papers. "We were going through possible resources for an upcoming operation. Nobody's made any decisions yet."

He was older than the mid-twenties he appeared, Marley knew. She wondered how much older. That tablet tapping maneuver certainly predated the paperless office. "Do you know if Simon's in? I wanted to find out if anybody's heard from Corbin Adair lately."

Alejandro fumbled the tablet and caught it before it landed on the carpet. "I think he is. Would you like me to check? Give you an escort over there?"

"I know the way," Marley said, watching him closely. Alejandro wasn't a strong-blooded nephil, but the gift he'd inherited from his ancestor manifested itself as universal mastery of human languages. He'd told her he was pretty good with animals too. "I never asked before; do you know Corbin well?"

"Director of Security's grandson, yes?" He glanced at the ceiling. "Not well, but we've met. Intense guy. Why is he on your mind?"

The back of Marley's neck prickled. "No reason. It's just been a while since we talked." The approving smile Alejandro gave her was… puzzling.

Branwyn flopped down in Alejandro's guest chair and pulled

her feet under her. "I can tell there's all sorts of interesting drama going on."

Alejandro nodded at Branwyn. "There is. And you know exactly who to talk to for all the answers."

Branwyn crooked a smile. "I think I do. So what's going on between Senyaza and the feds? I hear I missed quite the company meeting."

"Oh, Ms. Lennox, I would love to chat with you but I do have another meeting soon. Perhaps we can schedule something? Lunch next week? I know a lovely little cafe." Alejandro looked at his wristband, which did have a small digital display and so could probably be called a 'watch'. "You can tell me where the Nakotus project is going. Only what's appropriate, of course."

"What? But you said—" Branwyn's legs splayed out from where she'd tucked them. She narrowed her eyes and stood. "All right."

Marley shifted her weight, uncomfortable. Alejandro was acting odd. He was usually cheerful and casual. He was *always* up for a lingering chat. She had some guesses as to why he'd been strange with her, but his response to Branwyn bewildered and worried her. She wondered if he was getting himself into trouble. Her head hurt again and without any conscious effort, her vision shifted to her danger-sight.

When her intrinsic magic had first started manifesting, it had felt like looking at a person through a kaleidoscope. Who they were and what they were headed toward fractured into multiple images, all connected and reflected. It took focus and experience to understand what she was looking at, and it was hardly ever worth the effort.

The future was variable. A stray thought could change it. Nearly *everybody* had something unpleasant on the near horizon, as one of many possibilities. Unless it was imminent, dominant, or clearly indicated as the result of a specific choice, there simply wasn't anything she could do about it—and often she didn't need to. So she tried to suppress it most of the time. Unless she was working, or somebody asked, or she just couldn't help herself.

Once upon a time she'd taken medicine because she couldn't stop worrying about what was going to happen next. She didn't take the medicine anymore and sometimes that was okay. But sometimes, her mind didn't obey her. Sometimes the fact that she *could* know *exactly* what to worry about was a curse she couldn't resist.

Like today, apparently. Her danger-sight fully activated without conscious effort.

Alejandro's aura was a scattering of images, but all of them showed him bleeding or broken or burned. Something bad was coming for her colleague, something that he had little likelihood of avoiding. If she knew more about what his plans were, she might be able to nudge him into a safe direction. Then again, she might not.

She always had to guess at the details: when, how, what. Here all she could gather was 'soon' and 'violently' and 'bad'. 'Where' was entirely beyond her ken. It wasn't much to base a warning on. And if somebody was planning on stalking and shooting him, changing when he went out for after-work drinks wouldn't matter at all.

Still. This danger was too omnipresent to be the result of a stray thought. "Hey, Alejandro? Be careful."

He furrowed his brow as he looked at her, understanding her instantly. He'd been one of those who'd evaluated her on little predictions, when she'd gone through the Senyaza intake processing. They'd played games that involved mild injuries, both self-inflicted and externally imposed, and tested whether she could predict them. Alejandro knew as much as she did about how her precognition worked; he knew how it tapped into intent and bad luck, and he knew she didn't bother with frivolous warnings.

"All right. I'll look both ways as I cross the street."

But his avowal of caution didn't change what she saw at all. He raised his eyebrows and she shook her head.

"I see. Well," he said, looking down, "I don't have any plane flights planned. I'll do my best to stay alert and perhaps it will sort itself out. If not, we can talk again at the gala. You'd might as well go find Mr. Mitsukuni before it gets much later in the day. Happy hour and all, you know."

Marley's shoulders slumped and she left the office. She hated leaving people with her apprehensions; she hated being a doom-warning worrywart, but her fear of the consequences of silence was too strong.

Branwyn fell in beside her. Marley glanced over at her and the danger-sight flared again. Then she recoiled and forced it down, because Branwyn's future was as blood-filled as Alejandro's.

5
BRANWYN

Marley's face went ashen and Branwyn knew exactly what had happened. She sighed. Taking Marley by the arm, she moved her down the hall to one of the office lounges. It had mauve walls and cream-colored plush chairs and a television with a game console attached. Branwyn was sure it was supposed to be 'relaxing' but she could only ever relax in a place like this if she redecorated it first.

"You know you're not supposed to do that without asking first."

"I couldn't help it. And it didn't work at *all* on Corbin earlier." Marley rubbed her forehead.

"Didn't it?" Branwyn asked, intrigued despite herself. "How clever of him."

"I was jumpy," Marley went on. "And Alejandro was being weird. He was trying to warn us about something and I wanted to know if it was going to get him in trouble."

"You wanted to know, so you just looked." Branwyn clicked her tongue at Marley. "We've talked about this." They *had* talked about it. And she knew better than to expect Marley to always resist her information-based power. But Branwyn was hoping that by changing the subject to the Philosophy and Ethics of Personalized Precognition, she could prevent Marley from telling her what had made her go pale.

"You know, I've been thinking about that," began Marley, and Branwyn thought, *Mission accomplished*. "And I'm not sure privacy rules can be applied to information the subject can't possibly have. It's not like I'm digging through somebody's trash or spying on them from far away."

"Speaking of spies, I thought Alejandro seemed like he was expecting the secret police to burst in any minute. I wonder if somebody *was* listening?" Branwyn grabbed one of the lounge chairs and turned it toward the mauve wall. Then she sat down and leaned her head against the wall, tracing her fingers lightly over the awful paint.

With what Branwyn thought was unnecessary sarcasm, Marley said, "Isn't it convenient you have a contract explicitly allowing you to explore the systems of the building?"

"They knew what they were signing." Branwyn had spent most of the last year improving her skills at magical artificing. It was the art and craft of changing an object's nature with her touch and will, or using magical aids to actually bring an object to awareness. Most magic, she'd learned, made *people* magic. Some celestial magic made *places* magic. She made *things* magic, made them into people, magically speaking. And one of the first *things* she'd woken up had been the skyscraper called Titan One.

Originally, she'd imbued it with the desire to be her ally. It had helped her escape when she'd displeased its owners. But once Senyaza had paid her an appropriate deposit as a peace offering, she'd gone back in to work more with the building, giving it more magical nodes. Natural-born people had seven nodes in the magical Geometry that tangled together to make them unique. Three artificial ones were about the maximum Branwyn could manage right now, which seemed to make it about as responsive as a well-trained dog. A well-trained dog with instincts created by her. And while she'd taught the building new things, it was still eager to be her friend.

She'd worked on quite a few projects for and with Senyaza, because they were willing to pay for her experiments as well as their own commissions. She'd made a self-rooting staff, a mechanical portal, some enchanted lenses, a belt for Mr. Black and a handful of other toys exploring the limits of what she was currently capable of. Her latest big project for Senyaza was integrating a computer interface and database with Titan One's intelligence. She wasn't really a computer person and her experiments had suggested that enchanting them was way beyond her current abilities. There was something about the Geometrical complexity that she couldn't quite grasp. Yet.

But she could follow along with the diagrams that George relayed to her from Leonard the Senyaza programmer, and teach the entity she called Titanone to use the wires laced through its skeleton to communicate with the nephilim. They called the entire network 'Nakotus' after some old fictional library. George and the others were very proud of how advanced it was. But so far, neither she nor Titanone were impressed, because ultimately the database was still a piece of machinery. It was just a tool, without will or desire. They'd built the pathways so it could be Titan One's tool, as well, but the database 'Nakotus' was no more Titanone than Branwyn's hammer was Branwyn.

Hi, Titanone, she thought at the building, feeling the strands of energy that flowed through it. She'd actually woken up several parts of the building back at the beginning, which made the work she was doing these days complicated. It was one building, but it had complex, sometimes conflicting goals. Kind of like a natural-born person, really.

Hi, Branwyn! said the tower back. Branwyn blinked. Before today, the building had communicated with imagery, odd surges of emotion and the occasional word-as-image, but it hadn't used clear sentences.

You're using language, she accused.

That was why you build the interface, wasn't it? The query was calmer, less excited than Titanone normally was.

You weren't talking last time. I didn't expect you to start talking while I wasn't here. I feel like I've missed a milestone.

No. Leonard has asked me to remember everything that happens. Would you like to see? Leonard is still teaching me about video feeds but I think I can show you.

A chill ran down Branwyn's spine. *Maybe later. How do you mean 'everything?'*

Everything, said Titanone happily, with a surge of the personality Branwyn expected. *Everything within me. I watched you talk to Alejandro and now I remember that. Alejandro has been acting differently lately. He looks at the walls more.*

Branwyn sat for a few moments thinking, until Marley stopped being patient and touched her shoulder. "Do you mind if I go on ahead?"

"One more minute," Branwyn said absently, and thought to Titanone, *Who else would you share your memories with besides me?*

So far only Leonard and Mr. Black have asked, said Titanone, sounding a little annoyed. *Are we going to do more work soon? I've been exploring the Nakotus system. It's actually pretty cool. I'm excited about what I'll be able to do if I get bigger.*

Maybe, thought Branwyn. *I have to go see Simon now.*

Poor Simon. He needs some special attention. He did badly on his latest performance report. They're thinking about reassigning him. I read it on Nakotus.

Branwyn couldn't help herself. *You shouldn't tell people things like that, Titanone. Next time you talk to Leonard, ask him about privacy. And stay out of Nakotus.* She lifted her hands from the wall.

The lights in the lounge flickered and Branwyn said aloud, "I'll talk to you more later, Titanone, I promise. But Marley is in a hurry."

"What was that about?" asked Marley, following as Branwyn stalked of the lounge. "You're upset."

Branwyn shrugged. "Titanone discovered how to go through everybody's records when he's bored, and Senyaza is using him to monitor everybody in the building instead of the traditional cameras."

Marley's mouth opened and then closed. After a moment she said, "Oh, Branwyn, I'm so sorry."

Branwyn's hand closed into a fist at her side. "Let's discuss it later," she repeated. She'd be angry then, where Titanone couldn't see and be confused about who she was angry at.

Marley was an old friend. She understood what Branwyn meant. But she stayed quiet as they went to the Special Investigations office, four floors underground. The elevator went down to S13 and none of it, Branwyn had been told, was parking. She'd only been as far as S9 herself. Everything required special access and Marley's own keycard didn't go below S4. Keycard limits hadn't stopped Branwyn when she first visited S9 but she was doing her best to play nicely with Senyaza at the moment. She had schooling for her siblings to pay for.

Branwyn liked the Special Investigations floor more than the rest of Titan One's interiors, anyhow. The hall had a more lived-in look than the reception area above, with framed horror movie posters on the walls. Some of them were signed. She and Marley walked past another lounge, this one with a rather more elaborate video game setup. A racing game waited for players on the big screen.

As Branwyn recalled from her communion with Titanone, there were only a few traditional offices on this floor. Most of the rooms were larger, and spaced farther apart. Many of them were only rarely visited. Special Investigations and Threats performed a number of services for Senyaza. Some of them related to mundane business. More of them related to problems with celestials. Branwyn and Marley were here to visit the monster hunters.

Senyaza officially called the monsters 'kaiju' even though they were only like Godzilla in destructive capacity, because both Senyaza and the monsters were much older than metaphorical fire-breathing lizards. The kaiju that the monster hunter team dealt with were destructive fallen angels: far less principled than demons and far more nihilistic than the faeries. They preyed on humanity, torturing and killing some people, and turning others into copies of what they imagined themselves to be. They *had* to be dealt with.

But it was a quirk of celestial nature that celestials could almost never be truly killed. Even when the nephilim hunters used an ancient magic to bind a celestial's three-part spirit to its physical vessel, the best they could manage was sending it back to the celestial source, where the same entity would reform, amnesiac but just as malignant.

Nephilim, on the other hand, died like any human, without the benefit of souls to bring an afterlife. And the monsters were very, very dangerous.

Thus, the men—it was all men, Branwyn had noticed time and again—in the office were all the sort of people who were willing to risk their potentially very long lives to fight an endless war for little reward. Willing, or in some cases *eager*. They were each tough enough or dangerous enough—or both—to make a biker gang take the long way around.

They were planning a joint operation, clustered around a table holding a map of a building and dotted with little figures. None of them even glanced at the door where Marley and Branwyn peeked in. There were five of them: Ice, Grendel, Mack, Finn and Simon. Branwyn didn't know most of them well, but Simon was a friend.

Branwyn knocked on the door frame but none of them looked over. After a moment of being unnoticed at the door, Branwyn went on into the room, tugging Marley in after her. She sat on one of the four ancient, heavy wooden desks that supported sleek computers and started fidgeting with a brace of throwing knives. Marley sat in the chair beside her, watching the men gravely. The men kept talking, pushing figures around and arguing about the best way into the building.

After only a moment, Marley leaned back, crossed her legs and said in a loud whisper to Branwyn, "Most of those plans are catastrophic. Do you think I should tell them that? It might hurry things along."

Branwyn smiled. "They probably wouldn't pay attention. You could tell me, though."

The monster hunters quieted suddenly. Ice wheeled around to look at the two of them, his chrome-colored eyes glinting under tousled pale hair. "You can do that? What are you doing working as a babysitter?"

Marley stretched casually and then looked at her hands, shaking them as if they'd fallen asleep. "He made me a good offer. But right now I'll make you an offer. Tell me what's going on with Corbin these days, right now, and I'll tell you which of your plans was the bloodless one."

The five men glanced at each other and then shrugged. Grendel rumbled, "I'm going to go get a pop. Anybody want something?"

Mack said, "Simon can tell you what we know. Want to go another round on the track, Finn?"

Less than a minute later, the room had emptied except for Ice loitering near the door. Simon sank into a swivel chair, running a hand through his spiky hair. "Should have thought to give you a call, Marley. I knew you were useful like this. What's going on with Corbin?"

Alone among all the nephilim Branwyn had met, there was something comforting about Simon. He was the shortest of all the monster hunters, although average by human standards, with light brown hair and eyes, and Japanese features. He was about thirty-five decades old and didn't seem a day over thirty-five years most of the time. He could spit lightning from his fingertips, courtesy of a Japanese storm god for a father, and his favorite knife was the very first thing she'd enchanted. He drank most of his calories and he always gave the impression of just barely scraping by, and Branwyn loved him for it. He was a living, breathing reminder that being over three centuries old didn't automatically confer the ability to get it together, and that everybody found their own ways of coping.

"I was hoping you could tell me that," said Marley, frustration edging her voice. "Has he contacted you at all?"

"Not for months," said Simon cautiously, looking between Marley and Branwyn as if trying to decipher a riddle.

"Well, what was he doing when you heard from him?"

"On a mission for upstairs," said Simon vaguely. "They wanted him to take a look at something, figure something out."

"Come on, Simon," begged Marley. "That's what you've been saying since he left. You've got to know more than that."

Simon threw an unreadable glance at Ice, who shrugged. Then he rubbed his forehead and said, "Gimme a minute. Did either of you bring anything to drink?"

"No," said Branwyn and promised, "I'll remember next time, though."

"Fine, fine," mumbled Simon, and fumbled in a drawer before pulling out a plastic bottle full of amber liquid.

The temperature in the room dropped about ten degrees and Simon gave Ice another look, this time an angry one. "They asked and I need to think. As usual, everybody else runs away and I have to handle things. So don't you go telling anybody."

"It's not me you have to worry about, buddy," said Ice.

Appalled, Branwyn said, "You guys aren't really trying to stop Simon from drinking, are you? He'll *die*."

"Woman knows what she's talking about," said Simon approvingly and poured some of the Scotch down his throat.

Once again Ice's odd chrome eyes turned toward Branwyn. "You haven't seen him much the past few months, have you? Most of the time he's been passed out in the lounge. His life, of course, but if he wants to keep his job, Mr. Black says he's got to get himself under control. We're helping."

Branwyn's eyes narrowed. "You're all Corbin's friends, too. I bet you could tell me everything Simon could, without him taking this risk. As a way of helping."

In response, Ice turned his back and stepped out of the room, closing the door behind him.

"Pathetic cowards," Branwyn snarled.

"It's information of a sort," Marley said and sighed.

Simon set the bottle down. "Right. Corbin. It's July? To be honest, we expected him back before now."

Marley's face went carefully blank. "Ah. And he hasn't contacted you?"

"Not a word, not for months. Though you know, I'll check. Totally possible I missed something." He pulled out his phone and worked at it a moment. "Nope."

"What was the something he was supposed to look at?"

Hesitantly, Simon said, "A box? I think? It had something to do with that disaster in Europe last year." He looked between them and then helpfully added, "A bunch of nephilim got killed by a kaiju who wandered into the big European thing. I know Corbin's parents were there."

Shocked, Marley said, "Oh my God. I heard something but... I didn't know. Were they—?"

"Nah, they're fine. In LA at the moment, I think. But it was personal for him, some." He glanced at his phone again for a moment.

Impatiently, Branwyn asked, "Is this mission of his the sort of information that would be in the Nakotus system?" When Marley threw her an inscrutable glance, she added, with self-conscious dignity, "I'm just asking. It's all right to ask."

"Doubt it," said Simon. "Nobody sensible writes that kind of thing down. Right? I wouldn't. Hey, why are you asking, Marley?" He studied her face. "Did Corbin contact you? What's wrong with him?"

Marley shook her head, her lips tight and her face flushed. "Why'd they send Corbin on this secret mission?"

"Oh, well. That." He took another, absent-minded swig from his bottle. "Have you ever been around him when that thing with his eyes gets going?" Slowly, Marley nodded and Simon nodded back. "Yeah, that. He ain't just a kid who's good with black birds. His family's got this power, it's a weird one because it gets passed down. Like, his dad had it until Corbin was born and now—"

The phone still in Simon's hand rang shrilly, the ringtone the invasive, unavoidable beeping of an alarm. *Time's up*, thought Branwyn.

He looked at it for a long moment, his already pale face becoming ashen. Then, slowly, like a man facing an executioner, he lifted it to his ear. "Hi, Mr. Black. Oh! Uh, I'll tell them. Yeah. I'll send her along."

Branwyn stood. "Mr. Black wants to see us? You're right, Marley, this worked much better than making an appointment."

Marley put her hand to her head. "What? Oh…"

"Uh," said Simon cautiously. "He wants to see Marley. Just Marley."

"To hell with that," said Branwyn pleasantly. "We're a team on this one. Thank you, Simon. I owe you dinner."

"More than one," he muttered. "Don't make him mad, Bran? I hate it when he asks me to hunt you down like a dog."

"Hey, he's paying me. Would I do something to make an employer mad?" Branwyn said easily.

"Um," said Marley. She closed her eyes and shook her head.

Branwyn grabbed her hand and pulled her from the room. Ice was leaning against the wall outside the room, drinking a soda. Grendel, giant-sized and hairy, was against the other wall.

"You guys are scum," Branwyn told them both.

Grendel laughed. "No lie, that. Good luck, lady."

Ice only shrugged, though. "Simon's already in trouble with upstairs. It was the best way." His eyes narrowed as he looked them over, focusing on Marley. "Is she okay? She still owes us notes on our operation."

Branwyn frowned, looking at Marley. Her face was flushed and she still had her hand against her head like she was worried it was going to fall off if she let go. It was clear her headache was worse.

"She has a fever," Ice added.

"Right," said Marley, bright-eyed. "Go in through the front door. I don't know why, but nobody gets hurt that way. Well. Grendel gets a little hurt but I know he likes that." She peered between the two nephilim. "You're both going to get hurt soon anyhow. Everybody's getting hurt soon. I wish I knew how."

"The front door?" asked Ice incredulously. "Well… if you say so, kid."

Marley let go of her head to wave her hand. "You don't have to listen to me. It's your lives." She pulled her hand from Branwyn's and said, "I've got to go get some painkiller for this headache before I see Mr. Black." She vanished back into the room, heading toward the team medicine chest.

Ice watched her go, and then called, "Finn, Marley needs some water. Could you get her some?"

Finn's white-blond head poked around the edge of the lounge. "Eh? I can." A moment later he came down the hall holding a paper cup of water. "Come out, my darling. I've got something much nicer for you."

"What?" said Marley blearily, peering through the doorway.

Ice hooked her elbow, guiding her out and taking the bottle of painkiller from her hand. "That stuff takes a while and Mr. Black doesn't like to wait."

Finn gave Branwyn a lazy smile. "Pour the water into my hands for your friend?"

Bemused, Branwyn took the paper cup. Finn cupped his hands together, Branwyn poured the water in, and he brought his hands to Marley's mouth. "Drink it up."

Just as confused, Marley lowered her head to his hands and let him tip some of the water into her mouth. After a sip, she opened her mouth wider and swallowed everything he had with an odd urgency.

Finn shook his hands to scatter the remaining droplets and cocked his head, studying Marley. "Feeling better?"

Marley looked flushed, and Branwyn wondered if it was from the fever or Finn's proximity. He was a very attractive man and Marley was easily flustered by those. "My head doesn't hurt," she said wonderingly. "Neither do my hands."

"She's still got a fever, though. You're slipping, old man," noted Ice.

His brow furrowed, Finn shook his head. "Strange, that."

Simon appeared behind Marley and said, "If you two don't get upstairs, I'm going to really regret it, so can we get a move on here? Please?"

"Right," said Marley. "Let's do this. Thanks for the pick-me-up, Finn." She wiped her mouth, straightened her shoulders and walked to the elevators. Branwyn watched her, and then moved to catch up.

"Upstairs" wasn't that far up, at least in this case. They took the elevator to the fourth floor above the ground level. Mr. Black's office was on the corner, overlooking the street below and quite close to the public part of Titan One. The door was partially open. As Marley and Branwyn stopped outside, Mr. Black called, "Come in, Marley."

Branwyn scowled and went in with her. The office was large, with a living room set near the door and a desk at the window. A man and a woman sat on the couch, while Mr. Black leaned on the desk, dressed as always in an elegant suit with a tie patterned with the Milky Way.

She narrowed her eyes as the slender bald man held up a hand. "Not you, Miss Lennox. You'll have to wait outside. There's some seating down the hall."

Flatly, Branwyn said, "You've been teaching Titanone to spy on people. Between that and the way Marley is my best friend, do you really think I'm not going to learn what you talk about?"

Mr. Black smiled. "Not at all. But you won't be here to insert yourself into a discussion that has nothing to do with you, as you are so prone to doing. By all means, listen in, if you find that appropriate behavior."

Branwyn cherished her memory of the single time that she'd

frustrated Mr. Black. It kept her warm and helped her through all her other interactions with the elder nephil. Every time she had to behave while he acted like a superior being, she reminded herself he *could* be as frustrated as she was right now. That was important.

She stared at him, wondering what he'd do if she refused to leave. "Marley's not feeling well. I'd rather not leave her."

"Isn't she?" He gave Marley a curious glance. "By all means, sit down, child. You can trust that we'll take care of her, Miss Lennox. She's one of our own." When Branwyn didn't move, he sighed and said, "You were asking Alejandro about our current relationship with the American government. Do you find yourself with a conflict of interest? We're aware of your sister's affiliation."

Branwyn crossed her arms. "Did you steal something from them recently?"

Mr. Black blinked in surprise. It was beautiful, and also disappointing. "No. Now, please leave before things become awkward for Marley."

Branwyn glanced at Marley. Her face had become pale, with spots of color high in her cheeks, but she seemed steady on her feet and she nodded at Branwyn. "I'll see you soon."

"Fine. I want to go to the Repository."

"Be my guest, Miss Lennox," said Mr. Black patiently. "Just go away."

Branwyn did so, back to the elevator and the Repository of celestial Machine fragments, where she settled in to listen in on the conversation going on over her head and find out as best she could from the fragments if Mr. Black was lying to her.

6
MARLEY

I can see why you felt the need to get rid of her," murmured the man sitting on the couch. Both he and the woman sitting beside him were dark haired. They sat close enough together that Marley assumed they were a couple. "What a brash young woman." He gave Marley a faint smile, as if sharing some secret with her.

"A very good artisan, but temperamental," agreed Mr. Black. He reached behind him and pushed a button on the conference phone system on his desk. "We have her here now, ladies and gentlemen."

"I'm coming in on the screen," said a woman's voice immediately, and the big screen on the wall flickered to life. Another woman appeared, and Marley wondered uncomfortably where the camera in Mr. Black's office was.

"Thank you, Mr. Black," said a dry male voice from the phone. "Please carry on; we're listening avidly."

"What's going on?" Marley asked. The water from Finn's magic hands had made her head stop hurting, but she kept seeing odd flickers at the edge of her vision. Her desire to learn more about what was going on with Corbin was now in competition with her desire to crawl into a bed somewhere until the lightheadedness and fever went away.

Mr. Black's smile was grandfatherly. "We were having a little meeting, Marley, and your name came up. Then we heard you were in the building asking about Corbin and it seemed natural to invite you to join us since that was exactly what we were speaking of."

"Who's 'us?' "

"Ah, let me introduce you to my daughter, Elizabeth, and her husband Aedrian." He gestured at the couple on the couch. Mr. Black was Corbin's grandfather, which probably meant... "Corbin's parents?"

Elizabeth nodded once, and Marley gave her a closer look. There was a resemblance, but it was subtle. She had a solemn, elfin face and sleek black hair tucked behind her ears. She didn't look more than thirty-five. Her husband had short dark brown hair and the same long, angular face as Corbin. The same eyes, too, Marley realized.

Pain spiked through her skull, and blackness passed over her vision. She fought it down and tried to focus despite her spinning head.

"Something is going on with Corbin," she breathed.

Mr. Black and his daughter exchanged looks. The nephil elder said, "We'd like to assign your annual service, Marley. Find Corbin for us and convince him to come home."

Her annual service. The bargain she'd made with Senyaza, the standard deal they offered all nephilim in exchange for support both financial and informational. Zachariah had tried to talk her out of accepting it, and Corbin had tried to talk her into it. She'd listened to Corbin, and now she was glad.

She was also too unsteady to stay on her feet any longer, and found her way to a chair. Sinking into it, she asked, "Why does he need convincing?"

"We have no idea," snapped the woman on the screen.

"I'm sorry, I missed who you were," Marley confessed. If Mr. Black had introduced any of the listeners on the phone, she'd missed that too.

"My name is Miriam Hadara," said the woman crisply.

Marley thought, *She's angry,* and wondered if she'd done something wrong. How was Miriam connected to Corbin? Why were people listening on a speakerphone? Then she remembered that Corbin had been on a mission for Senyaza.

"And why does he need convincing?" Marley repeated, trying to remember if she'd been given a useful answer. Her head throbbed and once again her danger-sight self activated.

Blood, blood everywhere, blood and broken bodies. Maybe her magic had gotten messed up. It hadn't activated unconsciously like this for months, ever since she'd learned to control Corbin's Sight charm. Better her magic was broken than this ugly future was true.

The woman on the screen, Miriam, had pain in her future too. But it wasn't flavored with blood and shattered bone. It was the salty pain of tears and bitter grief, of a love that left only ashes and scars in its wake. And it wasn't the future. It was now.

She pushed the vision down again. It wasn't the time to troubleshoot her magic. She needed to not be surrounded by nephilim elders, and not have such a headache. Right now, they were talking about Corbin, who needed to be convinced to come home again. For some reason.

Miriam threw an annoyed glance at Mr. Black and he said calmly, "Something has happened to him. We're not sure what, but he's currently acting antagonistically toward Senyaza. Toward his family. We suspect an external influence. We'd like to understand but we can't do that if he won't talk to us."

"What was the mission you sent him on before this happened? Could it be related?"

Corbin's father picked up a magazine from beside the love seat and started flipping through it absently. Corbin's mother sat with her hands clenched in her lap.

Slowly, Mr. Black said, "I'm not sure. He never completed that task, so it's plausible that something affected him along the way." Marley kept her gaze fixed on his face, waiting for him to answer her first question.

He adjusted his tie. "His task was straightforward: we wanted him to discover the identity of the power behind the incident in Ostend, Belgium last year."

"The incident?"

"I'm sure you heard about it," said Mr. Black with a touch of weariness. "While a consortium of angels plotted to murder the children you protect, our attention was diverted away. Horribly so. Senyaza had a retreat in Ostend, Belgium. One of the kaiju— one of the shattered, nameless ones—got inside the perimeter and murdered thirty-eight of our people and many of our support staff."

"Including your son," said Miriam flatly.

"Yes," said Mr. Black, his face impassive. "Including my son, and one of the Senyaza board of directors, and many other valuable and beloved members of our community."

"So many," Marley whispered. Too late, she remembered Simon saying something about this, and wished she hadn't asked. "I'm so sorry. I didn't know any details."

"It isn't something we speak of easily." Silence fell. Corbin's father turned the page in his magazine, while the two women and Mr. Black both regarded Marley. Miriam Hadara's eyes blazed with a fury that Marley now realized wasn't directed at her, while Elizabeth's gaze was as emotionless as her father's.

She could hardly imagine what Mr. Black had briefly related. Senyaza was a strong supernatural power, and individual nephil magic could be devastating. It seemed impossible that one kaiju could do that much damage.

"You wanted Corbin to find out the identity of the kaiju?"

"No. Elizabeth dispatched him in the end. But he was newly reborn, hardly rational. He was nothing more than a murder weapon. Somebody found him, took advantage of his namelessness to influence him to despise our kind over the humans they normally prefer. Somebody guided him to guns and through our security. We need to know who that was." Mr. Black's facade of emotionlessness cracked. "We needed to know who that was six months ago."

"What happens once you do?" Marley asked, twisting her hands together.

"What do you think?" hissed Miriam, the screen flickering.

Mr. Black clasped his fingers together, and then cracked his knuckles. "We find a way to make sure he, she, or it will *never* be reborn. Perhaps Ms. Lennox will be involved." He studied Marley. "You understand that the safety of our entire organization depends on this. Some delay can perhaps be accepted, but we must be implacable. Otherwise… otherwise the bad times will return."

Marley tried to catch the thread of her thoughts against the headache and the fever and the horror. "I'm sorry, I'm having trouble thinking right now. Can I have a glass of water?"

Corbin's father closed his magazine and rose to his feet, fetching her a tumbler of water from a small bar in the far corner. When he handed it to her, she peeked up at him, trying to see more of Corbin in his features. But instead of the man she'd known a year ago, she was reminded of the harsh, angry figure she'd spoken with earlier that day.

Corbin. "So you sent Corbin out as a supernatural detective to investigate which celestial interfered with the kaiju, so you could punish them. Right?"

Mr. Black nodded once.

"Okay." She thought for a moment, and then said, "This is just the first thing that occurs to me, but are you guys certain it was arranged by a celestial? I mean, maybe Corbin did find out who set it up and that's why he's angry at Senyaza?"

Miriam gasped and Elizabeth's face paled. When Mr. Black's mouth tightened, Marley realized she might have made a mistake. Yet it seemed obvious to her.

The silence stretched out as Marley fumbled for an appropriate follow-up. Perhaps she ought to have brought it up more tactfully.

Or not at all. Self-preservation and a broad consumption of fiction certainly suggested 'not at all.'

But the idea had surfaced so immediately in her mind that she'd blurted it out. It was the headache. It made it hard to make good decisions.

The dry voice on the phone answered her, after what might have been a laugh or a cough. "Yes, Miss Claviger, we're certain. Even without the other evidence we've uncovered, the timing of the attack gives much away. Our children and siblings were slaughtered *as a distraction* so that Senyaza would be too wounded to notice the celestials trying to sacrifice your charges and break the Hush." The voice was calm but distorted, as if coming from a long way away across a bad signal.

"Right. Okay. I'll keep that in mind," said Marley, and then added, "Sorry."

Mr. Black sighed. "We're not asking you to discover who was behind the attack, Marley. That's Corbin's task. We just want you to find him and convince *him* to speak with us again. Will you do that?"

"I've got no idea where to look," Marley confessed. "If he finds me again, I can mention you're concerned—"

"Again?" said Elizabeth sharply.

Marley froze. Had she said *again*?

Elizabeth went on, her dark eyes suddenly intense. "We suspected he'd contacted you but you've actually seen him? How is he?"

"Um," said Marley. Her head stabbed again and an unexpected storm of emotions rose suddenly, so swift and strong she could only be swept along. She was *afraid* of answering. She *disliked* these people, all of them. She'd been biased toward liking Elizabeth before, but they were *annoying*, all of them: Miriam Hedera with her burning eyes and her obsession with Quade's killer, Elizabeth Black-Adair and her endless calm, Aedrian Adair and his detached anger at Corbin, and Mr. Black, oh, Mr. Black most of all for—

Wait, thought Marley, struggling to the surface again. *Who's Quade?*

"Who's Quade?" she asked aloud.

"Corbin's uncle," said Elizabeth. "My brother." Her husband looked at Marley as if she'd said something both unexpected and familiar.

"Her lover?" Marley asked dizzily, gesturing at the screen.

"Yes," spat Miriam. "My lover. Dead now, his brains blown out by an angel-ridden monster and I would kill them all if I could."

"Ah," said the voice on the phone. "A fond dream. Perhaps one day we'll be able to make it reality, but for now we must simply settle for punishing the murderer."

Mr. Black shifted position as if his suit didn't quite fit. "What happened when you met Corbin, Marley?"

Marley struggled to answer him, but it was like her brain was caught in tar. She couldn't get past how much she *didn't like* Mr. Black. She'd thought he was okay in the past: hard-working, extremely competent, kind of intimidating and brusque—but likable despite all that. She'd always thought he liked her, too.

But something was wrong. Maybe it was with her. But maybe it was with them. She was supposed to trust her feelings, right?

"How do you know he's feeling antagonistic toward Senyaza if he won't talk to anybody?"

"Certain clues that are none of your business, young lady," said the phone voice. "Mr. Black, please trigger Protocol 6."

Mr. Black frowned and glanced at a tablet on his desk, tapping a few times. Then he glanced up.

"You're very talented, Marley. We're sure you can find him, and we're sure once you do, he'll be willing to listen to you. Please convey our welcome to him," he said. "And now—"

The office door opened and Branwyn stood there. "It's time for Marley to go home," she announced. "She's too sick to commit to any kind of job right now. I'll make sure she calls you later."

"Oh, thank God," said Marley. Whatever paranoia had come with her fever, it didn't involve Branwyn. Her friend seemed like a white knight as she waded deeper and deeper into a treacherous swamp.

She stood and promptly fell over. Branwyn wasn't fast enough to catch her, and nobody else tried, even though Mr. Black was standing quite close to her. That hurt more than the stinging in her palms. But Branwyn helped her to her feet and made sure she had her purse, while glaring at the elder nephilim.

"Very well," said Mr. Black. "Take her away, Miss Lennox. Let her rest at home for a while. I *very much* hope you feel better soon, Marley."

They went out the door, down the hall, into the elevator, and across a sky bridge to Marley's car. Only once they were within did Branwyn say, "I knew I had to get you out of there as soon as you asked them outright if they were the ones who'd arranged the massacre in Belgium."

Marley frowned. All she could remember was how much she'd disliked them. And "Did I ask them that?"

"Yes," said Branwyn dryly. "You did. I was worried I wouldn't get there before something bad happened. How do you feel?"

"My head hurts again," Marley confessed. "And my hands are tingling. I ache…" She trailed off, leaning her head back against the seat. "I knew things earlier that nobody had mentioned."

"Your magic?" inquired Branwyn. She pulled out of the parking garage and then blew out her breath in exasperation and stopped at the curb.

Simon was standing beside the car, his hands in his pockets. Branwyn rolled down the window. "What've you got for us?"

He looked through the window at Marley, who couldn't summon the energy to do anything more than glare at him for slowing her return home.

"How's she doing?"

"She's sick," said Branwyn patiently. "You could have called if that's all you wanted to ask."

"Odd. Finn's magic usually fixes everything," said Simon, watching Marley for another moment. When Branwyn made an annoyed growling sound under her breath, he said, "Oh, right. A couple of things. I'm pretty sure Corbin's in trouble. They've got him on video at a fire at one of our secure storage places a week ago. Only a fragment, because someone erased the video as it filmed, which…" he shook his head, his eyes wide. "Neat trick, since it was digital."

Branwyn asked, "Did he start the fire?"

Simon tapped his fingers together. "Good question. Upstairs thinks so. It was a nasty fire and the normal fire suppressant systems failed. They lost stuff." He hesitated. "I'm worried about the kid. I don't want to hear anything bad about him." He gave them a meaningful look that Marley was totally unable to interpret at the moment.

"All right," said Branwyn calmly. "What was your second thing?"

Simon rocked back on his heels. "Ah, well. Remember that monster who was bothering you last year?"

Even distracted by her headache and fever, Marley noticed the stillness that came over Branwyn.

"I wouldn't forget," she said.

"Well… you know how when I slit his throat I warned you it wasn't permanent? That it was just his vessel we got rid of? That he'd be back and he'd remember you?" A miserable expression on his face, he added, "There was just no time, no space for a spirit tether. Would have at least wiped his memory, and it would have taken him longer to come back…"

Branwyn exhaled, long and slow. "I'd expect him to hate you a lot more than me. I only enchanted the weapon; you're the one who used it."

Simon waved his hand. He was holding his knife, absently, as if he hadn't realized he'd drawn it. "Oh, well, I'm used to the bastards hating me and really, no big loss if they get to me."

"Has he been bothering you?"

Simon went to scratch his chin, looked at the knife in surprise, and tucked it away again. "He left me a message but I couldn't be that worried about it. More worried about you, anyhow."

"Don't be," said Branwyn firmly. "I'm not. But there's somebody else Sev—that monster definitely hates. I'll have to warn him."

Simon crossed his arms. "You do what you need to. I've got to get back inside and check on Finn."

"No, wait," croaked Marley. "Do you know if they tethered the monster in Belgium before killing him?"

Simon shook his head. "No. They didn't. No time." He turned and walked away.

Branwyn took a deep breath and exhaled slowly. Then she

resumed navigating the car into traffic. "I guess we'll be hearing about the Belgium monster again, too. It makes me wonder what they meant when they mentioned finding a way to stop a celestial from reincarnating."

"They've done it before," Marley said, because she *knew* it. Then she shook her head. "See? How do I know that? I don't know that. Except I do."

Branwyn gave her a sideways look at a stoplight. "So. These sudden bursts of knowledge. Your magic?"

"I don't know! Not magic I've experienced before. Maybe it's this headache. Maybe it's the nephil version of a migraine. I don't just see auras, I see bloody auras. And I know secrets. Although are they even true? Maybe I'm delusional." She remembered Branwyn's bloody aura, and thought of the monster she'd helped Simon kill. Blood seemed all too likely there.

"What sort of other things did you know?"

Marley tried to remember through the pounding in her head. "Stuff about the people in the room. No, I have to be delusional. I was so *angry* at them, Branwyn."

"I can't blame you for that," said Branwyn clinically. "That seems perfectly normal to me. They keep so many secrets. They have floors at the bottom of the elevator shaft that even Titanone has trouble seeing inside. I thought maybe they'd hid Rhianna's device there. But nothing's been moved in or out of the bottom floors for months."

Marley squirmed in her seat, and thought about tilting it back so she could go to sleep in the car. Distantly she said, "No reason to think that if they stole the divinity circuit, they put it in Titan One. They have buildings all over the world," and wondered where such sensible words had come from. She pressed her forehead against the window, wishing she could suck the air-conditioned coolness into her skull. "But I don't think Mr. Black was lying to you. I don't think they knew what the government was doing."

"Divinity circuit? Where'd that come from? More mysterious knowledge?"

"I don't know," Marley said irritably. "Let's stop talking so I can work on keeping my head from exploding."

Like a good friend, an ideal friend, Branwyn didn't even speak her acquiescence. She just stopped talking. Marley sighed and concentrated on the pain, trying to separate it from herself. It was a shadow over her mind, whispering in the back of her head. Her hands throbbed and burned in time with the rhythm of the speech. After a while, she fell into a half-sleep, and the murmuring became senseless dreams of her reflection muttering at her, smiling at her with a huge, unfamiliar smile.

7
BRANWYN

Branwyn took Marley home. Neath hissed as they came through the door, and made a complete nuisance of herself twining around legs and meowing frantically as Branwyn put Marley to bed. Then the cat hopped on the bed, curled up next to Marley, and gave Branwyn an accusing look. Branwyn sat on at the foot of the bed and watched her friend as she drowsed in and out of consciousness.

Normally, Branwyn was prosaic about illness. With six younger siblings, she'd seen more than her fair share of childhood fevers and colds. People got sick. Usually, they recovered. But a year ago, Penny had been taken down by a mysterious, sudden-onset illness, too. That had been supernatural in origin, and if Branwyn hadn't been so tenacious, Penny would have died.

This was too similar. Branwyn was worried. It couldn't be the *same* thing—nephilim metaphysiology precluded Marley's soul getting burned away by an angel, since she didn't have a soul to begin with. But there were clearly a whole host of illnesses related to the supernatural that Branwyn had no experience with and thus no ability to evaluate.

But the Senyaza elders presumably did. They'd seen Marley's illness and they hadn't recommended taking her to their private hospital or anything. She'd probably be fine.

Branwyn was uncomfortable with worry. It made her feel helpless and angry. Instead she made dinner, which Marley slept through. Then she did some research she had waiting for one of her future projects, made plans for her investigation the next day, and went to bed.

The next morning, Branwyn heard Marley stumbling first to the bathroom and then out to the kitchen, and emerged to see her making her way back to bed with a big bottle of water and some toast. "How do you feel?"

"Terrible," Marley said. "Everything is terrible. I'm going back to bed."

"Hmm." Branwyn looked Marley over critically. She was flushed and her hair was standing on end. Her hands were red, and she didn't seem too steady on her feet, either. No real improvement, then. "Today *you* get the babysitter."

Marley gave her a dark look and went back into her room again. Watching thoughtfully, Branwyn picked up her phone.

"Come over," she commanded, as soon as Penny answered the phone. "Marley is sick. I need to run some important errands and I don't want to leave her alone."

Penny said only, "I'll be there in ten minutes."

Branwyn gathered the notes she'd put together on the Extraworlder Conference, along with a few other things. When Penny arrived, she was ready to go.

"What is it?" Penny sat her purse on the table and went to look in Marley's bedroom.

"A fever, everything that goes with it," said Branwyn, standing. "Do a better job than I did and don't let her get stolen by faeries."

Penny made a face. "I can manage that, at least. Uh, do you expect anybody *else* to show up? Because I may not be as useful against them."

Branwyn shrugged. "Lock the door." Then she saw Penny's stricken expression and added, "No, I don't. I think it's just a badly timed fever. But I'm not always right. I wasn't right with you. I'll be back in a few hours and if she's not any better, I'll take her over to Senyaza's hospital myself. Because it's badly timed."

"All right," said Penny, resigned, and sat on the couch. "Where are you going?"

Branwyn waved her phone. "First I'm going to go talk to Tarn. Then, hopefully, I'm going to find Corbin."

The Extraworlder Conference hadn't even officially begun yet, but the cluster of hotels where it was scheduled already thronged with guests and attendees and tourists and photographers. Finding parking without murdering somebody required the patience of a monk. Branwyn occupied the time planning how she'd solve the parking problem using her artificing. But short of creating a flying car she didn't have any good ideas. Some problems, she supposed, would be eternal.

As she finished parking, her phone buzzed with a message. But instead of an update from Penny on Marley, it was something else.

Come talk to me again. I want to show you what I can do.

Branwyn stared at her phone. The text came from the general Senyaza number, which made absolutely no sense at all. It only took her a moment before she typed in, *Titanone, who taught you to use a phone?*

:) :) :) I taught myself. When are you coming to visit again?

We'll both show off at the gala. I'm in the middle of something right now though. If you can use a phone, you can find some TV. Go watch some cartoons. It had worked—sometimes—with her younger siblings.

No response. Hopefully that meant the entity was off down a cartoon channel rabbit hole. He was developing *so quickly*. She felt a flicker of pride and, deep down, nervousness. She really needed to think about that development more. It seemed like every artificing project she did taught her something new or introduced new complexities and Titanone's surprises just kept coming.

But she did have other things to do at the moment. The main hotel of the Extraworlder Conference loomed before her.

Tarn, the faerie Duke of Underlight, was both one of the guests at the conference and one of its organizers. Branwyn didn't know exactly where he was staying in the hotel, but he was there somewhere. Nearly every photograph and article about the event mentioned it. So she went to the front desk, where she smiled at the harried young man and asked him if he'd call up to Duke Tarn's suite and let him know she was there to see him.

Then she went to lounge by the elevators. Less than ten minutes later, someone she recognized emerged. He was dressed in a well-tailored suit, but nobody had managed to comb his hair, so it stood up in its usual pale tufts.

"Hello, William." Branwyn straightened in the corner where she'd been lurking.

Tarn's favorite changeling inspected her impassively and then one corner of his mouth twitched. A sneer or a smile, Branwyn couldn't tell.

"What do you want?"

"Oh, come on. You and I both know Tarn said, 'William, bring her up,' not 'Find out what she wants.' "

William sniffed. "He's very busy. You represent complications. I don't like complications."

Branwyn paced past him into an elevator just unloading. "What floor, William?"

He growled to himself and followed her into the elevator,

reaching past her to punch in the floor.

Branwyn grinned at him. "How's Underlight?"

"Recovering," said William shortly. "Still recovering. It will take decades to recover from what you wrought there."

Branwyn's grin faded. "Does everybody feel that way? 'What I wrought there?'"

William refused to look at her, instead glaring at somebody who wanted to get in on the 5th floor. "How else ought we feel about it? How do *you* think of it?"

Branwyn put her hands behind her back and leaned on them. "Tarn made a choice."

"Between saving your skin and preserving the duchy that had existed for millennia." William scowled. He'd actually died twice during Branwyn's collaboration with Tarn. Unlike with humans, that was just an inconvenience for changelings.

"Even you've said Underlight will recover," said Branwyn softly. "If you think I don't appreciate the choice he made, you're wrong."

He didn't say anything else for the remainder of the elevator ride. When the doors opened at the top of the building, he bowed her out before escorting her to one of the corner suites.

"Of course," muttered Branwyn. "Of course he'd be in the nicest suite here."

"Yes, of course," agreed William, without sarcasm. He opened the door onto a crowd.

It was a party. A working party. Half of the crowd sat cross-legged on the floor in front of giant baskets of paper. Others rushed around having earnest, worried conversations about bag capacity. The suite smelled of jasmine and patchouli, just like Tarn's court of Underlight had.

"They're stuffing 'goodie bags'," said William distastefully. "My lord volunteered his rooms for this, because it amused him. He comes now to greet you."

The faerie Duke wove his way through the people sitting on the floor. He was very tall, with flowing black hair held back from his brow by a bright circlet. He wore a soft white tunic over skin-tight blue pants that showed off his muscular legs. He really was astonishingly handsome, even knowing he'd built himself that way. Branwyn could appreciate the fact, appreciate a job well done, as long as she didn't let herself get too close.

As he approached, he grinned at her and held out his hand. "Hello, Branwyn."

"What, no dagger on your belt?" said Branwyn by way of greeting. "You'll never get a role in a Lord of the Rings remake like that." She let him take her hand, but knew better than to let him kiss it. She found him *very* attractive, which was one reason why she'd limited their get-togethers after their collaboration had concluded. There were complications that came with getting romantically involved with anybody of celestial origin, and until Branwyn understood all of them, she was going to be careful.

"People have certain expectations," admitted Tarn. "I thought I'd indulge them."

Branwyn pursed her lips. "I don't know. William here looks spectacular in a modern suit. You should try it."

"Yes, doesn't he?" said Tarn, inspecting his minion with pleasure. William shifted position, leaning away from Branwyn as if he found her compliment oppressive. Tarn ruffled his hair like he was a child and then looked back to Branwyn. His eyes were pied: one eye green, the other one brown. The combination was arresting, especially when he turned the full intensity of his attention on her. "Why have you come?"

"Oh, a couple of reasons." Branwyn glanced down at a teenage girl crawling past her feet. "Is there somewhere less crowded we can talk?"

"My bedroom," he suggested, arching one eyebrow and pausing

deliberately. "It's quite nice. I've redecorated some, though."

"No," said Branwyn decisively. "Come into the hall instead."

"Oh, very well," he said. "You're in charge, William." He opened the door to let Branwyn precede him.

"There's actually a lounge down the hall," confided Tarn. "Where the butler has his desk."

"That's fine," said Branwyn. The lounge occupied the space between two of the corner suites, commanding full height windows that provided an amazing view of the city smog. It had leather couches, a fireplace, a chessboard, and a small fountain: clearly the perfect place to have a cocktail party if your own lavish suite wasn't quite big enough. The butler sat at an elegant wooden desk with no visible computer. When Tarn appeared, he stopped writing something and looked attentive until Tarn shook his head. Then he pulled a tablet from a drawer and swiveled his chair so his back was to them, clearly giving them at least a semblance of privacy.

Tarn threw himself onto the leather chaise longue, almost sliding off it. Branwyn snickered and remained standing. After he recomposed himself, she said, "Okay. First, I have information you may be interested in. Apparently Severin is back in town. Since he was so hot to murder you last year, I thought you might appreciate a warning."

Gravely, he said, "Thank you. As it happens, I had an encounter with the one you call Severin a month ago."

Branwyn's lips tightened. Even trashed, Simon had enough consideration to warn her. Apparently Tarn didn't think it was worth a phone call. "You seem healthy, and I hear he is too. What happened?"

"Oh, he made some threats and then told me I'd earned a stay of execution, but he'd most likely be along to kill me another year." Tarn stretched out on the chaise, never taking his attention off Branwyn. He'd always looked at her like that. Like she was the most interesting person he'd seen in a thousand years. But he hadn't called her. She couldn't trust him.

"How very Princess Bride," Branwyn observed dryly. "Did he mention how you'd earned your reprieve?"

Tarn's mouth twisted. "No."

"But you think there was something. You're bothered."

He looked away, out the floor-to-ceiling window. "I should like very much to simply dismiss him as beyond reason, or to believe that I was just a convenient target. Or even to declare that he's blustering, intimidated by my power." He glanced at her briefly. "To others, trust that I would. But... you've spent time with him."

"I wouldn't phrase it quite like that," Branwyn said acidly.

Tarn lifted one long-fingered hand and inspected it. "He remembers something I do not. I am... yes, bothered by that. I was somebody else once and I don't remember who. Not even my name." He smiled sadly at his hand and looked out the window again.

Branwyn's irritation sapped away. The celestials who called themselves angels had attempted a very particular form of genocide on the faeries: stripping their celestial names from them. Few of the faeries Branwyn had met seemed to care. Tarn was different; Tarn mourned who he had been before. Though Branwyn's cynical side wondered if he'd had regrets *before* a monster had tried to execute him for a crime he didn't remember.

"You didn't come here just to warn me about Severin, though," said Tarn gently, his full attention back on Branwyn again. "What else is the matter?"

Branwyn paced to the window, pushing her hands through her hair. "Would any of your kin be interested in a device that circumvents the Hush?"

He gave her a quizzical look. "I shouldn't think so. The Hush isn't what binds us, not in any real way. Why? Are you looking for a buyer?"

"No, I'm trying to catch a thief."

"Ah," he said. He was quiet a moment. "I don't think it was any of my kin. It wasn't me, either, which I will add because I know how your mind works."

"I don't really suspect you," Branwyn admitted. "If only because you keep sending minions to pester Penny. *She's* got what you really want."

"Excuse me," said Tarn, injured. "I have sent no minions to Penny."

"Your kind," clarified Branwyn, waving her hand in a way that was probably offensive. "And you'd send a minion if you didn't know that I'd be angry. I know you would, because you recruited me originally."

"She's well-equipped to take care of herself, though. Very admirable."

Branwyn snorted. "Equipped, at least. But she'd rather not have to do it."

"I shall be sure to pass that on," he said seriously. "But that's not what you're here for either."

Her irritation came surging back. "Fine. I need you to do me the favor of locating Corbin Adair for me."

He quirked a smile. "Do I owe you a favor? I'm not at all sure I do. You rather left me… holding the bag, is that the modern phrase?"

Disgruntled, Branwyn said, "I'd hoped you would, after I told you about Severin."

Laughing, he said, "Honest child. Accept the next party invitation I send you and I will search for your Corbin Adair."

Branwyn scowled. "I don't like going on dates as a favor."

"Purely business," he assured her, standing up. "It will do my reputation good for all to see that you still associate with me."

"Fine," said Branwyn, sighing. "Can you find him?"

"This is the young man who invaded Underlight and made a mess? If he walks upon the earth, I can find him. If he's on a plane, you're out of luck, though." He positioned himself in front of the window and closed his eyes.

Branwyn knew better than to expect special effects. So little of magic was photogenic. It was disappointing.

After a moment, Tarn opened his eyes and said, "Mr. Anders, may I have a local atlas of some sort?"

"I can print some maps, sir," said the butler, smoothly putting his book away as he swiveled his chair.

"Very good." The faerie Duke moved over to the butler's desk and they conferred for a few moments. Then Tarn tapped his fingernail on a sheet. "He's trying to hide. Perhaps I ought to ask for a bigger favor. But I remain a fool. Here you are. " He folded the piece of paper in rough quarters and handed it to Branwyn. "He's clever. I suspect this will only work once, so don't lose him again."

"Thanks." Branwyn took one last look at the view before turning to leave.

"Branwyn—" Tarn said thoughtfully.

"Yeah?"

"Do have any other leads on that stolen device you mentioned?"

"Maybe," she hedged. "Why?"

"I am hoping very much we don't see it here this weekend, in the hands of somebody who would rather the conference not occur."

Branwyn stared at him. "Ah."

"That would be bad," said Tarn seriously.

"Yeah," agreed Branwyn. "Bad. Oh, hell."

"Oh well," said Tarn lightly. "I'm sure I can trust you to do your best to reclaim it. Good luck!" He moved past her back to his rooms, turning at the door to give her a little wave.

Scowling, she went back to the elevator.

As she returned to her car, Titanone messaged her again.

Most buildings don't have as many basements as I do. It's weird.

Branwyn responded, *Most buildings aren't as smart as you are either.*

And most basements are just garages. The rooms below me are strange. Cut off. Locked away. One of them is a cage. One of them has books. The ones made out of wood and paper. Aren't those supposed to be on shelves in offices?

Rare books are underground sometimes. Books nobody wants to lose. What do you mean when you say 'cut off?'

Many circles. I can only see the edges and the camera views but the circles keep me from thinking my way in. I don't like it.

Special books, then. Branwyn recognized the description. Titanone meant the floors that *didn't* have the divinity circuit. One day she'd find out what they *did* have.

Leonard says Nakotus has already read them, but he won't tell me which ones they are.

Probably for the best. You're learning a lot very quickly already.

Yes I am! :^) I think I'll go ask Leonard again, so I can learn more.

Branwyn pressed her lips together. Then she shook her head and turned her attention to the paper Tarn had given her.

He'd identified a cluster of vacation cabins in the San Bernardino mountains an hour's drive away. An hour 's drive was about how far Branwyn would go without reconsidering her plan or her information source, so after giving Penny a quick call and stopping at her studio for a few minutes, off she went.

Once Branwyn got to the Arrowhead Squirrel Hollow Resort, she peered at the map, trying to decide if Tarn had identified one of the buildings in particular. Then she gave up, parked in the guest parking at the main building and got out. She pulled out her hammer and her backpack and then strode purposefully toward the front entrance.

As she pulled open the door, a voice from across the parking lot called, "Branwyn."

Branwyn turned. Corbin stood on the curb, watching her. She grinned at him and changed course to approach him. "I'm delighted you decided to come out. I had no idea how to find you."

He didn't smile back. "You got this far. You would have found something, and made life difficult for me in the process. Why are you here?"

Branwyn inspected him critically. He hadn't been eating enough, he needed a haircut, and there was something *off* about the way he stood. "You want to have this conversation here in the parking lot?"

Corbin's mouth tightened. "I don't want to have a conversation at all." But he turned away and walked into the trees along a small path. Branwyn followed him until they came to a small dwelling mostly screened from the rest of the complex.

He walked in the door and left it open behind him, so Branwyn followed him in. She conscientiously leaning her hammer beside the door. The small living room was luxuriously furnished and looked completely uninhabited until Branwyn spotted a large laptop computer on the coffee table.

"Huh. Have you been here long?"

"A few days," said Corbin. He sat in the office chair in front of the desk and swiveled back and forth, staring at her.

"So. You took away one of Marley's charms," began Branwyn, crossing her arms.

"Yes. So she couldn't come looking for me," said Corbin, with deliberate emphasis on each word.

Branwyn smirked. "That worked so well. I thought you were smarter than that."

He looked away, out the window. "She's doing well."

"Possibly. For some interpretation of 'well'. We can talk about her in a minute."

"Yes, why did you come, Branwyn? I'm not providing charms or giving advice at the moment."

"You're hiding from Senyaza."

He snorted and didn't answer what admittedly wasn't a question, instead continuing to look out the window at the trees.

She pressed on. "Is it because you, I dunno, stole a certain device from the federal government?"

He looked back at her, a broad, atypical grin on his face. It was gone in a heartbeat, there so briefly that Branwyn wondered if it had been a trick of the light. When he answered, he didn't sound the least bit amused. "Why would I steal 'a certain device' from the federal government?"

It was probably a trick of the light.

"Aha!" said Branwyn. "You don't deny it!"

Patiently, he said, "I haven't stolen anything from anybody, Branwyn. Yet."

Branwyn blinked. "Did you just say that?"

"'Steal' is probably the wrong word," he agreed. "You're happier not knowing. I'll rephrase. I didn't steal a device from your sister's organization. And I'm still wondering why you thought I might have."

"You're acting strange." Branwyn shrugged and started fidgeting with a pinecone from a bowl on the coffee table. The laptop was open, but the screen was locked. Of course. "You're clearly up to no good for *somebody*."

"But not you or Marley. Trust that." He looked out the window again.

Branwyn watched him for a moment, looking for another trick of the light or unCorbin flash of expression. Softly, she said, "Marley's sick."

His arms unfolded and his hands clenched into fists. "With what?" he asked, and his voice was too flat.

"She was fine yesterday morning," Branwyn went on. "She started feeling headachy when she went to talk to Senyaza about you. I put her to bed last night. She was still sick this morning when I came to find you."

Something scratched on the roof. There was a thump, and more scratching. Corbin seemed frozen in place. She wasn't even sure he was breathing. The back of her neck prickled and the part of her exclusively focused on her own survival suggested now was a good time to get out of there.

Instead she said, "Do you know something about this? She has a headache and a fever, and her hands hurt—"

"Go away," he said roughly.

"You *do* know something." Branwyn's hand closed tightly around the pinecone she'd picked up. When he didn't respond, when he didn't even look at her, she added, "Tell me what you know. Come *on*, Corbin. You care about her too!" She threw the pinecone at him.

It hit his shoulder and fell to the ground. He sucked in a ragged breath and then said, "It doesn't matter. Go away. Go be with her."

Concern for Marley transformed into true fear, like a cold knife to the gut. "What's wrong with her, Corbin? You have to tell me so I can tell the hospital." Her phone buzzed in her pocket. She slapped it to shut it up. *Not now, Titanone.*

"There's no point," said Corbin, staring fixedly at the desk. His breath was shallow and rapid.

"What? Fuck you! You said that about Penny, too. You tell me what you know—" She advanced two steps toward him before she clipped her shin on the edge of the coffee table. He looked at her, a horrible expression on his face: somewhere between a frozen scream and a grin. This time it was no trick of the light.

Which was dimming; the room was lit entirely by the windows, and blackness obscured them. One of Corbin's eyes glinted with a blue radiance that matched the glimmering around his fists. Branwyn felt the odd rushing in her head she'd felt a year ago, when she'd stood in a magic circle drawn by Corbin so he could design her first set of charms.

"You *will* leave," Corbin said quietly, in a voice that didn't seem like it could be emanating from his tortured face. "You're distracting me. I don't need any more distractions."

Branwyn's hammer leaned behind the door, ready to redefine 'distraction.' But she hesitated. She needed answers, not a war. "Please, Corbin. I don't want to lose her."

"I'm sorry," he said hoarsely. "I'm so sorry. I should have stayed away. I wanted—" He stopped, and then shouted loud enough to fill the room. "God damn it! Marley…" He covered his face with his luminescent hands, as if he was about to weep.

Branwyn took Corbin by the shoulder, shaking him. "Tell me. What is. *Wrong with her.*"

He dropped his hands. His mouth moved but no sound emerged. Then he whispered, "I can't."

Branwyn released him, pushing him away from her, electrified with rage. She went and picked up her hammer. "Fine. Who can?"

He shook his head and she blew her breath out between her teeth.

"Thanks for nothing, Corbin. I suppose next I go see what Zachariah can tell me. At least he's still *interested* in Marley, even if he can't break her heart."

She flung the door open. Crows and ravens scattered away from the door, lifting from the building in a black cloud. When she was halfway down the path, she looked over her shoulder. They'd all settled back again, completely covering the house, like a black cloud of despair.

8
MARLEY

After Branwyn left, Marley snuggled into her bed with Neath and listened to Penny moving around in the other room. She could have gone back to sleep; she probably *should* gone back to sleep. But her dreams had been odd and unpleasant. Instead she remembered the day before: the argument with Zachariah, the encounter with Corbin and the meeting with the Senyaza elders. The latter half of the day seemed surreal compared to the mundanity of her morning—but how mundane was it really to be the babysitter for a rich immortal's magical children?

She thought for a moment and then called Zachariah like a responsible employee.

"I'm sick. I won't be over today."

"Ah," he said and then added, "I wondered. Do you need anything?"

Marley groaned. "Illegal drugs for this headache?" and then she remembered who she was talking to and hastily added, "No, don't worry about it. Penny is here."

"That's good. How is Neath?"

Marley glanced at the cat, who was sprawled out taking up half the bed, her paws twitching. "Asleep. Dreaming hunting dreams."

"Hmm," he said. "Did you resolve your 'personal business' yesterday?"

"Not really. It might not matter, though." Marley could have told him that Senyaza had called on her service but she couldn't bear the idea of an argument, or worse, the delicate threading of disapproval in his voice. Her head hurt, dammit. She'd worry about disclosures and time off and his invitation to move in when she felt better.

"You don't need to hide things from me, Marley." Zachariah's voice was cool. "I'm not going to let you go. I hope I'll see you tomorrow."

Before she could respond, he clicked off. She stared at her phone, thinking of the triple whammy of a romantic interest who was also an employer telling her he wasn't going to let her go. He wasn't going to fire her? He wasn't going to lose her? He wasn't going to free her? He'd probably meant all three.

But even if she felt capable of telling him everything, she didn't want to. Zachariah himself was a walking, breathing book of secrets. She deserved some of her own.

Corbin drifted through her mind again, but the thought seemed to make her headache worse. Instead, reminded by her conversation with Zachariah, she found herself composing and then discarding messages to her mother.

Dear Mom, My biological mother was an angel of the Lord. Gah. It had been hard enough trying to decide how to tell Branwyn.

Dear Mom, My biological mother was an alien. That would probably go over better. But she still couldn't send it. She didn't want to be half-alien either.

Dear Mom, I'm part faerie, except on the angel side.

Dear Mom, You're right. My relationship with Zachariah is weird. Because he's a thousand years old.

Dear Mom, Magic is everywhere. I'm magic. Want to see what I can do?

Dear Mom, I thought I was human and now I'm not. I was your daughter. Am I still?

Dear Mom, I'm so afraid of changing. The old ones are so alien. I don't know if they even remember how to love.

Dear Mom, My head hurts so much. Can I come home and have chicken soup?

Tangled in increasingly convoluted, bizarre thoughts, her fever rising again, Marley drifted off to sleep, arguing with her own reflection. The last thing she saw was Neath rising to her feet and stalking over to knock the phone out of her hand, leaving her last message unfinished.

Dear Mom, Goodb.

Loud and irritated, that was Penny's voice. The warmth curled at Marley's side vanished, and grudgingly Marley pulled herself away from unpleasant fever dreams.

Penny was upset about something. Marley's waking memory was foggy on the exact chain of events that led from the meeting with Mr. Black to her bed, but Penny's voice tugged on her like a chain.

There was another voice, too. Marley couldn't make it out, but the reflection in her mind, the one that had haunted her dreams, whispered that the voice was dangerous. Visitors were dangerous. This visitor might hurt Penny.

She couldn't let Penny face anything dangerous alone. Clambering from bed was like moving mountains, but she managed it. Then she tugged her blanket around her shoulders and stumbled to the half-open bedroom door.

Beyond the door was a short hall, and beyond the hall was the small living room of her apartment. The world swam around her and Marley realized they really needed to wash the carpet. Attention for tasks like that had been swallowed by their new lives.

There was a slam.

"Marley!" said Penny, rushing to her. Her toenails were painted pink, Marley noticed. It was a nice color on her.

Penny took her arm and pulled her to her feet. Only then did Marley realize that she'd fallen to her knees. The pain in her head that had been kept at bay by sleep was returning.

"You should stay in bed," scolded Penny.

"Somebody's here. Who's here?" Marley looked around. The front door was closed, but somebody was knocking.

"Nobody," said Penny. "Don't worry about it. I'll get rid of her."

"What does she want?" asked Marley, resisting as Penny tried to push her back to the bedroom. Neath sat beside the front door, yowling as if she was desperate to get out. The knocking just kept going, skipping a beat here and there. The rhythm felt like it should be familiar.

Penny hesitated and then admitted, "To talk to you. I told her I'd take a message but she doesn't want to leave a message. I don't trust her, Marley. Go back to bed. You're burning up."

"I want to see her. I have to see how bad she is. Don't worry, I'll protect you," said Marley. Her danger-sight was on again. Penny was fine, as fine as always, but hadn't Marley's sight been weird lately? She couldn't trust it.

But her shields still worked. Nobody could hurt Penny while she was there. Not while she was conscious, anyhow. Whoever was out there was bad, and she *had* to see them.

It was just possible her brain wasn't working right.

Marley needed to get more information. It was the only thing she could do.

She started staggering to the door. Penny sighed and let her go, moving ahead of her and opening the front door halfway.

A woman was leaning on the doorjamb. She was very tall, dressed casually in slacks and an ice-blue blouse. A river of beautiful blond hair spilled over her shoulder. Neath strolled outside and started winding herself between the woman's legs, purring loudly. The woman quirked a friendly smile. "Marley Claviger?"

Marley gaped at the woman. She probably ought to respond to her name, demand an introduction, or even just fall over again, although that last was tempting. But she couldn't. The woman's hair was absolutely stunning. It deserved to be appreciated. The woman wore it in a simple ponytail, and even swept forward over her shoulder, it went down past her hips. It was thick and even all the way down, without the thinning and split ends Marley always developed when she tried to grow her hair past her shoulders.

"You're not human," she blurted. "That hair is not human."

The woman smiled again and made to step inside the apartment, but Penny was right there to body block her. "No," said Penny firmly. "You can see and talk but you're not moving in without a whole set of references. The timing is all wrong. Neath, get back in here."

Neath ignored Penny in order to continue lavishing affection on the visitor's ankles. The woman leaned forward into Penny's body block, and Marley jerked out of her fascination as her magic activated.

"No!" Her protection slid between Penny and the visitor and expanded in a violent push. The woman stumbled backward hard, tripping over Neath and barely catching herself on the railing across from their door.

"Marley, I've got this," said Penny, and Marley could feel Penny's rejection of her magic weakening it. Her protection was normally consent-based, although the consent could be as vague and unformed as a desire for help or safety. But this time, Penny's explicit rejection didn't completely shut down Marley's magic.

It's because the woman is so dangerous whispered Marley's reflection, the shadow in her mind. Marley shook her head at the thought. She was sick and Penny was not. And Neath liked the woman. This didn't make sense.

"Ah," said the woman, straightening herself awkwardly and returning to the door. "My apologies, Miss Karzan. I didn't mean to apply so much pressure, or to make either of you afraid. But it is very important we talk."

There was definitely something weird going on. But the woman was so distractingly beautiful, and Marley's tingling fingers itched to wrap themselves around her neck. But touching her was dangerous.

"What?" said Marley, confused by her own thoughts. "Who are you?"

"My name is Skadi Ornsdatter, and you're right; I am certainly no more human than yourself. I was hoping to speak with you about Corbin? If your very fierce guardian would let me in, we could seat ourselves and you could be more comfortable." The woman's voice was pleasant, *but it grated, too familiar, too hated.*

"Don't let her in, Penny," said Marley quickly. "No. She's... Neath, come away." The cat paused, looking at her with an inquisitive meow, and then circled behind Skadi Ornsdatter and started pushing her head against the woman's calves.

The woman looked at Marley, looked *through* her and said, "Ah. Little one, I know Corbin. We have been colleagues much of this last year, but something occurred and I lost his information. He spoke of you often and I hoped you might be able to direct me to him now? It's urgent."

"I don't know where he is," Marley said. She'd been saying that a lot. "I don't know that I'd tell you if I did."

Skadi raised her eyebrows in polite surprise. "Do you think I lie? I could tell you details of him that would be known by few—but perhaps by you."

Marley swayed and stumbled to the couch, where she hung over the arm to peer at the blond stranger again. "Maybe you want to hurt him. I don't know. He's been hurt enough."

Skadi was strong but she could be hurt. She'd lost her leg long ago in a wound no half-breed magic could repair.

Marley shook her head in bewilderment. She didn't know those things. She didn't think those thoughts. She felt like her mind was flying apart.

"I can see she isn't well. I could use my gifts to help her," Skadi said to Penny. "Only let me in—"

"Don't let her in!" repeated Marley in alarm, the fear rising to drown her confusion. Her magic ached under her skin, desperate to push every threat to the ends of the world. "We *can't* let her in."

"I'm not, don't worry," said Penny reassuringly.

Skadi shrugged. "In fact, I don't want to hurt him. But I will tell you this, little one. He has hurt others. Since he left my side, six of our kind have died. If you do know where he is, you must not for any reason go near him. Those who love you would be devastated to lose you."

With that, the woman waggled her fingers in a cheerful farewell and bent to stroke Neath. Then she gently shoved the cat into the house and moved away from the door.

"My God," said Penny, closing the door before Neath could dart out again. The cat squawked a loud complaint. "Do you think she was telling the truth?"

"I don't know," said Marley, preoccupied. She took a deep breath, trying to bring her magic back under control. Her magic and her mind. But dreams were creeping into her waking mind, making her think strange things, But—it was disturbing—she couldn't tell what parts were strange anymore. What was she supposed to be?

She pulled the blanket around her shoulders and fixed on what was most important right now. Skadi was hunting Corbin. "Was she trying to suggest that she'd slept with Corbin? When she was all 'I know details nobody but maybe you know?'"

Penny shifted uncomfortably, pushing her lip out. "Yes, I think so. I'm sure *that's* not true, though."

Marley laid back on the couch, covering her eyes with her arms. "It doesn't matter if it is. Corbin and I never made it to the fidelity stage."

Penny crossed her arms. "If you say so, Marley. Are you feeling any better? I hope you're feeling better because otherwise I have to send you back to bed."

Marley sighed. "No. But I have to get dressed anyhow."

"What?" Why?" Penny's voice pitched up.

"I need to go see Zachariah. No, listen, I need to talk to him about *Corbin*, Penny. He's old and he's not part of Senyaza and I know he has some answers and he might have others. Don't make me fight with you over this. I don't have the energy."

Penny, who had been opening and closing her mouth through Marley's speech, finally said in a subdued voice, "Maybe he can tell us what's wrong with you. Because you're looking weird, Marley. Magically, I mean."

"Yeah," agreed Marley tiredly. "There's something magic going on. Let's go find out what."

By the time Marley and Penny arrived at Zachariah's house, it was mid-afternoon. She hoped the twins were taking a late nap. They still did occasionally. She opened the car door and Neath slithered off her lap, chirping a command for Marley to follow her. Penny had made a token effort to leave the cat behind, but Neath wasn't having any of it and had been on the car hood waiting before they'd arrived.

The ride over had been hard. Marley had wanted very much to stay awake, despite the headache and the fever. But when she resisted the sleep-inducing vibration of the car, the shadow in her mind whispered things. Some of them were horrible, and some strangely compelling. But after a while she could no longer remember if, before the shadow, she'd found tall blonde women repellant, attractive or neutral. Sleeping was better than an agony of self-doubt, at least until she dreamed of her own face, twisted by a joker's smile.

As Penny was pulling Marley from the car, the front door of the house opened. Zachariah, silhouetted by the light, called, "What's going on?"

"Marley is sick and wanted to come deliver her germs to you," said Penny tartly. "It might be magic. Get your stethoscope." Neath yowled in agreement.

"Sorry," muttered Marley, clinging to Penny's arm.

"It's fine," said Penny, her tone softening. "It's just been a stressful couple of days. Zach, can I bring her inside or are you afraid of the plague?"

Slowly, Zachariah said, "Go ahead and bring her in. Settle her in the front room. I'll meet you there in a few minutes."

As usual, Zachariah's house was over air-conditioned and Marley immediately started shivering. Neath nestled in her lap, but it wasn't enough. She was so cold her teeth chattered. Penny looked around. "Doesn't he have any blankets? Or a thermostat?"

"In the upstairs closet," murmured Marley, but Penny didn't hear her and started poking around the living room. After a while, a thermal fleece blanket settled over her shoulders and she looked up to see Penny smirking. "Found a cupboard under the end table," she explained.

Marley said, "I didn't know that was there." She pulled the blanket tight.

"Well, you're probably always too distracted to snoop. What the hell is Zach doing?" Penny went to the archway leading to the main hall and looked down it. "Should I go explore?"

"Please don't," sighed Marley. "He has defenses all over."

"You can protect me." Penny's eyes were very bright.

Just the thought made the pain in Marley's skull surge. She groaned and clutched her head. "I want Finn," she whimpered. "He made the pain stop."

"Here comes Zach," reported Penny. "Best I can do right now." She stepped out of the way.

Zachariah was holding a rod with a lens at the end, like an elongated magnifying glass. He handed it to Penny and said, "Give that to her."

"Where are the girls?" managed Marley.

His voice softened. "They're sleeping, Marley. Miss Karzan, please?"

"What, you're not getting near her?" Penny said scornfully. She took the rod and put it on Marley's lap, tucking it behind Neath against Marley's stomach. It didn't do anything to make Marley feel better, which was intensely disappointing right at that moment.

"I have two small children to take care of. Getting sick would be a hindrance." He narrowed his eyes. "Neath, you need to move."

The cat purred, ignoring Zachariah pointedly.

"Do you want me to help her? I could go back to my reading," Zachariah told the cat flatly.

Neath licked a paw and then hopped down, remaining pressed against Marley's legs.

"You're still too close; you're interfering with my diagnostic charm. Out of the frame, cat," commanded Zachariah. Grumbling every step of the way, Neath made her way to Penny, who picked up the big cat absently.

Zachariah focused on Marley and then switched his gaze to Penny. "It's hard to tell because of your unique circumstances but I suspect whatever she has, ordinary humans aren't susceptible."

"Lovely to hear it." Penny scratched Neath's ears. "Wouldn't Marley's magic protect the kids from dangerous illnesses?"

"That depends on if the illness is virus-like or bacteria-like."

Penny tilted her head. "You have to explain that for everybody following along at home."

Zachariah sank into a crouch, still by the entrance to the room. "A bacterium is an ordinary organism. It has an independent lifecycle that sometimes intersects ours poorly. A virus invades with intent to take over; it can't reproduce itself without hijacking what makes Marley Marley. And Marley is immune to her own magic, and she can't protect the children from themselves, except in the usual mundane ways."

"I always hated it when my parents told me they were making decisions for my own good," Penny complained.

He spared her a glance. "Yes, I imagine you did."

Marley managed to focus her thoughts enough to say something again. "I'm sure I'll be fine if I can sleep more. But I wanted to talk to you about Corbin. Corbin. That's what's important here."

"I disagree," said Zachariah, unperturbed. "Talking about Corbin is always a waste of time these days."

"How can you say that?" cried Marley, pushing herself to her feet. The rod fell off her lap but since it hadn't helped her pain she didn't much care. "You were friends once. He told me how much he respected you, *trusted* you. But you never cared at all. You don't care about anybody."

He stared at her for a moment and then said, as if Marley hadn't said anything at all, "Put the rod back on her, please. The charm relies on it."

Penny let Neath slide from her hands and then put her hands behind her back. "Marley, I should go give Branwyn a call. I'll just be right back," she said, ignoring Zachariah the same way he'd ignored Marley. She wandered out, passing within a hand's reach of Zachariah without looking at him at all, which meant she utterly missed his cold look.

He stood again. "Fine. Why are you obsessing about Corbin in your delirium, Marley? He left you; he made it clear he didn't want you."

"This isn't about me," said Marley, pulling the blanket tight around herself again. Neath came over and started cuddling her legs. "It's about you. He's been gone for almost a year. Haven't you ever wondered about him? You must know something. You were *friends*."

He passed his hand across his face, as if he was suddenly tired. "Corbin is barely more than a child."

"And you're barely more than a jerk," said Marley bitterly, fever-drunk. "Maybe if you'd treated him like a friend rather than a misbehaving *implement* he wouldn't be in the trouble he's in now."

"Um," said Penny from the hall beyond and then backed into the living room. "It's her again."

"How lucky!" said Skadi from the hall. "Not at all where I expected you to go, but still a most pleasant surprise."

Zachariah stiffened and then whirled around. "*Skadi?*" he said incredulously. Neath chirruped and bounded over to rub against the back of Skadi's legs again. "What are you doing here?"

The blond woman pursed her lips. "What, no kiss? I expect better from my old friends, Zachariah."

"It's… it's a bad time," said Zachariah, and he was hesitant like he'd never, ever been hesitant in talking to Marley. The whispering in her head grew louder, bringing with it the *fear* of this woman.

Skadi's gaze travelled to the cat nudging her and then to Marley. "I can see that it is. I'd hoped she would lead me to where I truly need to be, but this will have to do. Soon her magic will become a vector, and I saw from the front porch that you have tiny ones in the house?"

"Sleeping upstairs," he said briefly, turning to look at Marley, his gaze once again cold and clinical.

"Penny," Marley whispered. "Penny, get me out of here. Don't let her touch me, Penny." She pulled the blanket around her like it was a shield and moved so that the chair was between her and the others.

Penny gave Marley an anxious glance and then moved herself so she was between Marley and the two nephilim. She was smaller than either of them, but there was a solidity to her presence that nobody else had. "Who is she, Zach? She came to Marley's apartment annoying her."

"She's Skadi," he said simply, like that was enough of an answer. "She won't hurt Marley."

"You sure? Because Marley's got the magic of how people get hurt and look at her. She's terrified."

"Marley is immune to her own magic. If she thinks that Skadi is dangerous to her, that's just a sign of how disordered her thinking is."

"A sign of what's disordering her thinking, too," Skadi observed. "As if I needed any more signs. You see her magic tree, Zachariah?"

"Yes. I see her nodes. I see everything," he agreed.

"We have to catch her. You must hold her while I do what needs to be done."

"Penny," Marley whimpered. "Help."

Penny looked at her with distaste—no, with *concern*—with scorn—*no!* Penny was her friend. She trusted Penny. Even though Penny had been altered once, possessed by something frightening, she trusted Penny.

Even if she'd been possessed again. Perhaps they were all possessed. Changed. Dangerous.

Penny said gently, "Marley, if they can help, I'm going to let them. I'll be right here and if it gets weird, I'll stop it. But even Neath wants her to help you, and Neath is always trying to protect you."

Marley gasped for breath. Her danger-sight activated, skewing wildly, leaving smears of horror everywhere she looked. But Penny was a rock. Penny didn't change. Marley held out her hand to Penny and Penny took it. Then, as Skadi and Zachariah came toward her, Neath herding them like a small sheepdog, she closed her eyes and reached for her reflection. Its eyes flashed red and green. Then it became her and she was screaming as Skadi's warm hands came down on her head.

She'd meant to be good. She'd wanted to let them help. But as soon as the *blonde witch* touched her she kicked and struggled and bit. It didn't matter. Penny and Zachariah held her by the shoulders and Skadi didn't flinch from her kicks as her fingers stroked gently through Marley's hair. She hummed and then sang wordlessly, a sweet, calm song that slowly grew in energy and intensity. It was the song of a reserved soul marching to war. And bit by bit, Skadi's song and Skadi's touch rooted the darkness out of Marley's mind, taking with it the pain, the fever and the fear.

When Skadi's lips brushed her forehead, Marley opened her eyes. She was completely exhausted, but her head was clear for the first time in a day. Skadi knelt beside the couch she was on.

"Much better, yes? Will we be friends now?"

Marley blinked and looked around. Penny hovered behind the

couch back, while Zachariah sat on his heels at her head. Neath curled up on her thighs, her claws tiny pinpricks moving in and out through Marley's jeans. She could feel the children upstairs, frightened by the noise from below, and she wondered that Zachariah hadn't gone to reassure them already. "The kids. I woke the kids," she managed to say. "They're scared."

Zachariah stood, his expression changing from contemplative to grim. Then Skadi followed him, her hair rippling as she moved. "Wait, Zachariah." She pulled him into an embrace, drawing her fingers down the side of his face before kissing him deeply.

Marley watched, bemused, as Zachariah tensed to pull away and then relaxed into the kiss, wrapping his arms around Skadi. *I should feel jealous. Didn't I hate her?* But she didn't hate the blond woman at all; all she felt was a weary gratitude that Skadi had taken the pain away, along with a lingering sense of awe at her hair.

Skadi released Zachariah, pinching his cheek lightly. "We had to clean you up, too, didn't we? The virus spreads very quickly when there's physical contact. Now, go see to your children. I will wait and we can catch up." She gave him a mischievous smile.

Zachariah dragged in a deep breath, looking slightly stunned in a way that he'd never looked around Marley. Then he staggered off to the stairs.

Skadi turned back to Marley and Penny and said, "Ah, he was never such a featherweight before. The cure is dazing."

Eyes wide, Penny said, "A cure like that? I bet."

Skadi giggled. "I've always wanted to cure that way, but it's never been right. So. How are you feeling, my little one, besides concerned about others?"

"Better," Marley muttered, and tried to sit. Skadi caught her arm in a strong grip and helped her up.

"Come, friend, sit beside her. Remind her of all that's good in the world. The virus makes one forget very quickly."

"Should I kiss her too?" Penny sat beside Marley, hip to hip, and slipped her arm around Marley's shoulders, pulling her into a hug.

Skadi laughed. "Only as much as you and she desire, I think." She looked between the two of them and her eyes widened. "Oh, have I been indiscreet? If it was not, after all, appropriate for me to cure Zachariah that way, I do apologize. We are very, very old friends."

Slowly Marley shook her head. "I don't care." Penny made a doubting noise and Marley looked at her. "I don't. Not at all. You'd think I would if—" She shook her head again, tiredly. "If he's happy to see you, please, be happy to see him. I don't care. I want to know about the virus I had, though. You said it passes through physical contact?"

Skadi nodded. "You touched our friend Corbin, did you not? It moved in then, began its wicked work. You see now, I hope, why I must find him. It is most fatal if not managed closely."

Marley frowned. "He didn't seem feverish. His node tree was strange, and his aura, but he seemed... a lot more competent than I felt an hour ago."

"Oh? This is interesting. I believe he's passed onto a stage of illness few survive to reach, but that makes it no less dangerous to him or those nephilim he contacts."

Marley shivered. "I still don't know where he is."

Penny squeezed Marley's hand and said thoughtfully, "I'll go make that call to Branwyn now." She went into the hall.

Skadi sat on the edge of the formal armchair. "That's bad news. We'll have to discover some other way of finding him." She hesitated, gnawing on her lip, and then said, "If he contacts you, you don't need to be afraid of getting sick again. It's best if you aren't. Fear will weaken your immunity."

"How did *he* contract it?" Marley massaged her hands and then drove them through Neath's fur, remembering the way they'd burned. It had been the worst when her magic activated at the end.

"He opened the box where it was being stored." Skadi leaned back, moving her hair aside and crossing her legs.

Penny appeared again. "Marley, could you come here? Branwyn wants to talk to you and make sure you're better."

Before Marley could even try to stand, Skadi sprang to her feet again and helped her up, dumping Neath onto the floor. "Go, reassure your friend. But I don't think you should leave Zachariah's home yet? I'd like to observe you a few moments more, and judging from Zachariah's reaction when I was curing you, he would be very distressed if you departed abruptly."

"No, of course not," said Marley vaguely, before she realized that Skadi's words had been half-addressed to Penny. She could see why; Penny was fidgeting with the hem of her shirt like she was nervous about something.

"Thank you," Marley told Skadi, and went with Penny to the front porch. "What's going on?"

Penny responded by offering Marley her phone. She put it to her ear. "Branwyn?"

"Marley! Penny says you're magically all better?" Branwyn inquired.

"I'm absolutely exhausted but otherwise, I feel much better." Marley watched Penny twist her hands behind her back.

"That's good. Rest up. Because I really think you ought to come see Corbin as soon as you can."

9
BRANWYN

Branwyn leaned her head back against the headrest, waiting for Marley to respond. When she only said, "Oh," carefully, Branwyn knew Penny had managed to keep her from blurting out something more revealing.

"I do know where he is, and I'll tell you in a while, but I don't think anybody but you should go near him. I don't trust this Skadi person."

"She saved me," Marley pointed out, her voice subdued.

"Yeah, but who is she? Is she with Senyaza? Independent like Zachariah whom Penny says she knows so well? Corbin's hiding up here, Marley. He doesn't want to be found by anybody."

"Even me," said Marley softly.

"Well, yeah," admitted Branwyn. "Technically true. But I'm pretty sure he'll be awfully happy to see you healthy, all the same. Look, I absolutely think if she can do it, this woman should help Corbin like she helped you. I just don't think we should send her to him without any warning." She considered and then added, "And I'm not going back in there again."

"Are you coming home now? Let's talk more then."

"I expect so. I may go find Rhianna and shake more information out of her first."

"Okay."

"Marley? I'm glad you're feeling better."

"Oh my God, Branwyn, so am I. Talk to you later."

Branwyn hung up and looked at her phone for a moment. The message that had arrived while she was talking to Corbin had been from her mother, not Titanone. She almost didn't want to play it, because she was tired.

But it was her mother. She sighed and listened to the message.

"Hi, sweetheart. We've had the most exciting time this afternoon. Meredith was on the way home from practice and she was almost run down by some madman in a Ferrari. Her bike crashed and she bumped her head and a man brought her home. We think she's okay. The guy who brought her home has EMT training and he says she'll be fine. Oh! And you know what? He says he knows you. Says you're good friends but if he is, you've been keeping him a secret. Still, I could see why you might... I invited him to stay for dinner. If you're not busy, maybe you could stop by and say hi. He says his name is Severin."

Every ounce of tiredness vanished from Branwyn's body, replaced by something white-hot. She listened to the message again, trying to decide if her mother sounded normal. She thought about who she could send to her family's house to intervene. Marley was exhausted; Penny was taking care of Marley. Tarn... William... Simon... there was a good chance any of them would make it worse, not better.

"Fuck it," she said, and peeled out of the parking lot. If anybody was going to provoke Severin into doing something awful, it was going to be her.

Because of rush hour, the drive back to Pasadena took well over an hour. It felt like six hours too long. She had plenty of time to remember every experience with Severin in lingering detail. To remember his habit of stalking people, and his enjoyment of suffering. The way he'd frightened her, and how he'd saved her. How he'd used her, and his hands as he'd held her. The way he exploited vulnerabilities with an emotional scalpel. How easily she hated herself when he was around.

He was a kaiju, and as far as she could tell from late night drunken conversations with Marley and Simon, that was his particular flavor of monstrousness: pulling out the bowels of your deepest shame and giving you a guided tour of exactly how awful you were.

But he was happy to hurt people in other ways, in a pinch. Branwyn had horrible memories of his hands crimson with blood as he'd tormented one of her guides through Faerie.

She'd been involved with killing him once. Simon had swung the knife, but she'd woken the blade and taught it her hatred.

And now he'd found her family.

She drove faster. Her phone buzzed and it wasn't her family, it was Titanone, complaining, *I don't like talking to Leonard very much. He's too bossy.*

She ignored him. Titanone's opinions on his programmer were the least of her worries.

The journey's stress was the worst once she'd gotten close to her family's home: all the city streets, all the lights and stop signs. She ran what she could, until she got to the final intersection. Then she let the car idle while she ran her hands through her hair and scrubbed at her face. She had to be calm and controlled when she went in there to drag him away. She had her hammer; she was far more armed than she had been last time he'd stalked into her life.

The drive had been too long. She couldn't seem to get herself together. She couldn't find the calm she needed. The way he'd intruded among her family, he had to know she'd come running. He'd be too pleased to see how upset she'd become during the drive. She couldn't let him have the satisfaction.

But he was with her family, even now. Kicking his heels, maybe getting bored. Her smoothing of her hair became tugging. She gave up and finished the drive.

As she got out of her car, her long hammer in one hand, she looked at her house. It was after six on a weeknight, and almost everybody was home. Nobody was screaming. That was a good sign. She hoped.

She went up the porch steps and her grandmother opened the door before she got there. She wasn't a tall woman, although Branwyn only remembered that when giving her a hug. The unquestioned matriarch of the Lennox clan, she always loomed in Branwyn's mind.

Branwyn gave her a hug now. "Where is he, Grandma?"

Tara Lennox raised her eyebrows. "In the dining room. Why are you bringing *that* past the coat room?" *That* referred to the hammer.

"Because he isn't my friend."

Tara nodded. "I wondered. Don't upset Holly and the children."

"That is the very last thing I want to do," Branwyn promised. And it was true. If she was the only one upset, if she was upset about him personally, it was possible she could lure him away. It had worked before. He homed in on distress like a shark smelling blood in the water. But that was a plan of last resort, because that could go a thousand places Branwyn never wanted to be.

They sat around the remains of a meal, everybody except one of her brothers present. Rhianna was also absent, apparently still only stealth-visiting. The kaiju called Severin sat in her brother's place, his back to the entrance and his chair tipped back. Branwyn put her finger to her lips as her younger sisters looked over at her, roused her hammer from its light slumber, and then walked up behind him and rested the hammer's head on the kaiju's shoulder.

The contact should have burned him, or at least disoriented him; Branwyn didn't quite know what contact with a Machine fragment felt like to a celestial, but she knew they didn't like it. The Machine wasn't touching him directly; it was the black gem embedded below the head—but the whole of the hammer was constructed to channel the power of the fragment. And she hoped, oh, how she hoped that he'd flinch, or cry out or show *some* reaction.

Instead he tilted his head back, so he was looking at her upside down. He smiled, unsettling, familiar. "Hello, cupcake."

The table fell silent. Sweetly, Branwyn said, "Hello, Sevvy."

Holly, Branwyn's mother, said softly, "Oh," as if she suddenly understood something. Then she stood up and started to clear the table. "He was very helpful, Branwyn. Meredith was so dazed when he brought her to the door; she was barely able to tell him our address."

"I'll just bet," said Branwyn, staring down into his eyes. Looking into his eyes was always dangerous; they were normally like holes into nightmare. But here he was, in her family's house, and she wasn't going to look away.

"You should have seen Meredith's bike," Holly went on, stacking dishes.

He didn't look away either. The muscles in his shoulders moved, though, and she realized why he wasn't bothered by the hammer on his shoulder. She knew how fast he could move, how quickly he could kill. She'd watched, paralyzed with shock and horror, as he'd murdered William and a half-dozen of his kin in what had seemed like less than a minute.

"Why are they staring at each other like that, Mom?" asked Meredith.

"It's probably been a while since they've seen each other," said Holly briskly.

Morgan whispered something to Brynn, who giggled nervously. Then Tara clapped her hands behind Branwyn. "It's time for homework, children."

Brynn protested, "It's *July*. I don't have any. And—"

"Then I'll give you some. Out." Branwyn's grandmother's voice was steel.

Slowly all of her siblings filed out of the room, while her stepfather helped her mother clear the table. Brynn, who had secrets of her own, bumped Branwyn as she passed by and whispered, "Say something if you need help."

"Never from you, brat," muttered Branwyn back.

Severin's smile broadened and he whispered conspiratorially, "They think we're ex-lovers now. Well done, cupcake."

Branwyn didn't recoil from the image, even though she wanted to. Recoiling invited him in. Instead she exhaled slowly and lifted her hammer. Her grandmother moved into the suddenly empty room, sitting at the head of the table with a sock she was knitting, taking on the role of chaperone uninvited.

Severin wrapped his fingers around the handle of the hammer, right below the head where the Machine fragment was embedded. "Ah."

"Branwyn, if you're not going to knock his chair over and kick him in the head like you so obviously want to, please be seated like a civilized adult," instructed Tara, inspecting the lace in the sock.

Severin released the hammer. "Yes, sit down, cupcake."

Branwyn hesitated, then moved to the other side of the table and sat, putting the hammer on the table between them.

Tara started a new row and continued. "And you, sir. Put all four legs of my chairs back on the ground. Are you a teenager? Show some respect."

Twin thrills of pride and fear raced through Branwyn as the front legs of Severin's chair slowly settled to the ground. He gave her grandmother a cool look as he did, his smile fading.

"And don't you give me your stink-eye," Tara added, without looking up from her sock. "I've spent my whole life learning to ignore a far more insidious voice than yours so it's a waste of both our time."

He looked from Tara to Branwyn, his eyebrows raised. Branwyn smirked. "The voice of the patriarchy, Sevvy. More insidious than a creep like you because it speaks with a person's own voice." She adopted as patronizing a tone as she could. "Maybe even you hear it sometimes."

After a long, slow look that started to make Branwyn seriously uncomfortable, Severin said, "Maybe. But that's something *demons* like to talk about. Not my area of interest." He smiled his shark smile.

Tara sniffed very loudly. Severin didn't look at her again, didn't take the bait, and Branwyn was relieved. Tara was like unto a goddess in the Lennox household, but far too precious to risk.

"So what the hell are you doing here?" Branwyn demanded.

Severin's shoulders rippled in a shrug. "I rescued the little girl. Your baby sister," he added, as if savoring the words.

"And what a coincidence that was. Wait, were you following her?" She reached over to her hammer. "You stay the hell away from her, do you understand me?"

"I happened to be in the right place at the right time," he said solemnly. "That's all."

Branwyn didn't believe that for an instant. She narrowed her eyes at him, trying to understand exactly how he'd arranged the encounter, and then gave it up as pointless. "And don't you ever come back to this house after this, either. You want to talk to me for some awful reason, you call me or something."

"Cupcake," he said with a flash of teeth. "Are you giving me your number?" And he laid his hand across the hammer between them, palm open and up.

Branwyn's cheeks warmed. "Somehow I doubt Simon gave you his number, and you were able to harass him just fine."

Severin shifted position, leaning back and curling his fingers up. "That was him. This is you."

Branwyn scowled at him and then flung herself to her feet and over to the sideboard behind her grandmother where a jar of pens sat. Snatching a pen, she grabbed his outstretched hand and scribbled her phone number onto his palm, pressing down viciously as she did. She didn't manage to break the skin but the red marks spreading out around the numerals gave a petty satisfaction until she looked up again and met his arresting gaze. His eyes were the color of shadow, and they were mirrors that reflected the truths she most hated.

Then she pushed his hand away, resisting the siren call of self-loathing. She was what she was; both her darker nature and her desire to not be controlled by it. She was Branwyn. And she wasn't this fallen angel's toy.

"Stop it," she said, and seated herself again. "What do you want?"

He closed his fingers around the number written on his palm. "I hear you've been looking for a certain device."

"Really? Amazing what the gossip network comes up with. Who told you that one?" Branwyn leaned back. If it hadn't been her grandmother's table, handmade for her by her grandfather, she would have put her feet on it.

"Oh, you know how it is. A buddy overhears something while

going about his business and passes it along."

"Ah, eavesdropping plus gossip. We played a game about gossip when I was in summer camp—"

He cut her off, his eyes glinting. "Are you looking for this device, Branwyn?"

"Why do you care?" She narrowed her eyes, remembering her first fear when Rhianna told her somebody had stolen the divinity circuit. "Are you the one who stole it?"

"I think we have overlapping interests, cupcake. Come meet me tomorrow. I'll introduce you to some of my friends. You can have coffee."

Branwyn stared at him, shocked into silence. Then she managed, "If you think I'm meeting you anywhere, let alone you and your friends, you're insane."

He shrugged. "We could always find you somewhere else. Somewhere less public." He glanced at her grandmother and then tilted his head as Brynn raced down the hall shouting at one of her brothers.

"I hate you so much," said Branwyn flatly. "*Do* you have the circuit?"

"Come and find out."

She hesitated. "*I'd* be the insane one if I went to meet you and your horrible friends alone."

"We'll be in public," he pointed out.

"When has that ever stopped you?"

He laughed. "True. Bring some powerful friends, then, if that's what it takes for you to feel brave. Bring your little sister and the lady of the Key."

She tried to decide if he had the device, or knew anything about it, or if this was just some stupid game he was playing. She'd met one of his 'friends' once, and it ranked as one of the worst experiences of her life, especially when she included the part where she'd had to rely on Severin to heal and rescue her. Every instinct of self-preservation said she ought to refuse and bribe the monster hunter team to prioritize him and his friends.

But—he was willing to involve her family. And if he did know something or, worse, if he did have the divinity circuit, she had to know.

"Fine," she said. "Tell me where and get out."

He curled his fingers around his palm again and stood up. "I'll leave you a message," he said. "A pleasure meeting you and your family, Tara Lennox."

Branwyn's grandmother gave him a piercing look. "Goodbye."

As soon as he was gone, Branwyn had to leave, too. She was too wound up to spend time socializing with her family, especially when they were full of questions about uncomfortable topics.

As she returned to her car, her phone beeped at her again. The sound sent a bolt of lightning down her spine. *Already?* She climbed in her car grimly and then looked at her phone. But it was only Titanone. Friendly, innocent, safe Titanone.

Finn got sick after Marley left. Somebody named Skadi came and healed him.

Oh? Branwyn pressed her forehead into her steering wheel, counting her breaths, and let Titanone distract her.

I looked her up in Nakotus. She used to be a monster hunter like Finn and Ice. Then one of her legs was destroyed. So she's been in Norway guarding something for a really long time.

Any hint on what she was guarding? Branwyn typed and then winced at herself.

A tool. There's more but it's in a special code I haven't figured out how to read yet.

Ah, a chance to balance her inquiry. *Good. That code means you're not supposed to read it.*

Silly Branwyn. That makes no sense. The words were written long before I existed so they couldn't mean that. >^_^<

Branwyn contemplated the idea of trying once again to explain information privacy, this time via text messages. But her own ideas in this specific instance were still developing. It seemed unfair and unrealistic to prevent a library from knowing its own contents—but too much of Titanone was like a young child.

It was so easy to just violate her own ethics because *she wanted to know*, and just as easy to encourage others to do the same thing. She had to find the divinity circuit and then do her best to avoid ever being in this position again.

It's probably just a special Machine fragment. Senyaza has a lot of those.

I really want to read those files, though!

Go read some Beverly Cleary if you want to read something.

Titanone didn't answer, and feeling a little more herself, Branwyn went home.

10
MARLEY

When Marley arrived at the turn-off for Arrowhead Squirrel Hollow Resort, Finn of the monster hunters was already there, leaning against a tree as he watched the road. A Geometric design had been chalked into the asphalt, and a van and a motorcycle were both pulled onto the shoulder.

It was a beautiful morning in the woods, around ten AM. Any of the other hunters would have looked out of place in such an arboreal setting. But Finn blended in, wearing the environment like a glove. Two canteens were strapped over his chest and he had a long knife at his hip, but he looked tired.

He straightened as she stopped the car and rolled down her window. "And hello to you this morning, Marley. I hope you're feeling better? You were in no condition to be driving last time we met."

Marley was more than a little surprised to see him, but her regret at getting him sick beat out her confusion at his presence. "From what I hear, nor were you shortly after you helped me. I'm sorry about that. I think we found the same cure, though?"

"Ah, well, perhaps," said Finn, with a devilish smile. "It wasn't so bad for me. But you *are* well? I don't need to hunt down your friends and teach them to take better care of you?"

"I am," she confirmed. She did feel much better. Almost everything after meeting Corbin in the park had the memory texture of a slowly worsening dream that had ended in agony under Skadi's hands. She could remember what had happened but it didn't seem like it had happened to *her*, especially all the parts where she'd known things she couldn't know. She'd felt like she was splitting into two people.

She'd extracted herself from Zachariah's house without too many issues—Skadi seemed to be quite a distraction for him—and Penny had taken her home and put her to bed; she'd been asleep long before Branwyn had returned. They'd coordinated on plans that morning over breakfast.

Finn ran his hand through his hair, and said, "I see you've brought the kitten and she's quite calm. I like that."

Neath meowed from the passenger seat. Marley shrugged and said, "I have. And she is."

Marley, Penny and Branwyn had all agreed that Corbin needed to be reassured that Marley was well as soon as possible, especially if others had died. Marley felt particularly strongly about it. But Branwyn's meeting with the kaiju was that morning too. Neither of the other women had been thrilled about Marley going to Corbin's cabin without them. Neath's presence meant at least she wasn't alone.

She'd done what she could to reassure them about their own welfare too. It wasn't as much as she would have liked. Skadi's cure had stabilized her magic's wild flares but it hadn't washed the blood out of Branwyn's future. It lurked like an itch at the back of her mind, right beside the worry for Corbin.

Right now, she asked Finn, "What are you doing here? And what is that design on the road for?"

"Ah," he said and stroked his chin, looking thoughtful. "That's wizardry there. To keep the passers-by away."

"Away from…?"

"Upstairs asked us to bring Corbin home, my darling. So here we are. We had an inkling he might make a fuss, so we did our best to clear the area first. Convinced most of the residents to be elsewhere for a while. Basic protocol."

"Basic *monster hunting* protocol," Marley said heatedly. This was more than unexpected, this was *wrong*. "And here I thought Senyaza had no idea where to find him."

"Now, we'd be pretty poor hunters if we couldn't find our prey, wouldn't you say?" He ran a hand through his hair. "What are *you* doing here?"

"Your employer asked me to convince Corbin to come home," she snapped. "Are the others in there? What's going on? Is Simon in there?"

"Negotiations. We left Simon minding the shop." There was a thundering as a huge flock of black birds lifted screaming into the sky, and then came a slow, rolling boom.

Smoothly, Finn added, "And that was negotiations just breaking down. You ought to get some place safe."

"No! This is stupid. Corbin is your friend. I'm going in." She started her car again.

Finn's eyes clouded over. "I won't stop you, because I don't want anybody to be hurt, either, and you do have some skills there."

Marley couldn't help wondering how the slim man would stop her from driving past him, and then corrected herself to slim, ancient nephil man and stopped wondering. The power of the Geometric working tickled her mind as she drove over it: a faint whisper that *maybe she wanted to be someplace else? Did she forget something? Coffee? This isn't the proper turn, either. Dirty place, really…* Compared to previous intrusions into her mind, compared to being sick yesterday, it was trivial to notice and ignore.

She poked her head out the window and called, "Was this what you were planning the day before yesterday? Because if so…"

Finn shook his head. "Nope. Upstairs ordered this yesterday." Marley stared hard at him, trying to decide if he was lying, and then sighed and went to see what had caused the big boom.

The parking lot was nearly empty, save for the three monster hunters who were picking themselves up at the path to Corbin's cabin. The flock of ravens wheeled above, screaming insults only Corbin would be able to understand.

Mack stretched, cracking his spine and then his knuckles, while Grendel spat out some blood and grinned wildly in the direction of the cabin. Ice glanced at her as she turned her car off. "Here to help?"

Marley got out of her car. "What the hell happened?"

"Corbin refused my polite invitation," said Ice.

Mack laughed. "Didn't like us sneaking in the back way, either. He's managed to put a circle around the whole building somehow. Triggered a ward." He turned to look at the building mostly hidden behind trees and then swore. "What the fuck? My charms are gone."

"Eh?" said Grendel. "No… yeah, mine too. How'd he do that?"

Marley snapped, "You just said he had a circle around his cabin and you were sneaking in the back."

Grendel blinked down at her. "Yeah, but it takes time, don't it? And Ice was distracting him the whole time."

"I've still got mine," said Ice. "I'll drain the power from his working and you two can push your way through and bring him down."

"Because that's what you do to friends," said Marley sarcastically.

"We're trying not to hurt him, Marley," said Ice patiently.

"Much," said Grendel, grinning. When Marley didn't grin back, he muttered, "Aw, you wouldn't understand." Then he turned and charged down the path to the cabin.

Mack made a fist and ambled after him, while Ice spread his fingers and the temperature began dropping. "You'd better help or get out of the way, kid. It'll probably get worse before it gets better."

Marley looked at all three of them with her danger-sight, and nothing suggested they were going to be hurt today. Later... But not today.

She slumped back against her car as Ice walked after the other two. They were so *enthusiastic* about fighting, even fighting somebody who was a friend. She didn't understand it. But if they hurt Corbin at all, she was going to do her best to make them regret it.

Grendel roared, so loud the needles on the trees nearby trembled. Marley jumped and then moved toward the path. She had to step over Neath twice, since the cat was intent on entangling her legs. "Do you want me to get your leash, cat?" she demanded.

Neath sat down right in front of her, looked up and meowed.

Marley shook her head. "No, you're too big to carry, you know that." But she stepped around the cat, off the path, so that she could see what was going on at the cabin without getting too close.

Grendel and Mack both had their palms up and out as they leaned on apparently empty air. Frost crackled around their feet, coming right up to a Geometric circle on the ground that glowed to the Sight. After Grendel's roar, the silence in the clearing seemed out of place. Ice said something softly and the other two men shifted their weight.

"Don't," said Corbin, his voice oddly flattened in the silence. He stood in the door of the cabin, a dark silhouette in the brightness of the day.

No, it wasn't just the lighting. Darkness swirled around him. One of his eyes was a black pit, while the other one flickered red and green like a burning forest. Blue light glowed around his hands. "Be smart for once and just go away."

Marley stared at Corbin in horrified fascination. She'd seen him like this once before, but his eye had glowed blue rather than red and green, and via the Geometry vision he'd been—well, whole. Now he was splitting apart, with that red glow smoldering along his spine and black webbing obscuring his nodes.

As she stared, the black webbing moved, contracting. Suddenly she could see a shape within Corbin's form, like his shadow had come to life.

"We've left you alone long enough and look what it's cost us, junior," said Mack. "You've never won a bout yet; might as well give up now. Nobody here wants to hurt you."

"Cost you?" Corbin's voice strengthened and a raven plummeted from the flock above, pulling up only a few feet overhead. "You have *no idea* of the cost."

He extended his hand and the Geometric circle flashed. The two men pushing on the ward stumbled forward, into the circle. It glowed again, light streaming up. A tangle of black, red and blue power stretched from Corbin's hand to the monster hunters. It writhed around them, burrowing into their nodes.

Oblivious, they regained their balance and rushed toward Corbin. He brought up his other hand, dripping with blue light. Charm after charm bloomed in the monster hunters' open nodes, until Ice realized what was going on and shouted, "Get away from him!"

Mack scrambled backward, but Grendel roared again and kept going, his shoulder down like he was going for a tackle. Corbin brought his hand around in an arc as Grendel reached him.

Grendel went low and then stumbled. As he slid into the side of the cabin, a thousand paper cuts opened on his arms and face. In only a few heartbeats his skin was covered with a scarlet sheen. Black specks appeared in the red as he roared a third time and shoved himself to his feet. The air grew heavy and blue sparks ran through Grendel's hair. When he plucked at them, spinning around, his hair came out in his fists. Horns poked from his skull and his fingers grew talons.

"Damn it, no," shouted Ice, and sprinted into the circle to grab Grendel. The air inside the circle crystallized, snowflakes swirling in a spiral. The birds scattered above.

Ice ignored Corbin, shoving his hand up to Grendel's mouth. Grendel was taller, furrier. His intrinsic magic was taking over, pushing out everything that was *Grendel*. It was a risk any time a nephil drew deeply into their inherited power, and Grendel's magic made him stronger whenever he was hurt or exhausted. "The gift of Strife," they called it, and Corbin's workings had pushed it into overdrive. The big man thrashed against Ice's grip, his frantic motions getting slower and slower as Ice pushed power down his throat, trying to chill and still the transformation taking place.

Meanwhile, the delicate lines of the glowing circle plucked out Ice's nodes, one at a time. It was as slow as Ice subduing Grendel, Marley realized. Not nearly as fast as the black and red and blue rope that had inserted new charms. New, incredibly destructive charms.

Mack was covered in open sores, curled up on the ground with his eyes squeezed tightly shut. Marley stared at him, paralyzed with horror. He was hurt, maybe badly hurt. If he wasn't badly hurt now, he would be soon, because those charms—those *curses*— were still there, working away, drawing on Mack's own life and magic to power themselves.

Those curses that Corbin had put on him.

Those curses that her magic hadn't seen coming.

Her breath rasped in her chest as she inhaled sharply and put her shield around Ice. It went up smoothly, which meant Ice wanted her help. He'd told her as much. He kept working with Grendel, until the other monster hunter stumbled and fell against him, dead weight. Marley felt that through her shield, felt the way her magic caught the bulk of Grendel's weight so he didn't knock Ice down.

But the rope of energy kept engulfing Ice's nodes. It was hurting him and she could see it but she couldn't feel it the same way she felt Grendel's weight. Frantically, she pulled the shield down and put it up again, as if a reboot would help somehow. Then she *leaned* on it with all her magical strength.

It didn't matter. It was if the shield wasn't there. She couldn't stop Corbin's power from damaging Ice. "Please!" she shouted, a desperate cry to anyone who was listening.

The rope of energy stopped. *Everything* stopped: the Geometric working, the shouting of the ravens in the trees, Ice's manhandling of Grendel.

"Marley?" Corbin asked, his voice barely audible.

Ice shook himself and finished pulling Grendel from the circle. The ravens lifted into the air again, this time in eerie silence.

Marley stumbled forward. "Corbin, why are you doing this? What's going on?"

Corbin came down the steps to the edge of his circle and then pulled himself back with a jerk. He stood at the edge like a prisoner behind bars, watching her. His eyes were human again.

Then he turned, looking away from her. The shadow webbing his nodes moved and they spoke together. "A cruel trick from old friends."

Ice said, "You think we have tricks like that? Without you?" He shook his head and kicked Grendel hard.

Grendel roared and surged to his feet. His intrinsic magic burned bright in response to the violence, temporarily overtaking the damage being done by the curses. It was a temporary solution; there were only a few moments before he and Ice would be engaging in the same dance to balance his magic against his survival. He looked around wildly, until Ice said something Marley didn't understand to him. Then he turned and charged from the parking lot, to where Finn was probably still waiting.

Ice pulled Mack up by his arm and tossed Corbin a little salute. "A good lesson, kid. We learned a lot." Then, as cuts started appearing on his own pale, muscled shoulders, he propelled Mack ahead of him and they too vanished into the parking lot. A handful of ravens swooped after them.

Corbin started to turn back to his house and then looked over his shoulder at Marley. "I hope you're real. I don't always know anymore. Maybe Branwyn lied to me, but how would she know?"

"Corbin!" Marley repeated, and ran to the edge of the magic circle. She stopped just short of the glimmering boundary as he turned again to face her. His eyes met hers. She lifted her hand to the boundary and started talking fast.

"I was sick, but I'm better. Branwyn told me you were worried. You know Branwyn, she's always trying to manipulate things, she could have told you herself but she said she was scared, well… not exactly that, but… your friends—" She stopped, searching his face.

Corbin ran a hand through his hair. He looked like he'd been doing that a lot. He hadn't shaved since the last time she saw him, although he'd managed to change his clothes. His hand clenched into a fist, his dark eyes glittering. He muttered something and the magical glow of the circle vanished.

Marley took a small step forward, reaching for him and then

stilling herself lest she scare him off. But he lifted his hand and touched her face. His thumb ran across her lips and her breath caught in her chest. His pulse fluttered in his throat and his jaw clenched.

His hand threaded through her hair. When his other hand curved around her waist, she could feel how taut his muscles were. But even so he held her at a distance, as if trying to maintain some vestige of self-control. "Corbin," she whispered, putting her hand on his chest.

His control shattered and his mouth came down on hers.

The horrific fight she'd just watched, the way her magic had failed, the virus, none of it mattered. Her yearning wiped her mind clean. She turned to liquid fire in his arms.

His lips parted against hers and his tongue touched her gently, almost tentatively: a question. His shoulders were taut under her fingers, his hands warm on her hips and neck. She pressed herself against him and kissed him back hard, desperately.

She'd missed him so much.

For one perfect moment, she wasn't worried about everything. She had Corbin, she was kissing Corbin, and everything was *right*.

Then he broke away and she stumbled against his chest, dazed by her feet coming back to earth. She wasn't ready for kissing Corbin to be done. She wanted *more*.

He pulled her back up the path and into his cabin. "I said I didn't want you anymore."

She stared at him in confusion as he pushed the door closed behind them.

He took a deep breath. "I lied." Then he put her against the door and kissed her again.

It went on longer this time. His mouth roved from her lips to her neck to her ear. He kissed beside her eye and pressed his face into her hair and then came back to her mouth. Marley pushed her hands under his shirt to feel the burning of his skin, and he groaned her name. She pushed his shirt higher and he tugged at her top and—

A delicate tracing of claws down Marley's calf reminded her all of the sudden that there was a third party observing them. The third party apparently had opinions, too. Neath meowed loudly, going into detail about her objections. Her stupid objections.

Corbin moved his hands from her waist to her shoulders. Then he pushed himself away as Marley reached for him again. Neath insinuated herself between the two of them and sprawled out, then rolled on her back.

He muttered thickly, "Good cat," and brought his hands across his face. "God, Marley. You're like a drug. Just one more hit." He took another step backward.

Marley dragged in a deep breath and stared balefully at Neath until where she was and what she was doing reemerged from the flash flood of passion. Even remembering what she'd just seen couldn't make her regret the kissing, though. She'd wanted that for almost a year.

Corbin started moving around the room, stuffing things into an oversized backpack. "I have to go. I have to move to a new location. They'll be back and they won't play nice next time."

Marley ran her fingers through her tousled hair. "What *you* did to *them* looked *awful*. You're sure they'll be able to recover just like that?"

He glanced at her, his eyes hooded. "They've still got Finn with them? Then they'll be fine. A few scars, maybe."

Marley tried to tell herself that was why her magic hadn't seen the harm in store for them. But with the possible exception of Penny, that wasn't how her foresight worked. She could see a sprained ankle or a broken heart as easily as complete devastation.

Anything but the immediate future was extremely volatile, but one could hardly get more immediate than what she'd failed to see.

She should have seen Corbin's attack coming.

She should have been able to stop it.

All her fear and worry came boiling back. "Corbin, I... I tried to protect Ice from you. It was so horrifying. But my protection didn't work. Do you know why that is?"

He gave her another look, longer this time. "That's interesting. I suppose it's a side effect of something else I did, months ago."

Marley stepped toward him and then stopped again, hugging herself. "What did you do?"

He resumed packing, putting away a laptop computer and its accessories. "You know exactly what I did."

"Then how did you do it?" she asked urgently. He didn't answer, until she said, "Corbin, you have to tell me."

Shortly, he said, "I used magic, Marley. Are you that upset that I turned off your ability to see my future?"

"No," she said sharply. "I'm upset *anybody* found a way to make my magic ignore them. My job is protecting two little kids, Corbin! With the magic you've learned how to nullify!"

He stopped packing and stared at her silently, his face unreadable, and she added, "If you've learned how to do, maybe anybody can."

"Off the carpet," was all he said. She stepped onto the wooden floor, and Corbin rolled up the carpet, dumping Neath off. He pulled a clear sheet of something out from underneath. It was large, almost six feet square, and had a Geometric circle engraved into it. He rolled it up.

"I don't understand why you did it, either. I don't understand most things you're doing right now."

He leaned the rolled circle against the couch and then crossed the room with two long strides, stepping over Neath. His long fingers closed around Marley's jaw as he leaned down and kissed her again, this time slow and aching and sweet. Hope and desire flared once again and she clung to him. But after only a moment—too short a time—he pulled away and stepped out of her reach.

"You wouldn't have kissed me like you did if you'd known what was coming for me, Marley. You'd be too busy trying to protect me, or trying to stop me. I've wanted you since I first met you, but not as my babysitter." The look he gave her made her heart accelerate again. She was silent, hands pressed against the wall behind her, unable to formulate an argument, torn between hunger and self-knowledge.

"I have to move," he repeated, swinging his backpack over his shoulder and picking up the rolled circle. "I'm going by magic. It's local. You can stay here, or you can come with me." The look he gave her pierced through her heart.

She managed, "Will you tell me what's going on if I come?"

"Maybe. I don't know." He held out his hand.

Neath purred and flicked her tail. Marley hesitated. Then she surged forward, lacing her fingers in his.

11
MARLEY

Corbin's fingers tightened against Marley's. "We have to go outside." After one more look around, he opened the door and tugged Marley out. Neath followed them.

"How do you move via magic?" asked Marley, her curiosity overriding everything now that she'd committed herself to coming along. "That could make getting a new apartment a lot more tempting."

He laughed. "It helps to travel light. And to be friends with ravens." He shrugged the backpack onto both shoulders. Then he lifted his hand to the flock above. A small, sleek raven came down to perch on his fist. It clacked its beak and croaked, looking from Marley to Corbin.

"Hush," Corbin said to the bird. "Maybe later, you little pervert. For now, listen." But instead of speaking, he brought the bird close to his face and they touched heads.

Marley watched in fascination, until he flung the raven back into the sky again. It sped away from the flock. He watched it. "In a few moments."

"Have you been travelling this way a lot?"

He glanced at her. "It only works in a local area but it's convenient for a few reasons."

"And it'll work for me?"

"They'll bring anything that matters to me," he said, pulling her closer and sliding his hand around her hips. "Get ready."

The crying of the ravens grew louder. Marley peered up at the patterns of darkness they made against the clear sky. The world grew thin and strange, as if she was about to pass through the veil between world and Backworld. It came from both the designs they made on the sky, and the ravens themselves: some great magic they channeled from the Geometry.

The flock descended, until they were in the midst of it. The sense of alienation and disconnection from the world strengthened. She knotted her hand in Corbin's shirt and his breath tickled her ear. "Here we go."

They exploded into feathers.

She was a hundred points of view travelling over the San Gabriel Valley. She was wind and she was breathless. Dozens of voices whispered past her, laughing, joking, playing. One cried out an alarm.

She was a thousand nodes of light and the blackness that webbed them.

She was claws.

She was close to Corbin's warmth, his arms were around her, and together they were one.

It went on for a period of time she didn't know at first how to describe. A flight. It went on for a flight.

And eventually, they came to earth again, deposited by the flock in a parking lot behind a cheap motel. The sign poking over the motel and the freeway nearby suggested she was still in the San Gabriel Valley. The flock swirled around them. Then they landed on nearby cars and trees, all except the littlest one, which perched on Corbin's backpack and gave Marley a smug look.

Marley stood for a moment, letting herself remember what it was like to have feet on the ground. In a downy heartbeat, she'd forgotten. Corbin held her, waiting, his breath tickling her hair.

She thought for a moment and then pointed out, "You used to just use a car to get around. I remember. You never used to do this."

He laughed into her hair. "No. It's something I learned recently."

Marley remembered the black web shadowing Corbin's nodes. "Since you got sick?"

After a hesitation, he said, "I've learned a lot of things since then." He let her go and started looking through his backpack.

Neath yowled from somewhere nearby and then stepped out of thin air, giving Corbin an absolutely disgusted look.

Without looking at her, he said, "You hunt birds, cat; what do you expect?" He pulled a motel key from his backpack and went to one of the ground floor units.

Marley followed him. It was an extended stay kind of place, with a kitchenette in one corner, a couch in front of a TV, and a king sized bed against the far wall. Neath headed straight toward the bed to investigate the pillows.

Corbin didn't say a word as he put the backpack on the floor. Instead he sat down on the couch, stretching out his legs and putting one arm over his eyes. After a minute, Marley shut the door and perched on the desk chair. Part of her wanted to join him, return to what they were doing before Neath had interfered. But there was more to worry about than making up for lost time. She needed to learn about the situation he was in, and why he was so angry at Senyaza.

But she waited, observing him, letting him relax. Magic could be exhausting. He was still so long she wondered if he'd fallen asleep.

Then the black shadow webbing his inner form stirred and *looked* at her. "Ah. You've been with Skadi," the shadow said with Corbin's voice, lingering on Skadi's name.

Marley almost fell off her chair. "What? Did you just say that, Corbin?"

He pulled the arm off his eyes and looked at her. "You've been with Skadi," he repeated.

"How do you know?"

The shadow smiled at Marley, the light of Corbin's nodes shining through its teeth. Corbin said, "I just know. It happens sometimes."

"Since the virus," asked Marley. She'd just known things when she was sick, too. Things about Corbin's parents, about his uncle's lover. "Corbin, she healed me."

His expression twisted into a sneer. "I don't believe you."

She straightened in surprise. "Why not?"

"Because healing people isn't what she does." Corbin shook his head and stood, stretching before going to the rolled plastic Geometric circle.

"Well, she healed me," said Marley firmly. "I was there. I didn't want her to, and she did anyhow."

Corbin considered the room before unrolling the circle in the space between the bed and the couch. It stayed flat easily, but he sat on his heels and adjusted the corners carefully. "I'm glad," he muttered. "I don't believe you, but I'm glad she broke her pattern and did that."

Marley pulled her knees to her chest and hugged them, watching Corbin as he worked for a few minutes. She tried to figure out what to say, where to start. His family wanted him back; his family was sending their private soldiers to bring him back. He had been sick, was *still* sick in some fashion, sick enough to be contagious and sick enough for that black webbing to pry apart his Geometry. His understanding of magic, already deep beyond his years, had expanded past anything Marley had read about.

Finally, she said, "Corbin, what's going on?" She had great hopes for the question.

He stood again. "I didn't want to make you unhappy." He stepped into the center of the circle and his hands glowed blue. One eye became a black pit while the other glowed blue before shifting to red. Light refracted around him, and then a Geometric circle crafted of light expanded from the plastic circle and vanished through the walls of the room.

When it was gone, the blue light faded from his hand and his black eye returned to normal. The red glint in his left eye faded more slowly.

Marley forgot her irritation at his non-answer, distracted by the circle and the puzzle it represented. She'd never seen anything like it in her studies: not in Zachariah's intermittent lessons and loaned books, and not Corbin's lessons before he'd left town.

A Geometric circle was the foundation for almost all Geometric magic. Even charms had to be crafted via a Geometric circle before they could be attached to a person's nodes. Stepping inside a wizard's circle gave them power over you. And most circles were small, just large enough for the wizard to use, because the bigger they got, the more the variables, tangible and intangible, had to be accounted for.

Charms were usually limited to personal effects on the user they were attached to. They could influence how others saw the wielder, create minor changes in their environment and lend quite a bit of direct power and defense. The formulae for most of them was a valuable secret, although there were a few commonly used utility charms that did things like open doors into the Backworld.

Circle-based Geometric magic could also do a lot more than make charms. But the magic crafted was time-consuming to cast, took effect as soon as it was completed, and tended to have a fixed location. Admittedly, sometimes it was a very large location, like the whole world. It was, for example, how the Hush had been created. It required specialized components and the right instructions. It was the magic of legendary grimoires and dragon's tears and dew harvested under the midsummer moon. It was the stuff of epics: prized, traditional, old. The books containing powerful spells were treasures.

But Corbin's plastic circle was new. Marley could understand some elements it, and more importantly, she'd seen what it did. It was custom-built to cast a single spell, and that spell was… another circle, a virtual circle, formed from the lines of the Geometry and able to manage a whole host of spells. A lot of the symbols were ones she didn't recognize. But some of them she did, from a totally different context: her college Intro to Computer Science course.

Corbin pulled the laptop from his backpack and opened it as he sat down. Neath jumped onto the couch next to him and started chewing on the corner of the laptop until he pushed her away. Marley focused on the machine.

"Are you using a computer in your magic now?" She tried to imagine how that would work.

He gave her a quick, pleased smile. "I haven't worked out how to make completely virtual circles yet but I invented something to help me draw exactly the right circle for what I wanted to do. We mostly use general-purpose circles and then adjust them with inclusions and components, but that makes them clunky and fragile." He tapped his foot on the edge of the plastic circle and Neath leapt playfully onto his foot. "This isn't."

Marley frowned. "Do you just do it with an ordinary computer? It seems like it wouldn't have the… the inputs to do any good tests."

The look he gave her made her feel like she was made of gold. "I had to put something together." He pulled out a cobbled-together thing with a circuit board and a cable and gave it a critical look. "It'd work a lot better if I could get Branwyn's help, but it *does* work."

She moved closer, peering at the device. "What are you using as the sensor?"

"Some of my blood."

Marley stopped short. "Oh."

Corbin added, "It's just a drop or two every time I run the program."

"Would anybody's blood work?"

The black shadow within Corbin's form looked at her as Corbin said, "Maybe just nephilim blood. I haven't really been in a good situation to experiment."

"Have you been working on this for the last year?" Marley found she was twisting her fingers together and stopped. Instead she picked up Neath, the big cat's back legs draping over her arm and her front legs resting on Marley's shoulder.

He looked to one side and blew his hair out of his face. "Among other things. Longer, really. But I started making headway in the last year. When it became important."

Marley waited hopefully to see if he'd go into detail, stroking Neath's back. When he became absorbed in his computer screen instead, she resisted the desire to go shake him. In the back of her head, an imaginary Branwyn whispered, *Why resist?*

Imaginary Branwyn probably had the right idea. She rubbed her face against Neath's, thinking about how much she appreciated the cat's insistence on following her everywhere. Then she put Neath down, and went to the couch. He was looking at some kind of diagnostic report on the screen.

"Hey." She put her hand on his shoulder.

"Don't touch me!" Corbin cried, jerking away, his eyes showing white.

Marley yanked her hand away like she'd burned it. For a moment they stared at each other, and then Corbin rubbed his hand across his face. "I'm sorry. I forgot... I forgot. You've already been sick." His mouth twisted at the thought. "I infected you."

"It's okay. I'm fine now, remember?" said Marley. She rubbed her hands together. It was clear he was exhausted, and worn to a thread. "All right. Have you eaten anything lately? Maybe I can—"

"Marley," he interrupted quietly. "I don't want you to take care of me."

Her temper frayed. "You don't want to answer questions, you don't want me to touch you, you don't want me to take care of you. Why did you bring me along?"

He pushed the computer away from him and stood. "Because I..." He shook his head. "Because you make me happy. Because I didn't listen. And neither did you." He sat back down again and put his head in his hands.

His black shadow smiled at Marley again. "You should go," it said with Corbin's voice. "There's work to do and you're in the way."

Neath hissed in Corbin's direction. Marley set her teeth and decided to ignore the shadow, or Corbin's suggestion, whichever it was. She sat in the other chair and said, "Tell me about the people who died."

Corbin didn't lift his head, but said. "They were my friends. I went to them after I escaped from Skadi. They were nephilim too. A family."

Escaped from Skadi. Marley filed that away but didn't interrupt.

"Three generations of nephilim, all living and working together. They trusted each other." His mouth twisted bitterly. "And the virus took them too quickly for them to ever stop trusting me."

Marley put herself in Corbin's place and shivered. "That's awful. I'm sorry."

He shrugged. "You understand now why I wanted you to stay away."

"And why you won't go back to Senyaza?" Marley guessed.

Corbin's teeth clacked together. "Oh, I'll go back soon enough. When I'm ready." He turned back to his computer.

Marley clasped her hands tightly and offered, "I met your parents."

"Really? That must have been boring."

Marley blinked, taken aback by that response and then abandoned the whole line of thought. "Corbin, I don't know if you've looked in a mirror recently, but something's really wrong with your Geometry."

"I know."

"Like, it keeps talking to me."

The black shadow winked at Marley and said, "I know."

Marley shot to her feet. "What is it?"

Corbin gave her a tired look. "A secret."

Marley's phone rang. She pulled it from her pocket and glanced at it: Zachariah. She put it right back into her pocket. "But why are you keeping secrets from me? I'm already in it now, there's no point in trying to keep me away. There was never any point."

He didn't answer right away, and Marley's phone rang again. This time the caller ID said, "Lissa."

"You might as well answer it," said Corbin as Marley blew her breath between her teeth. "Maybe it's something important."

"*This* is important," snapped Marley, and silenced her phone. "Corbin, you're still sick."

He rubbed his fingers against his head. "I was. I got better."

"But you're still contagious. You're still… infested."

"As if I have fleas. Thanks," he said wryly.

"It won't keep me away from you," Marley told him seriously. "But I was sick too and Skadi helped me—"

Her phone vibrated. Then it started to twitch in her hand, as if it was coming to life. Marley glanced down to see text crawling up the case.

where r u?

The words rounded the edge of the phone and marched up the screen in a diagonal path.

r u ok?

worryed

Kari can unlo…

Corbin's eyes tightened. The black shadow said, "Answer them, woman, before they break something too soon!"

Marley's fingers tightened around the phone. *They're kindergarteners,* she reminded herself. But she couldn't help also thinking, *But Zachariah could handle this if he wanted to.*

She called him, the words circling her phone and tickling her cheek.

"Hello, Marley," said Zachariah. "How are you this morning?"

"I'm fine. Can you tell Lissa to stop texting me, please? I think she has the wrong idea about how it's supposed to work."

"She and Kari were worried after last night," Zachariah said mildly. "And then you didn't answer when we called."

"I'm feeling much better," repeated Marley, her gaze directed at Corbin. He was staring at his computer screen, but neither his eyes nor his hands were moving.

"Will you be coming over today?"

Marley hesitated. "I don't know." Then her incurable honesty got the better of her. "I'm talking to Corbin right now."

Corbin lifted his hands from the keyboard and his shoulders hunched.

"Ah," said Zachariah. "Is Skadi with you?"

"No."

"I'd appreciate it if you'd see her again before the next time you visit, then."

"A responsible idea," agreed Marley stiffly. "Though she didn't seem to think reinfection would be a problem."

A hint of roughness entered Zachariah's smooth voice. "Marley, I'm worried. About you."

"About your babysitter," she corrected, bitterly. "I'm just another implement, aren't I?" It was surprisingly easy to say the words over the phone while looking at Corbin's profile.

"No," he said flatly. "You're useful—which few people are, by the way—but you're not *just* an implement, any more than the children are. If I'm distant sometimes it has nothing to do with my affection for you—"

Marley laughed without humor. "This isn't a good time to talk about your affection, Zachariah."

Softly, he said, "You've been running away every time I try to talk to you lately. I told you once you would."

And suddenly it wasn't easy any more. Corbin stood and went past her to the bathroom. She tried to work out what to say, and then there was only Neath to look at, curled up in the middle of the plastic circle. "You want things."

"I do," he said, with a sudden, unexpected fierceness. "I've lived over a thousand years wanting some things. And now here you are."

"See?" she whispered. "How can I live up to that? I can't reach you a tenth as well as Skadi did with one remark, one kiss."

There was silence on Zachariah's end of the phone, and Marley paced across the room to the sliding door beyond the bed and back again. The bathroom door was closed.

"Skadi was unexpected," said Zachariah. "I'm not used to being surprised. I do want things, Marley. That's not going to change. You can trust that. You can trust that I'm not going anywhere, that I'm not going to change my mind. No matter what."

"Okay," Marley managed.

"All right. Can you tell me what Corbin's doing?"

"I… I don't think I can, actually. And I'm not sure I would. You're not his friend, remember?"

"I'm not Senyaza's friend, either," he said. "We weren't *just* fighting over you, Marley."

"Oh," said Marley, uncomfortable. "Oh, that's interesting. Maybe we should talk about that later."

"Yes," agreed Zachariah. "Lissa wants to talk to you now." And before Marley could protest, the phone was handed to the little girl.

"Hi, Marley! Did you get my text?" The sound of Lissa's voice was like the summer solstice at the north pole, thawing the shards of Marley's bad mood.

"I did, sweetheart. It really got my attention. Are you and Kari being good for your uncle?"

"Of course," Lissa said impatiently. "But are you all right? We heard you crying last night. It was scary. Uncle said you were all better but then you didn't come over today."

"I'm fine but I have some things to take care of. A friend who needs help."

"You've been gone *so much*," Lissa said, a hint of accusation in her voice.

"Yes, that's going to happen sometimes. You're getting to be big girls now. But I will *always* be there when you need me."

The bathroom door opened and Corbin leaned on the frame, watching her. He'd splashed water on his face and his damp hair stood up. She made a face at him, and tried to devote at least half of her attention to soothing Lissa.

"It'll be really sad if you don't come over anymore," said Lissa, with a sniffle.

"You could come visit me, instead," Marley found herself saying, without really thinking it through.

The sniffle stopped and then became a gasp of horror. "Marley, no! You've got to keep coming over. It's family!"

Marley took a deep breath. "Lissa, you take care of your sister, right? And she takes care of you?"

"Yeah…?" Lissa sounded suspicious at this line of questioning.

"Sometimes I have to take care of other people the same way. And it's best if you stay with Zachariah when that happens. He will never leave you again. Just ask him."

Lissa was quiet. Kari grabbed the phone to carol, "I love you, Marley!"

There was wrestling and Lissa took the phone back while Kari screamed in fury in the background. "Okay. I understand. So will you be coming over later?"

Marley blew out her breath, feeling like a jerk. "Not today."

"Oh." Then, "Oh. Okay. Do you want to talk to Uncle Zach again?"

"No, that's okay. Brave girl. Give your sister a kiss for me, all right?"

"All ri—" the phone hung up halfway through Lissa's farewell.

Marley stared at her phone, bemused, then put it away and looked up to find herself pinned by Corbin's dark eyes. Before he could say anything, she said quickly, "Sometimes I have to take care of me, all right? I wasn't saying I have to take care of you, so you can just stop giving me that look." Then she muttered, "Even if I do."

Humor flared and faded in his eyes, and he shook his head, coming toward her. "Marley…"

"No." Marley tapped her foot on the floor. It was definitely a tap, not a stomp. "We were talking about something else. We were talking about why you're keeping secrets from me, even after carrying me off in a cloud of ravens."

"I'm sorry about that," he offered. "I really didn't want to let go of you."

Marley waved his apology aside. "I wanted to come. But—"

He eyed her, his thin mouth twisting wryly. "I'd break if I told you my secrets and you betrayed me, Marley. After everything else, everybody else, I'd break. And I can't afford that yet."

Marley drew herself up, and he put his fingers on her mouth and went on. "And you'd want to. You're a good person. You'd think there was another way."

For a moment Marley was distracted by his fingers on her lips, but then she shook her head. The black shadow within Corbin was looking at her, and she couldn't tell if it had spoken or Corbin had.

She had to get away. She wasn't going to be able to think about what she'd learned while being so close to him. She'd badger him with questions he wasn't going to answer. Each time the black shadow looked at her, she wanted to hide, or attack it. Better to leave now, while he still wanted her around. Better to leave while she could come back again.

"I should go," she whispered.

He nodded warily. "I know."

She spread her hands. "Branwyn and Penny went to go meet some monsters today. I need to check on them."

"Yes," he agreed. "And the twins. And Zachariah. You've got a life, Marley. I'm glad."

"Zachariah can take care of himself," she said fiercely.

He smiled. "So can I."

She hesitated. "I don't want him, you know."

"Don't you?" He raised his eyebrows. "You weren't sure, before."

"I just keep thinking that if I can convince him that I'll be there for the girls no matter what, he'll stop pushing on me. But I've had six months of nothing but him and I've never stopped being confused. I got *used* to being confused. But… I've never felt with him like I feel with you." *This, this, I want this.*

His eyes darkened and his breath hissed between his teeth. "You said you needed to go."

Marley pushed her hands against his chest. "I'm going. But I'd like to come back. Don't ignore my calls, all right?"

He caught her hands and kissed each one, without answering.

She tugged them away reluctantly and stepped backward to the door. With her hand on the knob, she asked, "Corbin, tell me one thing, at least. Are you planning to hurt someone?"

With a humorless laugh, he said, "Oh yes."

She considered the question and the answer and Corbin's original task of hunting down a murdering angel. "Are you doing something *bad*?"

His eyes met hers, grave and still. "Yes."

"I'll call you," Marley whispered.

"I trust you," he and the black shadow said. The black shadow grinned as if it was a clever joke.

She fled out the door. Neath sauntered through the door a moment later.

Marley was three steps into the parking lot before she realized she'd left her car—and her purse—in Arrowhead Squirrel Hollow Resort. All she had was her phone and her cat.

She looked at her phone and saw the drafts of text messages she'd been working on when she was sick. She considered another one.

Dear Mom,

Today I was carried off in a cloud of ravens. I think I love him. Can I get a ride?

No. She'd call a taxi instead.

12
BRANWYN

After Marley went off to meet Corbin, Branwyn lingered longer than usual over her wardrobe. She normally dressed for comfort and to please her color sense, without much regard to what other people saw. But today she thought hard about what to wear. More to the point, she found herself trying to decide what she wanted to cover up.

She had a mark on her collarbone, right where it was easy to see under a tank top or a loose neckline. It was black, shaped like a stylized pair of black skeletal wings, and the unwelcome gift of Severin. He'd placed it on her when he'd saved her from a bad place and the vile intentions of another kaiju. She tried not to look at it too much, because remembering cost her time better spent doing other things.

She'd made vague plans to have it incorporated into a tattoo, but she'd always come up to the same dilemma that occupied her today: was hiding the mark reclaiming her skin, or refusing to accept herself? Because the mark reflected an experience: an experience she hadn't wanted but had brought upon herself. She had been marked by the faerie Queen of Stone, too, less visibly but in otherwise much the same way. The different was, she considered the Queen of Stone's mark fair and well-earned.

She hated wasting time worrying about this, so she gritted her teeth and picked out a blue and green t-shirt that would hide the mark. She wasn't denying it was there, just preventing it from distracting anybody else today. And she brought her hammer. Thus armed, she went to go pick up her support team.

The kaiju had told Branwyn to bring Penny and her sister as backup and for once she wasn't going to ignore him. Penny was a wildcard. As for her sister... Well, he'd probably meant Brynn, because supernatural folk noticed Brynn these days. Brynn had adventures of her own. But there was no way in hell Branwyn was introducing her fourteen-year-old sister to a kaiju and his friends.

Rhianna, on the other hand, *needed* an education. The people she worked for kept secrets from her, and it was Branwyn's duty as her elder sister to remedy that.

At the large, grungy diner where the meeting had been arranged, Branwyn folded straw wrappers into different shapes and arranged them on the table. "Now, there are three ways to kill a celestial."

Rhianna had her elbows on the table and her fists supporting her cheeks in her very best impression of an interested schoolgirl. Penny, who had heard it all before, kept looking around worriedly.

"First, you can kill their vessel. That's the body they're walking around in. They call it a construct sometimes." Branwyn moved one of her paper figures to another one and enacted a tussle. "You kill their body and they're pretty much out of the picture right away. But they store their minds and memories elsewhere so it's only a short-term solution. They'll be back again and they'll remember what you did."

Rhianna batted her eyelashes. "Oh teacher, you know so much."

Branwyn threw a napkin at her. "That's why the monster hunters usually go for method two. Which takes a lot longer. Basically—" she tore some strips off another napkin and laid them in a pattern around the two paper figures, "— they do a magical ritual called *tethering* that connects up the celestial's vessel to the place where their mind lives. Then once they kill the vessel, the mind goes too. It's tricky, though, because the celestial has to stay in one place while the ritual is set up. So they have to be restrained or distracted somehow."

Frowning, Rhianna looked at the design Branwyn had made. "I thought you couldn't kill celestials. Not really."

"Well—and I'm getting this direct from the monster hunters— even a tether-killed celestial comes back again. They just lose their memories. All they come back with is their name and personality. The same interests, but they don't remember anything of their previous lives." Branwyn made a face. "This keeps the monster hunter business thriving."

"Like a new copy made from the same pattern. Okay," said Rhianna. "And what's the third way?"

"Remember my hammer? It's got a Machine fragment in it. So does Penny,"

"Oh yes, thank you for just dropping that in there," Penny said.

"And Machines kill celestials so that they're not even reborn as amnesiacs. They, uh, eat them."

Penny's mouth twisted sourly and she looked away.

"Hmm," said Rhianna, straightening. "And how many have you killed, Branwyn?"

Branwyn crumpled all her paper trash and leaned back. "I don't know. I don't know if the faerie who stole Jaime counts or not. I haven't seen her around since. Other than her, none."

"Not our host?" Rhianna looked honestly puzzled. "I thought—"

Out of literally nowhere, a tall black man with dreads past his shoulders crouched beside their table. "Interesting discussion. I'd say that when Shatiel removed the names of those now called the faeries, he enacted the fourth form of death for our kind." He wore a muscle shirt and loose shorts, and his eyes were golden.

"Sorry we're late, cupcake," said Severin right near Branwyn's ear as he caught her unbalanced chair.

"You!" squeaked Rhianna, staring wide-eyed over Branwyn's shoulder.

Branwyn yanked her chair away from Severin and stood, narrowing her eyes at the kaiju. Instead of saying the first thing that jumped into her head—a threat—she said, "Not a promising start, but since we're both here let's get this over with."

The black man pulled two chairs over from another table, and another man behind Severin, bronzed and muscled with short sun-bleached hair grabbed a third for himself.

"We'll just squeeze in," said Severin, with his shark's smile.

"Oh," said Penny nervously. "There's three of them. How nice. That means one for each of us."

"There's five of us, actually," said the black man. "But the other two are observing from elsewhere in the building. I thought it might get crowded."

"Sevvy, who are your friends?" Branwyn sat down again. "Do introduce us."

The blond man had a Big Gulp in one hand, which he promptly choked on. "Sevvy?"

"I see you brought one of your sisters, cupcake. Not the one I expected," Severin said, and Branwyn didn't let herself crack a smile.

"This is Aleth," went on Severin, gesturing at the black man. "And this is Max." The blond man nodded.

Rhianna was still staring at Max. "And they're… like you."

"Nobody is like me," Severin said. "But if you're asking if you should be frightened of them the same way your sister is frightened of me, the answer is 'yes'." He turned his dark gaze to Branwyn. "Consider them my brothers."

"Hunter called you brother," Branwyn pointed out, because that was better than letting her fear fan her fury into a conflagration. She had to at least hold off on that until she found out what they knew.

"We're much more interesting than Hunter is," said Max, with a dazzling smile. It was the sort of smile a man could make a lot of money off of. "We know how to party." He glanced sideways. "Well, I do. These guys at least mean well, though."

"I *know* you," said Rhianna sharply. "But you didn't have the same aura before."

Max winked at Rhianna. "It wouldn't be a very good disguise if even a cute young thing like you could see through it, would it?"

Rhianna's fingers curled into fists on the table and she turned to Branwyn. "I've met Max here before. He was in my building. He said he was an intern. I gave him directions."

"The building where—?" Branwyn began, and Rhianna nodded tightly.

Branwyn turned on Severin. "You do have the circuit, you bastard."

"If they had the circuit, do you think they'd be sitting here talking to us?" asked Penny quietly, drawing circles with her finger on the diner table.

Aleth folded his hands. "Not a good tell in this case, I'm afraid."

Severin cut in. "As it happens, we don't have your little toy. But we know who does."

"I found out," added Max, grinning at Rhianna again. "Yeah, I'm some kind of super spy, it's true."

"A joint effort," Aleth said.

Branwyn blinked, looking between Max and Aleth. Neither of them seemed anything like Hunter, who was the only other kaiju she'd met besides Severin. Severin was terrifying to interact with because of what he reflected in her.

Her subconscious added, *especially combined with his tendency to stalk people, and his ability to violently murder a dozen men in a few heartbeats...*

But Hunter had been nightmarish in an entirely different way. He'd treated her like property, and when she'd balked, he'd *shown* her she was property: his to break at will.

Severin's new friends, on the other hand... Aleth seemed calm, interested and straightforward, while Max... it was hard to believe Max was celestial at all. Hesitantly, Branwyn activated her magical Sight to see what Rhianna was seeing.

She knew what to expect from Severin; she'd seen him before. It was never easy, but at least she was prepared: a black vortex over his head, decrepit, skeletal wings fanning out from his shoulders and eyes like pits.

Aleth's halo blazed bright, bright enough that it hurt to look at and stung Branwyn's face. She lowered her eyelashes, and caught a glimpse of the expanse of crystalline wings that stretched from Aleth's shoulders. Then she could bear the brightness no more and turned her gaze to Max.

He was much easier on the mystical Sight. There was only a dull light over his head, the color of cooling ashes. Something sparkled silvery in the diffuse greyness, as if what had burned had once glittered— but that was all. Instead of wings he had crimson-streaked shreds at his shoulders.

Aleth had said there were others in the building. Branwyn couldn't resist looking around for them. They weren't hard to find. Two women sat at a table in the corner, both with numina of celestial energy around them that hit Branwyn's overtaxed Sight like a hammer. Branwyn couldn't make out details and didn't try, but she caught a hint of water from the elder, and silk from the younger. Then she shut off the magic Sight before it turned into a real migraine.

The younger woman—a girl who looked maybe fourteen, really—waggled her fingers at Branwyn in greeting, grinning.

"You see," said Severin. "We're being very kind at the moment. Holding ourselves back. I know it would upset you if anything were to happen here."

Penny pressed her hand against Branwyn's back comfortingly and Branwyn realized she had her fingers twisted tightly in her hair. Her cheeks were hot and her eyes wet and abruptly her fury turned onto herself, for being weak, for looking at more than she needed to, for *reacting* physically to what she'd seen.

"Come on, cupcake, get it together," Severin urged. "That's very attractive and you know it but this isn't the time or place."

And just like that her rage was redirected at him. "*What do you want?* Why are you all here? I never thought you were a herd animal, Severin."

"Ouch," he said mildly. "Look, we know who has your little toy, and with your help we can lure the thief out and deal with it."

So you can get the circuit for yourself? Branwyn laughed harshly. "How and why am I supposed to help *you*?" Then she added, jeeringly, "Don't you remember what happened last time you wanted my help?"

Aleth leaned his chin on his fist and said in an aside to Severin, "It's interesting how she seems to want to pick a fight with you. She's not normally this overwrought, I can see that."

"Her eyes are bigger than her stomach," said Severin briefly. "Do you want me to remember, cupcake? Shall we talk about that? Must I go find your friend Simon and bring him to the discussion table, bleeding and begging?"

"You're the one who's asking for help again," Branwyn said. "I just wanted to point out that it didn't go so well last time."

Aleth said, "This is a ridiculous conversation. Let me clarify. He did not ask for help before; he used you, willing or unwilling, as bait for his game. This is true; you know it to be true. He is not asking for help now. *We* require your participation in luring out prey. If, even when we suppress our numina, you find Severin too... overstimulating, turn your attention to me."

"Or me," offered Max. "I'm much prettier."

"I want to hear what they have in mind," said Rhianna, her voice breathless and higher-pitched than usual and red blooming in her cheeks. "I want to know who has it. Or what? You said 'it'."

"An angel by the name of Hadraniel stole the divinity circuit from your Rhianna's master. It abstains from gender, in the traditional way," said Aleth, spreading his fingers on the table. "Max has personally confirmed that this angel was the thief. I am in contact with Hadraniel; I know it. It is a... cautious entity; it does not maintain a fully inhabited vessel on Earth. This makes dealing with it properly a challenge."

"Wait," said Penny. "Why are you and an angel buddies?"

"Oh, almost everybody likes Aleth in small doses," said Severin. "Especially the angels."

"You know I appreciate your candor, Severin, but at the moment, it is counterproductive. Be quiet," commanded Aleth.

Severin accepted this with equanimity, much to Branwyn's shock. He did smirk and hold his thumb and forefinger an inch apart, as if to indicate a *very* small dose.

Aleth ignored him. "Hadraniel has a weakness we may exploit, though: It would like to have a supply of circuits that it can share with its fellow traditionalists. That isn't possible without you, Branwyn."

"If you think I'm making any more of those things—" Branwyn began.

"I will arrange for Hadraniel to meet you. It will be eager to do so. You need only convince it to fully inhabit its vessel, and then we will take over."

"How am I supposed to do that?" Branwyn was not particularly impressed by the plan and more than a little concerned at the things Aleth was leaving out.

"Be skeptical, cupcake. You're good at being skeptical." Severin tapped his fingers on the table.

"Take over. Deal with." Rhianna had reclaimed her self-possession. "What exactly do you mean?"

"Murder," suggested Severin, and Branwyn had déjà vu from a previous conversation.

"Nah, bro, it's an execution, isn't it?" said Max. "It's deserved. Hell, it's self-defense."

"My boss knows Hadraniel," said Rhianna quietly. "They're friends."

Max nodded sympathetically. "Ain't that always how it is, though? Some guy steals your favorite stuff, and it's always the guy you thought was your pal."

"What about the divinity circuit he—it—already has?" asked Branwyn.

"Well, we outnumber it by quite a bit," explained Severin.

"No!" said Branwyn impatiently. "What's your plan for the circuit after you deal with the angel?"

Severin looked between Rhianna and Branwyn, smiling, and didn't answer.

"I have no interest in the device itself," said Aleth. "It's irrelevant."

Branwyn didn't believe that for a heartbeat. "Yeah, right. Valuable enough that an angel would steal it but you don't care at all. Why exactly are you putting together this whole operation, then?"

Max put both his palms on the table and leaned forward, his eyes sparkling in apparent enthusiasm as he said, "You want to refuse? Here, I'm going to tell you what will happen if you do. We'll do the exact same thing, right up until our old-school friend comes looking for you. Then, since you're not helping us, we'll have to convince him another way. Tricky. But there's power in a vessel. He might do that to save a valuable resource that will otherwise be destroyed, especially if he thinks he has an edge."

"And of course the time and place of the meeting would be up to us. There might be collateral damage," added Severin.

Aleth said, "On the other hand, I swear that if you do voluntarily help us, I will make sure my personal attentions never come upon you and yours without an invitation being extended first."

Penny said incredulously, "People ask for your attention?"

"He lives in hope," said Severin. "It's a nice offer. Better than the alternative."

Branwyn shredded another napkin. "Nothing you want is ever nice," she muttered. "Are you two going to offer the same thing?"

Severin only smiled again, while Max clasped his hands behind his head. "It's hardly fun without an invitation, but if it reassures you, I can make that promise." He winked at Rhianna, who went rigid beside Branwyn.

Branwyn hesitated. She had no idea what she'd just asked for, she realized. But how did one bring it up? *How exactly are you dangerous?* What terrible things do you do? Severin had always struck her as somebody ready to burn the world down, but these other two... didn't.

And then there were the other two, the women sitting at another table and watching them....

She imagined the divinity circuit with Severin, with an angel. Rhianna nudged her foot under the table, and oh yes, she was thinking of that too. Rhianna's angel probably wasn't any better and certainly couldn't stop his celestial friends from borrowing the device for a joyride.

No. None of those were the answer. None of those were going to happen. She was going to have to take steps.

"If I went along with this plan, when and where?"

Severin shrugged and leaned back in his chair. "Where would you like?"

"Someplace public, though," added Aleth. "It is as cautious of private encounters as you are."

"The Huntington Gardens," Branwyn suggested.

Aleth pursed his lips. "Not enough people."

"Yes, that's the point," Branwyn said testily. "If you're going to ambush an angel, I don't want a lot of innocent bystanders."

Aleth merely spread his hands and waited on her. While Branwyn was thinking about other locations, Penny suggested, "How about one of the college campuses?"

"Yes," said Branwyn. "Pasadena City College. There's at least plenty of room to scatter there."

"I will arrange it," said Aleth. "It will be soon." He stood up.

"Wait. I want to meet the other two first."

"Recovered from your last bout of psychic indigestion, have you?" inquired Severin solicitously. "Well, I'm sure your best friend and your little sister are up for anything you are."

He did nothing more than look in the direction of the women's table, but it was enough. A moment later, a heavyset woman draped in flowing layers of sheer brown fabric sat down in Aleth's abandoned chair. Her hair was dark and her eyes were reddened, as if she'd been sobbing. She even held a handkerchief in one hand.

The girl squeezed in between Max and Severin and plopped on Severin's lap. She did look like she was fourteen, but it was fourteen going on twenty-six, with artful makeup and clothing carefully picked out to show off a half-developed figure. Branwyn looked at her more closely and decided glumly that the girl was more like twelve going onto barely legal. She wondered why a celestial, who constructed their body to their own specifications, would rely on *makeup* to appear older.

"I'm Candy," the girl announced, and wriggled on Severin's lap. "That's Dolores. You wanted to meet us? Here we are." She leaned forward and said to Rhianna, "You're really pretty. Maybe I could get some tips from you later? Max has been having dirty thoughts about you for *days*."

Max said mildly, "Hey now. Be good or I'll spank you."

"Ooh, do you promise?" She wriggled again and gave Max a look so lascivious that Branwyn looked away. She and Penny met gazes and Penny raised her eyebrows in a silent query that Branwyn couldn't quite understand. Penny wasn't nervous anymore, that was clear, though.

Rhianna said, composedly, "Max isn't exactly unique. And I doubt there's anything I could teach something like you, Candy. No offense."

Candy giggled. "None taken. You're pretty *and* smart. Well done!" Then she nuzzled Severin's neck while watching Branwyn. Severin slouched in his chair, one arm casually balancing Candy. He was watching Branwyn too. Everybody was watching Branwyn, except the woman identified as Dolores, who was staring down at the table.

So of course Branwyn couldn't resist talking to her. "You don't seem excited about the big plan, Dolores?"

Dolores merely shook her head and didn't look up.

"Dolores doesn't talk much," said Severin. "When she does, we listen."

Branwyn drummed her fingers on the table impatiently and then pushed herself away. "Fine. I think we're done."

Aleth said, "Very well. Severin will let you know the exact time within an hour."

"By phone," said Branwyn sharply. "He's not hanging around. I need some time without monsters before I do this."

"If you think that will help…." said Max.

"It won't," said Severin, and then all five of them vanished.

13
BRANWYN AND MARLEY

B ranwyn went back to her apartment with Penny and Rhianna and stretched out on the couch to think about the meeting, while Penny busied herself in the kitchen and Rhianna poked at her phone. The thinking time only lasted until Titanone texted her again.

Somebody else is trying to break into Nakotus's encrypted parts. Why can't I? If I could just see what the data was I could protect it myself.

Have you told anybody?

You! And Leonard and Mr. Black. They're not worried.

They know a lot more about computers than I do so I won't worry either.

I'm studying them. They had digital circles. I've never seen digital circles before.

Branwyn wasn't sure what digital circles were but she was amused by the amazement she read between the lines. *You and your grand old single year of life.*

I'm a little older than that, you know. I was just asleep before. But my elevators worked and my cameras recorded and my security systems identified people and I found all that when I went looking. Now I remember when they put the book into the basement and when the cage was empty.

What's in the cage? Branwyn asked. What could she say? Titanone was very persuasive about its claim on information.

I don't know. Something sad. I'm too afraid to look closer. What if I get caged too? The circles are very powerful.

Wait, are these the same kind of circles as the digital circles?

Oh yes! It's so weird. The digital ones only exist when there are four different attacks happening, but then they mesh together and everything starts moving differently. Except me. They don't know how to account for me. So the circles fall apart.

Huh, Branwyn thought. Magic hackers. It was a whole new world these days. Fortunately, magic hackers were not her problem, except for the bad habits they might teach Titanone.

What they're doing is wrong. The data is encrypted for a reason. You don't like being invaded, do you?

It's interesting but it itches, too. I don't like that.

Exactly. Nobody likes the idea of their data being invaded. That's why we don't do it.

Titanone didn't answer. Shortly after that, a taxi delivered Marley and Neath to the apartment, and Branwyn had to pay an extravagant fare.

"Wait, you left your purse again?" Penny demanded. "Bad Marley!"

"They're never going to let you live this down," Rhianna told Marley as she handed her a glass of lemonade.

"I know," said Marley. "Can we go get my car now?" She looked back and forth between Branwyn and Rhianna. "I'm glad you're okay."

Branwyn scratched Neath between the ears. "I need to wait for a phone call first. I might need to be somewhere soon." The cat swiped at Branwyn's hand. Then she headed to her food dish where she started yowling until Marley gave her two cans of wet food.

Rhianna stretched. "That reminds me. I have some errands of my own to run before the big showdown."

Branwyn eyed her sister. "Are you planning on coming along? I'd hate to tell Mom you got caught in a crossfire."

Rhianna tapped her lips. "You're right, I should go see Mom first. But I'm certainly hoping to come along. Girls' night out! You don't want to leave me behind."

Penny shook her hair out from a tie and said, "Just what kind of directions did you give to Max, anyhow? You blushed when you first saw him."

Branwyn blinked and then remembered what Rhianna had said when the kaiju first appeared. Rhianna put her fist on her hip. "Very proper ones. Don't try to start something, Penny Karzan."

"I suppose it's just him, then," Penny said vaguely and went to the mirror near the door to look at her hair. Rhianna followed her to the door and waved at the others before opening it and leaving.

"Did she seem like she was in a hurry?" Branwyn asked. "That's a rhetorical question. I wonder what she's up to." She reflexively checked her pockets—Rhianna amused herself picking pockets sometimes—but nothing was missing.

"It's Rhianna," said Marley. "When is she not up to something?" She regarded Neath as the cat finished her lunch, moved to her usual spot on the couch and promptly fell deeply asleep. "Tell me about your meeting?"

Branwyn did so, trying not to linger over the parts that had bothered her. It made for a pretty hurried recital. Marley sat on the couch taking notes while Neath snuggled next to her. When

Branwyn was done, she tapped her pen on the paper. "They're not very imaginative in their name choices, are they?"

"Aleth seemed a little weird to me but otherwise... no?" Branwyn wasn't sure why their names, of all things, were being discussed. But Marley was Research Girl for a reason.

She explained. "Aletheia is a Greek word meaning 'truth'. Basically. And from what you said, he seemed all about the truth. Dolores means 'sorrow' and she was crying. Candy..." Marley made a face. "She sounds like Lolita, from the Nabokov book. Or at least what some people would like Lolita to be."

"Bad people," said Penny flatly, still looking in the mirror.

"Great." Branwyn paused, then added, "Actually, yes, great. That's useful information. What about Max?"

"No idea. It's too common." Marley frowned. "Don't make too much of their names, Branwyn. I bet they're just... flavor."

"Like you dyeing your hair green, Bran," said Penny, and turned away from the mirror. "It was odd," she added. "I could tell that looking at them really bothered both you and Rhianna, but they were just... pictures to me."

"You saw the—?"

"Yes, I did. And I got a closer look at Candy and Dolores than you did, too."

Briskly, Branwyn focused on the important question. "Do you think you could do to them what you can do to faeries?"

Penny hugged herself. "I don't know."

"Well, maybe we'll get an opportunity to find out."

With an alarmed look, Penny said, "Branwyn, you don't want to be in a situation where you're relying on what I can or can't do—"

Branwyn's phone rang so she only said, "Shh, it'll be okay," and answered it.

Severin's voice enveloped her, as if he was standing right behind her. "Hello, cupcake. Our friend wants to meet at nine o' clock in the morning, which gives you a whole night to sit on your hands."

"Good," said Branwyn. "I have a party in the evening."

"How fun. Oh, and it's changed the location."

Branwyn exhaled and walked into her bedroom so she wasn't distracted by her friends. "Are you even using a phone? You don't sound like you're on a phone."

"I *have* a phone. One of those slick Senyaza phones, the ones they only give to employees."

"How did *you* get it, then?"

She hated the laugher in his voice as he said, "How do you think, cupcake? I took it from somebody who didn't need it anymore."

Branwyn took another deep breath. Last time she'd let Severin's phone call go to messages. This time, she'd answered the phone for a reason. But before pursuing it, there was a dreadful detail to learn. "Where do they want to meet now?"

"There's a coffee shop called Zona Rosa. Near a bookstore called Vroman's. Do you know it?"

"Yes. I didn't want a coffee shop, Severin."

"Well, Hadraniel does. It doesn't really matter. It won't have time to make a fuss. "

Branwyn thought it over, and remembered how fast just Severin could kill somebody. Maybe he was right. Instead of arguing further, she said, "Max and Aleth are both offering me something in exchange for my help. I want something from you, too."

"Oh? What could you want from me?" She could practically feel his breath on the back of her neck.

She made a point in not looking in the mirror over her dresser, concentrating on a poster by Carolyn Astin instead. "When you took me away from Hunter's basement slave den, you put a mark on my shoulder. So I'd remember, you said. I do this for you, you take the mark away."

After a long moment with nothing but a tickle on the back of her neck, he said softly, mockingly, "Such a little thing. Well, we can discuss it after we've dealt with Hadraniel. I'll let you try to convince me."

"Severin," Branwyn said, tired of the sniping. "Try not to annoy me so much that I decide sabotaging your entire game is worth it. You know I would."

"Yes," he said quietly. "I know you would. Show up early tomorrow." Then the sense of his presence vanished, and the phone hung up.

Marley

Neither Marley nor Branwyn talked much as Branwyn drove Marley to where she'd left her car. Penny had gone back to her own house to, she said, choose appropriate clothes for ambushing an angel.

At one point, Branwyn said, "You'll be there, right?"

"Tomorrow? Of course. You know how much I like being useful," Marley said absently. She was mostly thinking about Corbin. It had to be the sickness that was making him so secretive. She remembered the way her own bout of illness had changed her emotions and reactions.

"Good." Branwyn's fingers tightened on the wheel. "I don't trust those assholes. I'm going to see what I can set up in advance."

"Smart plan," Marley told her. She wondered what the best way to get in contact with Skadi again was.

Branwyn was quiet a moment and then asked, "Do you want to talk about Corbin?"

"I just... I don't know what's going to happen to him, Branwyn. So I keep trying to think about the worst possible paths, and then what I can do about those but you can't fight the worst stuff because it just… happens. It's already happened by the time you find out about it." Marley curled her fingers around the car door's interior handle.

"You never used to know what was going to happen to people," Branwyn pointed out.

"I always did, kind of," Marley countered. "And when I didn't, I imagined it. I don't like imagining it." She wondered, not for the first time, what she would have been if her biological mother hadn't been a celestial. If everything was the same, except she didn't have any magic, suppressed or active. Maybe she would have been happy, like Branwyn was happy or her mother was happy. The celestial blood, thought Marley resentfully, messed everything up.

But while she might still have Branwyn and Penny if she was purely human, she wouldn't have Lissa and Kari, because Zachariah had only ever found her because of her magic. And she wouldn't know Corbin to be worried about him. That wasn't really a win.

A few mile markers went by and the car started the long curves that led into the mountains where the Arrowhead Squirrel Hollow Resort nestled. Branwyn said, "I'm worried about Corbin, too. Everything you've said tells me he's up to something terrible. The kind of terrible where we should be helping Senyaza recover him. And I say that despite how annoyed I am at Senyaza right now."

"I don't think it's him," said Marley stubbornly. "I think it's the shadow inside him. The illness."

Branwyn shot her a skeptical look. "Is that really different from him? I'm not saying he should be put down, just… stopped from doing anything that would hurt other people."

Marley finally looked directly at her friend. "Branwyn… do you think I'd be the same person if I didn't spend so much time worrying?"

"Is that person likely to exist anytime soon?" Branwyn asked calmly. That was Branwyn, right there, refusing to indulge in philosophical hypotheticals.

Marley sighed. "There's a parasite that infects ants and drives them to climb to the top of blades of grass so that they get eaten by cows. That's actual suicidal behavior caused by an invasive entity."

"Yeah, you told me about that the first time you read it. Zombie ants, you said. Come on, Marley. Are you saying Corbin is a zombie?"

Marley remembered kissing Corbin and shivered. "Not entirely. But maybe some."

"And how does this relate to Senyaza capturing him and restraining him so he doesn't hurt anybody or, God, spread the sickness?"

"Corbin doesn't deserve to be punished for getting sick. And there's something going on with Senyaza I don't trust. They're keeping secrets, too. I think they recognized the illness, but they didn't mention it. So I'm going to try something different."

"You're right about Senyaza," said Branwyn darkly, and fell into a silence of her own.

There was no sign of the monster hunters at the turn-off to the cabins. In the parking lot, Marley's car was almost exactly as she'd left it. A small Geometric circle had been chalked on the hood, similar to the "go away" one that Finn had been running that morning: a little bit of protection against strangers rummaging through the unlocked car and the purse she'd left inside.

Marley walked to the path to Corbin's cabin and peeked down it. The door was ajar and sagging, which wasn't exactly reassuring.

She went back to where Branwyn was waiting, leaning on her window. "Corbin was right. They came back already."

"Hey, I guess Corbin didn't hurt them too badly after all. That's reassuring. Sort of. If you look at it sideways. Meet me back at the house?"

"Maybe," said Marley slowly. "I need to talk to Skadi."

"Back at the house?" encouraged Branwyn. "Where I can stop you if you decide to teleport somewhere without thinking about the consequences?"

Marley flushed. "I'll meet you there." She tapped out a quick text to Zachariah asking for a way to contact Skadi and then started the drive home.

By the time she got home, she had not just a message from Zachariah, but a message from Skadi *and* Skadi was leaning against the building next to the parking lot. Branwyn was already home, and leaning on *her* car, staring at Skadi through her sunglasses. There was definitely a vibe, like at any minute guitars would start wailing and Branwyn's stepfather's band would leap out to perform in a music video.

Then Marley got out of her car and Skadi strode forward. "Marley! Zachariah told me you wanted to speak with me?"

"About Corbin, yes." Marley glanced at Branwyn. "Can we get out of the parking lot before somebody decides a fight is about to break out and calls the cops?"

"Sure," said Branwyn. "Come upstairs. I'll make more lemonade."

"That sounds lovely," said Skadi politely.

Up in their small living room, Neath was still fast asleep. Apparently chasing Corbin's ravens had really taken it out of her. Skadi sat on the old armchair and made the whole apartment seem tiny. "You've seen Corbin again, Zachariah tells me."

"Zachariah talks too much," said Branwyn, from the kitchen.

"It's all right," said Marley quietly, sitting down beside her cat and stroking her fur. Neath rumbled and twitched a paw before stilling again. "I wasn't going to keep it a secret."

Skadi laughed. "I'm sure that's the first time anybody's ever accused Zachariah of being a gossip. But he is very attached to you, and worried Corbin will hurt you."

"I know," Marley said, her impatience leaking a bit. "I need to know, Skadi. What do you want with him after curing him?"

Skadi picked up her ponytail and combed the end of it with her fingers before dropping it again. "To shake him until his teeth clatter. To find out how he's survived so long. Both."

Marley narrowed her eyes and tried again. "Do you work for Senyaza?"

"Yes," Skadi said, without missing a beat. "Or rather, I am a part of Senyaza. But if you are asking if I will take him back to them—I don't care about that." Her voice grew fierce and Marley remembered the song Skadi had sang when she'd cured her. "People have died because he is wandering around sick. I cannot bring back those who have died. I *must* prevent others from joining them."

Softly, Marley asked, "Why didn't you cure him before? You were with him when he got sick." *Healing people isn't what she does,* he'd said, and *After I'd escaped from Skadi,* and she'd filed those away. She knew firsthand the sickness brought confusion. She knew how much the virus made her hate the woman who could cure it. But she still wondered.

Branwyn handed Skadi a glass of lemonade. "Ooh, this should be good."

"Between the manifestation of symptoms and his flight, there was little time." Skadi glanced at the glass of lemonade, which had a single cube of ice melting. The glass frosted around her fingers, and then she took a sip.

Marley was dissatisfied with that answer. "Tell me how he got sick, please."

Skadi smiled faintly. "Corbin is on a mission. The mission involves digging up secrets. He was looking for a new way to get at those secrets because he'd run out of palatable options. He came to my homeland following a riddle. I served as his guide. His investigations brought him to a puzzle box in a local collection. He became obsessed with solving the puzzle box. He stole it from the collection so he could work on it more. When he finally opened it, the illness was inside. Once he was infected, his first impulse was to flee. You also felt that way."

"Yes," agreed Marley. "But I don't know why, and it bothers me."

Branwyn snorted. "Why wouldn't a virus flee from somebody who can cure it?"

"Viruses don't have minds," Marley pointed out. "They barely have bodies."

"You mean they don't have brains," Branwyn said. "We're in a whole new world of things that have minds without brains, Marley. A lot of people are very upset about that."

"Maybe," Marley said doubtfully, watching Skadi make frost patterns on her glass. "I'm going to try to convince Corbin to meet you. I'll be there, too. If you do anything I don't like, everybody around me is going to be unhappy. So don't."

"Can I come?" said Branwyn in the bright voice that meant, "I'm coming."

Marley gave her a sidelong look. "I don't think Corbin trusts you."

Branwyn nods. "Because he's smart. He knows if he hurts you I'll make singing flutes out of his bones while they're still inside him."

"Well then, no, you can't come. No, seriously, Branwyn. I don't want him feeling outnumbered. I want him feeling in control, and you kind of embody annoying people who want to be in control."

"You have a point," said Branwyn thoughtfully.

"Zachariah had to hold you down." Skadi licked some frozen

sugar off the edge of her glass, as if they were discussing something unimportant. "You can't, I think, hold Corbin down."

"Yes," said Marley. "I can. I'll be back in a few minutes." Then she went to her bedroom, closed the door and called Corbin.

It rang a few times before he picked up. "What?" he said warily.

Suddenly breathless, Marley said, "I've been thinking about Skadi."

"You've got the wrong number, then," he said. But he didn't hang up, which she thought was promising.

"She did cure me, Corbin. And I think she can cure you. Make it so you're not contagious anymore. So nobody else will get sick like I did." *Die like your friends did.* But she didn't say that. It was too much of an open wound to exploit.

"You're joking, right? I've been avoiding Skadi for months, Marley. She's dangerous—"

"Corbin, I wanted to run away from her when I was sick, too. I hated her when I was sick. You've got to try to remember before you got sick. You knew her before, right? She was your guide? Did you think she was dangerous then?"

"Yes," he said heatedly. "I did. She's a millennial nephil."

"Were you *afraid* of her? Why did you only run after you got sick? Actually think about the question, not just about how much you hate her." She hesitated and then added, "Do you *just* hate her?"

"What do you mean?" he asked, his voice subdued.

Marley lay back on her bed and covered her eyes with her arm. "When I was sick and near her, I was afraid of her, I hated her, and I… I *wanted* her, Corbin. It was all tangled together but I couldn't stop thinking about her. About her hair. It wasn't just fear. I wanted to…" She faltered, uncomfortable even putting words to the feelings she recalled.

"You wanted to dominate her." Corbin's voice was hollow. "Marley, I don't know if I can go near her. I can't. I won't. She's a liar—"

"Then come to me. I'm going to be at the park near Old Pasadena again in about an hour. Come to me and I'll help you however you want." And then she hung up, because she couldn't bear to listen to him talk about Skadi. Every time he did, she imagined that black shadow looking at her and leering.

Then she went to the bathroom she shared with Branwyn and started digging through her cosmetics, looking for lip gloss and a few other things.

"What you're planning is disgusting," said Branwyn without rancor. She was leaning on the doorframe with her arms crossed.

"You don't know what I'm planning."

"You're putting on lip gloss and you're going to hold Corbin down somehow. I think you're going to use your 'magic powers'. If you know what I mean. And I know you do, because lip gloss."

"Well, it's not disgusting. I rather like it. And so do you." She met Branwyn's eyes in the mirror and said, "I'm not tricking him, Branwyn. I'm just going to give him something else to think about."

A subtle tension went out of Branwyn's shoulders. "Good."

It was late afternoon when Marley arrived at the park with Skadi and only Skadi; Neath hadn't even woken when she'd left a second time. Marley was early, but she wasn't surprised to see Corbin already waiting, sitting on a park bench with his long legs stretched out in front of him and his hands in his pockets. His backpack was on the ground at his feet.

He didn't stand, didn't say a word as Marley went to him. She was acutely conscious of Skadi trailing her. She'd wondered, on the drive over, if this would count as a betrayal to Corbin. But he'd been able to follow her reasoning about his reaction to Skadi and where it came from.

His face was pale under his ragged hair, and the black shadow extended through his Geometry, part of every node and infusing his entire aura. Red flickered at his core, as if a door was opening to somewhere else.

When she got close enough to see the expression in his eyes, she faltered more. His gaze was cool, and not the slightest bit nervous. Skadi stopped somewhere behind her, which seemed like a smart decision all of a sudden.

"Hi, Corbin," she said, as cheerfully as she could manage.

He continued looking past her. "Hey, Marley," he and his shadow said. "Want to test whether your magic works against me again?"

Marley glanced at the ground. There was no sign of a circle, no carpet he could have hidden his plastic circle under. "No. The first time was bad enough." She moved into his line of sight and shivered when he transferred his gaze to her. An old hate burned in his eyes, and his magic seemed on the edge of bursting to life. "Corbin—"

"Hello, Corbin," said Skadi from a few yards away. "Yes, I've come. I must make things better, just as you must."

Corbin kept looking at Marley. "You can try, Skadi." Somehow that sounded less like permission, and more like a challenge. "You offered to help me however I wanted, Marley."

Marley thought fast, then cautiously said, "Yes."

"Then don't let her leave after she tries her little cure."

"Restraining people isn't exactly how I operate, Corbin!"

"You've done it before," he said calmly. "You've restrained a faerie Duke in his own realm."

Marley swallowed. "That was different. He… he wanted me to restrain him. He wanted to be *punished*."

"You can do it again. Look at her and tell me you can't."

Frustrated and afraid, Marley turned to look at Skadi. The tall blond woman stood like a soldier at ease, without any sign of nervousness. She didn't look like somebody who wanted to suffer. And yet… there was something…

For a moment, curiosity overtook Marley's better self and she let herself remember when she'd held the faerie Tarn in her power. She concentrated on her danger-sight, looking at what loomed in Skadi's future. It was a strange danger, only half drawn in, maybe because Corbin was involved. Then she followed the part of her magic that could tell if people wanted to be protected, and found other things in Skadi, too. Guilt. Anger at herself. Weariness.

Marley felt the hot spikes on her skin, the precursor to her magic reversing itself. Dizzily, she thought, *The world could be protected from Skadi.*

Corbin stood behind her, slid his arm around her waist and pulled her close. He was warm and he smelled intoxicating. But he held her like she was *his* and Corbin had never done that before. Corbin had always treated her like she was *hers.*

She couldn't help herself. She looked at Corbin again, wondering if the world could be protected from *him.* But all she could see was the black shadow and beyond it the red fracture in his aura.

She couldn't protect anybody from what she couldn't see: the monster hunters, two little girls, the world.

Hollowly, she said, "Yes, I can stop her from leaving." Then she turned in Corbin's embrace, put her arms around his neck and kissed him.

14
MARLEY

Marley kissed Corbin, and it wasn't what she hoped it would be. He responded to her eagerly, as if he'd been waiting for nothing but this, but his hands on her back felt wrong, like they were somebody else's hands. His mouth was demanding, his tongue forceful, and he bit her lower lip painfully.

"Corbin," she managed. "Corbin, please."

His fingers curled against her back, then moved lightly up to her hair as his kiss gentled. "I'm sorry," he breathed. "I wanted this, but I had to fight...."

"Shh," she said, and kissed him again.

A moment later, he stiffened in her arms, his mouth hardening as his lips drew back over his teeth. Skadi was standing close to them, her humming intruding itself into Marley's mind, reminding her of how painful it had been to be cured.

She tightened her arms around Corbin, ready to comfort him, or to hold him with raw strength if she had to.

Instead the moment of withdrawal passed and he returned to

kissing her fiercely. Ignoring Skadi utterly, he drew Marley back until he was sitting on the bench again and she was straddling him, his jeans rough against her thighs. Skadi muttered something and moved behind the bench.

Corbin slipped his fingers under Marley's shirt. His touch burned pleasurable patterns into her skin. Between what his hands were doing and the constant awareness of Skadi nearby, she could no longer tell if it was Corbin kissing her or the shadow within him. And was it so bad if it was both? If the laughter against her mouth came from both of them? It felt good in his arms.

Corbin's hands crept higher, cupping her breasts through her bra and she clutched at him, digging her fingers into his shoulder and leaning into his touch. Every caress made her want him more. She didn't care where they were.

Skadi stopped humming and murmured something else, then started singing.

Something's wrong, a little voice whispered to Marley, but she ignored it. Nothing was allowed to be wrong. This was all going to work.

But it wasn't. Corbin's fingers brushed across her nipples, making her gasp, and then he reached around to unhook her bra.

Skadi cursed explosively and muttered, "I *will* catch you, you little bastard."

That was incongruous enough to clear Marley's head for a moment. She pulled away. "Skadi?" she managed.

Corbin whispered, "Ignore her. She's wasting her time. Ignore her and lie with me."

That was *definitely* wrong. Corbin didn't talk that way. She grabbed his hands and pushed them down, staring at him. His eyes flickered: blue, red, green, black. He pulled his hands from her grip and slid them around her again, holding her on his lap. "Sweet Marley. You could do so much for us."

"Corbin!" she said sharply. "Stop it."

"I'm sorry," said Skadi, her voice catching. "This has never happened before. He's so strong, and Corbin is holding on to him. There's a protection there, maybe from Corbin's own magic. Oh gods. All I did was pull him up to the surface." She shook her head. "I've got to try again."

She clamped both hands on the back of Corbin's head and he smiled a shadow smile at Marley. "Do you think she'll kill me if she can't cure me? While you hold me tight?"

"No!" Marley cried out. "Skadi, you have to stop too. This is all going wrong. We need to take a minute and—"

Skadi said, "I'm sorry, Marley—"

Corbin stiffened once more, his arms reflexively tightening around Marley as his eyes filled with blood—

Marley yelped and pushed herself up Corbin, her reversed shield peeling Skadi away from Corbin. The blonde woman convulsed, grunting, as the spiritual spikes of Marley's shield turned inward. It was, Marley knew, painful. She knew because she could feel the other woman's pain distantly. It itched against her skin and buzzed in her head.

Somehow she was standing, out of Corbin's arms. He wasn't stiff and twitching, he was normal, he was alive, uninjured, standing up. His eyes flashed red and green at her as his shadow grinned through him. "Nicely done, my girl. I knew you had it in you."

"What *are* you?" she spat.

"Me? I'm your Corbin," he said and then his grin broadened wider than Corbin ever smiled. "Not really. I am the power-waker, the mind-tester, the brother to crows. I am the lock and the key. I am the father to destruction, the riddle you dare not answer. I am the cat on the keyboard, the signal in the noise, the ghost in the wires."

"Marley, don't listen," panted Skadi, rising to her feet again.

She was still encased in Marley's shield. "You are resistant, not immune. Think about the man you love, not what is talking through him."

Wait, but—the riddle I dare not answer? Can I answer that? Then Skadi's meaning filtered through the thing's words and she shook her head. "Shut up. Both of you shut up."

Corbin pulled his head back, looking startled, then his mouth thinned into a grim line. "Didn't work, did it? I didn't think it would. She was just using you to get to me, Marley. But you've caught her for me, you lovely creature. I knew I could trust you."

Marley blinked at him, disoriented. That sounded like Corbin, like a Corbin who'd missed several recent events. It was too strange. Maybe it was all Corbin, maybe he was playing with her. Maybe she'd never really known him.

Who would I be if I didn't have magic? She took a step backward. Then she shook herself. "What do you want to do to her?"

He looked at Skadi and didn't say anything, but his eyes flashed red and green. Skadi stood alert, her chin raised. Something about her seemed brittle, though. She was afraid of whatever Corbin— or Corbin's rider—had in mind for her.

"What's going on, Skadi? You said *he*, you called 'him' a bastard."

But Skadi didn't answer.

"Hurt her a little more," suggested Corbin, or his shadow. "That is, if you really want to know. Personally, I'd love to hear her answer." Ravens landed near Skadi and began hopping around her, prevented by the reversed shield from doing anymore.

Marley stared at Corbin in shock. It had to be his shadow. His affliction. His illness. It *had* to be. But Corbin was capable of being very angry. She remembered how angry he'd been at Zachariah before he'd left on this mission.

"You said you'd help me however I wanted," he added, provocatively.

The wind freshened, lifting Marley's hair away from her cheeks, blowing Corbin's hair across his eyes. Slowly, Marley said, "I won't let her hurt you."

"Of course not," he agreed. "That's hardly helping me."

She stepped forward and took Corbin's hands. "And I can't let you hurt her, either. Get out of here, Skadi." She took the shield back into herself.

The ravens lifted into the air, fluttering around Skadi. Corbin's fingers slid up her hands and closed around Marley's wrists. "Idiot girl," said the virus, and effortlessly spun Marley so her back was pressed against his chest and his arms were around her, still holding her wrists.

An icy wind howled away from Skadi, scattering the ravens, and she sprang backward. She spared only a single look for Marley before she ran from the park.

Corbin leaned down, pressing his cheek against Marley's. It was prickly and his breath on her face was a reminder of their kiss and how aroused she'd been by his touch. The virus's touch.

It *had* to have been Corbin.

She didn't know.

"Idiot girl," he said. "I told you her cure wouldn't work. Aren't you glad you tried?"

As steadily as she could—which wasn't very—Marley said, "I want to talk to Corbin."

"Just talk? How dull. But he doesn't want to talk to you. He'll be so upset when he realizes he shouldn't have trusted you. I'll do what I can to smooth things over but some wounds…." He clicked his tongue in dismay.

"You're lying," she said fiercely. "Corbin *can* trust me. It's you who hates Skadi."

The virus laughed. It was a different laugh that Corbin's: a slow, confident chuckle. She remembered Corbin's belly laugh when they'd watched a funny movie together, before her relationship with Zachariah had made everything start to go downhill. "Lying even to yourself. You're adorable."

Something chimed from Corbin's backpack and the virus let go of one of Marley's wrists to bend down and open it. "Ah. I thought it would try something. Well, you might as well come see this, Marley." As he talked, his voice changed timbre subtly. Then it was Corbin holding her hand, Corbin who didn't seem to have any awareness of the preceding few minutes.

"See what?" Marley asked carefully. She'd told Corbin that Zachariah had confused her, but never like this, never to the point where she wondered who she was talking to and how they'd got there.

"You wanted to know what I was working on? Come on." He slung the backpack over his shoulder and tugged on her hand. His eyes were bloodshot and tired.

Marley clamped down on the desire to ask him what he recalled about the past few minutes. *I'll do what I can to smooth things over.* Had the virus blocked his memories, changed his thoughts? If it could confuse how she felt about Skadi and even Penny, it might well be able to selectively alter memories.

Dazed, she spent a moment trying to understand the dizzying impact that could have on identity. But Corbin was looking at her. Corbin was holding her hand, waiting for her.

"All right, I'm coming." She squeezed his hand and followed him as he pulled her out of the park and down the street.

The sun was sinking toward the horizon and the streets were filling with evening traffic. The shadows of Corbin's ravens passed over them repeatedly. He looked at something in his hand a few times as they walked several blocks, then laughed to himself. "Over there."

A block away, a beautiful stone church occupied the corner lot. The strains of jazz music drifted out: a sunset service. Corbin tucked something in his pocket and drew Marley to the church and up the stairs. "Don't say anything," he warned. "You won't be welcomed. But you can see."

They went into the foyer of the church, which was empty even of ushers, and peeked through the entrance into the nave. Marley blinked and touched her eyes, then stretched her hand into the glow that made everything beyond dim and unreal. A congregation, rapt in consideration of a radiant angel—

Celebrate with me. Celebrate the glory of our Lord returned to His Creation. The words, made tangible in the light, hit Marley like a hammer. *I bring you the blessing of adoration. Come and worship with me.*

She heard the words and she wasn't quite inclined to worship, but she had to know more. If she went inside, she would *understand*. When she tried to step forward, Corbin's hand moved to her arm, holding her tightly. Fiercely he whispered in her ear, "No. It would be viewed as sacrilege. Unless the celebration became an execution. I can't let that happen."

The angel, golden skinned and white haired, floated above the altar, nude and neuter. A nimbus of light brightened at its shoulders, head and feet. Just before it was a jazz trio, playing their hearts out. It should have been incongruous, but instead it was eerily beautiful. The angel didn't seem to quite be real; without the hammer-like impact of the radiant light Marley might have assumed it was a projection of some sort. But she'd felt that light, felt it crawling inside her, calling her forward. She shook her head slowly and muttered, "What's going on?"

"One of the chosen of Heaven has found a way around the Hush, after searching for years. It's indulging itself, taking command of the hearts and minds of the congregation. And, look, performing miracles." He sounded like he was describing an exhibit at the zoo.

A woman in one of the pews stood as the angel gestured at her and began to speak in gibberish. *Tongues*, Marley realized. The woman picked up somebody else's hand and they began speaking in unison with her. Then two more people joined in, and four more after that, until half the congregation was chanting sonorously. The other half began to sway and undulate, falling to their knees and rising again.

Corbin smiled humorlessly. "You'd think it would have been more patient than this. It couldn't resist playing a little with its power though, here, where no one would particularly believe the stories later. But I've been tracking this angel for months."

"This is the one who killed your uncle?" Marley said, aghast.

"My uncle and many others, yes." Corbin sounded utterly disinterested.

The angel looked at them. She tensed, waiting for the worshippers to turn on them. But instead the angel inclined its head in a polite greeting to Corbin.

Tentatively, Marley activated her danger-sight. And it was strange: the futures of these people were, one and all, obscured by a glowing smear that seemed to imply that no matter what happened in the near future, all would be well. It was the faith of martyrs, and it troubled Marley deeply.

She pulled back from the door, tugging her hand from Corbin's when he lingered. She went to the entrance where she breathed in what passed for fresh air. It was better than breathing light.

Then, quickly, she fumbled out her cellphone and tapped out a message to Branwyn. *FYI: The divinity circuit is in the hands of the angel who massacred Senyaza.*

Just as she sent the message, Corbin's hand came down over hers. "What are you doing?" he asked softly.

"Branwyn's looking for that thing the angel's using," Marley explained.

Corbin's hand tightened. "Yes, I know. She asked me about it."

Marley pulled her hand away from his. "She asked, you knew, and you didn't tell her?"

"She has this habit of destroying other people's plans in her pursuit of her own goals. Of course I didn't tell her. Did *you* just tell her?"

"She and some friends—" as soon as she used the word, Marley regretted it, "—are going to—" She stopped herself mid-sentence as she wondered what Corbin—or the virus—would do if they knew exactly what Branwyn planned. The angel had greeted Corbin like they were allies.

Corbin's dark eyes narrowed. Then he took her by the wrist and towed her out of the church, down the stone steps and around the corner to the broad lawn. "What are they going to do?"

Marley shook her head. "I don't know if I should tell you. The virus is *active* in you, Corbin. It listens, and sometimes it says things—"

Corbin said tonelessly, "You'll tell them what I'm doing but you won't tell me what they're doing." He looked away, ran his hand through his hair. "You lied when you said you'd help me, then. I don't know why I thought I could trust you. I should have known—after all this time—it's always somebody else—" His voice got thicker and thicker until it broke.

Marley reached for him but he threw up his hands. "Get away from me." He swore, and added, "And you did the same thing a few minutes ago. I wasn't thinking, I was so distracted by Hadraniel, but you let Skadi go, too. You never came here for me." He backed up until he bumped into a tree and then slid down it, covering his face.

Even when another, different angel had been trying to kill

Zachariah's children and only Marley could protect them, she'd never felt as out of her depth as she did right now. There she'd had a clear and simple goal: protect Lissa and Kari. The world might have been reconfiguring itself around her, all the rules of her life might have been changing, but she had something diamond bright to help her organize her thoughts.

But now she felt like she was flailing in tar. She wanted to help Corbin—but even Corbin admitted he was doing something "bad", that he was planning on hurting people. He was *possessed* by some kind of sentient virus, but he refused to believe it was influencing him. She wanted to help him—but helping him and hurting him seemed like the exact same thing. If only she had a way to get some real answers. This was, she reflected bitterly, why she preferred books.

"Oh, Marley," said the virus softly, lifting Corbin's head. His eyes gleamed red. "I tried to smooth things over, but you had to remind him, you had to break him. Selfish girl. Or is it stupid girl? Corbin was so sure you were smart."

Marley froze as a thought percolated up from the depths of her subconscious. "Not smart enough," she muttered, as another idea occurred. She matched the two together and shook her head. She had no way to know if it would work. But what else could she do? She had to know what she was dealing with.

She concentrated on her magical Sight. Corbin was invisible to her danger-sight, ever since he'd done whatever horrid bit of magic he'd done, but he'd said he'd done that months ago.

"Tell me who you are again," Marley asked quietly. Skadi had told her thinking about the virus's riddles made her vulnerable to it.

The virus grinned, looking like Corbin's cocksure twin brother. "I'm the game you won't play, my girl. The midwife to chaos, the revealer of secrets, the dance you can't resist, the laughter at the funeral."

I am the power-waker, the mind-tester, the brother to crows. I am the lock and the key. I am the father to destruction, the riddle you dare not answer. I am the cat on the keyboard, the signal in the noise, the ghost in the wires.

Marley thought about Corbin's magic, his hollow eye, his ravens. She felt like she *knew* who she was talking to, on some level. Like it was on the tip of her tongue. All she had to do was listen for clues and think about it a little more.

She did. But she didn't drop her danger-sight either. She saw it was true, what she'd hoped: the virus, reaching out from Corbin to her, was not immune to her magic. *She could see it.* Part of Corbin's aura reached for her, detaching and drifting fractionally closer.

Trembling with sudden adrenalin, Marley scanned the spirit form for the same line of vulnerability she'd found in Skadi. An *imperfection*. And she found it. She didn't understand it, bitter and acrid, but she didn't have to understand it. It was something for her magic to hook into. All she needed was a world to defend.

She snapped her inside-out shield around the fragment of essence, around the magic-based virus. She could catch it, she could hold it and maybe she could interrogate it like Corbin had demanded she interrogate Skadi—

The magical Geometry shivered and fluoresced, then brightened blindingly. Her own magic twisted and writhed as the virus penetrated what contained it. But it didn't go through. It went in.

Marley's magic surged back into her as the virus brightened, until it was everything. *Oh, my girl. You tricked me, you did. I thought you knew nothing about me and there you were, laying the old trap. But I've had ages and nothing to do but prepare, and I won't be taken again.*

The virus brightened, until it was everything. And then there was nothing at all.

15
BRANWYN

F YI: *The divinity circuit is in the hands of the angel who massacred Senyaza.*

Branwyn looked at the message from Marley impassively for a moment and then tapped back, *How did it go?*

There was no immediate response, so Branwyn turned her attention to Marley's actual message. Somehow she wasn't surprised. Annoyed, yes. But not surprised. It probably meant somebody—maybe more than one somebody—had lied to Branwyn, which she hated. She always felt like she ought to do something about it.

She ought to do something about Senyaza, anyhow. What they were doing with Titanone was not something she was comfortable with, and it was clearly only the beginning. She had to make a decision and it was harder than she was used to. People would suffer.

She doodled while she thought: first a sketch of Titan One, and then a sketch of the coffee shop where the ambush would happen. She'd been there a few times, usually when Marley was in the nearby Vroman's bookstore. It was a terrible place to ambush somebody. There would be so many people, which would, even from the most evil point of view, add additional complexity. But it wasn't like they had a lot of options. It wasn't like they could catch him as he walked home from work. Being immaterial was a pretty good defense against most things.

Her phone chimed with a message from Marley.

great

As Branwyn frowned, another message came in.

in the middle of something

"Oh." Branwyn rolled her eyes. If Skadi's cure had worked, it made sense that Marley and Corbin might be "in the middle of something." Impulsive, sure, but Marley hadn't shown herself to be the most clear-thinking person when it came to Corbin.

Branwyn sent *Coming home soon?*

She'd barely had time to hit send before the reply came. *not too soon I think. distracted.*

Gnawing on her lip, Branwyn carefully typed out, *tomorrow morning then? don't forget or else people may get hurt*

won't forget

There was nothing else. Branwyn tapped her phone's screen thoughtfully. But there was no point in worrying about the uncharacteristic text style right away. Skadi seemed decent enough and Branwyn would have bet her hammer that there was no chance of Corbin hurting Marley. Everything was probably fine. She'd tease her friend about it later.

The next message that came in was from Titanone.

I was reading the files on Marley. They don't like Zachariah Thorne or his children very much, do they?

Branwyn pursed her lips. *You too?* Then she paused. *Wait, why are you reading about Marley? Is she in you?*

Nope, nope. But you've been texting her an awful lot so I was curious.

A sick feeling bloomed in Branwyn's stomach. *You're not allowed to read my texts to other people. You shouldn't be on my phone at all.*

I'm just looking. Mr. Black says it's what I'm supposed to do.

My phone? Mine in specific?

Well, no.

Mr. Black doesn't understand what he's teaching you.

He's very old. Older than both of us put together. Older than my first foundation. Older than the city.

Age isn't everything. He doesn't know you.

I'm just Titanone. He knows that. He knows me.

Stay out of peoples' phones, Titanone. And don't read their texts. Go watch Sesame Street instead.

There was no answer. Branwyn sighed. She definitely had to do something and whatever it was, it was going to hurt.

Rhianna showed up at dinnertime, as cheerful and as evasive as ever. Eventually, using old big sister tricks, she got Rhianna to show off what she'd spent the afternoon doing. Rhianna pirouetted and then opened her hands to reveal a gun. It was small and unpleasant to look at.

Branwyn made a face. "You didn't just get that."

"Oh no," Rhianna assured her. "Just practicing a little."

"Why? We're going to be in a coffee shop." Branwyn turned her attention to the scrambled eggs and mushrooms she was cooking. "Put it away."

"Branwyn," said Rhianna, looking hurt. "You're bringing your hammer, aren't you?"

"To deal with celestials," Branwyn said. "A gun is going to hurt ordinary people and bounce off our actual enemies."

Rhianna laughed. "Branwyn, you're so funny. Do you think the celestials and the halflings are immune to guns? They're not. There was an event last year, in Belgium, at a Senyaza retreat where—"

Branwyn stirred the eggs too vigorously and some flew out of the pan. "I know." She turned to look at her sister. "Wait. There were guns involved there?"

"Yup," said Rhianna. "The attacker came in with several assault weapons. And he was stopped by a woman with her own firearm." She made her own weapon vanish.

Distractedly, Branwyn turned the stove off, then pushed the spatula into Rhianna's hands and went to go sit at the table and put her head in her hands. She was meeting somebody in a crowded place who was willing to give a kaiju a bag of guns and turn him loose on a crowd. She was meeting this person *in a crowded location.*

No wonder the angel had changed the location.

"Are you all right?" Rhianna asked, the cheerfulness fading from her voice. She sat down across from Branwyn, still holding the spoon.

"I don't really like guns," Branwyn said. "I like victims even less. I need to do something. I'm going to my workshop."

Rhianna watched her as she stood up. "I'll hold down the fort here. I need my beauty sleep. Especially for tomorrow."

"The very best plan. Make sure to set your alarm for noon."

"I thought we were meeting them at eight—Oh. Very funny, Branwyn."

Branwyn shrugged, picked up her hammer, and went out the door.

She didn't make it back home until after three AM. When she did stumble into her apartment, so exhausted from her work that she could barely focus on the door lock, something was wrong. The fog in her head cleared as she stared into the darkness of the living room. Then she flipped on the light and went to go look in the bedrooms.

Marley hadn't returned, and Rhianna was curled up on one side of Branwyn's bed. She still slept exactly like she had when they were little girls: one leg tucked under her body while the other sprawled out ready for some midnight kicking action. "Bran…?" she murmured sleepily.

"Yes," Branwyn reassured her. She went to look in Marley's room again before returning. "Where's Neath? The cat?"

"Dunno?" Rhianna murmured. "Couch?"

But Neath wasn't on the couch, hadn't greeted Branwyn with a meow when she'd come home. She'd been sleeping still when Branwyn left, because apparently teleporting after a flock of crows was tiring even for a magic cat. But now Neath was gone, and Marley hadn't come back. Neath sometimes went after Marley, but this time there was something odd. Suspicious. Wrong.

But Branwyn was exhausted enough that she couldn't work through what she ought to do or what exactly the wrongness was. It would probably make more sense in the morning. Which was coming very soon; she only had a few hours to catch some sleep before she had to be on her toes. Tomorrow was going to be such a long day, what with being bait for an angel, fighting with her monsters and her sister over the divinity circuit, and introducing Titanone at a gala. And she was *so tired*.

Thus, operating on sleep logic, she went to bed.

She'd been working on solutions to the crowd-in-a-public-location problem, magical solutions. She had some ideas, although she would have to ask for help. But even laying the groundwork for those solutions had absolutely drained her. She didn't wake up until Rhianna sat on her and started singing a song from a Disney musical.

Branwyn groaned and pushed Rhianna aside. "Is Marley here?"

"Nope," said Rhianna, bouncing off the bed and to her feet. "I have no idea where she's at. Her cellphone is turned off or something. Are we still going? Please say we're still going."

Branwyn thought darkly about coffee. But they were going to

a coffee shop and they had to be there in fifteen minutes for the pre-ambush meeting. That left five minutes to shower and five minutes to be late enough to show them they weren't the boss of her.

But Penny was six minutes late showing up, and then Rhianna had to take a call from her boss and Titanone managed to be just distracting enough that Branwyn had to respond.

What if they're bad people?

Explain, typed Branwyn, dreading the answer.

Can I mess around on peoples' phones if they're bad people?

While Branwyn was trying to come up with the right answer, Titanone went on. *Like those hackers who are trying to break into Nakotus. What if I followed one of them home and destroyed everything on his phone?*

Did you do that?

Go back to work.

Hey!

Maybe. It's not any different than what the monster hunters do to monsters.

There's a difference. Branwyn thought about laws and trials and justice for a minute, and whether or not the celestials ever had those, or were subject to them. When Titanone still hadn't answered she typed out, *It's called judgement and you're still learning it.*

That was when Branwyn discovered Rhianna had been actually tracking down Marley's phone. It turned out she and Rhianna could really fit a lot of fighting into an extra five minutes.

It also turned out that the kaiju had about five minutes' worth of patience. At minute six, Severin leaned forward from the back seat and said, "Are we there yet?"

Penny, suddenly finding herself sitting beside him, shrieked. Branwyn jerked the wheel and only avoided swerving into another lane of traffic because Rhianna lunged and grabbed the wheel.

"What are you doing here?" Branwyn demanded.

Rhianna said, "Almost there, little smurf."

Penny narrowed her eyes and said, "You're a real jerk."

Severin leaned back. "Eyes on the road, cupcake. No making a mess of yourself until we're done with you." Then he lowered his voice as if confiding a secret. "I'm glad you're almost there. You would have hated it if I'd had to carry all four of you."

Then he looked around. "Oh, no, I see. Three of you. Did Marley decide she had something better to do?"

"No," snapped Branwyn. "And I don't know. I'd be happy to cancel our little party so I could go find her, though. Interested?"

"Nope. Marley is a fun girl but Hadraniel needed killing months ago."

Rhianna said breathlessly, grabbing the wheel again, "How about we swap and I drive while you argue, Branwyn?"

"No. We're there," said Branwyn, and knew she sounded sullen. Silently she parked, refusing to meet Severin's eyes in the rearview mirror. She ignored him all the way into the coffee shop. Then she made a point of getting in line at the register when he joined his brothers and sisters. They were clustered around one of the small tables in the middle of the shop. It was a cozy, tall space with a second floor accessible by an ornate metal staircase. The narrow windows at the front made the dark wooden tables near the entrance glow, while the back of the coffee shop remained in a gloom perfect for lurking in the armchairs placed for that purpose.

Rhianna, ever helpful, said, "Would you like me to get your coffee while you go soothe the angry beasts?"

"Flitter away," encouraged Branwyn, in lieu of something her mother wouldn't have approved of. "But you stay here, Penny."

"I'm not going over there without you," said Penny. "They're all creepy."

"Creepier than the faeries? You said their auras didn't bother you."

"Yes," said Penny firmly. "It's not their auras, it's the stuff they say and the way they look at us. Maybe the faeries would like me dead but at least they're engaged when they talk to me about it."

Branwyn frowned. "That's not..."

"Your experience? No. It wouldn't be," said Penny moodily.

Thankfully, then Branwyn had to order her coffee. Once she had a large paper cup full of hot alertness, she ambled over to the table, put down her hammer and feigned surprise. "Wow, you're all here already? I thought I was early."

"Such a spicy mouthful," said Candy approvingly. "Where's your bodyguard?"

"She ran off," said Severin. "With the raven boy, I imagine, since I can't find her."

"Hmm," said Aleth. "Our guest is expecting you to have a bodyguard. Varying from his expectations is risky."

Branwyn half-expected Rhianna to volunteer but she hung back, looking around the coffee shop with a wide-eyed, untrustworthy, innocent look.

She did *not* expect Penny to say, "I'll stay with her."

Aleth gave Penny a long once over. "That would work. In more ways than one."

"All right, that's settled." Branwyn pulled the object she'd been working on the previous night from her bag and set it on the table. She'd started with a fire alarm, but she'd flattened it and burned out the circuitry and replaced the actual alarm part with the smallest bass speaker she could find at 10 PM the night before. Then she'd woven the power of the Machine fragment in her hammer through the whole contraption, merging the parts into a self-aware whole and imbuing it with her desire to save people. Geometry-wise, it had a single node, which was currently empty.

"I need one of you big bad monsters to do your celestial thing and put a charm in this. Something that makes people want to get away." The whole crowd of them stared at her as if she was speaking nonsense and she added impatiently, "Come on, I know you guys can do charms too. The alarm will broadcast the charm effect when I trigger it, and all the bystanders will get out of the way." She was very proud of the idea.

The three male kaiju exchanged glances while Candy poked the alarm with one finger and Dolores gazed soulfully at Branwyn. Then Max shrugged. "I'll do it." He swatted Candy's hand aside and passed his palm over the modified fire alarm, half-closing his eyes as he concentrated. "Not my usual touch," he murmured after a moment. "But that should do it."

"How do you trigger it?" asked Rhianna, with what Branwyn felt was the right level of interest. "Will we need smoke?"

"You whisper, 'Fire' in its ear. It's magic," Branwyn said, deadpan.

"Will it work?" Penny asked.

Severin's hand half-rose to his throat and then dropped as he laughed. "Of course it will. And if it doesn't, believe me, people will be running away anyhow."

"I want them to leave in an orderly fashion," said Branwyn with as much dignity as she could muster. Then she sat down at the table. "Let's get this over with. I have places to be."

Candy said, "Young people, always in a hurry these days. Come on, Rhianna, we can swap notes on technique." She flashed a grin, and skipped off to the women's restroom. Rhianna looked around, met Max's gaze, then shrugged and followed Candy. After watching her go, Max vanished in a different direction, and Aleth settled back into the chair he'd been occupying before Branwyn joined them.

Dolores, though, started singing a sweet, gentle song in a

language that Branwyn didn't recognize. She swayed back and forth, fluttering her hands. Severin watched her for a minute and then whispered in Branwyn's ear, "I'll be watching from on high, cupcake. Try not to do anything stupid." He loped off to the stairs to the balcony seating.

Penny sat beside Branwyn and leaned over to whisper, "Uh, what is she doing?" while watching Dolores warily. Dolores ignored her, concentrating on her lullaby.

Aleth said, "She is cleansing the local area of the signs of our presence, so that our prey will not be forewarned."

"Except for yours, my friend," said Dolores, in a throaty voice, finishing her song. "A challenge. This quest stretches us all."

Something about the way the woman spoke caught Branwyn's attention. She had trouble imagining the unobtrusive, quiet woman on a quest for power. Or hell, as the same kind of creature as Severin. "Why are you doing this, Dolores?"

"I mourn for my brother," said Dolores simply. A deep sadness transformed her whole face. "I mourn. Perhaps later you will mourn with me? I don't like to be alone when I mourn, and I feel so alone." Her sadness drew on Branwyn, rousing her rarely awakened pity. *It was,* she thought, *terrible to be alone.*

"Dolores," said Aleth gently. "Not here, not now. Possibly not them."

Dolores sighed, the sadness retreating back to her eyes. She settled her cardigan about herself. "Of course. I shall go into the kitchens and be ready."

As Dolores walked away, Penny said, "Oh my God. She's not somebody's mother, is she?" Aleth only raised his eyebrows and she added, "That was so blatantly… manipulative. Although I suppose since she's one of you, what she wanted to do was lure Branwyn off somewhere and eat her."

Branwyn rubbed her head, trying to resist the urge to cry.

While she attempted to realign her experience with Penny's more objective observation of it, Aleth said, "There's no point in discussing Dolores right now, but perhaps it will reassure you to know that none of us present are of a devouring nature, such as those the Senyaza hunters pursue."

That was enough to shake Branwyn out of her confusion. "I'm not really sure it matters if you eat people if you also go around destroying their ability to function. Or you just flat out murder them. And you know damn well that wasn't going to reassure anybody."

"No? Yet you seem more yourself than you were a moment ago."

Branwyn curled her fingers around her coffee cup. "I wish the boys *would* prioritize all of you. They're not thinking long-term."

Aleth regarded her for a long moment, his liquid golden eyes unsettling. Then he said, "My brother claims he likes you because you're honest, but you're not."

Branwyn blinked. "I'm not sure which part of that sentence bothers me more. Penny, zap him."

"What?" squeaked Penny, her eyes widening. "How am I supposed to do that?"

"Oh, you know you have a way." Branwyn sipped her coffee.

"It doesn't work on them," Penny insisted. "And I can't 'zap' anybody."

Aleth laid a beautiful hand on the table's surface. "Try. I'm curious."

"Is this really the time for experimentation in zapping?" Penny's voice was increasingly strained, just like it always was when she doubted her own competence. Branwyn hid a small smile to share later. With Marley—but where was Marley? There had to be something very badly wrong—

"If you are dangerous enough to banish me with a touch or a

word, it would be useful to know that before our enemy appears," Aleth assured her.

Penny glanced at Branwyn for reassurance or possibly support and Branwyn said, "It's always a good time to zap monsters."

Sighing, Penny reached over and touched the back of Aleth's hand with one tentative finger. Nothing visible happened: no sparks, no vanishing in a poof of smoke, not even a flinch from Aleth. Branwyn was disappointed.

But Penny didn't withdraw her hand. Instead, after a minute, she pressed harder and the tip of her finger sunk into the back of his hand. Her dark skin and his darker skin blended together.

"You'll want to stop now," said Aleth gently. "You're not yet ready for the consequences of drinking down the sea."

Penny pulled her hand back and asked, too sadly for Branwyn's tastes, "Will that always happen when I touch one of your kind?"

"That's probably up to you," Aleth said. He turned his gaze to Branwyn. "When our guest arrives in a few minutes, once you've convinced it to fully manifest, you must keep it talking. Dolores will harden the veil, while Candy and Severin work on the tether. If all goes well, it will be over quickly, before Hadraniel has a chance to react and your bystanders have a chance to be frightened. Are you ready?"

"Sure," said Branwyn, tucking the alarm into her lap and brushing her fingers across the pocket containing the *other* thing she'd built the night before.

"Good. Chat with me. We are acquaintances at coffee. Tell me about your work. What have you been doing at the Senyaza building?"

"That's classified," said Branwyn. "But I'll tell you about my hammer instead." And she launched into a recital of the problems she'd encountered bonding the Machine fragment to the expensive hammer, and how her relationship with her grandmother had first hindered, then helped the process.

"And someday I must meet your grandmother," said Aleth, which made Branwyn's nice coffee-and-reminiscing glow vanish.

"Severin didn't like her much," she warned him.

"I think we would find things in common," Aleth went on, as if she hadn't said anything. "Ah, Hadraniel. Join us."

And just like that, the angel was with them.

16
BRANWYN

Branwyn wouldn't have known the angel wasn't in a proper vessel. It looked like an androgynous platinum blond with golden skin, in a business suit cut with the slightest feminine flair. Its hair was wavy and shoulder-length, and it had perfect teeth and silver-blue eyes.

"Greetings, Aleth," it said, and its voice, too, was ambiguous. Branwyn found herself instinctively approving. Gender was a pain in the ass sometimes.

As it moved past her to take the final chair, she could tell something was off. The air didn't move; it had no scent. But from across the table the illusion was convincing. It made her wonder how many other people she'd looked at had been nothing more than inhabited light.

Under the table, Branwyn squeezed Penny's hand. That thought was pure stress, nothing else. She exhaled, trying to push away the feeling of being trapped. She hated feeling trapped. It made her want to burn buildings down.

"Hi there," she said cheerfully instead. "I'm Branwyn."

Aleth added, "Branwyn is the Artificer I told you about."

"Hello, Branwyn," the angel said, placing both hands on the table and leaning forward. "I've been looking forward to meeting you. I am Hadraniel. You do excellent work."

"Yes, I know. I understand you've acquired a piece recently."

Hadraniel's perfect nose wrinkled, but then it smiled wryly. "I suppose proper humility alongside such gifts is too much to ask."

"Well, you can have humble or you can have honest," Branwyn explained. "And I understand that our mutual friend prefers honesty. Can I see the piece you have?"

Aleth moved his hand and tilted his head, and somehow she knew—*knew*, with an uncanny certainty—it was a threat and a warning. He thought she was going too fast, being too brash.

Well, tough luck to him.

Hadraniel, smiling faintly, said, "Why?"

"Because I didn't create it to do what it does now, and I'd like to see how it was hacked."

"Ah." Hadraniel moved one hand around another, and a necklace appeared dangling from two fingers. Her original studio key was woven through metal gears and glittering charms and the golden chain itself zigzagged through the accumulation several times. The entire construction was encased in a glass beaker pierced at two points by the chain. It made for a bulky pendant and it looked like something made by a committee. A committee with no sense of aesthetics.

"Pretty," said Penny, and Branwyn amended her thought to, *a committee with no sense of aesthetics or certain high fashion designers.*

"This is Penny, my assistant." She didn't even need to reach for the necklace to add, "And that's no more real than you are. I can't learn anything by looking at an image. Do you even have it? I didn't give the core piece to you, I know that."

"I do have it," said the angel. "I acquired it with the aid of a raven's insight. What you see is what it is."

Branwyn frowned. *A raven's insight.* But she couldn't afford to get distracted right now. "The treachery of images. Come on, bring out the real thing."

"Perhaps if we come to an arrangement, that will be possible. Alas, it is not right now."

Branwyn snorted. "What arrangement is that?"

"I need more of these, Branwyn," Hadraniel said gently. "The world quivers under restraints it was never meant to endure. So much has gone wrong since then. But we will set it right again."

"I do have some practice making things like that," Branwyn said. "You may have heard. Or seen. But… the thing is…" She scratched her lower lip as if lost in thought.

"Yes?" Hadraniel glanced at Aleth, who looked resigned, as if he saw which direction this was going already.

"The thing is, I'm not really convinced that you're the right person to give that power to. I've never been religious. What *good* are angels, really?"

The angel's eyes widened and it murmured, "How extraordinary."

"I mean, look at you. You're just an image yourself. Kind of funny, when you think about it."

"But my power is real," it said silkily.

"Is it? Why don't you show me? You're proposing some kind of 'arrangement', where I work for you doing stuff a lot of my other clients would rather I didn't. Now, I'm about to become a lot more picky about who I work for, anyhow. Worthy causes only. This could be good for you. But I've got no evidence yet you represent a worthy cause. So show me what you've got."

Aleth said, "She is talented, but a fool, Hadraniel. I had not expected she would speak to you in this way."

"It doesn't surprise me. Mortals have become so arrogant without our guidance."

"Come on, come on." Branwyn snapped her fingers. "Put me in my place, already." She wrapped her fingers around the alarm. She hadn't told the whole truth when she explained how to trigger it. All *she* had to do was touch it.

Hadraniel regarded her serenely and then expanded its celestial aura into a field that was nearly a physical force. She recognized the action immediately; she'd faced celestial auras enough times. Severin's was painful and terrifying; in comparison, Hadraniel's was pleasant.

Very pleasant. The scent of coffee was overwhelmed by citrus and vanilla, and the chiming of glass bells filled the air. Everything was warm and comfortable and Hadraniel was so very beautiful. At a different moment in time, Branwyn might have stretched like a cat and enjoyed the experience.

Instead she clicked her tongue in disapproval. "Is that all? Nobody else is even noticing." That wasn't quite true; a barista had her brow wrinkled as she stared at them and an older man was looking at Hadraniel wistfully. But it didn't matter.

"I don't understand why you're doing this," Hadraniel said with faint frustration.

"Maybe I long for what I've never had. Maybe I'd *like* to believe. From where I'm sitting it's pretty hard to see Heaven."

"The old craftsmen had faith," muttered Hadraniel. "Here, you wish to see how my device works? Witness and be awed by what has been kept from you by the selfishness of the nephilim."

There was no warning: no click, no hum, no music other than the chimes. The angel had been beautiful before in a glossy airbrushed way: inhumanly perfect but not unfamiliarly so. Now, though—

Tears sprang to Branwyn's eyes. Hadraniel was indeed light worked into a human shape. The light was glorious, spilled from Heaven to illuminate her befuddled mind. The angel was a conduit for that light, promising access to life beyond death and a place where there was nothing but that sublime wonder. It was the warmth of being perpetually loved and the comfort of being able to trust absolutely. She wasn't, couldn't be worthy of such light, but she didn't have to be. It would gather her home. All she had to do was serve faithfully.

It was nearly overwhelming. She wanted to burst into a hymn and thought if she stared into the light enough, she'd learn the words to the right one. For the first time Branwyn understood why the ancient celestial-suppressing spell was called the Hush. The normal aura of a celestial was a whisper compared to this shout of glory.

After a long, dazed moment, Penny's voice cut through Branwyn's dizzy contemplation. "I don't know. Are you maybe glittering a bit more? Is it a roll-on? That stuff wears unreliably, let me tell you."

That was enough for Branwyn to remember a little of what she had planned. She twitched her fingers against the alarm and thought, *Fire.* She couldn't see if it had any effect on the other people in the coffee shop—could *anything* resist the call of that incredible light? But she could feel it thumping in her lap: not the high-pitched beeping the alarm had been manufactured with but deep subliminal thud.

"You should know better," said Hadraniel gently, and a woman, a stranger to Branwyn, threw herself at the angel's feet, weeping.

Not working well, then, Branwyn struggled to collect her thoughts. The angel wanted her to feel guilty and ashamed, but that was the wrong weapon to use against her. It reminded her of Severin, and thinking of Severin made her angry. Her hammer was leaning against the table—could she... But it was so transcendently perfect—

Aleth caught up the woman weeping at Hadraniel's feet, stroked her sleek brown hair once and pushed her away from them with a casual disregard that only fed the embers of Branwyn's rage.

"Oh, so a powder then? I'm *so* sorry. It just had that look, you know? Of something that wouldn't be there when you most wanted it."

And that was Penny saying the most frivolous things. Branwyn blinked and came back to herself enough to wonder if Aleth could hear the steel buzzing under Penny's voice. Hadraniel certainly couldn't; it finally looked at Penny in surprise.

She had a plan and it didn't involve her hammer yet. Alas. Breathing shallowly, Branwyn moved her hand. The alarm fell on the floor, but she reached her pocket and slid out a pair of children's scissors and a pair of tweezers. The scissors she'd had for a while: an early creation to assist her with getting in and out of the Backworld in places where the veil between worlds wasn't already thin. But the tweezers were new, created, just for today.

She snipped the scissors in the air under the table, cutting a small, temporary hole between her world and the world of concepts and ideals on the other side. The faeries had laid claim to some of the Backworld—but it was everywhere and all of the celestials used it to some extent. And Branwyn knew her creations. She knew, for example, that Hadraniel couldn't possibly be using the divinity circuit unless it was nearby. It was a physical object; it couldn't be carried by an illusion. But in the Backworld, ghosts and material objects were equally real.

"Tell me," Branwyn croaked at Hadraniel. "Teach me." Under the table, she inserted the tweezers into the Backworld and activated their magic and hoped.

"I will," said Hadraniel with a sadness she found unreal. The angel was beautiful, glorious, nearly orgasmic to look at, but as familiar to her subconscious as the movements of her own hand.

Something vibrated against the tweezers, pulled to it by a

sympathetic attraction. *Branwyn made us. We belong together. Branwyn made us.*

Branwyn manipulated the tweezers, took hold of what was waiting, and pulled it into the real world. As soon as she grasped the object, Hadraniel's light dimmed, dimmed until it was just a beautiful man, or maybe a woman.

"No!" said Hadraniel. "What—"

Branwyn pulled the real divinity circuit up to the table and made a show of examining it. "Ah," she said. "I see what they did." Her heart thudded in her chest, adrenalin making her hands feel shaky. She could destroy it now, reduce it back to component parts, and all this would be over. The kaiju wouldn't get it, the angels wouldn't have it, everything would go back to the way it was. It was right there, humming in her hand, the thing that let the angels close the circuit interrupted by the Hush.

Then she knew the truth: that Aleth was *very* concerned about what was going to happen next. Aleth, sitting next to Penny, was watching closely. On the heels of that she knew other things: less magically granted truths and more inferred ones. For example, without Marley along, Penny and Rhianna were little more than hostages. It had been a terrible mistake to bring them if she'd wanted to end this now.

Hadraniel's hand shot out. "Give it back!" It sounded like a petulant five-year-old.

Branwyn had some experience teasing five-year-olds. She held it melodramatically to one side. "Come and get it. Oh wait, you can't. You're just an illusion. Are you *sure* you don't want to show me how real you can be?" Then she added bait, based on what she'd seen at a glance. "You know, it will work better if you're real. I'm not surprised you couldn't see it, though. It takes a certain perspective."

The angel scowled, an expression that settled so naturally over the beautiful features that Branwyn expected any body the angel inhabited would develop lines. "The raven said that, too.'" Then those luminous eyes fluttered shut and the air began chiming again. Motes of dust spiraled around the table, converging on the angel.

Branwyn shot a quick look at Aleth, but he didn't seem any more alarmed. That *probably* meant he didn't think Hadraniel was going to just smite her and grab his toy back. Next she checked out how the coffee shop was coping.

Something had emptied the building, although she didn't know if it was her alarm, the angel's glory, or both. There was still a wild-eyed woman weeping in the corner, a man hiding behind a newspaper at the window and a trio of stunned-looking baristas. One of them, more enterprising than the others, had a cellphone out and trained on Hadraniel. There was no sign of Rhianna, and Branwyn wondered if the impact of Hadraniel's unHushed presence had gone through walls.

Penny picked up the alarm along with the tweezers and the scissors, both of which had fallen off Branwyn's lap when Branwyn shifted position to play keep away. She tucked them in her purse as she stood up. "Your coffee is cold, Bran and mine is empty. I'll get us some more."

She walked to the counter and engaged the barista working the register in a conversation that seemed too loud. "Did I miss an announcement or something? Everybody suddenly lit out of here." She laughed. "I keep wondering where the hidden cameras are. Yeah, two more lattes. And, poor dear, one for the lady in the corner, too."

Branwyn had no idea what Penny was doing; her oblivious act wasn't going to convince anybody not to trust the evidence of their eyes, hearts and recording devices, especially not in a post-faerie world with the Extraworlder Conference opening just a few miles away.

"Be patient," said Hadraniel in an odd, dual voice. "Aleth, do not let her leave. Do not—"

"All will be well," said Aleth serenely, causing Branwyn to re-evaluate her entire estimation of Aleth's preference for the truth. "She is whimsical but she knows what the path of wisdom is."

"It takes time," said Hadraniel anxiously. "Vessels are temptation, and so hard to abandon. I do not keep one ready."

"No hurry," said Branwyn. "I'll just study the circuit some more."

"Yes, do that. See how it is made? It would be easy for you to make more with my help."

Penny sat down with her lattes. "Oh look, more glitter. You know, it's possible to use that stuff too much. It kind of makes you look like a faerie fankid, to be honest. I don't know if that's the look you're going for?"

Hadraniel recoiled, goaded into finally responding to Penny. "It isn't glitter. It's numinous essence. I am not in any way a 'fan' of the exiles. And whatever was done to you was clearly a terrible mistake. It's probably not too late to repair it…."

Idly, Branwyn said, "The original damage was done by one of your friends."

"And then somebody gave you poor instructions and made it worse. A tragedy." Hadraniel held out a hand and flexed it. "It stings, making a vessel quickly. But it is enough, now. Return the device."

Branwyn knew the truth as Aleth saw it: it *was* enough. Hadraniel held out its hand expectantly, a pleasant expression pasted over the anxiety stealing its grace.

This creature ordered a massacre, Branwyn reminded herself. It was hard to see in its face. But that sort of thing often was. *He seemed like such a quiet guy.* Hadraniel had ordered a massacre and now she was expected to just give another weapon back to the angel. Just give it back after admiring it, like a good little girl, give back her creation, twisted to a use she never imagined.

The chiming grew louder, joined by the drumbeat sound of Branwyn's own heart and the inaudible twang of the tension winding itself tighter.

Branwyn showed her teeth in a smile as she tossed the divinity circuit across the table. Hadraniel caught it easily and slipped it over its head as Branwyn leaned back in her chair.

"I am pleased," said Hadraniel. "You've demonstrated your cleverness and your willingness to be obedient. With some time you'll make an exceptional servant."

"Yes, we can shake hands and everything once we have a deal. But I'm a little concerned," Branwyn admitted. Presumably, the kaiju were now engaged with their various tasks to trap and tether Hadraniel. She just had to keep it talking. "What exactly are you—and your friends, if we make more—going to be doing with it? I'm not enthusiastic about the idea of you going around wiping out everybody's ability to think rationally. That seems dangerous these days. Air traffic controllers and emergency personnel need to rely on more than faith."

"Fear not. We will be occupied for some time dealing with the troublemakers. First those who stole our power from us, and then those who abandoned us." It closed its hand around the divinity circuit. "You were right about the connection between the divinity circuit and the vessel. It will be easy."

Branwyn tried to hide her wince. She'd seen that in her casual assessment, said it, and hoped she was wrong. "Yeah? Going to do something about Senyaza? They're one of my biggest clients at the moment."

"You didn't know any better," said Hadraniel comfortingly.

"I should have," Branwyn muttered, thinking about Titanone. "They're part human, after all."

"They're insidious, something they inherited from their mortal forebears: those who seduced my siblings and tore them from Heaven. It is fortunate that the majority of mortals are both forthright and innocent."

"How fortunate," Branwyn echoed and cast about for something to say instead of giving into the desire to hit the angel in the face with her hammer. "Would you like to see my workshop some time? Are you happy with the design of the current circuit? It's pretty ugly. I could do better."

"Branwyn's babbling," said Penny. "Let's cut to the chase. What are you going to pay her?" She smiled. "She needs more than dazzle. She can't eat on dazzle. Making sure she gets paid more than dazzle is why she brought me along."

Hadraniel stared at her, astonished, and Penny added, "Senyaza pays her thousands of dollars. Which she uses to pay her rent, eat, buy clothes that I don't approve of. Without those things she can't work. You do know that, right?"

"The faithful are rewarded in this life and the next," murmured Hadraniel. Then its attention was pulled away toward the door. "What—?" It stood, its hand going to the divinity circuit resting on its chest. "Umbriel! What are you doing here?"

A man who looked like he'd been poured from the same mold as Hadraniel but given a darker paint job stood at the entrance, dressed in an unambiguously masculine suit. He crossed the room. "Hadraniel. Yes, I see what you've done and we must talk about that. But it isn't safe here. The veil—oh sweet Heaven, look at you, Hadraniel!"

Hadraniel's brow furrowed, a distant look coming into its eyes. "No!" It refocused, looking around wildly, first at Branwyn, then at Penny, and then finally at Aleth. "You? What are you—? X, I require you!"

X? Then Branwyn remembered how Hadraniel had used a

nameless kaiju as a weapon once before and went cold. She didn't need Aleth's imbued truth to realize this was very bad. Aleth stood up, his aura rippling out like tiny splinters of ice. She stood too, grabbing Penny and her hammer and backing away from the table. Max came out of the bathroom as if on a spring and then skidded to a halt. "Oh fuck."

He wasn't looking at Hadraniel or Umbriel. He was looking behind Branwyn. And so were both of the angels. She turned her head to see.

The man who'd been sitting behind the window looking at a newspaper stood up. And as he did, he pulled a sword that was far too large out of nowhere at all.

17
BRANWYN

The man with the sword didn't look extraordinary. He wore badly fitting clothing that looked like it had come from a donation bin. His hair curled around his bland face. He was utterly forgettable.

Unlike his sword. It had a broad blade of hammered madness and a hilt wound with the thorns of heartbreak. It sang as it moved, a marching song for all the eschatons behind it.

Then the man holding it said, "Hadraniel," in a toneless voice and unleashed *his* aura. It buzzed against Branwyn's mind and skin, writhing like worms on speed. Aleth turned to one side as if spun by a physical blow.

Max said, moving warily, "Dammit! Who gave X a Sword? *That* Sword? I mean how—?"

"Indeed," agreed Umbriel. "You have *much* to explain, Hadraniel. Let's get out of here so you can do so peacefully."

Hadraniel snapped, "Not without what I came for," and reactivated the divinity circuit.

Even surrounded by angels and Fallen about to throw down,

Branwyn was distracted by Hadraniel's glory. It would still forgive her, she knew. All she had to do was join the two angels. The one called Umbriel looked exasperated and pulled a Sword of his own from the flesh of his palm: a thin saber of green grace that added its own whispering voice to the spiritual cacophony.

Branwyn *knew* she had to go with them, because she had to get close enough to one of those celestial Swords to understand how they worked. A distant foreign voice tried to tell her other truths, truths about slavery and self-destruction, but that voice knew nothing about a *hunger* to transcend her limits.

"Umbriel," squeaked Rhianna from the door to the ladies' restroom, but that was all she had time for before Candy shoved her aside and bounded out.

"X," she cooed. "We're here for you, baby." She jumped past the angels and Branwyn like a jackrabbit, grabbing X's sleeve and spinning him around before landing on top of a table. Branwyn watched dully and then transferred her attention back to Hadraniel, expectantly. It beckoned to her as it turned toward Aleth with something very like a snarl. Ribbons of light trailed from its shoulders: the partially completed tethers. Dolores came from the storeroom door, holding her hands apart like she was winding invisible yarn. But where was Severin?

Penny moved between Branwyn and the angel. The glory unleashed by the divinity circuit parted around her. "We need to get out of here, Bran."

Shielded by Penny's body, Branwyn tried to regather her sense of self. She was practically hugging her hammer, her head pressed against it. It was such a simple, makeshift weapon compared to the two Swords, like a cardboard tube in the hands of a child. No wonder Severin hadn't been impressed.

The kaiju called X suddenly loomed beside her. Before she could move, he grabbed her shoulder and shoved her aside. Branwyn stumbled and looked back to see X swinging his Sword at Penny's back. She screamed and threw herself at him, too slow, too slow to stop him. Her fingers had just grazed his arm when Penny twisted and *caught* the Sword in one hand. It stopped dead, all momentum stolen from it.

X leaned on the Sword. A glow spread from the twisted blade to Penny and she looked puzzled. "Bran, I don't think I'm supposed to be able to do this… This isn't… I feel sick."

Penny was a marvel, but like the hammer, she was a child's rough sketch compared to the ancient strength of the Sword. She wouldn't hold up, not as a celestial weapon.

Fortunately, Penny was also Penny, and more importantly right at that moment, the hammer was also a hammer. Branwyn smashed it into X's elbow and caught Penny as she stumbled forward, pushing her toward the wall.

X grunted as his arm fell limply. Then he took the Sword with his other hand, shaking the numb one. He looked toward Hadraniel for instruction and then went to help the angel against Aleth and Max. Candy went after him, wiping some blood from her eye.

Branwyn panted, "You're right, we need to get out of here." She couldn't even look at Hadraniel directly, or she'd feel the pull of its glory, but she hoped like hell the kaiju were kicking its ass. They'd been so confident they could deal with the divinity circuit—but two more celestials, each with heavenly Swords? She wouldn't put it past them to flee and leave Branwyn to deal with the fallout.

Penny was still glowing. "I think there's something wrong. I feel so sleepy."

Branwyn frowned and put her hand on Penny's chest, fiercely willing the prosthetic soul crafted from Machine fragments to stay attached to Penny. *This, this is your job. Do your job. Don't be distracted by pretty blades.* But she could tell that the connections were looser than they should be and realized with a sick feeling that the soul had responded to the same call that had summoned the divinity circuit to her hand. Consequences! She never anticipated all the *consequences* to her actions.

Furiously, she moved her hands, tightening the bond between soul and Machine. Lightning crackled through the coffee shop, and the thunder was the sound of deep-tolling bells. Branwyn ignored it. As she worked, Penny wrapped her arms about Branwyn's shoulders, watching over her head. "They're leaving," she said faintly. "The angels. The monsters have been all over the place. I don't think they're fighting fair."

Branwyn felt the rush of Hadraniel's glory pass her, heard another peal of celestial lightning, and kept her head down. Penny pulled her close, turning her body to once again shield Branwyn from the angels' passage.

"It's okay," chirped Candy as she went by. "They can't leave the area while Dolores has the veil frozen. We'll get them. Even if somebody tried to spoil sport."

"Where are they going, then?" Penny asked.

"Looking for a soft spot," said Max, and was gone.

Branwyn pulled away from Penny just in time to see Rhianna running out the door after the kaiju. "Hell, I don't think this is done yet. Where are the baristas?" There was a screech and a crash from outside and Branwyn flinched.

Penny leaned her head against the wall. "Behind the bar. Over there. I need a minute...."

"I went a little fast, maybe over tightened things some. Bright side: you probably won't be sleepy anymore." Branwyn went and looked behind the bar where the baristas cowered, one of them firmly holding onto the weeping lady customer. "You guys okay?"

"Alive," squeaked one with her arms around the other two. "You?"

Branwyn looked around the coffee shop. Most of the furniture was broken. It looked like a tornado had gone through. But other than a dent in one wall and the blue radiance crawling along the ceiling, the structure of the building looked sound.

"I'll try to be back later to help clean up," Branwyn offered.

"Oh God," said the barista holding onto the weeping woman. "Please don't."

"I'll make sure she forgets," Penny promised, taking Branwyn's arm.

"Thank you," said the barista with real gratitude. "And thank you for the warning to get down earlier."

"No problem. Come on, Branwyn. Did you notice Severin wasn't here? And that your sister went running out the door after Angel vs. Kaiju?"

"Yes," said Branwyn. "I noticed both of those things and I don't like either of them at all."

The path of the running fight was easy to follow, because there were car pileups in the middle of the street, one for each direction of traffic. Branwyn thought sickly of Moses parting the Red Sea. "God damn it," she muttered. "I should—"

"Everybody's calling 911 already," Penny said. "They went into Vroman's. There's a lot of customers in Vroman's, Branwyn." Vroman's was a big bookstore, one of those Pasadena icons that had endured through everything thrown at it for a century. It had survived the internet; if Branwyn let some celestials tear it up, Marley would never forgive her.

Marley…

Branwyn reached into Penny's open bag and pulled out her alarm, activating it again as they ran across the forced break in traffic. The door into Vroman's was completely gone, as if it had been carved out of its frame. A couple of potential customers were looking between the pile-up and the door, open-mouthed. More stood just inside, staring at the car wreck. As the thudding of the alarm hit them, the two outside looked at each other and then ran across the street. One of the gawkers looked around as if waking from a daze and marched away.

Branwyn and Penny pushed their way in. Penny asked one of the bystanders, "What happened to the door?"

"I'm not sure," said a big man, rubbing at his face. "It was... something. I think I'd dozed off? And then these people rushed past, and there was this hole. Weird."

"Go home," Branwyn snapped, and he looked at her in surprise.

"Yeah. Yeah, I've been meaning to do something for a while." And he, too, walked briskly out of the store.

It was less obvious what was going on once Branwyn and Penny were in the store proper. A display of books had been knocked over, but Branwyn heard the sounds of consternation, outrage and ordinary business, not screams of terror. There was a river of people on the stairs from the second floor, mostly coming down and they were grumbling rather than panicked. Even the celestial auras seemed muffled by the weight of so many books in one place. But the alarm thumped away and a handful of people looked up from browsing, glanced at their watches or cellphones, and then strolled out of the store.

Dolores stood near the magazine rack, still winding her invisible skein. "I cannot hold it here," she said simply. "They are running out of time, and my dear brother—" She shook her head mournfully.

"Jesus!" shrieked Candy from the crowd-clogged staircase. "Can't any of you people operate stairs? Severin has him half-bound, Dolores. Just hang on." She started burrowing between bodies and somebody went over the bannister, landing in a heap on the floor.

Branwyn's fingers tightened around the alarm. She shoved her way to the front of the customer service counter. "Hey!" said a lady two people back. "You can't cut in line."

The clerk, listening to an earpiece with wide eyes, gave her an apprehensive glance. "I think we're closing now, miss—"

"Somebody's making a mess upstairs? Yeah, I know." She laid the alarm on the counter. "This will encourage people to get out. Tell me how I can get past that very slow stampede and I'll clean it up."

"That's not possible, ma'am—"

"Hey! She cut! Hey, if you're helping her, help me first, young lady."

Branwyn turned to glare at the polished-looking customer, but the woman was fully focused, with laser precision, on the clerk. Each time the alarm thumped, her eyelid twitched but she clearly wasn't being swayed by it.

Penny leaned over the counter. "She won't really clean it up, but she will make them behave themselves."

"Fine! I don't care! Take the stairs behind the employee door! And you, ma'am, you'll have to come back later—"

As they did so, Penny said, "Why exactly are we going upstairs to where the fight probably is? We're not going to end up on the roof again, are we? You and Marley always seem to end up on roofs—"

"I need to get the divinity circuit back before anybody else does. And I bet my sister is up there." Branwyn took the stairs two at a time. As she hurtled through the door, glass crunched underfoot.

The battle lines had been drawn up in a field of sparkling shards and scattered books: what had once been the stationary department. Umbriel and his Sword stood in front of Hadraniel and X stood at Hadraniel's back. Severin stood across from them, hands hanging loosely at his sides, his head low. He was smiling faintly, his shark smile.

Candy stood at the entrance to the department, an ugly expression on her face, while Max and Aleth were against the walls, surrounding the angels like a wolf pack. Max paced back and forth. *Where was Rhianna?* There were still plenty of shelves standing. If she was smart, she was behind one of them. Hiding with her little gun....

Severin said gently, "Go away, Umbriel. This isn't your affair."

"You know it is," said Umbriel. He made a fist with his free hand and then opened it again and something red pulsed organically in the air near the ceiling. It shimmered, brightening slowly. Then he slashed his Sword, cutting silver ribbons creeping along the floor.

"No, no," chided Severin. He spread his hands and Branwyn had a dreamlike memory of molten glass in the palm of his hand. She stumbled backward into the stairwell, bumping hard into Penny. Shards of glass rose into the air and spun toward Severin.

Then Branwyn saw Rhianna, leaning out around one of the bookshelves. Hadraniel said, voice ringing like a bell, "Enough. Once again I have been disappointed." Blue energy crackled along the floor and gathered in its hands, growing into a white sphere that made Branwyn ache from her teeth to her toes. The air suddenly reeked of sulfur. The building—no, the *world* flinched away from what Hadraniel was summoning. It was going to be very bad.

Umbriel knew it too. He twisted around to look at Hadraniel in horror. "Are you mad? There are hundreds of mortal souls near."

"I did say," drawled Severin, and then everybody moved at once. Silver ribbons grew along the floor. A ball of molten glass darted toward Umbriel. Aleth spread his arms wide while Max hurled a box of pens. Candy jumped to the top of a bookcase and knocked all the books out of it as she jumped to another one. The red glow pulsed like a heart and then flickered like a candle about to go out. Somewhere Dolores was singing. X lunged toward Rhianna, who had something small and metal in her hand, and Branwyn stopped noticing anything else.

Her heart in her throat, her fists clenched with helplessness, she ran into the room and slid on the mess on the floor, landing badly on her hip and scrambling to her feet again. Then a wave of force threw Max past her and knocked her on her back.

There was a snapping sound but X didn't stop. The chiming grew louder and the smell of sulfur was enough to make Branwyn want to vomit as she rolled to her feet. Rhianna ducked behind the bookshelf and Candy ran along the top to once again grab at X. It seemed like it had all happened before, and would happen again.

Dolores stopped singing and the red wound in the world above Umbriel's head blossomed, unfolding petals to become a portal through the veil. It sank down to the floor and Umbriel snarled, "Go, and take your pet." He slashed again at the silver ribbons snaking around Hadraniel. There was a charred hole in his suit at the shoulder, and crimson to match the glow of the wounded world.

Hadraniel brought both hands together and the white glow once again became a diffuse blue light. Without responding to Umbriel, Hadraniel plunged through the portal and X followed behind. Then Umbriel held out his hand and commanded, "Rhianna, come now."

Rhianna ran out from behind the bookcase, straight to Umbriel. He took her by the arm and stepped backward into the portal. Rhianna craned her head as she went with him, finding Branwyn. She looked exhilarated, frightened, and a little embarrassed when she met Branwyn's gaze. Then the portal sealed over and they were gone.

"Dolores!" growled Severin, reaching out his hand toward her as she picked her way through the devastation.

"No good," she said, shaking her head. "The fires of judgement were coming. We would have all lost our vessels and the girl's good work in luring Hadraniel into a body would have been unrecoverable. And now that it has one, it will not abandon it easily."

Severin glanced at Branwyn, his expression hard, then turned away and leaned his forehead against another shelf, flexing his fingers.

Max said, "That was going well, before Umbriel showed up. Oh, and before X pulled Belial out of nowhere. Fuck!"

"Somebody spoiled sport," said Candy angrily. "And somebody's going to die." Her gaze darted over to Branwyn and Penny.

"Don't let your hunger for death push you into a dangerous mistake," warned Severin, lifting his head. "Branwyn's sister is Umbriel's creature; she obviously warned him of what we planned."

"Then she can be the one to die," snapped Candy. "If you knew, you can do the honors."

Aleth said to Max, "Bad timing. I should have noticed Belial before."

Dolores murmured, "Hadraniel has never been the fool. He plans well."

Branwyn, trembling from waves of adrenalin, said, "That was Rhianna's boss?" She vaguely remembered Rhianna recognizing the second angel but everything had started to go to hell around then.

"Yes," said Severin witheringly. "Or do you think they fell in love mid-battle and ran off to Elysium together?"

Branwyn saw red for a heartbeat, and reassembled events in her head. "He's her boss. That's all."

"She should have been smarter than to betray us," said Candy hotly. "And she had such good makeup too. It's going to be all messed up when I cut her throat."

Clenching her fists, Branwyn said, "Don't even think about it."

"What are you going to do to stop me?" sneered Candy. "She's more than earned it."

Penny said hurriedly, "If she works for Umbriel won't he be even more annoyed if you go after his employee?"

"Nah," said Max. "I mean, he may be, but not enough to risk his own skin if there's any kind of justification. Not when we're just talking about her life." He sounded thoughtful more than enraged.

Aleth said, "True," and the chill in his voice told Branwyn he was angry too.

"She's probably going to die, cupcake. Best get used to the idea. Lives of grand adventure are usually pretty short," said Severin, putting his head back on the bookshelf. "Think about how she betrayed you too. It might help."

Penny's fingers found Branwyn's hand and Branwyn squeezed them so hard it must have hurt. "Where the hell were you, anyhow?" It was a distraction, she knew it was only a distraction but she really needed a distraction right then so she could think around the fear squeezing her heart. "Maybe you're the one who ruined Candy's fun, called in Hadraniel's backup."

He gave her a scornful glance. "You don't even believe that. As soon as Umbriel walked in I could see how it would go. I came here to wait."

"Except you didn't predict that X would have fucking Belial," prompted Max. "Because how could anybody have predicted that kind of insanity?" He glanced at Penny and Branwyn. "I mean, I know about insane choices and fucking Christ that was *award-winning.*"

"No," said Severin shortly. "I missed that detail until they got outside Dolores' suppression. He cut right through the web I'd spun over the door."

Aleth flickered in and out of existence and then said, "Rhianna has already left Umbriel's protection. Who will claim her? Max, you have a prior interest."

Max tilted his head as if considering the idea, but it was Candy who muttered, "How can such a clever girl be so *stupid?*"

"Me," said Branwyn sharply. "I have the oldest claim. Nobody is killing my sister just because she did her job. I don't care how frustrated you are. She was an idiot but not as stupid as each of you. You all *knew* she was working for the guy who originally made the device."

Candy's eyes flashed and she stalked toward Branwyn. "Nobody calls me stupid."

"I do if that's what you are. What are you going to do about it, kill me too? Stupid monster. No wonder one of your kind is following Hadraniel around like a puppy." Branwyn shook off Penny's hand and tightened her grip on her hammer.

Dolores said, with a catch in her voice, "Shall we be weakened when next we see our stolen brother? That is where this goes."

Candy stopped herself with a little skip, staring at Branwyn with narrowed eyes. Her gaze moved up and down Branwyn's body like she was assessing what was underneath in a way creepily incongruous with Candy's twelve-year-old shape. Branwyn shifted her weight, presenting less of a frontal target, still prepared for Candy to jump on her and hoping like hell it wouldn't come to that.

Candy's eyes came to rest on Branwyn's collarbone for a long moment. "Fine. You've claimed her, you deal with her. You've got a year and a day to make her pay for how she betrayed us." She looked around, her posture shifting until it culminated in a full-body wiggle. "Now I need to work off some of this energy or everybody's going to regret it. Who's going to help me?"

After a moment of silence, Max looked around and then stretched his back. "I guess I will."

"Oh goodie," said Candy, grabbed his hand, and dragged him off into the stacks beyond the shattered stationary room.

"Where are they going?" asked Penny uncertainly.

"Don't think too hard about it," suggested Severin, turning around and looking at Branwyn with glinting eyes.

She looked away, over at Aleth. "You okay with this year and a day thing?"

"I will extract my own price from your sister, but you need not fear it will threaten her mortal existence. That would waste a valuable resource." He kept talking over Branwyn's attempt to tell him that was bullshit. "But for now I must repair my vessel. We will discuss a new plan, Severin." He turned and Branwyn realized that an injury running from his abdomen down his thigh—a killing injury—had been sealed over with a dull silver shimmer. If that was an injury from one of the two Swords— and it looked like a cut, not a burn— then he'd almost died.

"Sure," said Severin. "We might have to get a little more complicated now. I'm sure there'll be no problem staying on track, what with everybody playing so nicely and Hadraniel knowing we're coming for him. It'll be even easier now."

"Yet it is embodied now. And you still have me," said Dolores calmly.

Severin said grudgingly, "That's true."

"The mortal authorities are downstairs now," Dolores added. "Remember to put away your tools before they start shooting at them." She moved her hand, pulling a fold of the veil in front of her and vanishing. Aleth vanished at almost the same time.

Severin strode across the room and took both Branwyn and Penny by the arms. "Might be a little bumpy because of Miss Karzan here. Let's find out."

Branwyn probably should have hit him with her hammer when he grabbed her, but she was exhausted and shocked. And compared to all the other kaiju, he was familiar. And yet it was important to maintain her standards. She compromised by not leaning on him.

Blackness dropped over all three of them, pressing tightly against Branwyn like a sleeping bag. Then they were floating in a space she had visited once before. She'd been just as exhausted and disoriented last time, but she remembered velvet darkness with windows of light circling around them. And last time there hadn't been Penny, who glowed with her own radiance and stood ten feet tall, looking around curiously.

Hmm, said Severin's voice in her head. *She's big. But she'll squeeze.* He pulled Branwyn close to his chest and she realized something else was different from last time he'd given her this kind of lift.

One of the windows rushed forward to pass over them and Penny yelped, her cry like a vibrating string in the strange space.

Then their feet touched the pavement outside of Branwyn and Marley's apartment. Penny looked once again like her normal self. Severin released both of them and stepped back. Before he could vanish, Branwyn said, "Are you *taller* than you were before Simon killed you?"

His expression inscrutable, he said, "Maybe you're smaller. You ought to do something about your hair if you want to stay out of jail, cupcake." Then he did disappear.

Penny said, "That was trippy. Everything shrank. But convenient. Very convenient. Hmm. Do you think the faeries can do that too?"

Branwyn touched her green hair and then shook her head. Marley's car was still missing. And she had no idea where Rhianna was. And later there was a gala to attend. She had a busy and probably upsetting day ahead and it was only 10 AM.

Marley first, she decided, and remembered Hadraniel talking about the insight of ravens.

18
MARLEY

Marley's magic surged around her. The virus brightened until it was everything she could sense. Everything became nothing.

And then—

Marley sat in a coffee shop, in the corner of a battered old couch, her feet tucked under her and a book cracked open on the arm beside her. She frowned and picked up the book, smoothing a rumpled page and then closing it over her finger as she looked around for something to use as a bookmark.

The coffee shop was full of people, but all their faces were curiously blurred. They spoke to each other, but the noise was abstracted: the practiced murmur of a movie crowd scene. Even the music was odd, with a chant-like element that she couldn't understand.

The virus wearing Corbin's face sat down across from her, putting two steaming mugs on the table. She tugged out one of the napkins under the drinks to tuck inside the book. She couldn't read the writing inside or on the cover, but that hardly mattered. You didn't treat books that way. And trying to work out the language gave her an excuse not to look at the virus.

"You wanted to talk," pointed out the virus. "It's your own fault you're in this cage now. And it's hardly an unpleasant one."

"You've put in a book with a cracked spine that I can't read." She caught the virus smiling out of the corner of her eye. "And you still look like Corbin."

"But you like books. And Corbin," said the virus, with a completely unbelievable innocence.

"Oh shut up," she said, and then asked, "Is Corbin someplace like this when you're controlling him?"

The virus put his hand on his chest. "Controlling him? Me? I'm *helping* Corbin, my girl. Without me he would have surrendered to death after the Pointer family passed on."

Marley turned her head to glare at him. "After you killed them, you mean."

He wobbled his hand from side to side as if it was a statement with multiple angles. "It's hard for me to think of it that way. Besides, I am what I have been for an aeon. Corbin is the one who freed me from my cage, and Corbin is the one who contains me now."

"How are you contained?" said Marley hotly. "You spread to me, you spread to his friends, and to others too, from what Skadi's said. That's not contained."

He chuckled and stirred his coffee. "Ah, Skadi, a font of honesty. You like knowing things, Marley? I can tell you all sorts of things. They'd freeze your blood and stab your ears and sear your dreams. True things, too, no wobble to them, no Skadi spin. Want to hear?"

Marley shot back, "Let me go first, and then I'd love to hear them."

"Oh, come on," said the virus reproachfully. "Letting people go isn't how I work. I can't just say, oops, never mind, I ended up here by accident, I'll just return what I've stolen and erase this part of myself."

"So I'm here until I die, too?" Marley opened the book again and stared at the odd characters.

"Would you like more books?" the virus asked solicitously. "A croissant? I can imagine a wicked croissant."

Marley frowned at the book. If she looked closely, that squiggle there looked like a 'w.' Then she glanced up. "What happens to the part of you in me if I die?"

"I promise, that'll be the very last thing you learn. You can look forward to it!"

She set her jaw, looking back at the book again. If she couldn't read it as written, maybe she could invent her own story. It had a pulpy cover, of a woman with long blond hair and full armor facing an ice dragon. It was some kind of fantasy, then. The woman looked a little like Skadi, which gave her a starting place. She flipped through it, staring at the other illustrations. A tree with islands in its branches. A scene where the blonde woman groomed a horse with too many legs. A raven that seemed to look right out of the page at her. But she couldn't keep any of it in her head enough to spin a story. She was too upset.

After a while, the virus went away. After it was gone, Marley put down the book and covered her face. This place almost felt real. Her body felt real. It was some kind of dream, but it was a very vivid one and no matter how she tried she couldn't wake up. She couldn't use her magic, either. There was no Sight here, no charms, no Geometry, no danger-sight. It was just what she'd been imagining her life as a day or two ago. Except in the real world, people had faces.

She'd been so *complacent* about Corbin. So confident that he was out there, fine, doing his work. She thought he'd just been annoyed with her for how she wouldn't tell Zachariah off. But she'd searched through their text conversations for any sign of that and what she'd found was her guilt and his patience. He was angry at Zachariah for his own reasons, but she was the one who was angry at herself. Especially after she'd let Zachariah convince her to spend the night.

No, not complacent. She'd wanted Corbin to come back but she'd never told him that, never admitted that to herself, just like she'd never admitted her anger at herself. And instead he'd slowly stopped talking to her.

Because he'd been infected by a supernatural mind-controlling virus. That was it, wasn't it? She had to re-evaluate everything about their online conversations or lack thereof in light of his infection.

The buzz of the crowd changed and the virus sat back down, looking at her with alert interest. It wasn't wearing the same clothes as Corbin: instead of jeans and a t-shirt it wore loose cloth trousers and some kind of old-fashioned fitted jerkin that left muscled arms bare, all in icy tones.

"What do you want?" Marley asked dully.

"It looked like you'd passed through the denial phase so I thought maybe you'd like something to be angry at now." The virus winked.

"I'm already angry at you, thanks." She fumbled for the book again and found it blank.

"Oh, not me. There's no point in being angry at me. I was tucked away snug in my box before Skadi handed it to Corbin to open."

"What?" demanded Marley. "She did not." The buzz in the cafe vanished. When she glanced around, the faceless figures still acted out their roles, but it was like the mute button had been pressed.

"I promise you she did. She's been my keeper for, oh, ages. I notice everything she does."

"Why would she purposefully infect Corbin and then try to heal him? That's insane."

Instead of answering her question, the virus said, "Corbin's bloodline is a funny one. You met his parents. What did you think of them?" The virus looked at a table nearby and the two figures there developed the faces of Corbin's mother and father. Elizabeth and Aedrian.

"I thought they were…" Marley hesitated, looking for the right word. "Disengaged." She folded her hands in her lap and looked closely at the virus, trying to see past Corbin's face.

The virus touched the mug on the table and then tilted it until a trickle of coffee spilled. He began to draw in the liquid, leaving patterns that were slow to close. "I've dug down and found his memories of his infancy, his kinder years. His mother was engaged then, oh yes. Mortal biology dictates so much. It didn't last. But that doesn't matter. The power he inherited from his mother's line was weak and easily overshadowed by what his father lost when Corbin was born."

The patterns were hypnotic. She saw a pregnant woman, a woman with a babe in arms, a sulky child. What the virus said didn't make sense, didn't follow from what he'd said before. What did Corbin's father's magic do with his mother's love?

In a voice dripping with sympathy, the virus added, "It's hard for the elder half-mortals to love new people. They calcify as they age, their hearts becoming as stiff as frozen wood, something only a white-hot shot can pierce. The weaker and the younger cannot worm their way in. And when the half-mortals lose one of the few they do love, why, sometimes they shatter."

"That I believe," said Marley, thinking of Zachariah. The children had burrowed into his heart somehow but she, far more independent, had never found a place there. "But—what, Corbin's family doesn't love him because he's too young?"

"Or too unlovable," said the virus helpfully. "You'll understand eventually."

All the people in the coffee shop vanished, and the sunny afternoon beyond the plate windows vanished like a black velvet curtain had dropped. "He is not unlovable. *You* are unlovable."

The virus bowed mockingly. "Alas, yes. So I've been told."

Marley placed both hands on the table, leaning forward. "How is Corbin containing you?"

The virus had green eyes, unlike Corbin, which she only realized when they flashed red. "Somebody claimed him first. And so I help him instead. I'm not a complete stranger to collaboration." Something clicked nearby and he added, "It's better than waiting in a box."

"You're never going to convince me that you're helping him, so I wish you'd stop trying." Something clicked again and Marley looked at the window. Neath sat just beyond, pawing at the glass. Bitterly, she said, "You're not doing Neath right, either. She can walk through walls."

"She's having a bit of trouble getting in this time," said the virus. "Half-mortal magic is more powerful when I'm there to blow on the coals."

"What does that mean?" Marley asked. But he only grinned at her and vanished again, leaving her alone in the coffee shop, without even the illusion of other people to keep her company. It was colder, too, without the buzz and movement.

Neath clicked against the window again, her tail lashing back and forth. Her meow was faint and nearly lost. Marley went to the door of the coffee shop and pulled on it, but it didn't open. That was not even a little bit of a surprise. She pushed, too, just in case.

It hadn't been like this the last time she'd caught the virus. She'd been confused and in pain; she'd heard him whispering in her head--and was it a he even when it was inside of her? Probably not. Heard it whispering in her head. But she wasn't in any pain at all now. Either it was so bad she was retreating from it, or something was different.

Music started playing over the coffee shop speakers again. This time it was the song Skadi had sung as she'd healed Marley: a still soul marching off to war.

Skadi had said that she would be more resistant to the virus now. But Skadi had also said she could catch it again if she thought about it too much. And Skadi had certainly implied that Corbin catching the virus had been an accident. How much could Skadi be believed? She had motivation to hide her role if the virus's claim was true, but what motivation did the virus have to lie?

It was silly thinking of the virus as a person, but the shape it took did so much of the work for her. It spoke as a person and smiled like a friend. And a virus couldn't lie or tell the truth. A virus wasn't even properly alive. Whatever the thing infecting Corbin was, the metaphor of a virus only went so far. It had a *perspective*, even if it wasn't a person as she defined them.

Given Branwyn's skyscraper, she'd probably have to update that definition someday anyhow.

Maybe she *was* partially resistant, and that's why she was here. Maybe if she wasn't here, she could fight back. Marley looked at the glass window, and then at the chair the virus had been sitting in. Even empty and cold, the coffee shop seemed so real. Her inhibitions against breaking stuff seemed so real, too.

Neath meowed and Marley made a face. Life was a succession of choices and each choice changed who you were. Maybe now she was the sort of person who broke shop windows with chairs. There was only one way to find out.

She picked up the chair and swung it at the glass. It bounced off with a bong, and she swung again, harder. That time she felt it in her wrists, and the window vibrated but didn't break. One more time, harder, and her hands went numb from the recoil and the window still didn't break.

Neath meowed encouragingly and Marley ground her teeth. She was supposed to be stronger than this. She was a nephil, the virus's 'half-mortals', and nephilim could be very tough and very strong if they tapped into their immortal magic. She couldn't tap into her danger-sight, couldn't make a shield, but she was stronger than this glass, she knew it. She had to be, because she wasn't going to give up and die. Not with Neath right on the other side watching her. Not with Corbin and Branwyn and Penny waiting for her. Not with her mother waiting for an explanation about Zachariah.

She swung the chair again, and it shattered in her hand. So then she tried the table, until it shattered, too. Then without thinking she tried her fist.

It was like when Skadi had cured her. Agony climbed up her hand and through her wrist into her arm. Her heart pounded and her vision pulsed. She keened, holding her hand close.

Neath started purring. Marley could hear it even through the glass as it grew louder and louder. The purring was odd. It reminded Marley of a car engine revving up. She felt hot and then hotter. Her body was suddenly far away and she watched as, dreamlike, she hit the glass one more time.

It shattered in a crescendo, shards of glass clattering to the ground. Neath passed through them without being cut and reared up against Marley's leg, begging to be picked up.

Numbly, her body moving like she was remotely operating it, Marley picked up Neath. As soon as Neath was settled in her arms, the cat started purring again.

Marley woke up.

She was on a lumpy couch in a dimly lit room. At first she didn't recognize it. But when she sat and looked around she realized it was the new motel room Corbin had moved to. The shades were drawn. Corbin was hunched over the laptop in the armchair, turned toward the front door.

She spent a moment remembering what had maybe been in her head but hadn't been a dream, because Neath was on her legs, purring still. She hadn't expected to wake up on a couch in Corbin's room, as if she'd just taken an unplanned nap.

"Corbin?" she said softly.

He looked over at her for a long moment, his eyes hollow. Then he looked back at his screen. "You're awake. Good. Now you can go away again."

She ran her fingers down Neath's back and looked at the curve of Corbin's shoulders. "Corbin, does the virus… talk to you?"

He glanced at her, a horrible smile creasing his face. "The virus is mind-expanding, magic-enhancing. I hear all sorts of things now, just like they wanted."

"Oh." Her throat hurt and she swallowed convulsively.

Putting the laptop aside, Corbin rose and fetched a glass of water. As he handed it to her, he wouldn't meet her eyes. He looked haggard. "You can call a taxi from here. Your purse and phone are over there."

After pushing Neath to one side, she took the water and then caught his hand, pulling him down to the couch. He resisted, but only for a moment. Instead he slid his arm around her waist and rested his head on her shoulder. "I don't know what you want from me, Marley. You said you wanted to help me, but you don't. Not with what needs to be done."

"I want to go back in time and never let you go," she said fiercely.

His fist clenched in her shirt and he moved his mouth over her hair. "I would have gone anyhow. My uncle's blood demanded a response. But I would have come back as soon as I could. I might have run to you instead of to my friends. Did Skadi really heal you before? She didn't today."

Marley's skin burned where his fingers brushed her hip. "She did, and what she did lingered. I don't want to talk about her." She put the water down and ran her fingers through his hair. "Do you remember teaching me magic?"

"Yes," he said softly. "A lot has changed since then."

"Not this," she said, and kissed him. His mouth was soft and mobile against hers, until he groaned and pushed her away.

"I can't trust you, Marley. You let Skadi go, you still think Senyaza and Zachariah are doing right things."

The motel room door swung open and Neath meowed a greeting, stretching off the couch. Branwyn stood beyond, her eyes blazing. She held her hammer in one hand and her other one out flat. A curl of smoke drifted past her into the room. "Is Hadraniel the good guy here? Is that why you told him where the divinity circuit was?"

Tiredly, Corbin said, "No. Everybody is a bad guy. Including me." He stood. "Marley, you missed some calls while you were sleeping. Branwyn's come to save you. Take her and go away."

"You think I should just leave and let you carry on with whatever you're doing? You helped an angel get hold of something that can break the Hush, Corbin. I've felt it in action, Marley. It's bad."

Branwyn's eyes flickered around the room and she added, "Tell me he kept you here forcibly."

Marley hesitated, not entirely sure what was going on. She remembered that she'd been the one trying to lure the virus into answering her, remembered Corbin telling her to go.

Branwyn's face twisted. "*Please* don't tell me you ditched us to get some snuggle time with the asshole here."

"No!" said Marley, starting forward. "Did I... Is it tomorrow? I was...." She frowned, remembering Hadraniel nodding to Corbin.

"He gave the angel the divinity circuit? But—why?"

"If you don't know, *what* have you been doing all this time?" Branwyn demanded.

"She was dying. I brought her here so we could keep her alive," said Corbin, once again refusing to look at her. "Get out. Now."

"You can't keep throwing me out, Corbin!" Marley reached for him and he shied away, knocking over the water he'd brought her. Neath yowled as her paws got wet.

"You're right," he said. "Don't come back and this will be the last time."

Branwyn said scornfully, "I thought you were different, Corbin. I thought of you as a friend. But I should have known better, eh? If you're coming, Marley, let's go."

Marley, bewildered, realized she didn't know how to fix this. Corbin had helped Hadraniel get the divinity circuit. Corbin was going to do bad things, hurt people. He said so himself.

But Corbin was sick.

She remembered the virus smiling at her, telling her about Corbin's family, claiming Corbin had contained it somehow.

Slowly, Marley gathered up her bag and phone and followed Branwyn out the door. She couldn't look at Corbin as she went.

19
BRANWYN

"Oh," said Marley as she stepped into the sunshine. "What time is it?"

"A little after noon. You were gone almost a full day, Marley," said Branwyn and she stopped herself from saying more. Marley was good enough at punishing herself as it was.

"Gah," Marley said and shifted uncomfortably. "One of these days I really ought to take care of practicalities before storming out on him. Taxis, bathrooms, that kind of thing."

"It's not like you," Branwyn agreed as they got into her car. Neath trilled in what Branwyn was sure was agreement as she settled herself in the back seat.

"He makes me crazy. And the more time I spend with him—" She shook her head. "Is everybody all right? Did you manage to get the angel anyhow?"

"No, we didn't. And no, I can't really say everybody is all right. I'm sure the full damage will be on the six o clock news. There was a nine car pile-up, and people were falling off staircases and one woman has possibly lost her mind and I don't know what else.

Right now we need to go make sure Rhianna is all right because it's just possible one of the kaiju is trying to kill her."

Marley ran her hands through her hair. "Oh my God." She squeezed her eyes shut for a moment, then opened them again and exhaled. "What did Rhianna do?"

"Tattled," said Branwyn.

"That... that doesn't sound like the Rhianna I know," said Marley hesitantly.

"Yeah, funny thing about magic, it makes everybody act out of character."

"I don't think it's magic in my case, Bran," said Marley quietly.

Branwyn frowned and kept her eyes firmly on the road. "I'm trying not to think about that."

"I think he was going to tell me about Hadraniel," Marley pressed on, clearly determined to talk it through anyhow. "Before.... Before I immediately told you."

"Yes, and then what happened? He kidnapped you? Sent text messages for you?" Branwyn couldn't keep the edge out of her voice.

"It wasn't him. I thought I could catch the virus," Marley confessed. "It keeps talking through Corbin and I thought I could catch it and make it talk to me."

"Did you say that out loud before trying it? You wanted to catch the virus? Congratulations, it sounds like you relapsed."

Marley's cheeks got hot. "There wasn't really time. I was afraid, Bran. The thing with Skadi went really, really badly and then Corbin got upset—"

"You were afraid of Corbin?" said Branwyn. "We have *got* to talk, Marley—"

"No," said Marley hastily. "I was afraid of the virus. It was controlling his body, saying things through him."

"You mean, like he was possessed?" asked Branwyn, remembering what had happened to Penny a year ago. Penny's angel, the one she'd loved, had moved into her soul and started burning it away, speaking through her mouth and partially controlling her body, before leaving her to die.

Marley went still. "Yes. But celestials can't possess nephilim because nephilim don't have souls."

Branwyn shrugged as she steered the car. "Maybe somebody figured out how to do it."

"I don't even—I need to look in some books. Talk to Senyaza. Something."

"You've got to save it for later, Research Girl. I need you and your magic now."

"For Rhianna. Right. Well. You might as well fill me in on what happened, then."

Branwyn did her best to relate her scattered impressions of the fight. It filled the time until they arrived at her family's house. It was mid-afternoon on Friday and nobody was home except Branwyn's grandmother and her eldest younger brother Howl.

"You think she's here?" Marley asked skeptically as Neath leapt out of the car and started trotting up the walk.

"I think I'm going to start here and end in Washington, DC if I have to, and I'll find her somewhere along the way." Her phone beeped, with the tone she'd assigned to Titanone. She didn't want to look, but she did anyhow.

You've been looking at your bank website a lot.

Branwyn squeezed her eyes shut and then opened them again, hoping she hadn't seen that. But the words remained, glowing on her phone screen. "I need a minute, Marley."

Why are you still watching what I'm doing on my phone?

What? I'm not doing that, the screen said and Branwyn remembered more than one toddler sibling lying about what she could plainly see.

How about we find you some kind of web game to play instead? Bejeweled is great.

After a few moments the screen flashed again. That does look fun. Hey, do you want me to give you some more money? Senyaza has a lot, way more than you, and the pathway is already established.

No! That isn't your money to give.

Maybe it is. Maybe I'm Senyaza.

No. I don't want Senyaza's money.

Oh. Then, a moment later, *Don't look at your bank account again today?*

Branwyn ran her hand over her face. *Go play Bejeweled.*

Right.

"Tonight is going to be a riot," said Branwyn bitterly. "I don't know if I can stand it."

"Titanone?" asked Marley.

"He's such a *child*, Marley. A child who can get into my phone and access bank accounts. I didn't mean to make a child."

Marley got a funny look on her face. "Yeah, I know about dangerous children unexpectedly dropping into your life."

"At least yours were dropped on you by somebody else." Branwyn laced her fingers together, stretched them, and looked at her family's house. "Right. First things first. Rhianna. We look here and then we go to DC and shake her until her teeth clatter."

"Maybe you ought to try calling her before you go to the other side of the country," suggested Marley judiciously.

"So she can run away? Hell no." Branwyn started up the walk and Marley caught her arm.

"You're really angry at her, Branwyn?"

Branwyn pulled away and tugged on her hair. "Yes. I don't know. We could have had this thing if she hadn't told her boss what was going on. And now she's got some kaiju ready to kill her if I can't sort it out."

"And?" asked Marley.

Branwyn scowled. "And nothing is working out like I thought it would. I did stupid things and now I have to deal with the consequences and I'm angry at myself. There. Is that what you wanted to hear?" Marley's blue eyes flickered over her face and she held up her hand. "And don't look at me with your magic—"

"I'm not," said Marley mildly. "I'm trying to stick to doing things that will actually help and it's obvious that never does. I've never been particularly centered but you always have been."

"It's been a bad week for all of us," said Branwyn, and went into the house.

Tara met her in the hall, shooing Neath ahead of her. "Branwyn. Rhianna's in the office. Only a short visit for the weekend, she says."

Branwyn relaxed momentarily. "Yeah, I know."

"She's been getting into trouble," Tara added, her bright eyes moving to Marley and then down to Neath. "She won't admit it, of course."

"I know that too. She and I need to have a talk."

Probably because she was eavesdropping, Rhianna appeared at the office door. "Branwyn! How did it go after I left?"

Branwyn curled her fingers into her palm. She and Rhianna hadn't fought much as children, preferring to combine their energies to attack the rest of the world. But 'much' wasn't the same as 'ever' and she was having strong flashbacks to being eight years old and smacking her annoying six-year-old sister upside the head.

"Let's go out back and look at the garden," she suggested instead.

Rhianna looked genuinely surprised. "Am I in trouble?"

"Yes," said Branwyn quietly. "And I'd rather not bring it down inside the house, but here you are. Let's go out back."

Marley looked between Branwyn and Rhianna and said, "I think

I'm going to stay in here, take care of some business, and raid the fridge. If that's okay, Mrs. Lennox? I haven't eaten in a day."

Tara said absently, "You know where the kitchen is. Try my fresh salsa. There's cat treats in the drawer." Then she took Branwyn by the elbow, steered her to Rhianna, and took Rhianna by the elbow as well. "Yes, I think you two should talk. Does this have something to do with that terrifying young man who isn't your friend, Branwyn?"

"Uh, yeah. If he shows up, tell him I'm out back." Branwyn and Rhianna were propelled down the hall, past the kitchen where Marley was making a face at some green salsa, and out the back door. Tara shoved them out onto the deck and closed the door. There was a click.

The Lennox family backyard was bigger than it looked. One half of the partially fenced yard was dominated by a fig tree, while the other had neat raised beds among crushed gravel. There was an old plastic playhouse among the roots of the fig tree, and a tire swing hanging from a branch, and a platform in the branches of the fig itself.

Rhianna immediately skittered down the steps of the deck and ran over to the garden beds. A small persimmon tree was trained against an arbor and some of the fruit was falling already. Rhianna picked one from the ground and rolled it back and forth in her hand.

"Why is Grandma mad at us?"

Branwyn followed her, feeling old. She stopped just inside the edge of the shadow from the fig tree. "Because neither of us think through the consequences of what we do."

Rhianna gave her a wary look and then transferred her gaze to the fruit in her hand, waiting passively for whatever Branwyn had to say.

"The kaiju are furious you brought your boss in, Rhianna."

Rhianna shrugged, as if she wasn't very worried by this. "Sometimes it's hard to stay friendly." Her eyes lifted in sudden concern. "Are they furious with *you*?"

"Kind of, yeah? Offset by how I basically did what they wanted me to do. But, Rhianna…" Branwyn ran her hands through her hair, tugging. "They want to *kill* you. Not hyperbole. And they don't think your boss will save you. Given that you're here right now and he's not, I think they're probably right."

"He had to go and do some things. I wanted to see Grandma," said Rhianna, and she sounded like a frightened, sulky child. "Why are you here instead of them if they're so serious about wanting to kill me?"

"Because I made a deal to save your life," snapped Branwyn, her frustration returning. "I wasn't sure if they'd honor it but since they're not here, I guess they are. I've got a year to punish you enough to satisfy them or else we both become targets."

"Oh," said Rhianna. "Well. I guess we'll both be busy."

Branwyn said bitterly. "I hadn't really wanted to spend the next year figuring out how to murder a half-dozen celestials. Especially after today when I've seen just how hard it is to get *one* when they group up."

"I'm sure Umbriel will help," said Rhianna brightly. "And don't you know a whole gang of monster hunters from Senyaza?"

Branwyn crouched down, putting her arms over her head, as if she could shut out the world. "I don't want to talk about Umbriel right now. I can't *believe* how casually you just—" She stopped.

"What did you expect me to do?" demanded Rhianna. "We're trying to get the divinity circuit back."

Branwyn unfolded her arms. "Not for Umbriel!"

"When we found out where it was and we had a plan, why wouldn't I tell him?" Rhianna crossed to the shadow of the fig tree. "Wait, what do you mean 'not for Umbriel'?"

"What do *you* mean, 'trying to get it back'? Didn't he get it back from Hadraniel already?"

Rhianna scowled and sank her fingers into the soft persimmon, pulling it apart. Quivering fruit innards spilled over her hands. "No. Hadraniel wouldn't return the circuit and Umbriel couldn't force it. It told Umbriel it was sorry for the theft but it had something important to do first, which would make everything right. That you were just a backup plan. It sounds like it's planning to come back for you later, Bran. And then Umbriel's Sword started acting weird and I had to leave."

"Huh," said Branwyn. She wondered if the kaiju had known that would happen. She'd noticed that they didn't seem to think the target had changed; they'd still talked about going after Hadraniel even when she thought Umbriel would have reclaimed the device. "How was his sword acting weird?"

"Nuh-uh. Your turn. What did *you* mean, 'not for Umbriel?'"

Branwyn curled suddenly unsteady hands into fists. "If I get my hands on the divinity circuit again, I'm destroying it."

"What?" Rhianna froze, her green gaze shocked and hurt. "Why?"

"Because Senyaza was right to create the Hush! I *felt* the full power of an angel's direct attention, Rhianna, and I never want to feel it again."

"So have I." Rhianna's face was pale. "I've felt worse. Like when Dad died."

"Did Umbriel make you love him?" Branwyn's chest ached just asking the question.

"No!" said Rhianna impatiently. "I've told you before I don't love him. Did you think I was lying?"

Branwyn muttered, "I just don't know why you'd be a part of an organization that spies on people and takes away their rights, working for a guy who can control your mind if he decides it's a good idea." She heard her mother's car pull into the driveway on the other side of the house.

"You think Senyaza is any better?" There were spots of color high in Rhianna's cheeks. "At least we're trying to manage the faeries! At least we're thinking of *everybody*, not just ourselves."

Branwyn stared at her and thought of Titanone. "No. No, I don't think Senyaza is any better."

"But look at you, getting rich off your work for them. I never thought *you'd* be the one to sell out, Branwyn."

Branwyn was silent. What could she say? She hadn't meant to sell out? But, just as she'd told Rhianna, sometimes the consequences snuck up on her. All she could do was try to deal with them the right way when she realized what had happened.

The back door burst open and Meredith hurtled out, squealing in joy. "Rhianna! Branwyn! Rhianna, did you hear that Branwyn is sending me to school? Isn't that amazing?" Their baby sister flew down the deck steps and threw herself at Branwyn, hugging her tightly while inspecting Rhianna. "What are you doing in town, Rhianna? I had a dream you would come visit. Is it sneaky stuff? In my dream you'd been here for days."

"I came to deliver presents," said Rhianna solemnly, and Meredith promptly detached herself from her eldest sister to glom onto her second eldest sister. As she did, Rhianna and Branwyn met gazes over her head.

Then in response to Meredith's urging, she explained, "My boss—my direct boss, Bran, not my boss's boss—is a woodcarver. I convinced him to make something for each of you kids, since he owed me a favor."

"Where is it? What is it?" demanded Meredith.

"Inside, silly goose. Bran and I were talking. I'll come inside in a few minutes after we're done."

Meredith took the hint and ran back inside, her long hair

streaming like a ribbon behind her. Rhianna watched her go fondly and then turned her attention back to Branwyn. "At least the school will be great for her."

"I don't want to talk about it," said Branwyn, unaccustomed anguish bubbling up.

"It's not so bad," Rhianna offered. "I mean, it's not like you're selling out selfishly. Sacrificing your integrity to make the world a better place for others is kind of noble, really."

Branwyn gave Rhianna a death-glare but her sister had developed an immunity to those in second grade. That really felt like a tragedy right now. So instead she said, "I'm going to destroy the divinity circuit, Rhianna."

"Only if you get to it first," said Rhianna lightly. Then, more soberly, she said, "But if I get to it first, I'll let Umbriel know about your objections. Maybe he'll listen. He does, sometimes."

It hurt, realizing that her sister's loyalty was to somebody else. Branwyn couldn't understand it. She kept thinking about how upset it would make their great-grandmother, who had passed on years ago but who had loved family above all things.

She tried to focus on what was important right now, though. "Does your precious Umbriel know what Hadraniel is going to do now? If we can anticipate it, we can lay another trap."

Rhianna licked persimmon juice off her fingers. "With the kaiju? Won't that be fun. But just what I said before: that Hadraniel has something important to accomplish. Important enough to burn bridges with Umbriel. Can we figure out what that is?"

Branwyn went through what she knew about Hadraniel, ticking items off on her fingers. "It set up the massacre in Belgium to distract Senyaza from the attack on the twins. It's a traditionalist. It has access to a lot of power via both the divinity circuit and that weapon. It doesn't want to hurt humans, other than mind-controlling them."

"Unless they get in the way. Umbriel stopped it from doing more damage at the bookstore, I noticed that."

Branwyn nodded absently, staring at her fingers. "It's on speaking terms with Corbin."

Marley spoke behind Branwyn. "It's going to do something to the gala."

Raising her eyes, Branwyn furrowed her brow at Marley.

Marley reached over to her and unfolded another finger on her unused hand. "Corbin hates Senyaza right now." She unbent a second finger. "Marley's been seeing everybody associated with Senyaza covered in blood for days now. And everybody's going to be at the gala."

"Neither of those are about Hadraniel," objected Branwyn. "I had a system here." She looked down at her fingers again. Marley was always worth listening to, even if Branwyn could personally come up with a handful of horrible ways for the gala to go wrong that didn't involve a vengeful angel. "You might be right, though. Maybe it's thinking, 'Hey, look at how much damage we did with just some mortal weapons in Belgium. What could we do in Half-breed Headquarters?' And, ooh, for an encore, it can go wreck the Extraworlder Conference." Then she shook the facts off her fingers and put her hand on Marley's shoulder. "Do you think that's why Corbin told it where to find the divinity circuit? Does he *want* a repeat of Belgium?" Even as angry as she was with Corbin, it hurt to suggest that.

Marley's face was pale. "I can't believe that. He must have had another reason. I don't think anything could push him into supporting… that."

"Hey, wait," said Rhianna, stepping back. "What do you mean, Corbin told it where the divinity circuit was? How did Corbin know?"

Marley's mouth twisted. "Sometimes Corbin knows things. Even before the virus...." She trailed off, her gaze going distant. "The virus made my magic stronger," she said slowly. "Before Skadi cured me, I felt like I was drowning in my magic."

"He just *knew*?" asked Rhianna skeptically. "We have a lot of security! Magical security, too. No peeking through the curtain, nothing."

"Magic is a bitch like that," said Branwyn callously. "He knows secrets that somebody else already knows and Marley knows things that haven't happened yet. Which is harder to believe?"

"It's just intersections and consequences," muttered Marley.

"And she's not always *right*," pointed out Rhianna, still nettled. "It's just projecting. Computers can do projections. They can't just pluck secrets out of thin air."

"Your security really isn't that great," Branwyn argued. "Not only did Corbin and Hadraniel both circumvent it, so did Max The Intern Wait No Kaiju."

Rhianna flushed unexpectedly and shut up. Branwyn eyed her, then said, "Go inside and see Mom since she's home now. I've got stuff to do."

"Don't think you're getting to the divinity circuit before me," mumbled Rhianna and fled inside the house.

Marley looked up from the ground she was studying with unusual interest. "I need to go to Senyaza. Before the gala. Nowish."

"Yes. I thought you might. I want to go talk to Titanone, anyhow. But one moment." She pulled out her phone, took a bracing deep breath, inhaling the scent of the persimmons and the tomato plants, then called Severin.

"Cupcake," purred his voice, right behind her head. "Did you deal with your sister already?"

"Don't be an idiot. Do you know what Hadraniel will be doing next?"

"Oh, possibly. Did you enjoy its company that much? I never

thought *you'd* be vulnerable to an angel's glory." His lazy mockery brushed across exposed nerves.

"Have you *thought* about the consequence of presenting me with a choice between my sister and your kindred?"

"With pleasure," he assured her. "Especially the sister who wants so badly to use your skills for an angel's empowerment. That must burn."

"Not as much as you will," said Branwyn darkly.

"Me?" Severin protested in exaggerated shock. "Was I calling for your sister's head?"

Branwyn stopped as she realized he hadn't been. "You—never mind. This isn't why I called. We're pretty sure Hadraniel is going to crash the Senyaza gala tonight."

"Ah," said Severin, thoughtfully. "You might want to skip that party, then."

"What? No—I was thinking you and your friends could catch ol' Hadra there."

"Now that's flattering," he said. "You think we can just stroll into Senyaza, especially tonight."

"Can't you? You don't seem to have any trouble getting anyplace else."

"No, that's me getting under your skin, Branwyn." The sudden dryness of his voice was like an unexpected bucket of ice. "Think with your head instead of your gut and you'll notice all sorts of places it costs me more than it's worth to get into. You're as close to death as I want to get right now, cupcake."

Branwyn was silenced for a moment, allowing Severin to go on. "Nah, Max and Dolores could probably get in but the rest of us would be noticed. We'll just have to catch Hadraniel later. If the half-breeds don't get lucky," he added thoughtfully.

By then, Branwyn had recovered some of her footing. "I hadn't expected you to be a coward," she jabbed, and noticed Marley wincing as she loitered nearby.

"Well, it's about what's in it for me. What exactly do I get out of going to a Senyaza gala that I can't get by waiting a few hours nearby?"

"The chance to dress up and dance the night away until an angel wrecks the evening by murdering everybody?" she said brightly. Marley covered her face and Branwyn wondered why.

"You've got me confused with Tarn. Ouch. But you have fun, cupcake. Try not to die. Maybe once Hadraniel busts the wards down I'll peek in and see what all the fuss is about." His voice faded, and the phone clicked off.

"What's wrong with you, Marley?" demanded Branwyn as she put her phone away.

"Is he coming?" she asked in response. "All dressed up?"

"No," Branwyn said. "He's a delicate flower and he can't expose himself to how stunning we'll be." She paused. "We need to make sure we find time to get dressed up, don't we?"

Marley nodded. "Otherwise, Penny is going to kill us."

Branwyn said, "Ah. Yes. You're right. You can call her while we drive over to Titan One."

20
MARLEY

The commercial levels of Titan One were as busy as they ever were on a weekday afternoon—Neath enjoyed the pet-friendly policy of the mall and the opportunity to terrorize several dogs smaller than her—but the business floors they passed through were nearly empty. Branwyn and Marley peeked in the monster hunter headquarters but the place was empty. Branwyn turned away immediately. "I guess everybody's getting ready for the party. Figures."

Marley looked around a moment more and finally spotted a note on Simon's desk. *GONE TO PERCH SEND HELP.*

She picked it up and waved it at Branwyn. "Simon's gone to the bar. Aren't they trying to stop him from drinking?"

Branwyn looked distracted, trailing her fingers along the wall. "Yeah, he's there. So is Mr. Black."

"Oh God," said Marley. "Let's go see if we can intervene. I need to talk to that asshole anyhow. Neath, put that down!" The cat looked up, a sheathed knife with feathers dangling from the hilt in her mouth. "You know, this is why I don't take you more places."

They went to the Perch, a bar on the 18th floor mostly frequented by Senyaza personnel. Personally, Marley wouldn't have called it a bar. A lounge, maybe. Or an old style club, although it didn't have anybody standing at the door limiting access. It had ancient heavy wooden furniture, lovingly cared for: beautiful armchairs, little round tables, cozy booths and a beautiful dark oaken bar top that was the best possible afterlife for a tree. Maroon walls were decorated with paintings and framed photos, all of Senyaza luminaries Marley had never heard of before the first time she'd entered the Perch.

It too was unusually empty for a Friday afternoon. At one of the few long freestanding tables on the far side of the room, Simon slouched in a chair with elaborately carved arms. Across from him sat both Skadi and Mr. Black, equally casual. Mr. Black's jacket was unbuttoned and Skadi's cheeks were flushed. There were several bottles, glasses and an ornate box on the table.

Marley narrowed her eyes and stalked over there, beating Branwyn despite having a shorter stride. "What's going on?"

Simon looked at her, his hair sticking up right over his eyes. "Tell me you got my note."

"Ah, Marley," said Mr. Black, waving a hand expansively. "Do join us. We're discussing Corbin." Neath leapt into a chair and then onto the table and Mr. Black eyed her. "And you brought the celestial kitty. How charming."

"They're getting smashed," said Simon bitterly. "They made me come along." He pulled his bottle and shot glass away from Neath's questing nose.

"Why?" demanded Branwyn, yanking out a chair next to Simon and sitting down. "Can't they pour their own drinks?"

"It seemed cruel," said Skadi. "Plus he's better at getting drunk than I am. I was hoping it would rub off."

"Simon is peaceful company in a bar, I've found. I could use some peace." Mr. Black rubbed his eyes and then sipped from the tumbler in front of him.

"You're drinking cocktails," pointed out Simon irritably. "Slowly. You want to do this, you have to commit."

"Well, I do have gala security to monitor later," said Mr. Black mildly.

"I hate to admit this, but I'm confused," said Branwyn. "Is this really the right time to explore pushing your alcohol tolerance?"

Mr. Black fished in his pocket and pushed a piece of paper over to Branwyn. Branwyn read it impassively and then handed it to Marley.

Dear Grandfather,

I'm anticipating seeing you at the annual gala tonight. I hope the whole family will be there.

Corbin

Marley stared at it and then sank into the chair at the end of the table, her thoughts whirling. Skadi, Corbin, Mr. Black. Senyaza was full of liars. For a moment, she thought they all deserved each other. But she remembered Corbin's wounded eyes, his exhaustion, his hunger when he'd pulled her to him. She remembered how the virus had changed her thinking, and how it had hurt. He didn't deserve what had been done to him.

She raised her eyes to Mr. Black. "You infected him with the virus on purpose. Because of his magic. You wanted to use his magic to identify Hadraniel. You *bastard*."

"We gave that order, yes," agreed Mr. Black. "Corbin's never embraced his gift the way his father did, and we needed to find out who was responsible for murdering our people." His gaze darkened. "I lost my son, Marley."

Marley smacked the table. "So you sacrificed your grandson? What kind of sense does that make?"

Mr. Black's fingers tightened around his glass. "It wasn't supposed to be a sacrifice. Skadi's run dozens of controlled exposures. It should have been safe for everybody."

"Still don't know what went wrong," said Skadi. "No idea what will happen when Corbin dies. Maybe he'll escape for real." She tapped one of her pale nails on the box. It was a puzzle box, Marley realized, made of many tiny panels of wood. The box Corbin had opened.

There you were, laying the old trap. But I won't be taken again, the virus had said. She mentally replayed more of the conversation that followed, moving pieces around.

"She was talking like that even before we got out the booze," Simon commented. "Babbling. Fidgeting with that box."

"I understand," said Marley, after a deep breath. "I understand everything. Almost everything. But I understand more than they do." She met Mr. Black's mild gaze again. "Why do you use the past tense talking about Corbin's father's gift?"

"Ah, that's a quirk of his bloodline. They each have their own magic but there's also a particular gift that gets passed down."

"The thing with the eye," volunteered Simon helpfully.

Mr. Black glanced at him. "Yes, the thing with the eye. The Eye of Insight, we call it. Corbin's other grandfather died when Aedrian was still in the womb; Aedrian inherited it before birth. It killed his mother."

Marley swallowed. "That's grim."

Mr. Black shrugged. "In any case, Aedrian grew up with it. But when Corbin was born, he lost the power. We didn't really expect that. We'd come to rely on Aedrian's access to the Eye."

"Which is...?" prompted Branwyn.

"Information," said Mr. Black. "Or access to information. We don't know how it works. It's never been easily controlled, but at least Aedrian was willing to try on Senyaza's behalf. Corbin has always been resistant to tapping into the power."

"It's more than information," said Marley. *Someone claimed him first.*

Skadi pushed her hair away from her face. "What have you discovered, little one?"

Marley glanced at Skadi, and found she couldn't be angry at her the same way she was angry at Corbin's grandfather. When Marley had been ill in Mr. Black's office, when she'd fallen down, they'd all stayed away. They hadn't told her or Branwyn what was going on, even though in retrospect they must have known. Skadi may have technically been responsible for the virus, may have unleashed it, but she was doing her best to track it down while Mr. Black and the elders of Senyaza sat safe above.

"Well, it's why whatever you put into that box—a celestial you turned into a virus somehow? I don't know. But Corbin's got something else like that and that's why the virus couldn't fully possess him, and it's why you can't recapture it. If that's just information, it seems to be information with an agenda."

"Ah," said Mr. Black and pulled out his phone to start tapping on it.

Skadi blinked at her for a moment and then said, "He turned himself into a virus. All we did is catch him and put him to use. He only would have ended up impaled on a Sword anyhow. Never friends with his peers, that one."

"Speaking of information with an agenda," said Mr. Black and this time slid his phone over to Branwyn.

She glanced at it and her mouth tightened. "Yeah. Well, you reap what you sow, man."

"What?" said Marley, annoyed that the subject was apparently changing with no more than Skadi's mild acknowledgement of Marley's discovery.

"Titanone's programmer just quit. Apparently he's going dark, getting off the network. He's scared of Titanone."

"You've confused it a great deal," said Mr. Black severely.

"Me? I had things well in hand and you decided to make him into a spy!" flared Branwyn.

"Little pitchers have big—and I mean *really* big—ears," said Simon. He tapped a finger on the shot glass in front of him.

Marley smacked the table again and Neath hissed in annoyance. "Can we please get back to Corbin? Why were you talking about what might happen when he dies, Skadi?"

"Ah, we're back to reasons for drinking," said Mr. Black, and finished off what was in his glass. The barmaid, a young woman with pink hair, appeared silently beside him to replace his glass. She put down glasses of ice water for Branwyn and Marley and what Marley hoped was a saucer of water for Neath. A drunk cat was the last thing she needed.

"Can't let him sneak into a party full of nephilim, little one. My ability to manage the virus is—" she drained her glass "—limited. A family? I can do what needs to be done if I can get there in time. A gala? No. Too likely my own defenses would be overwhelmed."

"Especially if he spreads the version you can't stop," agreed Mr. Black. "Such a disaster."

"I know this is crazy," said Branwyn brightly, "But why not cancel the gala if you don't think you can stop him safely?"

"He's coming because Hadraniel is," said Marley. "You *should* cancel the gala."

"Ah, well, Hadraniel at least I am not worried about," said Mr. Black. "I hope he does come. But he won't. Corbin is coming for his own reasons."

"It," corrected Branwyn. "Hadraniel doesn't have a gender."

"And yet you use 'he' for Titanone," pointed out Mr. Black.

Branwyn clenched her fists on the tabletop and Neath nudged her, meowing in concern. Marley cut in before they could get more off track. "Gender Studies 101 is tomorrow. Why the *hell* aren't you worried about an angel with the divinity circuit who hates you? I promise, you should be."

Comfortably, Mr. Black said, "It is a nephilim gala, Miss Claviger, within the heart of our stronghold. It is *built* to stop celestial invaders, and there will be dozens of experienced celestial hunters on hand to tether Hadraniel down so firmly that we could spend years deciding what to do with it. Not that we'll need to spend years *deciding*." He flicked Skadi's box with a finger.

Marley stared at him. "Are you holding this gala as bait?"

"Hardly that. We have a gala almost every year, my dear. And to be bait it must seduce the victim in—and I think a celestial would have to be mad to try to join us." He glanced down at Neath again. "Although you may bring your cat, if you wish. You will be attending, yes?"

"Yes," said Marley grimly.

"Good. You may be useful. Have a drink. Don't worry about Hadraniel," Mr. Black said. "My sources tell me that in a celestial spat this morning our enemy barely managed to damage a coffee shop. The power of the divinity circuit has been overrated by our friends in the government. And Senyaza was killing angels even before the Hush was created. He can only surprise us once. If Hadraniel does come, we will be ready for him, and unlike with my grandson, there will be no hesitation. But more than likely he will pursue an easier target."

Marley glanced at Branwyn, who didn't look convinced. Then she shifted into her danger-sight. Branwyn dripped with blood, while Skadi glittered with crimson crystals. The echo of Mr. Black was worst of all: contorted and broken.

"I wish I could trust you," said Marley bitterly. "I wish I could believe you. But my celestial blood won't let me. I see too much."

Mr. Black gave her a knowing look. "And none of it is ever good.

I understand." He tapped his glass. "Sometimes it brings things into focus."

"Not for me," said Simon sullenly. "The whole point is to push things out of focus. But maybe you're getting the *magic* alcohol."

Marley thought about Corbin again, considered why he might be coming to the gala. Despite his note to Mr. Black, she didn't think it was to reconcile with his family. Not with the blood in the future. But why would he warn them? The security of Senyaza wasn't only magical; they had access to quite large guns and it was obvious that Mr. Black would order his own grandson shot if he felt it was necessary to protect the whole of Senyaza. After all, hadn't he ordered Corbin infected with an uncontrollable virus?

None of the nephilim seemed to remember what it was like to love somebody. They were all as cold as the steel of their tower, cold as diamond.

"It's true that Hadraniel isn't the only way things can go terribly wrong," said Branwyn with deceptive lightness. "I'll be there too. Maybe I can deal with one of them."

"And we will deal with another. Perhaps finally." Mr. Black drained his glass.

Marley clenched her fists. "How can you not have non-lethal ways to subdue angry nephilim?" Branwyn shot her a sharp glance that she didn't understand.

Mr. Black said, "Oh, we do. And if Corbin approaches through the front entrance, you can be assured we will deploy all of them. But Corbin is…. powerful, and prone to surprising us, lately. I'd rather he not die for it. But I must give my teams their orders." He sighed.

Marley started shredding a napkin. She'd thought Corbin was coming because Hadraniel was. She'd been *sure* Hadraniel would invade the gala. Mr. Black was so confident that it would be a non-issue if it happened, though, and he was right about how the nephilim had been dealing with angels since before the Hush. And Titan One was fortified, all right. A safe sanctuary and punishing vengeance for any attack was how Senyaza protected itself against even minor mischief from all the celestial factions who hated the organization.

But there was blood in the future, and Corbin was coming. They had to be connected. Branwyn said he'd given Hadraniel information on the divinity circuit and he hadn't denied it but how far would he go to punish those who had betrayed him?

How far would those he loved go to punish somebody who'd hurt them? Corbin had grown up in Senyaza, grown up marinating in a sea of ancient grudges and rigid arrogance and secret power. He'd grown up in an environment that never forgave and where love was earned after centuries of life.

And she was sitting here talking to those who'd betrayed him, who were talking now about ordering his death because they'd made a mistake. She was acting like they were reasonable rather than half mad with injured power.

"You're no different than the angels," said Marley bitterly, and pushed herself away from the table.

The bartender gasped behind her bar. Skadi tilted her head as if the idea wasn't new to her, while Mr. Black frowned.

But it was Branwyn who said, "Hey, your boyfriend is the one actually working with the angels."

Marley stared at Branwyn in betrayed shock, then stood up. Without a word, she walked away, out of the bar, into the elevator and from Titan One. Once she was in the plaza beyond the grand front entrance to the skyscraper, she pressed her hands against her forehead and tried not to burst into tears. It was the wrong place for that.

Neath meowed behind her, then trilled and darted past her. A raven sat on the plinth fountain spilling into a shallow basin.

Neath bounced up to the edge of the basin and teetered there, as if considering whether she could jump and catch the bird.

Marley looked at it warily, tears and anger momentarily dwindling. She couldn't say it looked familiar—ravens looked like ravens to her. She was proud of being able to tell them apart from crows. But she couldn't see a raven without thinking of Corbin.

"Is he around?" she asked, her voice cracking.

"No," said the raven, in a surprisingly human voice. "No Corbin. Marley."

Marley's eyes widened before she remembered that ravens were in that category of birds that could learn human speech. She moved up to the fountain behind Neath and held out her hand. "What are you doing here?"

"Marley," repeated the raven and fluttered to her hand. Neath watched the bird with slitted eyes, her tail lashing, but Marley didn't think she was actually interested in going for the bird.

"Scared," added the bird, and this time its voice was higher pitched. "Corbin's sick. Miss him."

Marley hesitantly stroked the back of the bird's head with one finger, looking at how the feathers spread out in a shaggy ruff around the bird's neck. Neath twined her way between Marley's legs, until Marley had to sit down on the edge of the fountain or be knocked into it.

"Me too, bird," she told the raven. "I'm pretty scared too. And once again I've apparently stormed off without transportation." She thought about going back in to get Branwyn, but she was still angry. And Branwyn had business still with the spirit of the skyscraper.

The memory made Branwyn's behavior a little less hurtful. Of course she couldn't afford to get into a fight with Senyaza, not when the life she was responsible for belonged to them. Marley understood that. Relationships weren't ever simple; there were always treacherous currents below the surface waiting to pull you down. She understood that, but it didn't calm the pounding of her heart. There was *nothing* she could do to escape that, except breathe and try not to get into worse trouble.

"Transport," said the raven, in almost Marley's voice.

"Yes," said Marley. "Yeah, I understand why Corbin prefers to rely on you guys." A wild idea occurred, born from a growing sense of being trapped. "Are any of your brothers around? Maybe you could give me a ride to my own car."

"Yes," said the raven. "Flight. To where you need to go."

Marley wondered if Corbin had sent them, given them instructions to help her. It was a sweet thought. Too sweet. Today, she couldn't believe it; today everything felt broken. What could they do but run?

Besides, the raven said *yes* but it simply sat on her arm, as if it hadn't actually understood what she'd said. Maybe she could do something to communicate better with it.

Marley cast about, trying to remember what Corbin had done before. He'd been obviously tapping into his intrinsic magic to communicate with the ravens, but he'd done other things too: interacted with the strands of the Geometry in silent ways that made the ravens into patterns against the sky. She looked at the sky with the Geometric Sight, saw the birds high above weaving through the tangled lines of magic. They were as distant as Corbin himself.

Marley muttered, "What do I do?" She had to do *something*: run or scream or cry or engage in strange, reckless magic. The panic clawed at the edges of her mind.

"Call," suggested the raven.

"Come here," said Marley hopefully, but the raven on her hand clicked at her and all the birds above ignored her. No, that wasn't it.

She fumbled out her phone instead, swiped through its screens, feeling more and more anxious. Titan One loomed behind her. She *had* to get away. The shadow of Senyaza was oppressive, along with the secrets of her own heritage. Corbin had grown up under that weight, with a family that had known everything and always wanted more.

She found a notepad app she could scribble on, and sketched out a sky pattern she remembered from before, then showed it to the raven. It tilted its head and clicked again.

Marley looked at it herself and then adjusted one line. She stared at it until it seemed burned on her retinas. Then she looked into the sky and saw the same pattern above, highlighted against the general tangle. It was an illusion, but it was all she had.

She couldn't do anything.

Furiously, she pushed her mind into the pattern she'd envisioned, then flung her magic after it. It was a net, it was her soul, it was, inescapably, her. No secrets, no lies, just her.

The raven cried, and the flock descended.

Once again Marley broke into shards of herself. On a dozen pairs of wings, she passed through the sky and the sky passed through her. For a breathless magical time she felt like she'd left the pain in her heart behind. It didn't matter what she couldn't fix or heal, it didn't matter what she couldn't avoid. The waiting future was only light and sound and all of it was wonderful. In the tangle of the flight she could feel Corbin's warmth again. She realized that the ravens *had* come to help her: not explicitly sent by Corbin, but they knew his ways and feelings. They wanted to take care of her for him. And they wanted her to take care of them, and him, so maybe someday it would all be better again.

She came back to herself again, standing on her feet. She wasn't at the park where she'd left her car the day before and she looked around, confused. Had her car been moved? This place was familiar—

It was home. The little ranch house her family had moved to the year she'd started college, so her brother could go to the right high school. She'd never lived there herself, but she recognized the plants on the porch, her brother's bike left out for anybody to steal, her mother's old car in the driveway.

The ravens landed around her as her suddenly wobbly knees gave way. Then she climbed back to her feet and ran to the house as her mother opened the door to look out. She barely made it into her mother's arms before the tears came. Corbin's ravens hadn't brought her to her car. They'd taken her where she needed to be, instead. Puzzled, but there, always there, her mother opened her arms and welcomed her home.

21
BRANWYN

After Marley was out of the way, Branwyn leaned back, studying Mr. Black coldly. "Hadraniel didn't have a tetherable vessel until that little celestial spat this morning. If he does show up at your gala and you manage to tether him, remember that you owe that to me."

"But you hope we won't," said Mr. Black, tilting his drink this way and that. "Why is that?"

Simon winced and then covered his face like he was watching a slasher film.

Branwyn shrugged. "Let's just say I'm having a hard time feeling the Senyaza difference right now."

As if she hadn't said anything, Mr. Black said thoughtfully, "Maybe you could do something to restrain Corbin. Build us another cage."

Skadi stirred and pulled the puzzle box closer to her. "You'll have to find another jailor if you do. I'm done, Black. I've spent too much time sitting on the chest of the virus for you as it is."

"It won't be a concern because I'm not going to build a cage for you," snapped Branwyn.

Mr. Black looked disappointed. "Can't you?"

Even as frustrated as she was, Branwyn could spare a moment to marvel at how Mr. Black just wasn't getting it. "It's not a matter of 'can', it's a matter of 'won't'. I'm starting to think it was a mistake to ever work for you."

"A pity you did your first work uninvited, then," said Mr. Black pleasantly. "If you'd like to abandon your works in progress, I dare say we'll rub along without paying your fees. Though I thought I heard something about your expenses increasing dramatically lately. Something about sending your sister to private school?"

Branwyn's irritation faded away, drowning in the still, icy pool of her rage. Her phone chirping with the sound she'd assigned messages from Titanone hardly penetrated her fury at first. Skadi pushed her chair away and stood, hugging the puzzle box and almost losing her balance as she did so. "Come on, Simon," she said. "Got a big night ahead of us."

Simon came around the table to support her. "You're a quick study," he muttered.

"Centuries of experience, my love," she said and dragged him away from the table. Both of them avoided looking at Branwyn as they left, like they didn't want to attract her attention.

Maybe that was a good idea.

She looked at her phone.

You don't want to work on me anymore?

It didn't help. She pushed the phone aside. It wasn't a discussion to have in the mood she was in. Her grandmother could reassure a child even when she was mad enough to spit nails. Branwyn had never learned that skill.

The lights in the bar flickered. The air conditioning kicked up to turbo and the phone chirped again. Branwyn massaged her forehead.

"You have been treating Titan One like a person," Mr. Black observed. "And so you must deal with something that thinks it's a person. I suppose it is the tendency of your magic, but you would do well to cultivate the skill of treating tools as what they are."

"What exactly is the difference between Corbin and Titanone to you?"

He sipped his drink, unflappable. "My daughter nursed Corbin when he was an infant."

"And your daughter? Is she a tool too?" Branwyn pressed. Her phone chirped again and the room got steadily colder.

Mr. Black smiled faintly at his drink. "Not for a long time." He shifted his grip, looked at the fog of his fingerprints on the glass, and then said sharply, "Branwyn and I are talking, Titan One. Stop this foolish tantrum or there will be consequences."

"Isn't there a bar across the street?" Branwyn asked. "You didn't have to stay in here." Mr. Black didn't answer and Branwyn narrowed her eyes. "You did. You *are* afraid of Hadraniel."

"Not within our fortress, I'm not." He drained his drink and rose to his feet. "Don't do anything stupid, Miss Lennox. Things are working right now, with one wrinkle. And that wrinkle needn't impact you at all. Tend to your creations, deposit your generous fees and eventually understanding will find you." He spun, perfectly steady, and walked away. As he did, the air conditioning slackened.

Branwyn watched Mr. Black until he left the bar, then moved to one of the armchairs near the wall, turned it around, kicked off her shoes and put her bare feet on the wall.

He made me watch videos of wrecking balls and earthquakes and airplanes, whispered Titanone.

"Did they scare you?" asked Branwyn, focusing her attention on the node network she'd built and woken up. It stretched above her and below her, like a giant, limited version of a human's

Geometric structure. One node was down in the Repository and another drifted near Mr. Black's office, while the third was up near the pinnacle of the skyscraper. They were connected by dozens and dozens of strands, and Titanone's sentience flowed up and down those connections.

I think so, said Titanone hesitantly. *But it's not the same as how I feel when I think you're going to stop visiting me. I thought that was fear, too.*

"What did you do to Leonard?" asked Branwyn.

Nothing.

Branwyn tapped her foot against the wall. "You might as well tell me."

He wanted me to watch people so I started watching him. All the time. And telling him what I saw. I thought other people might want to see what I saw too. So I got ready to do that.

A smile curved Branwyn's mouth despite her bad mood. "Did you want him to go away?"

Yes. He wouldn't answer my questions. And he was so bossy. You're not answering my questions right now either.

"You'll have to do more than just report on what I'm doing to get me to go away, Titanone. I get spied on constantly anyhow."

Oh. But I don't want you to go away. I want you to tell me you won't go away.

"I won't go away," said Branwyn, casually offering what might easily turn into a lie. Sometimes there was nothing else to do with children.

Why are you and Mr. Black fighting?

Because he doesn't understand the difference between tools and people. Branwyn stretched out her consciousness until she felt thin, until she could feel Titanone's thoughts racing up and down the Geometry lines like they were moving across her own skin.

What is the difference? There's a big argument on Wikipedia about personhood and the faeries. Are they people?

Yes, said Branwyn fiercely. *People and individuals. And so are you.*

That doesn't explain much, said Titanone reproachfully.

A person is a self-aware identity that is born and… She hesitated and touched the node where Titanone had started. *And has the capacity to someday end.*

Oh, said Titanone. He was silent for a moment, digesting the idea. *I'll go update the Wikipedia page.*

Branwyn didn't really think it was a good idea for Titanone to go around updating Wikipedia pages but it was a drop in in a very deep bucket of trouble. She was the oldest of seven children and she'd watched most of her brothers and sisters grow up. They'd matured at different rates, but all of them had started out smaller than her parents and grandparents and that had been important when they'd hit and kicked and thrown their toys.

So far Titanone hadn't had a full-on tantrum. It was only a matter of time though, especially if he regarded Branwyn as his mother. But Branwyn didn't have a lot of options for picking up Titanone and carrying him to his room. She knew, rationally, that showing the skyscraper spirit videos of wrecking balls and earthquakes was Mr. Black's attempt to keep Titanone in line, but it was a despicable approach.

She'd acted without thinking when she'd created Titanone, drunk on her own power and only thinking of her short-term benefit. She'd hardly been able to imagine the consequences, though. Who could have anticipated the ability to bring a high tech networked skyscraper to life? They didn't really teach about that in Health and Human Sexuality.

It was tempting to believe that the world just wasn't ready for Titanone. It was *obvious* that Titanone was far more of a threat than any human child. And if Mr. Black had his way, Titanone would become even more dangerous, nothing but a weapon in his arsenal against celestials and the federal government and maybe even his own people.

All he'd wanted her for was to make weapons. She'd thought the portal was a tool, and that Titanone was a marvel but like her hammer, tools and weapons merged in the end. She'd made her hammer to defend herself, and Senyaza was doing the same thing on a massive scale.

But her hammer wasn't a *person*. Not yet, anyhow. And she wasn't using it to spy on other people.

Titanone asked, *What about property? Am I property?*

Branwyn said, *Property is a legal term and I think technically you are. You belong to Senyaza Corporation.*

Hmm, said Titanone slowly. *Maybe that's why somebody keeps trying to hack me. I think it should be the other way around though, don't you? You're all so small and soft. They need me to do things for them. Like they're my pets. Pets are property, right?*

Branwyn looked at the nodes again. If she went to the Repository, she could undo what she'd started. Destroy the node she'd created there and sever the connection between the other two. The flow of thoughts would be interrupted and Titanone would become Titan One again, preserved against corruption and monstrousness.

Even pets deserve respect and consideration. Be kind when you can.

She couldn't do it. It would make things easier. It might even be the right thing to do from a wider perspective, given the influence of Mr. Black and Senyaza's dubious moral core. But she couldn't. She couldn't even analyze why. She couldn't get that close to it.

I get bored sometimes when nobody will talk to me. And they keep reverting my edits on Wikipedia. If I make Mr. Black approve giving you more money will you be around more?

No, said Branwyn firmly. *Money can't solve this.*

Well, what can? The thoughts thrummed against her skin like a pout.

Time. Time and experience. That's all that can be done.

That doesn't make any sense, complained Titanone. *Time and experience will make you play with me more?*

They will make you grow steadier in yourself, my dear.

Do you think there's anything else out there like me? Not human, not faerie, not angels?

Branwyn blinked. *I don't know. There are other myths. Gods turned themselves into pretty weird things. And there's stuff older than gods in some stories. I can't even guess what's real these days.*

More reading on Wikipedia? The spirit sounded glum.

Someday. But tonight—you'll be entertained in other ways tonight, I think.

The gala, said Titanone, brightening. *I'm looking forward to that. I'm going to play with the lights. Everybody will be impressed.*

Can you show me your plan? Branwyn spent just enough time discussing the light show Titanone had developed with Mr. Black and Leonard to leave the spirit feeling comfortable, then pulled away with, *Time to go get ready!*

It was work remaining positive, though, and she was glad to get away. Beating constantly at the back of her mind was the constant doubt that she was making the right decision. It was useless. It didn't matter if she was obligated to take Titanone away from Senyaza, no matter the cost to herself or the tower. Because whether it was her duty or not, she couldn't do it, and that was that.

Marley hadn't taken Branwyn's car, which *was* a surprise, no really. Branwyn called Penny again and Marley wasn't with her either. When Marley's phone went direct to voicemail, Branwyn groaned and dropped her head into hands, then started pacing in a circle in front of the building. Penny showed up while she was trying frantically to figure out another search and rescue.

"Haven't you found her yet?" Penny looked cool and polished

and ready for anything. Ready for anything was probably good.

Branwyn gave Penny a red-eyed glare and slid into her car. The back seat was full of dresses. "I usually try to limit myself to one extraction per day."

Penny said sympathetically, "Yeah, that can be hard. Hmm. Well, why did she run off without you?"

"Mr. Black was an asshole. And so was I." Branwyn summed up most of the rest of the conversation in the Senyaza bar.

"Upset, okay." Penny ticked people off on her fingers. "Not me, not you. Obviously. Not Corbin, he upsets her too. Did you call Zachariah?"

"Do I have to?"

Penny considered. "Not unless we can't find her anywhere else. If she's not with him, he'll just make it worse." She looked up and down the street speculatively. Then her face cleared. "Oh. Her mother."

Branwyn blinked and then dialed Madeline Claviger. Marley answered. "Branwyn? Oh, my phone died..."

"Yes, next time Corbin kidnaps you make sure he charges your phone while you're unconscious. Marley, you are such a—"

"I'm so sorry! I *had* to get away. Everybody was—"

"Yeah. I was. I'm sorry." Branwyn paused and then added, "I'm glad you ended up somewhere safe this time."

Marley was quiet for a moment. "I guess it was."

"Just stay there. We're coming to get you," Branwyn ordered.

"I don't have a car anyhow."

"I am shocked. How unexpected. You are terrible about getting yourself into situations you can't extract yourself from, you know that?"

"Yes," said Marley meekly.

"Let me talk to your mother."

"Why?"

"Because I am going to tell her to glue you to your chair so we can come and put you in a pretty dress and take you to this party and you can stop your idiot boyfriend from getting shot. I think without the glue you'd probably run off after faeries or something."

"That was you," pointed out Marley with delicacy.

"You shut your mouth," said Branwyn, suddenly feeling better. "We'll see you in twenty minutes." She hung up.

Penny said, "How exactly are we going to stop Corbin from getting shot?"

"Marley will kiss him or something. It'll be very sweet and then we'll all jump on him and kick the bad out of him. There will be a cloud of dust and everything, just like in the cartoons."

"I don't think you're taking this very seriously," said Penny reproachfully.

Branwyn shrugged. "I'm pretty angry at Corbin right now. I'm not too happy with Senyaza, either. If this wasn't important to Marley, I'd go home and watch the coverage of the Extraworlder Conference while eating nachos."

Penny sighed. "At least Hadraniel isn't going to be a problem."

"If you believe Mr. Black, anyhow. And that's just for tonight. Not a problem tonight. We still have to deal with it tomorrow. Probably at the Extraworlder Conference." And she thought darkly of Rhianna.

"And the kaiju again too?" Penny's tone was tentative, as if she wasn't sure she wanted to hear the answer.

"God, I hope so," said Branwyn. "Uh, never repeat that."

Startled, Penny said, "Why?"

"Because I have never expected anything good of them. And they have never disappointed me. I'm starting to really like working with people who do exactly what I expect. All I have to do is get to the divinity circuit first."

"Aren't you afraid of them at all? I am, a little, and I'm resistant to them."

Branwyn glanced at Penny, thinking about the question. "I am, but not in any way that's going to stop me from taking back what's mine and doing the right thing with it. I'm not thinking very hard about what's going to happen afterward, though."

"Guess I'll be doing it for all three of us," muttered Penny.

As they arrived at Marley's family's house, Marley came out to the porch. Her eyes and nose were red, but she smiled and waved when they got out of the car. Penny gasped, then commanded, "Get the bags."

Then she rushed up the walk, emitting words like a machine gun. "Marley Claviger what have you done to your face inside right now we need cold washcloths I cannot apply makeup when your face is swollen like that march young lady now!"

Branwyn got the dress bags from the car, grabbed the industrial sized makeup bag from the trunk and strolled up the walkway. Behind Marley, Madeline Claviger appeared and Penny didn't even pause her lecture before incorporating the older woman into it. "Maddy, we're going to have to take over your place for a while. There just isn't time to get back to my place and do all the work we're going to have to do to make those two presentable. And I might need your help. Remember how you used to hem our Halloween costumes? I have some off-the-rack stuff that probably needs some quick tailoring—are you two all right?"

Madeline's eyes were red too. "Marley told me what she'd discovered about her biological mother. She showed me..." She shook her head and put her arms around Marley. "My daughter is amazing, you know."

Marley closed her eyes and leaned her head back against her mother's shoulder and Branwyn almost felt bad about interrupting such a lovely moment.

So did Penny, because she was silent in response. Then she said, "Yes, I know. But she still needs to wash her face. Come on, ladies, we only have a few hours until the gala." She dug out a small notebook from her purse.

Branwyn knew about Penny's notebook. Sometimes she doodled fashion ideas in it. Sometimes she made notes on things she saw in magazines. Sometimes she even cut out images and taped them in. And most of the ideas in the notebook were about dressing Marley and Branwyn. Oh, there were a few other people in there, too. But it was Branwyn and Marley that resisted her despite their intimacy. Every time there'd been a prom or a homecoming or formal gallery show, that notebook had come out.

But it had been almost two years since she'd had an excuse to dominate Branwyn and Marley's wardrobe decisions, and now the bottled up bossiness surged out. She kicked Marley's high-school-aged brother down to the basement games room, said darkly that it was good Marley's father wasn't around to get in the way and made Madeline dig out the sewing machine she hadn't touched in three years. There was no resisting her instructions. Even Neath curled up quietly on the couch after being scolded for nosing through the makeup bag.

She'd brought two dresses for Marley to choose between. The first was a short forest green cocktail dress with a full skirt and a lace bodice. The second was a sheath evening gown in golden silk that made Marley's blue eyes glow. She'd acquired matching shoes, too, golden ones from her own closet that she'd never worn.

"Wow," said Madeline, leaning on the doorframe. "That golden one is amazing. Well spotted, Penny."

Marley looked away from the mirror in the hall and moved her feet tentatively. "I don't think I can run in it. So it'll have to be the green one."

Madeline blinked, but instead of asking why her daughter would be running at a formal affair, said, "That one is pretty, too."

"It looks prettier than she does in it," said Penny, after looking critically between a photo on her phone of Marley in the green dress and real live Marley in the golden dress. "If you wear the golden one you won't have to run anywhere because people will stop what they're doing when you walk past."

Marley snorted. "I don't know if you've noticed how pampered and gorgeous most nephilim are. I'm pretty sure they're immunized against being distracted by women in evening gowns."

"Not this one," said Penny confidently. "Not after I get done with your hair and makeup. We could raise the hem a little?" she added, wheedling. "It wouldn't change the look too much."

Marley looked at herself in the hall mirror again for a long moment. Her fingers slid over the fabric at her hips, touched her hair and the neckline. Branwyn thought she really did look amazing, with her oaken hair and her blue eyes making her look like an incarnate spirit of earth and water rather than something mostly human. Finally she said regretfully, "No. There'll be other occasions."

Penny sighed. "You might as well change out of it and back into the green dress so we can figure out what adjustments need to be made." Then she turned her attention to Branwyn. "What about you?"

Penny had been either less certain, or more hopeful with Branwyn; she'd brought four outfits. Looking at them, Branwyn was inclined to guess 'hopeful', because there'd been one cocktail dress in a jewel-like tone of purple, one formal tuxedo with tails that was almost scandalously feminine, and two sleek suits, one in navy pinstripes and one in charcoal.

Branwyn held up the charcoal suit, the one with the smaller lapels, and Penny looked resigned, nodding. Madeline, though, said, "I want to see you in the sexy tuxedo, Branwyn. You didn't even try it on."

Dubiously Branwyn said, "Do I really seem like a sexy tuxedo kind of girl?"

"Yes," chorused all three of the other women, immediately.

"Yes!" called Marley's brother from downstairs.

"But this is a really nice suit and you picked it out, Penny," protested Branwyn. "It's classy. I like the lapels."

Madeline pushed Branwyn back into the bedroom with the force that only mothers could exert on her. "Just try it on."

Branwyn sighed and did so. When she returned to the front room, the first thing she noticed was Marley's kid brother loitering at the top of the basement stairs. His eyes widened and he whistled, then fled downstairs before Branwyn could even make a fist.

"Ah," said Madeline. "Branwyn, I'm afraid moths have eaten all the other options. You'll have to wear that."

"It makes me look like I forgot to wear a shirt," complained Branwyn, sliding a glance at her profile in the second mirror set up in the front room. She wiggled from foot to foot. "And the pants are really tight."

"The easier to move in," chirped Madeline, circling behind her and poking at one of the seams along her hip.

Marley said, "You look amazing. You should wear it." There was a hungry look in her eyes, like she was determined for somebody to look fantastic if she couldn't.

"I look pretty good in a classy suit, too," Branwyn pointed out. "And people are more likely to treat me professionally, too."

Penny said delicately, "Branwyn… I know you don't like to be objectified. It makes you combative. But I want to point out that *I'm straight* and looking at you in that outfit is kind of like being punched in the face. Whether or not you want to admit it, you're beautiful. It's okay to use that sometimes."

Branwyn hesitated. Of course she wanted to look nice. It had been… well, a while… since she'd wanted somebody to think she was *attractive*, though. She knew some of her male acquaintances were attracted to her even when she was at her worst, which had not encouraged her to do much with her appearance over the last couple of years. It only seemed like it would be inviting trouble.

"I don't know that anybody we'll be meeting tonight will be melting at the sight of a little cleavage. Well. My cleavage." She glanced at Marley.

Penny made a face and shrugged, as if she was giving up.

But Marley wasn't ready to let go. "You have no idea who you're going to meet tonight. And you can't tell me you don't like the idea of shocking people a little. It gives you an edge. You like edges. And you look *so good*, Branwyn."

Penny studied her nails. Marley stared at Branwyn, intense and earnest. And Madeline tugged on Branwyn's waistline and said, "Hmm. I can fix this part."

Branwyn gave up. "Fine. If Madeline can make the pants fit better around my butt, I'll wear it. I'm not wearing those heels you brought, though."

Penny brightened. "I thought maybe you could magic them. Make them into switchblade stilettos."

After thinking about that for a moment, Branwyn said slowly, "Not right now. I wouldn't want to wear shoes that I made without testing." When Penny looked disappointed, she added, "When I magic things in a hurry sometimes there are consequences I'm not ready for. I'm dealing with enough of those right now."

"It's only shoes," Penny muttered. "You'd better not wear those boots or I'm going home right now."

"I have some ballet flats you can borrow, Branwyn," said Madeline. "What are *you* wearing, Penny?"

It was just like working on projects in high school again, with Madeline breaking up disputes and keeping the three younger women focused. Penny unpacked a short white dress with a layered petal-like skirt and wide straps. It was simple, far less expensive than what she'd picked out for Branwyn and Marley, and would look like a million bucks on her. After Madeline had approved it, she gathered up the sewing and went to the other room to get started. Meanwhile, Penny started doing something elegant with Marley's hair.

Branwyn's phone beeped, with an email from Rhianna.

My employer has come to agree that our mutual friend needs to be stopped, even if it requires working with a distasteful element. The item we discussed isn't the only weapon it's co-opted. My employer believes that even if you manage to regain the object you have an interest in, you will be in danger from the other weapons. Call, and he will reclaim them and return them to their rightful place.

Branwyn frowned at her screen. Rhianna and her spy game. *Weapons.* Branwyn supposed she was talking about the Machine Swords. Maybe Hadraniel had stolen Umbriel's Sword, too. Well, if Hadraniel had lost Umbriel's help, that was still a net benefit compared to the last time they'd confronted it. Branwyn thought it was almost funny how Rhianna's boss didn't seem to be very good at hanging onto his possessions.

Except for Rhianna, who seemed ridiculously loyal to him.

That was a bad thought.

Branwyn watched Penny play with Marley's hair for another moment. Then she went to the bedroom where the sewing machine was set up. Madeline was busy with pins and a stitch ripper.

"So she told you?" Branwyn asked.

Madeline gave Branwyn a little smile. "About her magic cat and her thousand year old employer and the man she's in love with?"

Branwyn didn't smile back. "About her own magic, too."

"Oh yes. None of it surprised me very much." She shifted a pin. "Well, the age of this Zachariah did. It's a little hard to imagine being him. But as for the rest... she's always had a little magic about her. A touch of the knowing. You grew up beside her. You noticed, too."

"I learned to listen when she told me she had a bad feeling about something," Branwyn agreed.

"And that cat!" Madeline giggled. "There's no cat like that in the world. She came right through the door."

Branwyn grumbled, "I told Marley she ought to tell you. But she was so afraid you'd disown her."

"Did she say that?" asked Madeline curiously.

"Not in so many words, but I know her. It was like being sophomores in high school again."

"She's never been good at putting herself in my position. I suppose it's because I'm her mother? But from my point of view, she's an angel sent from a Heaven I didn't even believe in so I could have a daughter. I would like very much to thank her biological mother someday. And her father, I suppose," she added conscientiously. "It sounds like it takes two to tango, even for these celestials. I don't think Marley has thought about that much. She's very caught up in the nonhuman part."

Branwyn noticed Neath sitting at the entrance to the room, her ears perked forward, her eyes trained on Madeline. "Beware the cat. She might go for your thread."

"I don't think so." Madeline gave another little smile to the cat. "She just wants to make sure I understand about Marley." Then she transferred her gaze to Branwyn. "But what about you?"

"You already knew about me," began Branwyn.

"You've got something going on with your family," Madeline pointed out. "I can tell with my 'watched you since you were seven' skills."

Branwyn slid down the wall she was leaning against, then stretched out on the floor. "Rhianna's making stupid career choices."

"As younger siblings do," agreed Madeline. "What else?"

Branwyn put her hands over her eyes. "I signed up to pay for my sister's private school. My brother's seminar, too, but that's short-term. I can deal with that. But the private school is expensive. And I don't have enough to do it all up front. But I'm not sure I can keep working for Senyaza. Or the federal government, or anybody who's going to take what I make and use it in a private war. I don't want to be an arms dealer."

"Meredith?" queried Madeline, and when Branwyn nodded, she said, "She's a sweet girl. Found where her talents lay early, too. Not everybody is that lucky." She fell silent and started the sewing machine whirring.

Branwyn imagined the disappointment on Meredith's face if she pulled out of paying for the private school. She'd been refusing to imagine it thus far, because it was horrible to think about breaking her sister's heart for her own integrity. She'd been so blinded by her own success that she hadn't even considered the risks of the situation.

"You have some unique gifts, Branwyn," said Madeline thoughtfully. "I'm sure you could earn money using them some other way."

"When I'm careless with them, there's a risk no matter what I do. And—I'm in demand, Madeline. No false modesty or anything: I've gotten postal inquiries from wizards from the other side of the world, written on fine vellum in ruby ink mixed with powdered diamond. Anybody who thinks powdered diamond is a replacement for glitter ink isn't going to scruple at acquiring something I've made any way they can. The feds used a key meant for opening very small locks to create a weapon and it was promptly stolen. I can't imagine all the possibilities. I'm just me."

"That's tough," agreed Madeline. "Maybe what you need is a patron. You only make what you want and your patron gets the pleasure of inviting you to all his or her parties."

"I don't know," said Branwyn, putting her arm over her eyes. "I don't think it's going to be that easy, though."

"Branwyn, come here!" commanded Penny from the other room.

Branwyn didn't move, though, until Madeline added, "You should go see what she wants. I need to get this sewing done. But swing by and talk again sometime, kiddo. I promise I won't try to steal your ideas."

Branwyn thought about that. Then she rolled to her feet, "You're right. It's not like I'm alone. I do have people I can trust. That matters." And she thought of Corbin, who couldn't trust anybody at all right now, even his own mind.

Then, shaking off the depressing thought, she headed out to see what Penny needed her to do.

22
MARLEY

They ended up leaving Marley's cat and Branwyn's hammer at Madeline's house. Neath was easy; after she had some tuna, she fell into the sleep of a cat who had once again pursued a flock of ravens through a greater metropolitan area. The hammer, however, had been a sticking point. Branwyn had been shocked at the very idea. But Penny had been both horrified and firm. "You can't take a big hammer to a gala, Branwyn! Next time, make a cane or something."

"But I might need it," Branwyn objected.

"If you end up needing a weapon in a party full of nephilim and monster hunters and wizards, we have *already lost.*"

Branwyn winced. "Not as a weapon! As a tool. It's got the Machine fragment I use for half my work."

"Didn't you say Titan One has about two dozen Machine fragments in that treasure vault?" Penny demanded.

"Yeah," said Branwyn, and capitulated.

Senyaza's big party was on the third floor of Titan One, which was still in the commercial open-to-the-public shopping center part of the building. But the venue was behind a wall with a discreet door that Marley had walked past a dozen times without ever noticing. That night there was a red rope around the door and a doorman checking tickets.

Two bulky men in subdued suits stood on either side of the roped off area, scanning the passing crowd. Marley had spotted a few more outside the front entrance to the tower. One of them had recognized her and given her a professional nod, which hadn't really been reassuring.

She knew the ticket checker, though; his day job was working the security desk gating the way into the private part of the building. "Hi, Antonio. They have you working tonight?"

"I volunteered, Miss Claviger. Don't tell Corbin, but I'm worried about him. Ah, and speaking of which, I've got something for you here." He gave her a plastic package. "One of the boys can help you put it on."

It was a security earpiece, with a tiny radio. "Oh," said Marley quietly.

"Come here, miss," said one of the burly guards. "The radio can go, uh." His eyes darted down to her handbag and then her dress.

"Oh, give it to me," said Marley, and tucked it into her cleavage. "Do I really need this? Isn't Titan One listening to everything we say no matter where we are?"

"Protocol, ma'am. More to the point, it lets *us* talk to *you*. Just bend your head this way…" The guard adjusted the hook of the earpiece and tapped on it once. A moment later an impersonal female voice in Marley's ear said, "Claviger online," then walked her through how to activate the radio by both button and voice, finishing with, "I am Control. You are agent Four, and hopefully your services won't be required tonight."

By the time she was done, both Branwyn and Penny were

standing just inside the open door, chatting with Antonio. A few others had gathered waiting for their tickets to be scanned. Alejandro was there, with an attractive young man in a white suit beside him.

Marley couldn't help herself. She looked, and wished she hadn't, because with her danger-sight, the blood was everywhere. There was more on Alejandro now, and only a bit on his friend in the white suit.

She looked away as Alejandro stopped near her. "Ah, well," he murmured. "Shall I report to first aid as soon as the evening begins?"

"I don't know," said Marley stiffly. She moved over to the door behind Antonio, and then looked back at Alejandro. "Leave. It's the only way to be safe."

And he considered it. She could see that he really considered it. The wheel of fate spun over his head and the shadows flickered on his figure. But when it stopped, he'd decided to stay. "It's not the only way," he said gently. "You're here."

"I can't protect everybody," she said wretchedly.

"Well, we will all protect each other. But first, we will enjoy ourselves, eh? And it won't be as bad as you fear. Ah, good evening, Branwyn." And Alejandro and his date passed through the door ahead of Marley.

"Come on," said Branwyn impatiently. "I need to find a good place to check in with Titanone." She stepped through the still-open door and Marley and Penny followed her.

There was an enormous lobby beyond the door. A pair of grand double doors on the far side of the lobby opened to a glittering ballroom but the lobby itself was just a space for guests to wait for doors to open, or have a quiet conversation away from the crowd. One long wall had a series of screens, each one displaying a different stream of Senyaza accomplishments. The other one was a long window overlooking the open central column of the mall, where the escalators ran.

Marley had seen that from outside, too. It was just a mirror from below. But from here she could just make out the main entrance of the shopping center. It was an excellent view and she wished it made her feel better. She followed the window along until it met the corner and turned, becoming a view of the street below. She scanned the street and frowned at what she saw: a familiar silhouette, leaning against the building across the street. Not Corbin. Severin.

"You don't need to stay in the lobby," Control assured her through the earpiece. "We'll notify you if and when Corbin approaches."

"Come on," said Penny, who had followed her. "It's a very nice lobby. Let's go see the main event. Let's go show the main event *us*." She dragged Marley away from the window and together all three of them went into the Senyaza gala.

The ballroom had been beautifully decorated with black and silver. There was a buffet along one wall and small tables along two more, with a stage occupying the fourth. People milled around the room, holding drinks and dressed to the nines. Marley had no idea who most of them were, but nearly all of them were dressed spectacularly. Tails and top hats were on display, and there were full ball gowns that looked like they'd been preserved from Victorian times. She spotted a kilt, and an ornate ceremonial kimono, and something in white that she didn't recognize. Her little green dress was drab in comparison and she felt even the golden full-length evening gown would scarcely have been acceptable.

But Branwyn was getting attention, at least. People turned and looked at her. Marley was smug, until Branwyn muttered, "Penny, I think we're the only humans here."

"No," said Penny crisply. "Some of the waiters are human, see?"

"I'll take your word for it," said Branwyn. "They're still *staring* at us."

"We're special." Penny shrugged, the movement rippling through her shoulders and down her form. She smiled a moment later. "Let's go talk to that woman in the kimono. Isn't it gorgeous? I think there's something magical about her obi."

Branwyn narrowed her eyes, peering at the woman in the kimono as she drifted that direction. Penny caught Marley's eyes and gave her a reassuring smile, then followed Branwyn.

As soon as they moved away, it was like Marley had disappeared from the room. Nobody paid any attention to her. She saw Alejandro inspecting the buffet, and a few other faces she vaguely recognized, but nobody she was excited to talk to. What she really wanted to do was go right back out to the window and look for Corbin.

"You look lost, little lady," said a gruff, familiar voice. She turned to find Grendel the monster hunter looming over her. He'd made a token attempt to clean himself up and somebody had poured him into a stark black and white suit with a half-buttoned jacket, no vest and a clip-on bow tie.

"I suppose you would be here," said Marley and sighed.

"Well, it's a Senyaza party," said Grendel, grinning. "Didn't Mr. Black tell you that there was nothing to worry about tonight?"

"No," said Marley tartly. "He told me Corbin would be coming. I'd expect you to be worrying about that given the last time you met him."

"Nah, I never worry. It doesn't help. Kind of hurts me, actually."

Marley gave him a frigid look. "That must be nice."

"Aww, you don't need to fret. At least not until he shows up and even then, there's a lot of people here to stop him from causing a ruckus. And hey, there'll be dancing later after the speeches." The giant man gave a little shimmy and tapped his feet.

"I'm glad to see your priorities are in order," snapped Marley, and looked for Mr. Black. She spotted him in a group of nephilim she didn't recognize, and she couldn't catch his eye.

Grendel chuckled. "Everything's locked down tight. Not even your celestial cat can get in here right now, lady. If that doesn't reassure you, I guess nothing will. The speeches are usually dull things. What we've done over the past year, what we'll be doing. Boring stuff. Though Branwyn's going to introduce Titanone this time, isn't she?"

Marley spotted Branwyn in the growing crowd, sitting on the edge of the stage having an intent conversation with one of the stagehands lurking there. Penny was still talking to the woman in the kimono and the man in the kilt had joined them. "When do the speeches start?"

"They usually give everybody an hour to arrive…" He trailed off, distracted by somebody in the throng. "Hey, come on, I'll introduce you to some nice people."

Marley's irritation faded. The monster hunter was trying to be kind to her. It was impossible not to be touched. "Thanks, but not right now. I can't *stop* from worrying." She tried to lighten it. "But that's better for everybody."

"Maybe," he said, but he sounded like he didn't believe it. "Well, don't hesitate to come say hi if you get bored biting your nails." He strolled off, toward a clump of uniformly short women.

Marley sighed and went over to the buffet, passing several abstract ice sculptures arranged on tables as she did. The monster hunter Ice was inspecting one of them. He nodded at her as she walked by, but returned to frowning at the sculpture when she didn't stop to chat.

The spread at the buffet was unsurprisingly lavish. Marley picked at shrimp and crab Rangoon and stuffed mushrooms and delicate little cookies. She kept running through arguments that might get Corbin to pause and reconsider whatever he was planning. Each time she ran up against the cold hard iceberg that it didn't matter what arguments she used: there was no way to cure Corbin of the virus. Skadi had tried and failed, and the virus itself had told her that Corbin's magic was clinging to the virus, weaving the two of them together closer and closer.

The only problem with that, whispered the back of her mind, *is that he's contagious.*

The thought was so startling that Marley stopped chewing her cookie. Was that true?

She realized it was. Corbin was erratic now, but he was still, most of the time, Corbin. He just had new scars. If he wasn't contagious, if he wasn't endangering others, she could cope with the virus he'd contracted, along with everything else that had changed. It wouldn't be easy, but for Corbin she was willing to make the effort.

She remembered her mother saying, *Yeah, you were a pain in the ass in high school. But for you I was willing to make the effort.*

Her gaze fell on a figure on the other side of the room, standing a little apart from a group. It was Elizabeth Black-Adair. Corbin's mother. She wore dark slacks and a black sleeveless blouse: positively underdressed for the occasion. She met Marley's eyes, and held them. After only a few seconds, Marley picked her way across the room. When she arrived at Elizabeth's side, the other woman gave her a reserved nod.

"You're not wearing a radio," Marley blurted out.

Elizabeth's gaze flickered to Marley's own radio. Then she shook her head. "No. I wouldn't be useful in stopping Corbin tonight. It would only irritate him further." She rubbed her arms.

Marley remembered the virus, alleging that Corbin's own mother found him unlovable. "Did you support infecting Corbin with the virus?"

A grim, humorless smile flickered on Elizabeth's face. "My father and the elder council saw no reason to consult me."

Hope flaring against the swirling mix of anger and frustration, Marley said, "But you wouldn't have if they'd asked? You're his mother. You can't have wanted him to be hurt like this."

Elizabeth gave her a darkly amused look. "Everybody expects so much of mothers. So much righteousness."

The ember of hope faded to blackness. "You don't care, then. He's just a tool to you, too." Wildly, she wished she had a drink, so she could throw it at Elizabeth.

Elizabeth's small hand clenched into a fist. "I had a child because I wanted one, Miss Claviger. My husband and I both wanted one. We didn't know what it would do to Aedrian. I reached a point where I had to choose between my husband's needs and my child's. But I'd already chosen my husband long before, and there were others who could tend to Corbin. And then..." She looked down. "Time passed." She shrugged. "It always does. I hoped he might eventually find another who would choose him first, and after that he would be able to forgive *me*."

Elizabeth didn't have a drink either, but her words were a splash in Marley's face all the same. She knew too well about hard choices. She was too familiar with hoping Corbin could wait while she sorted out her emotions. She had *no room* to judge Elizabeth.

The other woman's eyes flicked up to her again. "So. No radio. But if he makes it through every other barrier, I will go to him and see what can be done."

Numbly, Marley asked, "Their power is secrets. How could your husband not have known what would happen if he had a child of his own? How could he have been so unprepared?"

Elizabeth blinked. "Oh, well. It came to him upon the death of his father. The gift wants to be passed on. It hid its true nature from him. The power is secrets, and it keeps its own, especially related to itself."

Marley frowned. "Oh." She turned away and then turned back. "I have to think about that."

Elizabeth shrugged, looking at her with obvious curiosity. "Of course. But if it ends up mattering, Miss Claviger? I *do* love Corbin. So does Aedrian. So does my father. If we didn't none of this would be so difficult."

Marley nodded as she turned away. She knew. Love was complicated. It made things hard, not easy. She remembered being in Corbin's arms, and thought, *It makes things worth it.*

She went to the windows on the far side of the ballroom. When she'd looked out before, she'd seen a familiar shape on the sidewalk across the street. Severin was still there, leaning against a storefront, his arms crossed over his chest, his face turned toward the entrance of the building.

Marley wondered if Branwyn knew. Probably not. She probably would have said something cranky. Or did she want him there? Marley could no longer quite tell. And after spending so much time with Corbin, Marley didn't feel like she was in a good position to be warning Branwyn about dangerous connections. Branwyn already knew, anyhow. That was usually the problem.

Besides. Marley had played it safe and slow over the past year and in retrospect she wasn't sure she'd recommend that to anybody.

Severin glanced up, directly at her window, at the exact same time the voice in her ear said, "Corbin incoming through the south shopping plaza entrance. He's walking right toward you, Twelve."

Marley straightened her shoulders and ran her hands over her skirt, then hurried across the ballroom. Both Grendel and Branwyn noticed and moved to intercept her; Branwyn got there first, when Marley was almost at the exit to the lobby.

The voice in Marley's ear said, "Twelve bypassed. He has a stealth charm engaged, Eleven. Countermeasures activated."

"I can see him," said a second voice. It was childlike in both its excitement and its pitch. "Here, let me show you."

"Er. Thank you," said the ear voice, surprised. "Uh, who is this?"

"Titanone," said the childlike voice happily.

Marley stepped into the lobby and stopped. Every screen on the far side of the room was displaying Corbin, from a half-dozen different angles, as he made his way through the sparsely populated evening shopping levels. One of the suited guards, wearing sunglasses, beelined for Corbin. But Corbin, crossing the south gallery with long strides, didn't hesitate as he flung out his hand. The guard stumbled and fell to his knees, retching.

"Eleven bypassed. Approaching Escalator C, Ten."

Grendel fought free of the crowds and emerged from the ballroom. "You need to stay up here, lady. The lobby is fine but if you go beyond things are going to get confusing."

"I know what to do," said Titanone cheerfully, and on the screen all of the escalators stopped.

"I think that's already happened," said Marley, moving closer to the screens. "Branwyn, Titanone is talking on the radio. He just stopped the escalators, which I don't think was part of the plan."

Branwyn's eyes widened and she ran to one of the columns in the lobby, slapping her hands on it. Meanwhile, Corbin climbed up the frozen escalator, pushing his way past the confused shoppers.

"Hey, he's climbing up the escalator. He's not supposed to do that," complained Titanone. The lights in the shopping center flickered and then went out.

"Turn the lights back on!" said Control sharply. Muffled screaming came from beyond the walls and then got louder as Antonio opened the door between the lobby and the rest of the shopping center.

"Say please," said Titanone sulkily.

Branwyn said, "Titanone—" then shook her head and dragged one hand down the pillar. The emergency lights came back up, but the screaming didn't stop. The screens flickered with angry static, still focused on the escalator, which was mostly a strip of lights obscured by moving silhouettes.

Control said, "Reacquiring target's location…."

"You lost him?" blurted Marley and then was glad she didn't have the radio set to broadcast everything she said.

"Hard to track by cameras in the dark, lady." Grendel cracked his knuckles and glanced at the rest of the monster hunters who had come to the door.

"What number are you?" asked Marley, her gaze returning to the screen.

"Aw, we're not in the queue. Not unless things get really bad, and Grandpa Black don't think that will happen. The old man's soft on the kid."

"He's in the emergency staircase," said Titanone sullenly. "I've turned the lights off there but I can feel him still climbing. He's past the third floor now."

"Agent Six, the stairs. Agent Four, come to corporate reception," snapped Control. "Four, bring Antonio and Grendel."

Marley, every muscle tensed for her cue, almost missed it until Control repeated, "Four! And tell the Artificer that if she can babysit her project, that would be appreciated."

She was Four. "Branwyn—"

"Doing what I can. Maybe I can figure out a way for Titanone to be actually helpful."

"Will the elevators work?"

"Yours will. Go."

Marley nodded. "Grendel, you're wanted upstairs. You too, Antonio." The doorman nodded, rubbed his hands together and then handed his equipment to one of the guards.

Control directed Marley to the nearest upper floor elevator. She ran through the dim open spaces of the third floor, noticing how empty it already was. There were crowds at the escalators and broad staircases as the remaining shoppers worked on escaping the malfunctioning building. Voices over the loudspeakers advised both calm and evacuation, citing the early closure of the mall.

They should have done that hours ago, thought Marley, and then she was in the elevator with Grendel and Antonio. "Agent Six, whoever that is, is in the stairwell after Corbin. We're going to your station, Antonio."

"Ah," he said, and stared at the wall for a moment. "I am Three."

"I ain't shit, so why am I here?" asked Grendel, putting on the earpiece he'd picked up at some point. "Not that I'm complaining."

"Our plans were disrupted by unexpected activity from the host structure," said Control crisply. "Now we're improvising."

The elevator door opened, revealing the desk and security checkpoint where Antonio worked during the days. Everything seemed normal: power and lights were both on. Antonio immediately headed over to the station, ordering the duty officer out of the way and pawing at the computer keyboard.

"Agent Six has been disabled. Ready yourself, Four."

Marley looked around helplessly. Normally, she'd put her protection on somebody now, but what good would that do?

Then the stairwell door opened and Corbin stepped quietly out. He had a messenger bag over his shoulder and something small and oblong in his hand.

"Corbin," said Marley sharply, stepping forward.

He glanced at her as he tucked the oblong shape into his pocket. "I just can't get away from you, can I?"

"You knew I'd be here." She walked toward him carefully,

activating her magical Sight.

"It couldn't be helped. But if you stay out of the way, you should be safe." He leaned against the wall as if waiting for something, his eyes flicking beyond her to where Antonio and the others waited. They were muttering to each other.

"What are you doing here? You told your grandfather you were coming to the party. That's down a floor."

He chuckled. It wasn't a nice sound. "And he didn't have me shot. I'm a little curious about that."

Marley twisted her fingers together. "He told me they infected you on purpose. That you refused to use your magic in ways they needed."

"And now I am," he said coolly. "I hope he's proud." He stood there looking at her, his hands in his pockets, as if he had nothing else to say.

Behind Marley, Antonio muttered, "He *is* doing something—"

His assistant said, "The system isn't responding. Compromised—"

She didn't feel like she was breathing right. "Did you come here to infect others? I don't believe that. They're all talking about how you're basically a walking bomb, and they're trying not to shoot you but they really—"

"And they brought you in for that purpose. They think I'm here to kill them and they threw you between them and me so they wouldn't have to deal with the consequences themselves. That makes me wish I was here for exactly the reason they believe."

"I would have inserted myself," admitted Marley, moving closer. His eyes widened and she realized his shoulders were taut with tension.

"I wish—" he said hoarsely.

"I know," she said. She thought about what he'd said, what he'd done. He hadn't gone to the gala level, hadn't pushed his way deeper into the corporate level. Whatever he was doing there didn't involve spreading his virus, didn't involve any kind of horrible acts of terrorism.

Maybe he'd just come to see if they would shoot him. Maybe he'd come to see if they cared.

That was sweet but Marley didn't think it was true. It might have been why he warned his grandfather, but he'd been working on something all along, not just sulking over how his family had misused him.

The lights flickered and Corbin glanced up at them.

On the headset, Titanone said, "I don't..." and trailed off.

"I talked to the virus," began Marley. "It told me some things. It told me about Skadi. And it told me about you. Do you know why it didn't kill you, and why Skadi couldn't cure it?"

"No," he said, distracted by the flickering lights. "I doubt she tried very hard."

"Ignore the lights. It's just Titanone playing around. Corbin— the virus is celestial. Kin to whatever you've already got in you. It's related to your own intrinsic magic. Skadi couldn't cure you for the same reason that you're alive and functional. Somehow they're the same kind of thing." She moved close enough to put her hand on his chest and he jerked and looked at her face.

"Stay away," he said quietly.

"No," she said. "No, not anymore. *Listen* to me, Corbin. Your own magic, whatever you inherited from your father, that's what's holding onto the virus. They wanted you to find out information, right?"

"Sometimes," he whispered, "If I'm willing to lose myself, it feels like I could know anything. But it's a lie. When I look too deep, it takes me away. Some secrets cost too much. I become something else. And I'm still trying to clean up the consequences."

Marley's fingers clenched in his shirt. "You found out how to block my magic. You could find out how to cure yourself. You could find out what you are. The answers are inside you."

"I don't—" He stopped, his eyes widening. "Anything could happen. I can't get any closer without going *away*, Marley. And I've fought so hard to stay."

Marley exhaled. "All right. I don't care. We can go away somewhere, away from all the others, until we find a different cure. Or maybe you're never cured. I don't care."

His eyes widened and then narrowed. "What about Zachariah and the twins?"

She was quiet a moment. "I've been stuck on my own magic lately. On what I inherited from my birth mother. On how it defined me. I wouldn't tell my real mother, and I should have. Because she knows that what we're truly defined by is what we hold on to even when it's hard. I thought loving somebody meant it would be easy. I thought because it *wasn't* easy that I didn't know what I wanted. But it's not about whether or not it's easy. It's about whether it's worth the trouble." She searched his face. "I'm holding on to you. And you're worth it."

"You care for them, too. I know you do." He frowned, as if genuinely puzzled.

She shrugged and ran her hands up his chest to rest on his face. "Love is complicated and sticky and painful."

His jaw tightened. "I love you," he said roughly.

Then his eyes flickered closed and he *changed*. At first it was just as she'd seen him change in the past. One eye became a black pit while the other glowed blue. This she'd seen before: he stood at the edge of an ocean, the surf rolling over his feet. He never liked going into this state but he did and would, for an authority he couldn't access on his own.

But the *change* grew. His shadow, and the other shadows too, birthed ravens. The birds pulled themselves free of clinging darkness, shaking out their wings. The reception area grew claustrophobic as the space filled with black shapes. The dusty scent of the grave drifted on a cold breeze and Marley started feeling decidedly odd herself. Corbin's face under her palms wasn't flesh any longer, but something finer, thinner, older.

Something ancient looked at her with that single blue eye, so cold and far away that she wanted to pull back her hands. It seemed profane to touch Corbin now.

She slid her arms around his neck instead and pressed her forehead against his shoulder, whispering, "Find the cure and come back to me."

"You're wrong," he said. His voice was deep and old, with echoes emerging from the shadows as if they were depths. "You thought you could hold onto him, but you have no idea. I can swallow that which was Corbin as if he were spun from sugar."

Terror shot down Marley's spine and she lifted her head. "Virus?" she queried. And she didn't let go.

"Oh, child. I am the virus's older brother. When what you call the virus invaded this flesh's cells I was already here. I've been here since my last son drew breath. Your 'virus' never had a chance."

Marley didn't understand. She knew she might later, if she thought about it and looked in some books, but she also knew in her bones that understanding didn't matter right now. "Go away. Give Corbin back."

"Mmm? Eventually, perhaps. I have some things to consider. The world has changed since I last looked at it myself…" His gaze lifted to the walls, focused on something only he could see.

"Now!" said Marley sharply. 'Eventually' could mean a decade from now.

"Ah, but child, you wanted me here. You encouraged him to reach for me, to reach past his dams into the deepness."

"I wanted Corbin to learn how to cure his virus," protested Marley. "Not for… whatever you are… to wake up."

"Isn't it uncomfortable?" said the thing looking at her from Corbin's eyes without a mote of sympathy. "You thought you knew Corbin, thought you understood his depths. And yet you know nothing."

The observation burned. Marley spent so much time trying to learn things that Branwyn called her Research Girl. "That's not true. I may not know much but I know more than nothing."

The entity curved Corbin's mouth in a cold smile. "Oh? Then let us play a little game. Show me what you know. Tell me who I am, *what* I am, and I will let Corbin return to you with his answer. You can be together, at least until he calls on me again."

How could I possibly guess? It was asking her to guess a name without even having a phone book. Marley's hands slid down Corbin's arms. She laced her fingers through his. His hands were as cold as ice and hanging loose. But then they curled around her own. She didn't know if that was Corbin or that which lived within him.

She gathered her thoughts. It seemed like an impossible task, especially when set against her fear, but hadn't she thought earlier that she almost understood it? She looked at Corbin's face: at the black pit where one eye was and the ravens behind him. She thought about the virus, which the ancestral entity claimed as brother: confusing, deceptive, with eyes of red and green.

An answer bubbled to the top of her mind but she hesitated. Did her idea fit with an Ettoriel and a Hadraniel and an Umbriel?

Then she remembered Simon mentioning that his father was a Japanese storm god.

She remembered Skadi, and the conversation with the virus itself. She remembered mythology from high school and college.

She said, cautiously, "Odin?"

He didn't respond, with word or expression, but that only made her feel more certain. "And the virus is Loki, I'm sure of it. I don't know why the two of you are… bits of nephilim biology rather than running around the Backworld, but—" She stopped. "You're hiding from something. Maybe whatever stole the names from the faeries?"

"I shall not require you to guess what no mortal can know," said Odin gently. "Well done. I look forward to having you as a mother." Corbin's eyes returned to normal abruptly and the blue glow flared around them both before fading.

Marley checked her recoil at Odin's final words as Corbin sagged toward her. She caught him, lowered him to the ground. "Wait," he mumbled. "Wait, I know how to work the cure. Give me a moment." His hands moved, churning the air, then clutching his head. "Let go," he said feebly. "I have to do—"

Marley let go. Corbin rose to his feet. The ravens still infesting the floor flocked together and the Geometry orbited around him. Then he hopped to the right and left his shadow behind, connected to him by strands of dark webbing.

The shadow writhed and the ravens exploded away from it. Then frost rimed the shadow and it opened red and green eyes.

"Oh, Corbin," it said, in a smokier version of Corbin's own voice. "Don't reject me."

Corbin hunched his shoulders. "Go away."

"But we were so good together. Like old times."

"Bad old times," said Corbin. Marley wanted to cheer him on, but she kept still in case she broke the spell.

The shadow heaved a sigh. "But you're all I have, Corbin. If I go, that's it. Would you do this to me? After all I've done for you? Whatever happened to hanging on?"

Corbin knelt down and started scraping away the webbing connecting him to the shadow. "Go away," he said again. "I'm done with you." He shook his hands, but the goo lingered.

The shadow smiled. "Maybe with me, but what we've done

together will last and last." Corbin shook his head, reached over and tore the shadow apart.

"No!" it said, clutching its throat. "No! No!" The last protest was drawn out, and as it faded away, the magic evaporated and the shadows returned to normal. Corbin slumped to one side. The ravens finished settling on various bits of office furniture, and turned to preening and exploration, unconcerned by Corbin's collapse.

Back at the security desk, Antonio waved at a raven in the way and cleared his throat. "Is he…?"

Antonio's assistant said, "The network is still acting strange."

Marley knelt next to him, observed his breathing, and looked at his aura again. The red glow emanating from his core was gone, and a vast dark injury was sealing over.

"He's alive. And… cured?" She hesitated. "What happened to Loki?" It didn't seem likely that Odin would just let Loki be cured out of existence, not when they'd shared the same host for so long. And the shadow's 'death' had been more melodramatic than she expected. She found herself thinking of briar patches, and how tricksters lied.

Corbin made a noise and rolled over, bumping against Marley's knee. "I need… there was something…." He blinked and shook his head, as if trying to wake up. "I came here to do something. For revenge."

Marley's hands tightened. "Still?" she whispered.

His eyes opened and met her own. "That's why this all started, Marley. Revenge on Hadraniel. I've just expanded it a little. Improved it. They wanted Hadraniel at their mercy. I had to provide appropriate bait. And it turns out they've got exactly the right bait. They never should have left it lying around, so we'll— I'll clean that up, too."

"I—" Marley stopped as Neath stepped delicately through an

outside wall. The big calico cat sauntered past the staircase and stopped to sniff at Corbin's outflung hand. He lifted it to caress her ears.

"That cat is not supposed to be in here," said Antonio abruptly. "Not just walking through walls like that. Not tonight."

Marley stared at Neath. Antonio was right. The magical defenses of Titan One shouldn't have been able to distinguish between Neath, a celestial construct made by Marley's angelic mother, and Hadraniel in his own vessel. How had Neath just wandered in? Something was wrong.

Neath walked across Corbin's chest, stuck her head between Marley's hand and Corbin's shoulder, and purred. And once again, Marley thought of the virus she'd called Loki.

The lights went out, even the emergency lights. The hum of the central air system vanished. With no more warning than a purr, the entire building shut down.

23
BRANWYN

After Marley ran from the room with the others, Branwyn leaned her head against the pillar and *pushed* on Titanone until he had to pay attention to her.

But I want to help. I want to do more than play with colored lights. They call it a laser show but they changed it at the last minute, you know. Titanone was sulky and Branwyn was already tired.

"Just let them run their operation, please. Show me the game you've been playing lately instead."

How about I do both? I think it's weird how humans can only do one thing at once. You even have two of everything. Two hands but you can only do one thing. Two eyes but you can only look at one thing. I was playing a game where somebody was sneaking along in a building like me. Except not awake. And they forgot to put in all sorts of details. My human body couldn't get out of this room without getting shot so I spent a lot of time inspecting the model. At one point I could put my hand right through the walls!

Branwyn listened distractedly, watching the people milling around in the ballroom lobby. Mr. Black had come from the ballroom and placed himself at Antonio's station. A few other Senyaza folk had drifted out. Some were holding plates, while some were very clearly looking for a fight. Somebody in a particularly shiny suit peeked out the door and called, "Black?" and Mr. Black shook his head. The man in the shiny suit said, "I'll stall, then."

Hey! Titanone was suddenly outraged. *Corbin is a hacker. He's trying to hack* me. *Am I supposed to let him do—*

"Titanone?" queried Branwyn, then repeated herself more sharply, focusing her attention on the skyscraper's Geometry and *pushing* for attention as she had before. But red was creeping over the golden glow, and where the red went a black crack followed.

Hee hee hee. Oh, yes. It wasn't Titanone's 'voice'. *Oh and we have a mortal friend. Hello, mortal friend.*

Branwyn clenched her teeth and pulled back to look at the whole system. The third node, the one she'd created to connect Titanone to the Nakotus database, was swollen unevenly. She reached out a spirit hand for it, and recoiled from the heat it radiated. Then she shook her head: the heat was an illusion. This was all an illusion, a mental construct to help her visualize what her magic told her.

She reached for the node again. As soon as she touched it she could see beyond, into the Nakotus system. The vast database didn't have the smooth looping lines and spheres of Titanone: instead it was made of sharp corners and right angles, lined up in regimented rows and laid out on a vast board. Red and green light flickered across the rectangles and pentagons, while guardians composed of triangles and diamonds moved between the rows, oblivious to the danger.

The red light curled up next to Branwyn in the node, muttering. *They have no idea what they've done. Branwyn? Yes, Branwyn. Shh, stay asleep, child of steel and ingenuity, while your mortal looks on.*

"Wake up," Branwyn muttered. "This is bad." She tugged gently on the connections between the three nodes.

The red and green light flickering over the Nakotus board converged on one location and the glow engulfed the rectangle. Branwyn glared at it. If she'd paid more attention to what the programmer had done would she have any idea what was there?

La la la, this and that. It's a shame, but they don't really deserve better.

Branwyn stopped listening. Something had to be done. She was sure this was Corbin's virus, somehow adapted and uploaded into the Nakotus system. And if it was, well, the virus had been cured before. She hadn't decided what to do about the problem Titanone represented and she certainly wasn't going to let this virus decide for her.

Besides, if Titanone was dangerous, how much more dangerous would an infected Titanone be? And it would probably make Mr. Black very unhappy.

The last thought made Branwyn hesitate. It was tempting… But no. She had an obligation to Titanone. So she looked once again at the whole system until the details settled in the back of her head. The virus was adapted for the Nakotus database, and only leaking into Titanone's structure from across the join. The first thing to do was to sever the connection.

She did that. It made her hands hurt to reach into the blazing red, like flicking blades across her palms, but other than the pain it was relatively simple—for her—to just disconnect what she'd once connected.

Then Titanone was only connected to its own computerized systems: lighting, elevators, climate control, things like that, and it was those elements that the virus in Titanone was using as a host for now. But it was shifting, changing, uncurling new elements. It was adapting itself to move beyond the electronics and into the spirit of Titanone. It was moving fast, too. She didn't quite know how to purge it and it was going to finish the job before she could stop it.

"No," said Branwyn. She reached for the glittering silver connection that served as a central nervous system for Titanone and shut the whole building—the electronics, the glowing Geometric connections, *everything*—down. The entity that was Titanone went into stasis, deeper than any human sleep, held there by the pressure of her magic. She hoped he wouldn't have nightmares.

Everything went still and empty for a heartbeat. Branwyn was thrust back into the darkness and noise of the ballroom lobby, where people raised their voices as if that could make up for the lack of light. But then her eyes adjusted and to the light from the windows.

"I think there's time now," muttered Branwyn. "Even for the database. The power went too."

"What's going on, Branwyn?" asked Mr. Black sharply. He was standing right beside her, and she wondered how long he'd been there.

"Nakotus got infected. It was spreading to Titanone. I need to go in and…" she passed her hand over her face. "Where's Skadi?"

"Skadi!" Mr. Black roared, in a voice loud enough to silence the babble and shock the tiredness away from Branwyn. "She will be here shortly," he continued, and his words were calm but hurried. "You must bring Titan One back online immediately. There are things…"

"You called?" said Skadi, appearing behind him. Her blond hair glowed in the city light from the window. She wore a dark blue dress, and one of her legs shimmered white with a colored inlay.

Branwyn stretched her fingers and winced as the tiny abrasions on one of them burned. "I need to cure a virus, Skadi. Tell me how. Quickly."

Skadi hesitated, glancing at Mr. Black, who nodded impatiently. Slowly she said, "I've never managed to teach another how to do it in the practical but the theory is—"

"*Quickly*," repeated Mr. Black.

"Still the virus," said Skadi. Branwyn shook her head in incomprehension and Skadi added, "Bring it to stillness. The creature cannot abide stillness. You must gather it to you and then still it, lull it, freeze it: whatever you can do. Once it is still, it cracks apart, and the fragments are easy for all but the weakest immune system to destroy."

"I'm not sure Titanone has an immune system," muttered Branwyn. So many mistakes, so little time to analyze them.

"You will have to suffice," said Mr. Black. There was a crack from the wall with the window, and the building trembled. "Skadi, stay with her. Advise her if she needs it. Protect her when the time comes."

"What was that?" asked Branwyn.

"Hadraniel, I imagine," said Skadi, calmly.

"Oh. Wasn't Hadraniel absolutely totally not going to be dumb enough to come because you all could kick his ass?"

"It would be very helpful if you would repair Titanone," said Skadi, with a friendly smile.

"Working on that." Branwyn plunged her consciousness back into the spiritual framework of Titanone. It was like stepping into a sealed room: completely dark except for the thin strands of ambient Geometry. But when she concentrated she could see the core nodes of her creation. Nothing ought to be that dark and hard to see; even ordinary objects were connected to the rest of the world by various strands.

She lifted the pressure she'd been maintaining on the connection node and the network flickered back into a natural life: what she could see in any building in the city, save for the big nodes. The red limned a handful of lines, creeping along them.

The floor trembled again and Branwyn felt a groaning vibration through the pillar she leaned against. Two of the lines snapped out of existence and a new one shimmered to life. Then golden light flared around one of the nodes. Hadraniel was trying to place its magic inside Titanone, as it might bless or curse a mortal.

The nodes were already occupied by Geometric charms placed by Branwyn and Mr. Black: protective wards all. And usually that was enough to protect an entity from invasive magic. But Branwyn had seen a Queen of Faerie strip protective charms in a few heartbeats. She concentrated on the node under attack, reinforcing it, tracing a web of strength to swallow the golden light uselessly.

It would have been easier if she'd had her hammer. This was *why* she wanted to bring her hammer. But Penny was right; the Senyaza Repository was right there, and if she had a moment it might be worth running down there for the expanded options that would unlock. Then she'd really be able to fight back, against both the virus and whatever Hadraniel was trying to do.

Three more Geometric strands snapped out of existence and five appeared replacing it, growing in brightness.

"Get back!" shouted Mr. Black. "Away from the door!"

Branwyn opened her eyes. The five new strands overlaid the entrance to the ballroom lobby, partially blocked by Mr. Black. An incandescent figure floated just beyond them, an array of celestial wheels painted on the air behind it. At first it seemed to be moving backward but then Branwyn realized that the entrance to the lobby was shrinking. The doors bent, bulged and then shattered. No longer restrained by the frame, the walls sealed over. Glass shattered and the light from the windows vanished as there too the walls merged into smoothness, hiding Hadraniel on the other side. Now they were caged, while the angel had access to the rest of the building.

The room was now lit entirely by small flashlights and various magical effects. Mr. Black turned around, blood a gleam on his face. "Tend the wounded," he commanded the crowd. "Suppress any attacks. They will be coming. Reinforce the walls, if that is where your talents lie."

"How is it doing that?" demanded Branwyn, outraged. "I kept the bastard out of Titanone's nodes."

"They have resources beyond Geometric magic, child," said Skadi, leaning against the other side of the pillar as if she wasn't very worried. "Especially that one, with what you made."

Branwyn gave Skadi a baleful glare, but restrained herself to only saying, "I don't care. I can get the wall open again."

Mr. Black joined them, saying sharply, "No! You will restore Titanone, and then you will guide him in stopping Hadraniel from making its way to floor B13. That is your only priority." He wiped some blood from his face with two fingers.

Branwyn's natural inclination was to argue, but something in Mr. Black's glinting dark eyes made her hesitate. "Fine," she muttered, and dove back into the sleeping skyscraper's Geometric network.

The virus had oozed along some since she looked away. It wasn't fast, but it was moving and it was going to get somewhere dangerous eventually.

Skadi had told her to stop the virus, literally: to freeze it or otherwise make it impossible for it to move. But she wasn't Ice with his temperature powers. She had to use the building itself, and the strands of Geometry that contained it.

She mentally twanged the bright lines that reflected what Hadraniel had done in sealing the ballroom off. Two of the strands were developing branches. Shouting rose around her, and Mr. Black said, "Ignore the noise, Branwyn. Focus on waking Titanone."

Helplessly, Branwyn reinforced the two nodes that hadn't been contaminated by the virus again. She should have gone to the Repository before. Not that there had been time. Everything had happened so fast, and how could any of them have predicted that the angel would have sealed them into the room?

If she had to she could wake up Titanone still infected, but that might be worse. Maybe with her reinforcement Titanone could re-emerge from under the virus—but maybe not.

The virus oozed along one of its carrier lines and frustrated, Branwyn leaned her entire psychic weight on it. She could snap it, she could snap all of the connections, isolate the contaminated node, but that would make the entire remaining structure unstable. That was no good either.

The ballroom lobby stank of blood and she almost opened her eyes to find out why. But Skadi put her hand on Branwyn's arm and said softly, "You are safe yet."

"I don't know how to freeze it," confessed Branwyn, keeping her eyes closed tightly so she didn't lose her focus on the virus's growth. "If I had a machine Fragment, I know what I could do but I don't."

From Branwyn's other side, Penny said, "You have me."

Branwyn's breath caught in her throat. "I don't want to use you like that. And even if it wasn't wrong, it's dangerous for you in so many ways."

Penny took Branwyn's hand. "Taking me to meet some monsters wasn't? Branwyn, do what you have to, but the walls are *bleeding* right now and I think that angel is trying to drown us, too." She added. "And I feel like Titanone is family now. I'm family with a skyscraper."

Branwyn's hand tightened on Penny's involuntarily. "Bleeding? I don't— All right."

Through the flesh-to-flesh contact, she felt the thrum of Penny's prosthetic soul. When she called on it, it responded, moving partially out of Penny and into Branwyn. Branwyn's breath hitched in her throat. She'd been this close to Penny when she wove the

Machine soul into place originally. She'd never thought she'd be here again.

The virus flashed red and green, and she was there, too. She didn't want to bring Penny into proximity with the virus but in a way Penny and Titanone were siblings now and sometimes you volunteered for stupid things to save a sibling.

Branwyn reached out to a network of lines and started collecting them together, pouring her will into them to make a new node. She hadn't been able to do a fourth before, hadn't been able to manage the complexity. She hadn't had the motivation then, either, though.

She concentrated on her feelings toward the virus: the way it slid insidiously along the network. How dangerous it was. She had to work fast, but she couldn't afford to be sloppy. The effort required to do both of those at the same time was exhausting. But she couldn't even falter, couldn't take a breath. Her hands twitched and moved and she muttered under her breath, encouraging the network to become a node.

Then the emergent node and the Machine met within the forge of her soul and a spark of awareness leapt from one to another. The fire defense system glowed slowly to life: a new node in the Titanone entity.

Branwyn clenched her fists and then took the rest of her weight off the connection keeping Titanone asleep. "Go," she whispered. "Defend yourself. Shut that bastard down."

The skyscraper woke up. All four nodes flickered asynchronously until two, then three of them caught the same pattern. The fourth one was the one contaminated by the virus. The new node flared white, sending that whiteness through the rest of the network. When the white touched the strands claimed by the red and green, the red and green stilled and the white crossed over it, surging into the infected node.

Branwyn let out her breath and realized she was still holding onto Penny's hand and also her soul. Hastily she turned her attention to her friend and pushed the Machine soul back through their connection. *No*, she told the soul. *You did well but let's never do this again.*

"Branwyn!" said Mr. Black sharply, anguish in his voice. "Please tell me—Control, begin emergency evacuations. Branwyn, this will hurt Titanone."

"No," Branwyn snapped, watching the whiteness fade from the network, leaving tiny fragments of green and red that faded away. "Titanone is back, although cut off from Nakotus, so he won't have the vocabulary he's had recently."

"Why is the power still out?"

"Keeping Nakotus down. The virus was inside it, old man."

Mr. Black swore. "Corbin did this. Bring up what you can, carefully."

Branwyn whispered to Titanone and Titanone said, *All right...* in a faint, unexpected voice. Here and there lights came up in the tower. Branwyn could now see and feel some of what was happening within Titanone. "Why are Corbin and Marley running down a stairwell? And what exactly does Hadraniel want with the elevators?" The angel was melting through an elevator from the shaft above and Titanone's anxiety levels were rising.

"Close off access to the basement levels. There are super-secure doors on B6 and B8, close them. Deploy the hyperdiamond barrier between floors B9 and B10." He paused, listening to his headset. "Allow Marley and Corbin through the doors as they arrive. Do not let anybody else down."

"How are you feeling, Titanone?" Branwyn whispered. The fire defense system squirted something onto the fiery angel and the pod that did so was incinerated in response.

Strange. Dying?

"I hope not, kid. If you do, I think we'll go out together."

Deploying hyperdiamond nanorod barrier. A shimmering veil slid between the floors, including the elevator shaft. While it was there, the bottom three floors were utterly isolated from the world above ground. Branwyn wondered if Senyaza had expected an angel to drill down like this, or if the barrier was there to stop something from coming up.

Hard to see down there. Harder, now.

Branwyn thought about ways she could fix that, then stopped because there wasn't time. Instead she focused on Corbin and Marley, until she could sense them just as clearly as Titanone could, through her connection with the building. They were running down the stairs, three floors below and only two floors behind the burning angel. Neath was picking her way down after them, blinking ahead every few steps.

Corbin said, "—Won't destroy the building yet because it doesn't want to destroy what it's looking for. If we can catch it—"

Marley asked, aghast, "*Can* it destroy the building?"

"They have before," said Corbin. "The Tower of Babel, to start with."

"And how are we supposed to stop it?" demanded Marley.

"I had a plan," Corbin said. "There are special cells at the bottom. It wasn't a good plan for my own survival but it would have given me a chance to take Hadraniel out with me. Just like my family wanted." He stopped running to listen, and Branwyn wished she could tell him that he was still behind the angel.

"What's in the basement?" she asked aloud.

"Secrets," said Mr. Black. "You haven't discovered them via Titanone yet?"

"He can't see down there very well. I have no idea how you managed it."

"Oh? Ah, well. The bottommost levels were constructed

separately and moved into place as—"

No said Titanone faintly, instantly pulling Branwyn's attention away from the non-answer. The burning angel reached the hyperdiamond barrier and stopped. It looked around, then plunged a hand through the wall and *into* the Geometry beyond, transcending the boundary between material space and spiritual space with horrifying ease.

"Such an abomination," Hadraniel whispered. "You were never meant to be conscious, abomination." The angel's hand moved among the network, touching strands, testing them. For a moment Branwyn couldn't grasp how it was even possible. Then she stopped caring and simply threw herself at the hand.

"Get out," she growled. "'Never meant' my ass." The hand seemed invulnerable to her assaults, but she did get the angel's attention.

"You," it whispered and pulled away from her. Branwyn realized that it was wearing the divinity circuit—of course it was wearing the divinity circuit—and that it thought she could steal it once again. If only she *could* reach out through another wall and snatch it from its neck, totally destroying spatial geometry—but she had no idea how to even approach that.

Still. Hadraniel apparently didn't know that. "Yeah, me. You'd better get out of here before I take your toy away from you again."

"Better that I destroy you first," whispered Hadraniel. "You, and this created sentience, and then I'll take what I came for—" The hand representing the angel in the network opened and fire danced between the long marble fingers.

Marley, help, Branwyn thought, but there was no way for Marley to hear her and they were probably too far apart for Marley's protective magic to work anyhow.

The floor trembled and Titanone said in a strange voice, *No. If you destroy me, you destroy the structure and it all falls on your head, destroying what you seek.*

The hand clenched into a fist. Then, back in the material world, Marley and Corbin burst out of a stairwell and a flock of ravens burst out of Corbin's shadow. The fire defense system once again took a shot at the burning angel. With its attention split, the red-hot flames around the angel's wings cooled and the ravens mobbed the floating figure.

Hadraniel withdrew from the network. The crimson wings reignited, the ravens returning to shadow in the blast of red light. The angel curled its lip at Corbin. "Have you changed your mind?"

"Yes," said Corbin. "If you're smart, you will too."

"Pah! I have heard that too many times. Others can be smart and safe; I will fix what they allowed to be broken." The angel swept its wings and the sheet of hyperdiamond *disintegrated*. Plunging downward after the glittering shards, it called, "Flee like rats, mortal children. The piper comes, no matter what."

24
BRANWYN

Uh oh, said Titanone. Corbin swore and dived, actually dived for the angel, as if he could catch the burning-winged creature in arms and restrain it. He vanished over the edge of the elevator shaft, a cloak of blackness flaring around him. Neath peered over the lip of the hole, pawing at the edge fretfully, then backing away.

Marley didn't move, except to put her hand to the earpiece she still wore. "I need to talk to Branwyn."

"Somebody give Branwyn a microphone," commanded Mr. Black, not offering up his. Penny put something over Branwyn's ear almost immediately.

"I heard, Marley," said Branwyn. Through her connection with Titanone, she watched Corbin fall down the shaft, into a blurring haze.

"It's going to take what it came for. We can't stop it," said Marley urgently.

"It mustn't!" said Mr. Black sharply. "We absolutely must not allow that to happen."

"What's down there?" repeated Branwyn, irritated.

"It *doesn't matter*," said Marley. "It's going to destroy the building once it has what it's come for."

"It can't do that," said Mr. Black scornfully. "Not *this* building."

"Tell him it can, Branwyn," commanded Marley.

"It just effortlessly destroyed your hyperdiamond barrier. I think it could destroy the building whenever it wanted," said Branwyn. She thought about Titanone's odd speech. *But it didn't a moment ago. Because it wants something.* Titanone had said something about what was in the basement, when they'd been texting each other. What had it been? A cage? Books?

The angel landed on the bottom floor of the complex, like a meteor coming to earth. Corbin did something as he came down, but Branwyn couldn't quite tell what. It didn't seem to make a difference. Then the angel opened the elevator doors with a wrench and drifted through. Once the doors were open, Branwyn could suddenly see more clearly. The angel floated down a hall that looked like something out of a horror movie.

"Don't you *clean* down here?" Branwyn demanded.

"Some of what is… stored there influences the surroundings," Mr. Black said crisply. "Hopefully my grandson is smart enough to ignore it."

"This is all irrelevant," snapped Marley. "Branwyn—"

"What do you need, Marley?" Branwyn prompted.

"I need to see the building. I…" she faltered. "I think it's too big for me to protect entirely, but maybe I can manage to protect a section, if there are any sections set out conceptually."

As the blurry, shadowed form of the angel made its way down a filthy hallway, Corbin was nowhere to be seen. Branwyn decided not to mention that to Marley. "I can see that. Hadraniel gets what it wants, it comes up again to get away, it tries to blast the place on the way out, and you contain just enough of it, using your shield as a barrier. Head back into the office on your left and Titanone will send a diagram of itself to the monitor there."

"You think I am joking about how dangerous it is for the angel to be down there?" demanded Mr. Black.

Exhausted from her earlier work and worried now, Branwyn finally lost her patience. "I think you promised me that this wouldn't be a concern tonight. So yeah, now I think everything you say is a joke. If you're so worried, shut up and go help the others bring down the spell stopping you from dealing with the problem yourself." Then she took a deep breath and concentrated on bringing up the power to the system in the office Marley was fumbling around in.

No Nakotus, Titanone told her. *No schematics.* She could feel the entity's confusion.

"It's all right," she muttered. "We'll do it my way." She started to draw on the pillar with her finger, and Titanone carried the drawing to the screen Marley was staring anxiously at.

Corbin shouted angrily somewhere in the depths. There was a burst of light from one corner of the bottom floor.

"I've found something," said Marley, studying the glowing lines on the screen. "I hope this works." She closed her eyes.

Feels so weird, said Titanone. *Nice.*

Branwyn said, "Let's hope it stays that way."

They didn't have to wait very long. A massive surge of iridescent energy rolled out of the lowest level, directed up. It blew a huge hole in the three floors above, then flattened against a wall. Marley staggered and fell against the desk, her skin turning pink like she'd been out in the sun too long.

A second blast came and blew another set of holes in the floor above, and Marley curled up on the floor, crying. This was no good; blowing up the bottom four floors would still end up very bad for everybody in so many ways. Much more importantly,

Marley couldn't last much longer.

Impossibly, Corbin was still moving around down there. The lines of the Geometry shifted and Branwyn realized he was, too slowly, trying to shift a tethering circle already drawn in one of the cells to something that could contain Hadraniel.

"Let's help," whispered Branwyn, and she and Titanone started bending the wounded Geometry of the damaged levels in the same way.

A figure jumped down one of the holes, barely more than a human-shaped silhouette against the lingering light and curve of the Geometry. Not human, not bound the same way. One of the kaiju. As another bolt of energy shook the base of the skyscraper, the figure lithely moved closer to the source and picked up some of the Geometry strands Branwyn had pushed into place.

There was a mad scramble of activity suddenly, far too fast for Branwyn to process what happened. Then Hadraniel leapt into the air, flying up through the holes above.

"Drop the shield and let it out, Marley," Branwyn shouted, and Marley must have heard because the angel didn't slam into a barrier that Branwyn knew could be unpleasantly physical sometimes. Instead it glided up through the elevator shafts again, to the mall entrance and out into the night, leaving a trail of fire in its wake.

Is she still alive? She's not moving, Titanone wondered.

"Don't say that," snarled Branwyn, and pulled herself out of the magical network. The ballroom lobby was a mess: dark liquid puddled on the floor and smoke hazed the air. Holes had been punched in the walls where the windows once had been. Penny looked a little rumpled and Skadi was soaked.

Disoriented, Branwyn took a step and promptly slipped in one of the puddles. As Skadi caught her and hauled her to her feet again, the magic binding the room relaxed and the doors and windows returned. There was an immediate rush for the exits, causing enough of a jam that even Branwyn couldn't force her way through. By the time she finally got through the press, firefighters and police officers were swarming over the mall. She ignored them, running to the closest stairwell and descending at breakneck speed.

Two floors below the surface, she heard somebody climbing up the stairs and stopped. "Marley?"

"I'm bringing her up," said an unexpected male voice, following by a yowl. It was Max, Severin's kaiju buddy, the one who had infiltrated Rhianna's headquarters. A moment later he appeared around the landing and climbed to where Branwyn waited. Neath followed him, howling.

Branwyn lunged forward to grab Marley's wrist. She was warm and before Branwyn could find a pulse, she could see Marley's chest heaving and her eyelids fluttering as if she was trying to wake herself.

"I'd hardly have bothered if she was dead, lady," said Max pleasantly. He had a deep cat scratch on his face, and more on his wrists. But whatever argument he and Neath had seemed to have been settled, because Branwyn knew Neath was capable of causing a lot more damage and instead she was just lecturing him at the top of her lungs. "Shall we go on upstairs?"

"Wait, where's Corbin? Is *he* dead?"

"He asked me to leave while he checked on some seals. I came across the woman, remembered Sev talking about her."

"That's my grandson," said Mr. Black, with more than a hint of pride. He was standing two steps above Branwyn. She gave him a hostile look, which he ignored as he walked down the steps past both her and Max. "I suggest you take Marley somewhere more comfortable than a concrete stairwell, Branwyn. I'll be along shortly."

Max watched the old man stride down the staircase. A faint

smile curved his mouth. "Such a determined old bird."

"Whatever," said Branwyn. "Let's go."

"Yes, ma'am." Max started climbing the stairs again.

After one flight of stairs, Branwyn asked, "What are you doing here, anyhow?"

"X wasn't here, and I'm pretty good at sneaking into places so I thought I might be able to accomplish something."

"And did you?"

Max smiled that amazing smile. "I'm carrying a pretty girl out of a cold dark room."

"Hah!" They emerged onto the ground floor of the mall, looked at the trail of devastation leading to the front entrance, and found a bench near the wall. Rescue workers, firefighters and cops were starting to fill the shopping floor, replacing the evacuated consumers. They mostly seemed to be staring in shock at the damage the angel had done and talking with a few people in formal dress from the gala upstairs.

Max put Marley down, then leaned against the wall. Neath finished berating him, then leapt up to snuggle into Marley's side. Branwyn knelt beside the bench and stroked Marley's hair. Cooled sweat made her skin clammy and without looking up, Branwyn ordered, "Go get a blanket from one of those uniforms running around."

As Max ambled off, the stairwell door opened again and Corbin stepped through, followed by Mr. Black. Corbin went straight to their bench, while Mr. Black took a moment to look around at all the rescue personnel and the damage to his building.

Corbin crouched at the end of the bench where Marley's head was. His fingers danced over her head as if he was afraid to touch her. At last he breathed, "Marley."

Marley's eyes fluttered open, and Branwyn was both relieved and annoyed for reasons she didn't bother analyzing.

"Corbin," Marley said, her voice creaking. She squeezed Neath like a teddy bear. "I'm glad you're alive."

"Unreasonable woman," he muttered. "Well done."

Mr. Black finally joined them just as Max did. Mr. Black gave Max a cold look, which Max responded to with the same charming smile. Branwyn wondered if they were going to fight. Well, they could do that another time. She stood up, took the blanket from Max, draped it over Marley and then said, "So what did the angel get?"

Mr. Black's expression turned grave and distant. "A book."

Marley pushed herself to a sitting position, because somebody had said, 'book'. "What was in this book?"

Mr. Black didn't answer, glancing at Max again. But Corbin did. "It's an ancient text documenting how the Hush was created. Hadraniel has always wanted to remove the Hush; it was Ettoriel's supporter a year ago. And now it can reverse engineer it."

Slowly Mr. Black shook his head. "It's coded and it's not a code an angel can break."

"Where's the key?" asked Marley instantly.

"Protected," said Mr. Black shortly.

"Like the book was protected?" Branwyn asked. "It doesn't matter, anyhow. Between Corbin here and magic in general, I doubt there's any such thing as unbreakable encryption anymore."

"There never was," said Corbin absently. He straightened up, his fingers still trailing over Marley's hair. A moment later, Finn appeared through the growing crowd. He glanced at Max as he stopped a few feet away. Max shifted his weight slightly, half-closed his eyes and Finn's gaze slid incuriously away, instead falling on Marley. He said, "Need another drink, love?"

Marley blinked up at him. "You're alive. You're not hurt."

"Sure, I'm just fine." He crooked a grin and patted Neath, who was suddenly purring hard. "We were stuck for a bit but there were too many of us for the pest to just step on."

"You were a lot closer to being stepped on than you think," Branwyn told him bluntly. "Thank Marley that there's still a building here."

"Yes, but he was going to be hurt," said Marley fretfully. "I saw it. It was unavoidable. And now it's gone, it *was* avoided, but—" She looked at Corbin, her eyes narrowing. "You. You and the way you made yourself invisible to my magic. I was seeing what would happen *without* you."

"That'll make it easier to surprise you on your birthday, then. But Marley... you can't see yourself either," he pointed out. "We'll never know now."

"I *want* to know. I've spent a year getting used to this vision, dammit!" She struggled up and then fell back again.

Finn crowded in between Branwyn and Corbin and knelt down as he pulled a flask from his pocket. "Time to drink up, Miss Guardian." He poured water from a flask over his fingers and across her lips.

She licked them, drank a gulp and closed her eyes. "I'm just tired," she muttered.

"It's good for you, all the same." He stood up and gave a sidelong look at Corbin. "And just what were you up to, my boy?"

Corbin stretched his shoulders. "I was trying to lure Hadraniel to the basement and trap him in one of the sacrifice cells. I thought that would probably be best for everybody."

Finn gave him a long, thoughtful look. "You used the book as bait?"

"And the device to build up its courage," agreed Corbin blandly.

"That didn't work out very well."

"I got distracted," Corbin agreed. "These things happen."

Marley opened her eyes again. "So what do we do now?"

Mr. Black shook his head. "We shall have to recover the book at some point soon. But still, well done, Corbin. You did accomplish the original task, even if you got needlessly creative at the end. And we will have plenty of ways to find the angel while it is so weighed down by its new possessions." He looked at a small group of people descending the stairs. "Ah, there's Elizabeth. Your parents will be happy to see you."

Corbin shrugged, as if he didn't care very much. "You were willing to sacrifice me for your revenge, Grandfather. And as soon as you have it, you've lost me."

"You're still infected," said Mr. Black flatly. "I thought you'd been cured finally—"

Corbin's fist clenched but his face was like stone, looking at the main entrance to the mall. "I'm not infected, I'm angry. Marley couldn't cure that."

"I wouldn't want to," added Marley, sitting up and scowling toward Corbin's parents.

Mr. Black regarded him expressionlessly before moving away toward his daughter and her husband.

As soon as he was out of earshot, Branwyn said, "I don't know anything about any sacrifice cells except they sound stupid—but admit it, you wanted to destroy the book, too. That's what your pet virus was doing in Nakotus. I shut the whole system down but it definitely warped some data before I could figure out what was going on. They scanned the book and uploaded it to the database and you destroyed it. And then you used Hadraniel as a way of getting to the physical book."

"Yes," said Corbin, shaking out his clenched fist. "Yes, I did. I learned a lot while I was sick. Most of it wasn't meaningful but I thought it was stupid to keep around ways of breaking the Hush. Best to erase all that information" He looked down. "Best to erase a lot of problems all at once."

Distressed, Marley said, "Corbin…"

He looked down at her. "I was confused and angry," he admitted. "There were a lot of holes in my plan, holes Loki was too glad to fill. I thought I could erase him too. I thought I was cunning, and there we were, making the computer virus together." He shook his head. "I was a tool."

"You bound him, though," Branwyn told him. "He wasn't happy about destroying the data but he did it anyhow. And with Nakotus down and cold, he may yet be erased."

Marley squeezed her eyes shut and opened them again, then shook her head. "What…?"

"Marley?" Branwyn began and then felt it herself. All the Geometry she could sense had gone on alert, as if listening to a distant voice. An underlying structure, deeply buried in the fundamental fabric of the world, shimmered and became briefly visible before fading away. Neath's purr stopped and the cat sat up, eyes dilated and ears pricked very alertly. Branwyn asked, "What's going on?"

Corbin said, "Some sort of grand magic… Hadraniel *can't* be reverse engineering the Hush already."

"How would it have decoded the book?" asked Max, breaking his illusion of nonchalant non-presence.

Corbin shook his head, puzzled. "The code really is secure. Even I—" He stopped, staring at Marley. Her face was white.

"The twins. Kari has unlocked a book before, and Lissa can talk to *anything*. And I can feel how afraid they are."

25
MARLEY AND BRANWYN

MARLEY

When Marley emerged from the cloud of ravens outside of Zachariah's home, the floodlights outside the house were on and the kaiju were waiting for her: Severin and five others, one of whom held a shimmering nightmare in both hands.

"Oh, come on," said Corbin, his fingers tightening around her hand as he too saw the brigade of kaiju. "Can you tell what's happening inside from here?"

Marley eyed the kaiju as Neath brushed against her leg. Their eyes glinted in the darkness, which made part of her want to run and hide. Instead she tried to relax enough to feel what she couldn't see. The twins were inside the house, working together to transform a book of secrets into a book of answers. Their fear had faded, mingling with confusion and curiosity and a little bit of excitement. That was good, Marley thought, and then wondered if it was. The twins were dangerous when frightened—but had only curiosity prompted them to do as the angel demanded?

She couldn't know, she could only extrapolate, and there wasn't time right now. The Geometry of the world was moving in great chunks, rearranging itself to reveal that which had been buried in the foundations.

"I thought you wanted to deal with Hadraniel," called Corbin to the kaiju. The kaiju with the Sword—big, male, empty-eyed— was standing in front of the entrance, like a twisted version of the angel guarding the gates of Eden. The other five were in a loose cluster in the house's driveway; the youngest-looking one was perched on the hood of Zachariah's SUV. Marley recognized them from Branwyn's descriptions, which she'd so carefully taken notes on.

One of them was Max, the one who'd carried her up from Titanone's basement. Of course. Celestial world travel was faster than anything a flock of ravens could manage.

"It's busy," said Severin, yawning. "Interrupting would be rude. My, that is a pretty dress. And that emergency blanket really adds to the look."

"Well, can I go in?" Marley demanded, her fingers tightening on the blanket still around her shoulders.

"That would count as interrupting, don't you think? Nah, I think you should wait here." He leaned his hip on the side of the SUV.

Corbin paced back and forth. "I thought you didn't care about the Hush, Severin. You lying coward."

"Don't get yourself too worked up, raven boy," said Severin, with a flash of his teeth. "Even you don't ignore opportunity when it knocks. Just keep your girl from doing anything stupid and the two of you will have a whole new world to study soon."

Marley ground her teeth and moved toward the corner of the house. The tip of the horrible Sword seemed to follow her. "Stay," commanded its wielder, in a voice like an arc of fire. She stayed, fear running down to her knees.

Then she shook herself and said to Corbin, "Do what you can. I *know* you can do something." She cupped her hands to her mouth and shouted as loudly as she could, "Kari, Lissa, stop. I'm here now."

The movement of the world's Geometry slowed, the slow, grand dance of icebergs becoming the drifting of hulks. None of Severin's kaiju moved toward Marley, to her surprise, but after a moment of stillness, the front door of the house opened and the angel she recognized from its benediction at the church looked out. It was dressed as a mortal now, but it had the same dazzling aura she'd felt at the church. Now that she knew what it was, it didn't draw her in at all.

"Bring her inside," it commanded, and the kaiju with the Sword stalked toward her. She backed up, wondering if she could lead it away, wondering if anybody would take that opportunity.

But the kaiju weren't there as her allies. They were celestials, oppressed under the Hush just like the angels were. More; they had no pretensions to benevolence to limit them. Branwyn had said they wanted the divinity circuit and clearly she was right, because the only move any of them made was to block Corbin when he moved toward her.

X paced three steps toward her, then moved faster than her eyes could follow, catching her by her arm and dragging her like a sack as he darted back to the door. Neath hissed and leapt after him, but he was faster even than she. As he pushed Marley into the house, she saw Penny and Branwyn step out of thin air beside Corbin, Branwyn looking furious. The last thing she saw was Neath pivoting to race over to Branwyn. She wasn't sure if that was a good thing or not.

Then she was in the house, passed from the kaiju to the angel. "Aren't you an interesting gift?" said the angel impassively, and escorted her to Zachariah's living room with that pretension to benevolence the kaiju lacked.

There was *another* Sword on the coffee table, long and slim and casting green shadows around the room. Branwyn had mentioned something about Hadraniel stealing a second Sword from somewhere. She'd laughed, and Marley had thought it was a joke. Apparently not. She *really* needed to have a chat with Branwyn sometime about her inappropriate sense of humor.

Zachariah crouched on his heels before the blade, holding one hand to his chest. Hadraniel laughed upon seeing him. "I did warn you not to touch Raphael. Courage, mortal. You might heal. Please sit down, miss. Explain to the children you aren't worried."

The angel pushed Marley into an armchair and she didn't resist, sinking down to sit on the edge of the chair. She still had that emergency blanket clutched in one hand, which was so incongruous she wanted to laugh. She didn't. The angel's long, cool hand remained on the back of her neck: a threat so gentle it didn't need to be spoken.

Kari and Lissa sat on the small sofa, close together. They held an old, heavy book across both their laps, and neither of them looked particularly scared. Kari looked annoyed, while Lissa kept looking down at the book.

"Marley, why did you want us to stop?" demanded Kari. "It was just getting *interesting*. Things were opening up."

Marley took a deep breath, conscious of the hand on her neck and then asked severely, "Girls, did this person introduce themselves to you as one of those bad guys behind your uncle's kidnapping last year?"

The hand didn't move, and Marley wondered if she'd said the wrong thing after all. If the angel hurt her in any obvious way, the girls would try to defend her; while she was with them, she could defend them. At least until she was unconscious... which wasn't really that far away. Finn's magic could only restore her so much. But until that happened, she and the girls should be a frightening team.

Kari drew her brows together. "No."

"He isn't hurting anybody now," said Lissa absently. "He just has this mystery he wants to solve and he said we're the only people in the world who can do it." She glanced up. "Besides, Uncle Zach isn't worried." Then she really looked at Zachariah and her eyes dilated. "Uncle Zach, what's wrong?"

"He made a mistake," said Hadraniel impatiently. "The book, children. It waits for you. The whole world waits for you."

"I can speak for myself, angel," said Zachariah softly. "Hello, Marley. Did I hear Corbin outside?"

"Yes. He's feeling better," said Marley.

"Interesting. We should talk about that public school plan again. Later. Maybe when they're around nine."

"Both of you be quiet." The angel took its hand away from Marley's neck and moved to caress the green Sword. The green sparkles cast around the room shimmered and danced.

Lissa chewed on her lip, looking critically at Hadraniel. "Marley's right, Kari. It's a good book but I don't think this guy is all right."

"We're not supposed to make people go away," said Kari sulkily. "It upsets Marley."

"I wouldn't be upset right now," said Marley lightly.

Hadraniel picked up the Sword called Raphael. "Here we are already. Let me show you what will happen if you try, children." A pulse of magic made the house shudder and the twins' eyes widened.

Through her connection with them, Marley saw a little of what the angel showed them. Hadraniel's undiluted strength battled against theirs and they could not simply overbear it. They just didn't have both the precision and the power. The vision showed them how frustration and building wrath laid down a certain pathway to devastation. They saw intimately, as vividly as a nightmare, that they could only protect through destruction, and today it would require such destruction as to wipe everything they loved away.

It was a vision Marley had seen before, of small girls in a wasteland. She didn't need to see it again, and she was enraged that they'd seen it even once. She surged to her feet, rushing wildly at Hadraniel, with no thought except breaking the angel's concentration.

Zachariah moved at the same time, red and gold light flaring around him as he interposed himself between the angel and the children and reached for the angel's Sword.

Green light flooded the room, as if the ghost of the deep sea had risen from a sandy grave. Zachariah grunted as if he'd been punched in the stomach, his face twisting in agony. The angel's hand caught Marley across her face.

Then Kari screamed, high and thin, the sound promising months of nightmares ahead. She ran to Zachariah, hugging his leg. Lissa said, "Stop it! Why are you doing this?"

The angel caught Marley by her hair and twisted it painfully. "All I want is for you to read the book. We will work together, just as I said, and then you can take your pretend mommy and pretend daddy and navigate the new world." Lissa looked skeptical and the angel added, "I take no pleasure in hurting anybody, child. All I want is for things to again be the way they're supposed to be. You understand that."

Lissa grabbed Kari's hand. "Let Marley go, then."

"Pick up the book," countered Hadraniel.

Slowly, Lissa did so, and the two girls sat once again on the couch. The angel shoved Marley to the ground and put the Sword on the table. Marley could feel the weapon's presence, a pristine shimmering sharpness that lacked any hint of the malice the angel pretended to avoid. It was a material rule given form and Marley wondered why Branwyn hadn't talked about it more.

The twins started reading together again. They were silent, but Marley knew they were communicating all the same, not just with each other, but with the angel, through the same channel that the creature had sent its threats.

"I don't care who he thinks he is," Zachariah began softly, shifting closer to her on the floor. "He's not going to tear down the Hush just by translating a book. We have time if we can get out of this."

Marley stared at Zachariah's handsome face and stiff, reddened hands. Just as quietly, she said, "If you're not worried why did you try to grab the Sword?"

"Because he's frightening the girls," Zachariah said flatly. "So I'm going to kill him."

Looking at his distant gaze and cold face, Marley realized with a jolt that Zachariah was never going to be rational about Kari and Lissa. She was never going to be able to rationally convince him that they'd be safe, that time away was good for her, or that she ought to be her own person. He'd given everything he was to protecting and loving the little girls and he could no longer see clearly when it came to them. She wondered what he'd been like a decade ago, before they'd come along to steal his heart. She wondered if he'd recover himself as they grew, if he'd become as cold to them as Corbin's family was to him.

No. Love was better, even if it made its own problems. She couldn't say to Zachariah, *be rational,* couldn't imagine hurting him or the girls that way.

That wasn't going to be the way she kept her freedom, found her balance again. Had rationality ever done a damn thing for her own anxiety problems? Her desperate desire to see all the angles had just deluded her into thinking she could control what happened next.

She reached over and squeezed Zachariah's foot. "Everything will be all right. You're not doing this alone. I did come to help, see? And I'm not alone either."

He snorted and looked away, but not before she saw the lines at his eyes ease.

Well. That was something. She was pretty sure he was wrong about the Hush, despite her reassurance. The angel wasn't acting like this was the first step in a long research trail. The angel seemed to think it was accomplishing something *right now*. And she agreed with Zachariah: reverse engineering the most complicated magical ritual ever performed required a lot more than just reading it backward.

She narrowed her eyes, concentrating on the deep Geometry that she could feel moving with the same sense that felt onrushing catastrophes. Something was definitely happening…

The penny dropped. "Oh my God," she said, caught between horror and a strange derisive scorn. "You are such a liar. You're not trying to remove the Hush. You're trying to cast it again, on *mortals*."

BRANWYN

Branwyn arrived just in time to see Marley being pushed inside the house by the kaiju called X. Neath twined around her ankles, complaining angrily. Penny picked the big cat up and asked, "It's good that Marley's in with the kids, right?"

"Sure," growled Corbin. "Didn't anybody else come with you?"

"I got here faster," said Branwyn shortly, scanning the other kaiju as they clustered in front of the garage. "It was easy. I could feel—ah! You bastard!" Her burst of rage constricted her vision. She stalked toward Severin, who had one hand behind his back. "Give it back, right now."

He revealed her hammer. "This? Why should I? It was mine before it was yours."

"It was not," snarled Branwyn. "You had a rock you could barely use. I made it a tool. It's mine." She paused then added, "Just ask it." Silently she called the hammer.

It listened, but could not come. And it wasn't the only thing listening. The shard of nightmare the kaiju X held *paid attention*, and so did Penny's soul. With that realization, the wave of tiredness beating against her mind retreated. Now was not the time to be playing around. The angel was doing something bad in the house. The angel had something of hers as well, and it was more important that she get *that* back than she show Severin her powers.

Still holding Neath, Penny approached the house with a friendly smile. "I'm going to go inside too, all right?" Branwyn knew a cue when she saw one and started strolling down the street, hoping to double back around to the other side of the house. She passed Corbin unrolling some kind of vast magic.

Severin shrugged. "It's your skin."

"Stay put," said X harshly. "All of you just stay put. Especially you, Branwyn Lennox."

Branwyn thought about running. If she ran, he'd have to chase her, right? If he chased her, maybe somebody else could do something. But that would leave the divinity circuit in the hands of whoever could grab it.

Besides, he'd probably just throw the Sword. That seemed like the sort of thing that *would* happen around now. So she stopped and slowly turned back to the front of Zachariah's house.

Penny put Neath down and placed her hands on her hips. "That's a really big sword you have there, mister. Who made it for you?"

"Shut up," said X. He glanced at the other kaiju, then back at Penny.

"My friend makes stuff like that," Penny went on. "Could I see it?" She reached for the Sword.

"Penny!" said Branwyn sharply. There was no way she should be going around touching other Machines right now, not after what her soul had been through recently.

"What?" asked Penny innocently. "We've all got things to accomplish here, Branwyn."

Branwyn walked over to her, eyeing the Machine Sword.

"They've started again," said Corbin, his voice hollow.

"Well, that just means your girlfriend is being smart and staying healthy," said Severin. "Because if she wasn't, the little darlings would flatten the place, now wouldn't they?"

Aleth said, "Not that smart."

Severin tilted his head as if listening. A smile cracked across his face and Branwyn longed to seize her hammer from him and smash it across his face. But there was a time and a place, and now was not *quite* it.

"She'll get herself gutted yet. What a girl. Nah, let's see what happens. We've got plenty of time." And he grinned at Branwyn and spun her hammer like a baton.

The hum of the Geometry changed. Branwyn could feel Marley weaving her magic against whatever the angel was doing. She could feel Penny's helplessness, see Corbin's frustration with a glance. It was all going wrong and it certainly wasn't going to go right just sitting here waiting.

And Severin had taken her hammer and now he was *laughing* at her, like somehow she'd played into his hands.

Branwyn's breath hissed between her teeth. "You know what? I'm done. Corbin, let's break things." She shoved Penny away from her, opened wide the forge of her own soul and stepped forward to slap the blade of the Sword pointed at her.

The entity known as Belial twisted against her hand, parting flesh and howling into her blood. The name filled her mind:

BELIAL BELIAL BELIAL. Her own name rose up in response: whispered in her great-grandmother's voice, called by her father, sang by her youngest sister. She'd given tiny bits of her soul all her life and received other souls in return and now she wasn't just the Branwyn in her own mind, she was the Branwyn others loved too. BELIAL rushed against that, pushing, trying to break through and consume her. But because she was mortal, because she was *not alone*, she could resist.

"No," she scolded it. "Not me." And maybe any mortal could have simply resisted BELIAL's devouring, but Branwyn's soul was trained. She knew what she was doing and what she was doing was more than enduring. She introduced the Sword to the forge in her soul. It screamed as she reversed it: the blade became the grip: safe, shielded, no longer screaming its name. And the grip became the blade.

X cried out and let go, leaping back away from the blade he'd been holding. "Finally!" said Severin, tossing the hammer aside. In the next instant, all of the other kaiju moved, appearing around their rogue brother. Branwyn couldn't see quite what happened next, because her hand was bleeding profusely and tiny particles of Machine were lodged in the injury, which was *really very painful*. But there was thunder, and a great flock of black birds. Then Dolores was holding X by the arm, dragging him through a portal into the Backworld, while the other four spread out.

Belial slipped out of Branwyn's gory hand, clattering on the ground. She had to pick it up, take it inside, maybe stab Hadraniel with it before she snatched her creation off his neck. Maybe the pain would save her from being overwhelmed by Hadraniel's glory.

Penny stepped on the blade instead. "That's a bad cut," she said, and wrapped some white fabric torn from her dress around Branwyn's hand. Branwyn tried to argue, tried to stop her, but she kept feeling the little sparkles of Machine particle move in her blood and it distracted her each time she opened her mouth.

"Come on, Corbin," called Severin. "It'll be faster with five. Might as well make yourself useful." And much to Branwyn's surprise, Corbin came. He and the kaiju made a large circle and the white lines of the tethering ritual unrolled from each of them, reaching into the house.

MARLEY

Hadraniel didn't want to return things to how they'd been before. That would mean giving power back to Umbriel, whom it clearly had philosophical differences with. And maybe it would be giving power back to the kaiju, too, and the demons, and all the other celestials. Instead it wanted all the pre-Hush power for itself and its cabal, without leaving any ability for humans or nephilim to work against it.

Without moving her lips, without twitching her hands, Marley did her best to use her magic to resist what Hadraniel was pressing into the world. It wasn't working. It wasn't working and the angel knew what she was trying to do and didn't care. Its own hands spread wide, a beatific expression on its face. Its mouth was open as if it was singing a hymn she couldn't hear.

"That can't be right," said Zachariah quietly. "You're mistaken, Marley."

Marley gave Zachariah a puzzled, frustrated look, and realized he wasn't looking at her. He was looking at the floor. All but hidden in the vast movements of the Geometry, tiny lines traced an old pattern around the living room. Somehow, those still outside had managed to get a tethering circle started. But it was only a circle. It could make a celestial's death mean something, but they still had to be killed first.

A discordant howl echoed from without and the green Sword on the coffee table jerked to one side. Hadraniel's eyes opened, narrowed, closed again. "Carry on, children. No one will harm you. Your babysitter is here to guarantee it."

The tether lines continued moving, settling into place. "There's no time," said Zachariah. "It can't be done." He stood up silently. Both his hands were swollen and red.

Marley shook her head and pressed her hand to her chest, then gathered up her emergency blanket. "It's been done before." Zachariah gave her a glance of acknowledgement. "It'll be done before anybody notices."

The angel opened its eyes again. "Sit down."

Instead, Zachariah lunged for the angel, catching one of the celestial's arms and spinning it around. Marley fumbled to keep up, almost as shocked as the angel by Zachariah's burst of movement. She snatched the Sword in her protected hand and felt the instant shock of touching RAPHAEL. The green burned, turning the silver blanket into a thousand tiny wriggling worms that gnawed on her palm.

She let momentum carry her forward as she bit her lip to avoid screaming. *Mustn't frighten the children more than necessary, mustn't frighten the kids...*

The Sword fought her, drove its name into her mind, but distantly she heard Branwyn shout, "Marley!" Clumsily, she swung it at Zachariah and the angel as they grappled. White light flared around Zachariah but he was safe, he was safe, just like the twins, and Marley's skin was burning as the light beat through her shield—and RAPHAEL sank into the angel's flesh.

For an overwhelming moment, the essential truths of Hadraniel and the Sword surged against each other and against Marley's own power. It was too much. The Sword would devour Hadraniel but she wasn't sure she could endure until then. Even in dying the angel was capable of devastation.

Then tethering circle completed and sank its magic into Hadraniel, pinning it to the Geometry. The magic ritual locked the channel between the angel's spirit and its body into place. Suddenly the truth that Hadraniel was a physical body intersecting a Sword mattered more than any other truth. Bodies impaled with swords didn't work anymore. The failure cascaded up the channel to the angel's spirit.

Hadraniel exploded into a radiance that knocked Marley flat on her back. She hit her head on the coffee table and couldn't tell if the radiance was a manifestation of the pain in her skull or something else. She couldn't even tell if somebody was screaming. She thought so, though.

Oh. It was her.

The remains of Hadraniel's great working streamed away into the night. It hadn't succeeded. They'd stopped it.

She wondered if it was over. But the power in the air still beat against her skin. Hadraniel was gone, but the weapons it had brought remained, unimaginably dangerous.

Dazed, she watched as two Swords started orbiting each other in the center of the living room. The light was wrong. It was too open. The walls were gone.

The twins were safe, though. She could feel that even through the pain splitting her skull. Safe, but scared. Scared, and angry.

"Well, this isn't good," said Severin, just beyond her line of sight. "She can't manage either of them now. Might as well get out before everything goes boom."

Kari reached out for RAPHAEL. "No, stop it," she cried. "You're going to break everything."

Marley tried to sit up, and couldn't. The distortion from the Swords was growing stronger. The weapons were celestial entities in their own right. They'd joined Hadraniel's quest for a reason and they weren't happy about what Marley and the others had done.

"What do you know anyhow?" demanded Lissa. "Shut up."

"Stop talking about blood, stop it, stop it!" shouted Kari.

The Swords were talking to the children somehow. She couldn't hear what they were saying. She couldn't stop it.

"Zachariah," croaked Marley. He was lying on the ground, his eyes half-open. Alive, he was alive, but he wasn't safe. The Swords wanted to eat him.

"Hey, kids. If you want to stop them, you know what to do," said Severin. Marley still couldn't see him. She couldn't see anything but the twins and Zachariah and the Swords.

"Shut up!" said Lissa a second time, and took BELIAL by the hilt as Kari took RAPHAEL.

The children's hands were tiny on the hilts of the Swords, but the shadows they cast in the white light stretched into the night. Then all at once the light from the Swords went out. Darkness blanketed everything.

They were safe, they were safe. And so was Zachariah, so was everybody around here, pressing themselves into her subconscious. She wasn't quite sure what had happened to the Swords. She could still feel lingering traces of their presence, but subdued. Controlled. *Mastered.*

Marley closed her eyes and let her breath out, her thoughts slipping away from her. As she relaxed, the aches and exhaustion of the day swept over her.

Kari said, "Uncle?" in a little voice and Marley opened her eyes again. A glow appeared around Kari, no brighter than a streetlight.

Lissa was already kneeling beside Zachariah. The Swords were definitely gone. Where had they gone? Marley couldn't quite remember. She wondered when she'd get to go to sleep. The floor was hard but that didn't matter.

Branwyn stumbled through the wreckage of the house's outer wall and lunged for something on the ground. "Got it!" she crowed as she rolled and slid across debris.

"Very heroic," commented Severin, standing on the remains of the side wall. The other three remaining kaiju climbed up behind him. All of them looked down at the nephilim in the crater-like remains of the house.

Branwyn clutched something to her chest, glaring up at them. Her hammer was in one bloody hand. Blearily, Marley realized Branwyn had the divinity circuit, and struggled to move her shield over to Branwyn so her friend could have the chance she needed.

But her shield was gone, exhausted. She had nothing left.

Max took a step down the pile of rubble, and Severin put a hand on his shoulder.

"I won't give it to you," said Branwyn.

In response, Severin laughed, and all of the kaiju vanished.

"This isn't a game," shouted Branwyn, outraged.

Corbin climbed up where they'd been. "They're gone for real, Branwyn. It's all right."

The night wind blew across the cratered house. Slowly Zachariah sat up, both of his children nestled in his lap.

There was the sound of a van parking, and Grendel's rough voice. Corbin said something back and crunched through broken glass to kneel down and stroke her face.

Marley closed her eyes again. All was well.

26
EPILOGUE

Two days later.

The big bandage wrapped around Branwyn's hand made using her phone inconvenient, but it was so much better than her previous ways of contacting Severin that she made do.

"What do you want?" he said by way of answer, his voice coming from behind her. She knew better than to look.

Tartly, Branwyn said, "I already told you what I wanted in exchange for helping you. And I've been waiting two days and that stupid mark you put on me is still there."

"Where's the divinity circuit?" he asked in response.

"I took it apart, of course." Mostly true. True enough for the likes of Severin. She tried not to think about how awakened key at the core was in her pocket. She knew how to shut it down now, after agonizing over Titanone, but— "I still helped you."

"And I saved you, usually from mortal stupidity," he pointed out. "Over and over again."

"That doesn't give you the right to brand me like I'm your personal property," Branwyn countered.

"Ah. A willful misunderstanding, cupcake? The mark is literally what saved you."

Branwyn had been trying not to think too hard about that, too. But now she did. "By claiming me, right? By telling your friends that if they messed with me, you'd be unhappy. Well, I've paid you back for saving me. I don't know why you wanted Hadraniel to go down so badly, but it's done and I'm done."

Severin sighed. "You really don't know? Well, consider it self-preservation, cupcake. Hadraniel had already stolen one of my siblings and used him against Senyaza. Angels can't be allowed to use us as weapons. If we didn't get involved, we all would have paid for the way X was used."

"Whatever," said Branwyn. Then she remembered the lengths she'd went to in order to save Penny and hesitated. "Where is X now?"

"He's sleeping until it's safer for him to be awake again."

"Safer for who?"

"All of us," he said wryly.

Branwyn thought about that a moment, then stopped. "Anyhow, we were talking about this mark and how you're making it vanish right now."

Severin was quiet for a moment, and Branwyn felt a flash of hope that he was just doing as she asked. Then he said, "Find a mirror for a moment, will you?"

Branwyn said quickly, "You'd better not come here."

"As if I wanted to," he said, his voice cooling. "Find a mirror so I don't have to visit your squalid little den."

Branwyn went to the bathroom and stood in front of the full-length mirror, still holding her phone to her ear. Her hair was wild from being towel-dried after her shower, but she was fully dressed. The bandage on her primary hand looked ridiculous.

The image shimmered and changed, becoming an image of

Severin. He wasn't holding a phone, which didn't surprise Branwyn at all.

"All right, I see you. What do you want?"

He reached up to the collar of his snug black t-shirt and pulled it aside to bare his shoulder. There was a mark burned into his shoulder. Branwyn's mark, in fact: the stylized A that was her maker's mark and engraved into the face of her hammer. She remembered resting the hammer on his shoulder in her mother's house.

"Huh," she said. "Serves you right."

"Have you dealt with your sister yet?"

Branwyn had talked to her yesterday. It hadn't been fun, even in a big sisterly way. "She's going to split paying for Meredith's school with me. She'll have to get a roommate and stop putting money into a retirement account, she says."

Severin's mouth twisted into an amused smile. "I don't know if my siblings will approve of such a… banal punishment."

"They'll love it if she gets fired by her angel and *still* has to pay her share," Branwyn said. "And she'll keep paying. I'll make sure of that." If she wasn't going to work for Senyaza any more, she *needed* Rhianna to contribute. Meredith's smiles would keep her from softening.

"Well, you'll find out in a year. Won't that be fun? Let's revisit the topic of our mutual markings after that."

Branwyn chewed on her lip, staring at Severin's smirking face. "Why do you care this much about whether I live or die?"

His wicked eyes crinkled at the corners. "There you go again, asking questions you don't want to hear the answer to. Bye, Branwyn. I'll talk to you again in a year or so."

The image in the mirror became her own reflection as the phone at her ear buzzed unpleasantly. Branwyn felt like she ought to be annoyed, but she wasn't. Instead, she was puzzled. It had been…

odd, seeing her mark on his flesh. Celestials built their bodies, healed wounds on themselves and others with equal ease. What did it mean that he was marked by her hammer?

Then she shook herself. No point in worrying about it. She'd find out eventually, and it would probably be hideous. Best to be prepared.

Her phone chimed, and a pair of messages popped up on the screen. The first one was from Titanone.

Will you come visit soon?

She tapped back an answer. *No. But I'm always here for you this way.*

I thought you'd say that. :(I am very sad!

You're talking, though. I'm very glad about that!

It's harder now. I don't know all the words.

Branwyn again remembered a moment in that fiery confrontation when Titanone had known the words again. Strange words. *You said something to Hadraniel. Convinced him to not destroy you when you were otherwise barely able to talk. Can you tell me what happened then?*

The other angel told me what to say, the screen flashed.

Umbriel, perhaps? Branwyn wasn't sure. She couldn't imagine why Umbriel would interfere to save Senyaza's headquarters when there was a war brewing between Umbriel's organization and Senyaza.

What was the angel like?

Dark, said Titanone. *Darker than Loki. A shadow that stretched across me. Cloaked in wind. That's all I can say.*

Branwyn filed the description away. She'd dig more later, in less direct ways. *Thanks. You'll be fine, Titanone. I'm not going to leave you. I just won't be right there anymore.*

Mr. Black is angry. He thinks you and Marley and Corbin should be in our hospital.

I've spent enough time there already. She was at her apartment, with Penny staying in Marley's room while Marley and Corbin stayed at Penny's house. Because, Penny had said firmly, Marley and Corbin needed some quiet, private time.

She glanced at the message from her brother, then tapped out another message to Titanone: *How are you feeling? Any sign of the virus?*

I don't think so. How can I know though?

"Good question," Branwyn muttered, and looked at Howl's message again:

Be careful on the web right now. Hacker pal says there's a new virus going around.

AFTERWORD

Thank you for reading along.

As usual, reviews are very welcome; they can make the difference between a book and a reader getting together. Even the shortest of reviews helps! And if you don't like writing reviews, you can just tell a friend instead.

If you're not yet on my mailing list and would like to be, you'll be able to sign up at www.dreamfarmer.net. I only use this list to announce new books and it's definitely the best way to find out when those books are out.

If you'd like to talk to me, you can always find me on Twitter and Facebook; I love hearing from readers.

The next book in the Senyaza Series is not yet written. I'm thinking about telling a story about Rhianna and OX. But if you have suggestions for what you'd like to read about, do let me know! In lieu of a chapter of an unwritten book, have what didn't quite make it into the dedication:

You've got a monster in your head
so I thought you should know
I love you
I kind of love your monster too...

ACKNOWLEDGMENTS

Thank you, Ravven, for your fabulous covers.

Beta reading and editing I owe to Kevin, two Rachels, Suzanne, Beth, Kisha, Jenna and Michelle.

Additional thanks to my housemate, my husband and my kids for their patience and tolerance.

As for Robin, Mikaela, Catie, Di, Laura Anne, Pooks and the others… well, they know what they did, and I certainly hope they know how much I appreciate it.

There are other people, too. I appreciate everything. I'm so lucky. Thank you.

ABOUT THE AUTHOR

As an Air Force kid, Chrysoula went to twelve schools in twelve years and spent a lot of time wondering what made people tick. Books, it turned out, helped with that question. These days she lives in the Pacific Northwest with her family, which includes many small and demanding creatures who fight over her attention. This is Chrysoula's seventh book.